J B MORRIS

SETH

BOOK ONE

SETH

Cover, interior design, and formatting by
Buzzelli Design
anna@buzzellidesign.com

United States Marine
"No better friend No worse enemy"

Former Marine Corps Staff Sergeant Seth Collins was an icon to his special-operations team. Awarded the Navy Cross, he had six combat deployments under his belt. War was his business until called home.

But Seth's war wasn't over.

The Mexican Halcon Drug Cartel put their crosshairs on Seth. Their best assassin Angel swore, "He must die."

Contents

JB Morris

Chapter 1

His hair stiffened on the back of his neck.

Gun held at eye level in a two-hand, combat grip, Police Officer Seth Collins stepped into the warehouse away from the door and the outside streetlight. The empty, abandoned building didn't fit. Something was wrong—out of place.

Then a soft noise. Almost silent.

A shoe grated against a small pebble on the concrete floor.

Seth froze.

Dispatched on an anonymous tip of a possible break and entry, he thought he'd seen a faint light moving inside the building. The broken lock and sound confirmed his suspicion.

He wasn't alone.

Silence.

The intruder remained frozen in place.

Okay, you son of a bitch. You wanna play a game of hide and seek. Go for it. See if you can kick my ass.

Seth saw it in the shaft of a streetlight shining through the windows. The faint outline of a stub wall jutting perpendicular from the outside wall. Days of fighting house to house with the Marines in Fallujah taught him how to locate and identify the source of a sound. Someone was standing in the dark, fifty meters ahead, behind the wall in his two o'clock position.

3

After surviving six combat deployment in Iraq and Afghanistan his reflexing automatically kicked in. His mind cleared itself of all random thoughts, concentrated on his immediate surroundings. Ears listened for the slightest sounds. Moving the left foot one short step ahead, he balanced on the balls of his feet, swept his Glock 22 service pistol 180 degrees.

His peripheral vision, better than most, studied the dim outline of the interior wall. The streetlights revealed a floor covered with trash. With each silent step, he advanced by inches toward the hiding place of the person behind the wall.

Sound. Movement.

Seth froze again.

A coat rubbed against the wall. He was in trouble. Someone had moved into a better firing position. Squatting down deep into his calves, he waited. An impatient enemy was often a dead enemy. Seth's patience paid off. A pencil sword of flame spit out a 9mm jacketed hollow point bullet passed over his head and disintegrated into shrapnel when it hit a steel beam. He winced when a fragment bit him in the calf.

He dropped to the floor, yelled in pain, kicked the broken remains of a pallet. He inched his way up into a crouched position. Using his left hand to search the floor in front of him to avoid obstructions, he duck walked to a fifty-five-gallon barrel. Whoever shot at him was stupid. Seth knew his exact location. He listened for any minute sound of movement by the shooter. Time for patience—then payback.

The silence of the night exploded again with a second round smashing into the floor where Seth fell. He didn't return fire. Surprise was an ally in a gunfight. The shooter probably expected he had killed or wounded him.

"Did you shoot him, Julio?" a voice said from across the

warehouse.

"Yeah, I hit him," the shooter said. "You know I don't miss, Rodas."

Two of 'em.

Then a third voice said, "What the hell just happened, Julio?"

"Shut up, Arnie."

Dammit, Police Sergeant Arnie Pappas.

"You're supposed to protect me, Julio. Getting busted ain't part of the deal."

Julio ignored Pappas. "Rodas, come in from the side. Tell me when you can see his dead ass. I'll cover you."

Jesus Christ, Seth. You got yourself into a drug deal with a dirty cop.

Admonishing himself, he squatted behind the barrel, realized he'd made a grave mistake. Combat taught him never to expect the routine. It'd kill him every time.

Time for backup.

***

The dispatcher broadcast on the radio band of occurrence and the "J" band. "All available units. Assist officer at the Atlas Warehouse, 1287 Warren Avenue. Shots fired."

***

Squatting behind the barrel, Seth felt the burn in his leg muscles. The cramps waited to grab hold if he'd allow it. Moving to a more comfortable position was an invitation for another bullet. He believed Julio's boast he never missed.

Frozen in place, he ignored the pain racing down his leg

5

while Rodas advanced on his left flank, stumbling over trash. Seth wanted to laugh. The man wouldn't have survived five minutes on a combat patrol. He leveled his Glock, waited for Rodas.

Rodas was ten feet away when he saw Seth squatting behind the barrel. "I found him." He swung up his HK P30 semi-automatic pistol.

Seth shot him in the mouth.

"Did you kill him, Rodas?"

Silence.

"I'm leaving," Arnie said. "This ain't part of the deal."

"Shut up," Julio said and fired in Arnie's direction. The bullet ricocheted off a digester tank, smashing into the wall at the far end of the warehouse.

Screaming in terror, Pappas dropped to escape from a second bullet.

From his ten o'clock position, Seth heard Pappas's cries of anguish and gasping for air. Still, his trained ear captured the sound of a shoe brushing against trash on the floor. Julio moved. Had to be away from the wall. Lying in a prone position, Seth searched for him in the faint glow of streetlights.

Nothing.

Julio froze into place.

Seth remembered a similar situation in Iraq. Trapped in a building, he'd guessed when the terrorist would bolt for the open door. The terrorist died two meters short of the door. Okay you son of a bitch, Julio. Which way are you going to go? Are you going to the center or are you going to the exit door?

A shoe brushed a broken piece of glass.

So predictable. Julio, you're going to the door. You haven't any balls in this fight.

Seth leveled his pistol at the door entrance.

Without warning, Julio emptied his gun in Seth's direction. One bullet burned Seth in the right thigh. Twisting his ankle to the side, he was relieved there weren't any bones broken. Ignoring the pain and blood, he kept his focus on the door.

Julio slammed in another magazine, fired two more shots, sprinted toward the door. The bullets slammed into a wall ten meters away from Seth.

"Freeze," Seth shouted. The outside streetlights silhouetted his body. Julio fired once before Seth fired two 9mm full metal jacket bullets into his stomach. Julio dropped in place, a black duffle bag falling away from his feet.

Standing up, dragging his right leg, Seth wobbled to the front door. Losing blood, he bit his lip again to keep from passing out. Blood bubbled out of Julio's mouth. His eyes glazed over. The bubbles stopped.

Julio was dead.

Pulling out his tactical flashlight, Seth hobbled over to Pappas. The man's face was blue, his eyes unfocused. Seth called for an ambulance, but his mouth wouldn't work. Unable to resist closing his eyes, a surge of dizziness overwhelmed him. He heard someone yelling "police" before he closed his eyes, dropped to the floor.

***

Opening the car door, Police Captain Roscoe Drummond swung both feet down to the warehouse parking lot. A long sigh helped propel him into a standing position.

His eyes were red, and a brush missed some of his tousled, thinning, gray hair. The lack of sleep and a day-long murder investigation, without an arrest added fuel to his grumpy mood.

At the age of sixty-two, Drummond gave up any hope of being happy about receiving midnight phone calls. His wife and two daughters learned to sleep through the noise and Drummond's subsequent search for his clothes in the dark. Even his loud complaints of, "Where in the hell are my goddamn shoes?" failed to cause a stir in the household.

The thirty-plus years of being a cop, working long hours, not enough sleep, and gulping meals had aged him beyond his years. Adding to his seasoned appearance were drooping shoulders on a short, stocky frame and his usual rumpled blue suit.

Decades of high-speed pursuits and chasing suspects had also left him in a state of perpetual motion. Sitting at a desk was difficult. Standing allowed his arms and legs to move untethered.

His foul moods seldom landed on the shoulders of his fellow officers in the patrol division. They were "his boys," each of whom he had selected. They, like him, were honest cops who worked hard to keep the streets safe. His officers called him "Drummond." They argued, "Anyone can be a captain, but there's only one Drummond."

The usual recipient of his foul moods as he described them, was the "son of a bitch" who committed a crime forcing him out of bed. He barked and yelled at them to drop to the ground. Safely secured, he said he'd ask the judge to throw the book at them. He should have been a drill sergeant. Despite his diminutive size, he had a booming voice that carried for a block.

The DA loved him when he testified, leaving the jurors spellbound. Politicians were terrified of a scandal when he refused to release their sons and daughters who drove home drunk or were high on drugs.

Drummond's scowl announced his mood.

"Porter, this better be good."

"The body at the door," Police Sergeant Jeff Porter said, "is a known member of the Los Guerreros Cartel. Goes by the name of Julio. Had a bag full of money lying next to him. We've been counting it. Hundred-dollar bills. Still not done. Looks like we have a dirty cop too."

"Who?"

"Sergeant Arnie Pappas."

"Goddammit!" Drummond's voice was raw with anger. "Is there any honest son of a bitch left?"

"He—"

"Don't interrupt me, Porter. Where is the bastard?"

"That's him they're loading up in the ambulance."

"Shot?"

"No. Medics think it's a heart attack."

"What's his condition?"

"Not good. Unconscious."

"Who's the patrolman that broke up the party?"

"Seth. Took a bullet in the leg. He's in the ambulance that just pulled out."

"Gonna be okay?"

"Yeah, should be."

Drummond let out another deep sigh. Returning to bed wasn't going to happen. "He's a good cop. I'll stop by on the way home. What kind of drugs?"

"Ten kilos of coke," Porter said.

"Outstanding. Anyone else involved?"

"One deceased individual inside. Unidentified. Seth shot him in the head."

Drummond tugged at his ear. "You have everything under control?"

"Yes, sir."

"Good. I'm going to check up on Seth. I want you in my office at zero eight hundred. Tell me what you have."

"Yes, sir."

"One last thing," Drummond said, opening the car door. "Captain Turner and Sergeant Holman may show up. You call me if they even look like they want to be involved in the investigation."

"Sir, Captain Turner is my superior officer."

"Dammit, Porter. That's a direct order. Do you want to be on my bad side?"

"No, sir. Is there a problem I need to know about?"

"Yeah, there is a problem you don't need to know about. Just call me or you'll stand in front of my desk. Trust me. It will be an ugly experience."

***

Narcotics Sergeant Marcus Holman turned off the ignition, gripped the steering wheel. Shook his head in despair. He imagined a jail cell would be his new home before sunrise. He pushed back in the driver's seat, exhaled a protracted sigh. He tried to stretch his long, thin legs, on a six-foot-two frame, to their maximum length. The floorboard blocked any effort for relief. Frustrated, he removed his smudged glasses, wiped them on a rumpled white shirt. Earlier, he'd stuffed his soiled necktie into a coat pocket.

Eyelids wide open to reject exhaustion, he examined the sea of red and blue lights a block away. "Think they can see us?" he said in a flat voice.

"Nah. We're a block away," Captain Boyd Turner of the narcotics division said. "God, the parking lot is lit up like a Christmas tree. He grabbed the binoculars off the dashboard, searched for Captain Drummond.

The radio continued to chatter between two dispatchers and four units on patrol. One dispatcher directed officers on a car chase on Washington Street while the other dispatched a backup unit to assist officers in search of a suspect wanted for armed robbery of a convenience store. Earlier, parked in an unmarked police car at the intersection of Sixth Avenue and Ambrose Street, they were shocked to hear the dispatcher repeat Seth's call for backup at the warehouse.

Their biggest drug deal. Worth millions on the street. A total bust. Boyd and Marcus had argued earlier on who should pick up the drugs at the warehouse. Marcus wanted to use one of the two narcotics detectives in on the drug deal. He said Frank Coleman or Logan King, both in their forties, could escape from a trap. Boyd said no. Called Sergeant Pappas a friend who had picked up the drugs for three years without a problem.

Too slow," Marcus argued. "Pappas has a history of ill health."

Boyd disagreed. The argument ended. It didn't quell the distrust between them.

Marcus sighed, tried to wish away a debilitating exhaustion that left him slumped in the seat. "So, how long do we sit here on our butts?"

"Jesus Christ, Marcus, we just got our ass kicked. Now you want to go home. We'll leave when I goddamn well say so. We need to see if Drummond is on to us. Christ, for all we know, Pappas talked to him."

They didn't speak for five minutes. Marcus' weariness of

Boyd's temper continued to grow.

Bathed in sweat from the terror of jail or of being murdered by the drug dealer, Marcus needed a distraction from the black thoughts that plagued him.

"We have three new dealers on the west side."

"Where?"

"Around the four-hundred block on Powell Boulevard. Near the park."

"Do we know 'em?" Boyd asked.

"Some guy and two whores. Escobar roughed him up earlier. Dealer didn't get the message."

"Have Escobar make a return visit." Charged to protect the distribution of drugs, Escobar Padilla served as Boyd's enforcer. With impunity, he beat and maimed any competition. Two months earlier he'd murdered a fourteen-year-old dealer.

"I'll see him tomorrow," Marcus said.

"Good. My butt's sore." Exhaustion plagued Boyd following a heart attack eighteen months ago. He'd told the doctor fifty-two was too damn early for a heart attack. The doctor agreed, gave him a prescription to change his lifestyle. Add another fifty-two years. Boyd would have none of it. Death was acceptable when he decided. First, his daughter Alyssa had to give him a couple of grandchildren.

Boyd grabbed the bottle of Jack Daniel's from the floorboard. Another swig caressed his palate. "Goddamn, fine whiskey."

"I'll have some of that," Marcus said. Parched throat satisfied, he handed the bottle back. "So, how do you spend your money?"

"Alyssa."

"Alyssa?"

Boyd examined the one swallow left in the whiskey bottle. "No daughter of mine will be saddled with student loans."

"How did you explain all the money?"

"Told her it was an inheritance. Rich uncle in Tulsa. It worked."

"Yeah, but what about your wife? She knows better."

Boyd snickered. "Elena? Not a problem. She damn well thinks and does what I tell her."

"Where's Alyssa at in school?" Marcus asked. He flipped a spent cigarette out the window. Missed the telephone pole target.

"I put her through Ohio State. Now she's off to med school."

Marcus nodded receipt of the comment. "How do you hide your money?"

"Easy. I keep the money in a safe. Dole out little amounts so IRS won't notice." Boyd glared at Marcus. "You better be smart with your money."

Marcus threw both hands up. "Goddammit, I ain't stupid." Marcus grimaced from a sudden foot cramp. He wiggled his toes to will the cramp away.

"What the hell is with your attitude?" Boyd said. "Always pissin' and moanin'. I'm tired of it."

"Well, I'm goddamn tired of you treating me like an idiot."

"Bullshit." To ease the tension, Boyd said, "Marcus, I don't want to argue. We're in deep shit."

"Just dial it down, Boyd. You piss me off."

Boyd ignored the comment. Tried to offer a smile. Wasn't much. Lips never parted. "Tell me, Marcus. Whatcha gonna do with all of your money?"

Marcus answered the question to himself weeks ago. "I'm takin' on every woman east of the Mississippi."

"What about your wife and girlfriend?"

"They'll do until I find me another sweet young thing."

"Damn fine answer." Boyd picked up the binoculars, searched for Drummond. Seconds later, he said "Goddammit. I thought Drummond was leaving. He just got out of his car. Goddamn, straight arrow. Someday, I'm gonna kill that son of a bitch."

"Tough call. Too many people love his ass."

"He'll be so dirty when I'm through with him. He'll be toast."

Two more squad cars entered the lot while two paramedics loaded a gurney into the ambulance. "That's Pappas they loaded into the bus. By God, he better be dead."

Marcus grunted. "Pappas? Why am I not surprised. And you called him a friend."

Boyd laid the binoculars on the dash. "The hell with him. Pappas knows too damn much."

Boyd's father, a gambler by profession, and a thief at heart taught Boyd to pick useful friends. Someone to do his bidding or give him what he wanted. When they dried up, dump them. Their usefulness, like Pappas, had expired.

He learned another important lesson watching his father hustle from one deal to the next. How to make money the easy way. But making money paled to the most important one—don't screw up. His dad flunked the test. Two men murdered him over a gambling debt.

Emulating his father, he started small-time in high school. He stole from friends and their parents when invited to their homes. Boyd wasn't greedy. Steal enough from a purse in the hallway so no one would miss the money. A ten instead of an enticing twenty-dollar bill. Accused of theft, he'd dropped the friend, moved on to a new one. A budding new life of crime didn't leave his family immune. Who'd suspect him of stealing from grandma?

Not enough. He needed more than chump change. Life was expensive after high school. Gas for the car and money to entertain the young women before a nightcap of sex.

He spent a few years with eight-to-five jobs, but they left him tired, bored. Little money left for gas, and the women with expensive tastes avoided him.

An unexpected moment in a bar settled Boyd's life choice. He'd stumbled into a bathroom, witnessed the bartender pay off a police officer. He discovered a cop had easy access to drugs and money. Simple was Boyd's rationale. Smarter, more lucrative to be a dirty cop than spending a lifetime of hustling from one scheme to another. With so much drug money in the division evidence locker, no one would miss a handful in his pocket.

Years later, he became the captain in charge of the narcotics division and the kingpin for the Halcon Cartel in Hillsdale. Bribes paid to the police chief ensured protection from arrest.

"Marcus. I've seen enough. Let's get the hell out of here. I want you to go to the hospital. Pappas needs to be dead."

Marcus jabbed a finger in Boyd's direction. "Goddammit, you go. You've got the rank."

"Dammit, Marcus. That's an order."

"Don't piss me off with your orders. Remember, we're partners."

Boyd erupted in anger, stabbed Marcus with a finger. "The hell we are. I brought you in. You said you wanted money." Spit flew from his mouth. He stabbed Marcus harder. "You weren't a partner then, and you're no goddamn partner now. I make the decisions. Now go to the friggin' hospital."

"Someday, Boyd, you're going to push me too hard."

Boyd leaned into Marcus. "What? Is that a threat?"

Marcus escaped from his slump, leaned into Boyd "No. Just back off."

"Or you'll do what?"

Not a word. Their venom spent itself. They glared at each other.

Marcus raised his hands up in surrender. "Let's drop it. We have bigger problems. Drummond, for one."

"Drummond is the least of our problems. We're in trouble with Carlos." Carlos Torres was their drug distributor.

Boyd tried to relax with a sigh. The sharp heart pain left him struggling to breathe. He had to be cautious, or the next attack could kill him. "We'll be lucky if Carlos doesn't shoot us or Drummond doesn't burn us."

"You shouldn't have used Pappas."

"Are you saying again this was my fault?"

"I'm saying you should have used Coleman or King."

"You keep it up, Marcus, and you're out."

"Like what? You going to shoot me?"

Their anger returned. More intense, louder.

"Keep pushing, Marcus. You don't have far to go."

"This ain't over, Boyd. Not by a long shot."

Boyd ignored the threat. "Who busted up the deal?"

"Don't know."

"Goddammit, find out. I'm gonna to kill that son of a bitch."

Marcus chuckled. "He's a cop, Boyd. You're nuts."

Boyd grabbed Marcus' shirt, choked him. "Trust me. You don't want to call me a name again. Now drive me home and go to the hospital. I want Pappas dead. Are we clear?"

***

Boyd checked his rage on the drive home. He and Marcus had sold drugs for four years in Hillsdale. Marcus' usefulness had expired. He had little restraint left to keep his meaty hands off of Marcus' skinny neck.

Chapter 2

"Do you want anything else?" the Eastland Memorial Hospital nurse asked.

"No, I'm good," Seth said. "Thank you, ma'am. Appreciate if you would leave the partition open."

"The oxycodone will go into effect soon, and you have water on the nightstand. Press the call button if you need anything. Try and get some sleep."

Seth's quick examination revealed all he needed to know about his surroundings. Machines and outlets of all kinds, pale blue walls and a thin mattress that sagged under his 220 pounds of thick muscles.

Squeezing the pillow without his leg lighting up in pain, Seth closed his eyes, relaxed in the quietness of being the only patient in the eight-bed recovery room.

Alone.

Alone was good. Not the alone where he was away from people. More like the kind where no one slipped through into his heart. Gave him time to think—daydream about yesterday. Yesterday was gone. There were no further changes. Tomorrows proved hard. He couldn't escape from his anxiety of having no plans or expectations. He existed—one empty day bled into the next one.

Goddammit, Seth. Hell of a life you've picked for yourself. There has to be some reason to get up in the morning.

For most of his thirty-four years, alone marked his comfort zone. But idleness was his nightmare. It was the mother's milk that fed his demons.

He closed his eyes, willed the anxieties and pain away.

Daydreams.

He was seven again.

His parents didn't work out. Mom left. His dad Raymond woke up one morning to find her gone. No note. Her clothes were still in the closet, but her favorite blue dress was missing. They didn't know where she'd gone or if she'd left alone. They never saw or heard from her again.

Seth realized it was the same when she was still at home. Gone a lot. Neither he or his dad knew where she disappeared. She refused to explain her absences. She wasn't gone for days. More like putting on a modest dress, make up, and being gone for much of the day.

Seth struggled to remember her face. The coarse, uncontrollable, red hair was unforgettable. The rest, a blur. She asked him about school but never shared in any of his activities. Their family routine was Mom came home late in the day, fixed dinner, and watched TV while Dad sat in his rocking chair stone-faced. Seth saw first-hand his dad's broken heart and was powerless to help him.

Silence became the standard in the household. They tried to avoid asking her questions. She had little patience for them.

Years later, he realized Mom was mentally ill. Still, Seth was unable to forgive her. He'd never forget all the pain she gave to him and his dad.

Change was inevitable after she left. It became the tonic to help heal the household. Dad buried his grief in a private place and did his best to enter into Seth's world. He was there for the wrestling and football games, yelling encouragement with the rest of the parents.

For Seth, it was more of a struggle. He'd never acquired the skill to keep many friends in school. He wasn't a recluse. Friendship required opening up to others, exposing his secrets.

Unacceptable.

Classmates called him a loner. He was comfortable with the label.

"What the hell? If you don't know me, you can't hurt me," was Seth's motto. He'd learned it when he was a child. The lesson served him well.

Until Allison.

Seth described her later as, "That goddamn bitch of a whore Allison!"

He met her on a street corner in Rome when she stepped off a tour bus. Pretty thing he'd thought. Had to be about twenty. Laughed a lot, too. She'd told him how handsome he was with his Marine Corps uniform and a chest full of medals. He'd told her how beautiful she was with her blonde hair and an infectious smile.

Seth was a kid himself, twenty-two and cocky. Allison was the first one to explode his libido into overdrive. She'd abandoned the tour bus, and they ran away to a hotel room in Sperlonga, Italy. Seth was in love. She loved him too. Told him so.

Two months later, he finished his tour in Iraq and followed her back to Allentown, Pennsylvania, where she lived with her parents. Seth liked them. He believed her father tried to warn him about Allison. The father described his love for his daughter but worried she'd had many short-term boyfriends, sometimes two at the same time. Seth wondered later if he would have listened to him. Seth and Allison loved each other. Nothing more was needed.

They married three months later and moved into a billet at the Marine Corps Quantico Base in Virginia. For six months, they'd loved each other with unbridled passion and partied at the bars and nightclubs surrounding the base.

Four months after Seth shipped out for a tour in Afghanistan, a fellow sergeant and friend pulled him aside. "Just a heads up, Seth. You need to check in at home. Things are not going well."

The friend shipped out two months following Seth's deployment. He saw Allison with several different men, one of whom bragged he'd spent the night with her.

Seth escaped death the following day. Allison, who had slipped down into the goddamn bitch category, was with him instead of focusing on an incoming RPG. A fellow Marine saved him when he slammed Seth to the ground.

Allison was gone when he returned home. New tenants occupied the billet, and her parents were unaware of where she went. Her father called a month later to report Allison and another man died in a car accident in Alabama.

Life was bitter for several years following Allison's death. What little smile Seth had disappeared. Casual conversation also left him. His mood was black, his heart filled with rage. He loved Allison. They'd laughed, loved, and bantered the names of their two future children. He'd given her all he had—she'd rejected it. It broke his spirit for life when he realized casual sex was a greater draw for her than marriage to him.

The rage spent itself, leaving an emptiness in its wake. Nothing mattered. There weren't any hopes or dreams. Just existence. Seth began to fantasize about what would be the curtain call on his life. Death on the battlefield or buried in a remote grave without mourners? No matter. He didn't give a goddamn.

But Billie Spencer had other plans for Seth.

Why Billie? What possible reason was there for Billie to decide it was his job to save his emotional life?

Started innocently enough. Eight sergeants stood together in the Iraq desert following the deployment of the 2nd Battalion of the 5th Marines to Ramadi. Filled with bravery, the terrorists didn't have a chance. Billie was in the middle of the group, grinning like a Cheshire cat.

They sealed their friendship on a Sunday morning during the second battle of Fallujah. Trapped behind a burned-out truck, Billie and Seth escaped death when three insurgents emptied their AK-47s' at them. Knowing what would follow, they'd leaped up, escaped through a blown-out door into a house without a roof. A ball of flame from an RPG engulfed the truck, slammed them to the floor. Seth would never forget Billie's words and silly grin.

"Son of a bitch! Those bastards are serious."

Good days. Sometimes they were on the same battlefield. Other times, eight-thousand miles apart on separate tours. Whatever the distance, Billie and Seth grew close, like brothers. Billie skyped Seth almost every week and was able to make Seth laugh again. Billie hadn't given up on Seth.

The definition of time was change and for Billie, time was painful. Discharged early, he returned home suffering from Post-Traumatic Stress Disorder. For months, it was Seth's turn to help his friend. He called Billie several times a week to help him with his depression. The calls worked. Billie was better for a few days before his demons returned with a vengeance.

Unlike Billie, Seth managed to hold his demons in check.

Still, he worried one day he would follow Billie's lead and his demons would consume him. Demons wearing face masks of his dead comrades.

Noise.

Seth opened his eyes, checked his surroundings. He heard two nurses talking. Seth bit his lip from the sudden pain when he attempted to move his leg to a more comfortable position. Daydreams gone, he glanced at the clock on the wall. Time to call Billie again. Seldom sleeping, Billie's depression kept him awake during the night. Unable to find his phone, Seth pressed the call button.

"I have to make a call," Seth said. "I can't find my cell phone."

"You should be trying to sleep," the nurse answered.

"Ma'am, it's important, or I wouldn't ask for it."

"It's in your patient locker. I'll bring it in."

"Thank you."

He wondered how much longer he could hold off the Billie's depression before it destroyed him.

***

Taking off his overcoat when he entered the ER, Captain Drummond saw a familiar face.

"Drummond. Haven't seen you for a while," Doctor Bryce said.

"That's good, right?"

"Guess so. Thought you'd retired."

"What a sweet thought." Drummond threw his overcoat over his shoulder. A strong antiseptic smell filled the room. "You look dead tired, Doctor. Long shift?"

Rubbing his eyes, the doctor said, "And then some. You here

for the wreck or the police officer?"

"Wreck?"

"Four teenagers in a VW hit a tree. Lost the two boys. Trying to save the girls."

"Hope they make it."

"Me too. You must be here for the officer. He's in the recovery room. Just for a minute, Drummond. He needs to rest."

"Thanks, Doc. Good luck with the girls."

"They're going to need it."

Drummond headed down the hallway. The discovery of Sergeant Pappas at the warehouse confirmed his worst fear. The corruption, centered in the narcotics division and the chief's office, spread into the evidence room supervised by Pappas. Enough was enough. Time to act. He was determined to clean out the corruption. Seth's military experience was essential to help him. When Seth returned to duty, he'd reassign him to work out of his office to take on Boyd, Marcus, and the chief.

Seth had served under Drummond in the Patrol Division since joining the department two years earlier. Drummond realized the chemistry between them. Never understood why just knew it was there. Somewhere along the way, they had also become friends without either one of them declaring their relationship. Drummond sensed they had a mutual respect for each other's service to the public. He was pleased their minds worked in sync. When an incident occurred, Seth had already responded before Drummond could issue an order to lead.

He found Seth in the far dark corner of the recovery room next to a single nightstand lamp. Stepping through the curtain, he stopped at the foot of the bed. Eyes half closed, Seth waved an index finger.

"Won't ask how you feel. A drug dealer once shot me in the

arm."

"Smarts," Seth said.

"I can award you a Medal of Valor if you want it," Drummond said with a wry grin. He laid his coat on the bed away from Seth's leg. "The ladies will love it."

"Screw the medal."

Drummond sat in a chair next to the bed. "Knew what you'd say. Seen your military record. Can't put the medal in the same room with a Navy Cross." Drummond let out an infrequent chuckle. "Didn't pick up a medal either. Wouldn't help me with the ladies. Already married."

Seth's lazy smile was a rare experience for Drummond.

"Know anything about what happened, Seth?"

"No. Walked into an ambush with a dirty cop. What do you know?"

"More."

"Did you know about Pappas?" Seth asked.

"No," Drummond said, leaned back into the chair. No relief. He was still weary. "Pappas was a surprise. I knew we had a problem, but I didn't know he was part of it. You're a good officer, Seth. One of my best."

"Thanks. We had a corporal in Iraq selling dope. Cost us one outstanding captain. I hate dirty cops. Hate dirty Marines more."

"Me too. Cop gives an oath. I haven't any tolerance when they break it. Get well, Seth. I'm going to call on you."

Seth raised up from the pillow. "What do you mean?"

"I want you to help me clean up the department."

Ignoring the pain in his leg, Seth said, "Sorry, Drummond. Not available."

Drummond jolted out of his exhaustion and the chair. "What do mean you're not available?"

Despite becoming drowsy from the oxycodone, Seth said with a finality in his voice, "I'm checking out, Drummond. You'll have my resignation in a couple of days."

"Quitting?" Drummond was incredulous. No one quit on him. He'd cajole, threaten, or take whatever steps were necessary to ward off an unwelcomed resignation. His powers of persuasion usually paid off. He raised his voice, wrinkled his nose. "You can't just up and quit. I have a department full of dirty cops."

"Sorry. I spent too many years fighting someone else's war. I'm done with that."

Drummond felt his face turn red with the flush of anger. Anger management had never been his strongest suit. "What the hell are you talking about?"

Despite the pain, Seth scooted up in bed. Eyes cleared, jaw set, he said with venom in his voice, "I served six deployments fighting the goddamn president's wars. And what did the son of a bitch give us for support? He tied our hands behind our backs. Said we had to fight a politically correct war. He and his goddamn rules of engagement. His insanity killed too many outstanding Marines. I'll be damned in hell if I'm going to fight somebody else's war again. Enough of that bullshit."

Drummond pulled back from Seth's rage, retreated to the bed footboard. He had to regain self-control, or there wouldn't be any chance of Seth helping him. Dropping his voice, he said, "Seth, I'm not the president. I understand it has been—"

"Goddammit, Drummond, you don't understand. Dad had a stroke, needed me at home. I joined the department to pay the bills. None of this, 'I'm gonna clean up the streets of Dodge.' That's your gig, not mine. Dad doesn't have much time left. When he's gone, there's nothing left for me here. I'm sorry,

Drummond. For me, being a cop is just a job. For you, it's your life. I'm going to spend some time with my friend Billie. Then I'll figure out what's next."

The consolatory, "I understand" approach didn't work. Drummond returned to his preferred loud, commanding, in your face approach to winning an argument. "Goddammit, Seth. You're a cop. Cops don't quit. They finish the job, then go to the next one." Drummond was losing it. He wanted to express his concern to Seth. Accepting a resignation was not part of the script. "I'm asking you for help, and you're telling me to go to hell. That about it, Seth?"

"You can yell at me all night long. Won't change a thing. I was going to quit. Tonight sealed it."

Drummond had to find a new approach, but he couldn't dump the anger. Didn't want to either "Okay. What about your dad? You going to quit on him, too?"

Seth slapped the bed hard. "Damn you, Drummond. That was a cheap shot."

Drummond said nothing, wouldn't back off the argument. The department was at stake. So be it if meant pissing off Seth.

Seth backed off from his angry voice, but the anger remained in his eyes. "Dad's dying, and there's nothing left when he's gone. What do you want me to do?" he said, "Stick around, write traffic tickets?"

Drummond struggled. He was running out of arguments. "No, you self-centered, selfish son of a bitch. I want you to do your goddamn job, I—"

Pulling back the drawn curtain, an angry head nurse barked, "Gentlemen! Lower your voices. You are in a hospital." Scowling at Drummond, she warned, "One more outburst, and I'll ask you to leave."

"Sorry ma'am."

The nurse left. Drummond's anger remained. "So where are you going?"

"I don't know."

"Oh, that's cute. From here to there. Hell of a well-thought-out plan, Seth." Drummond shook his head in frustration.

Fading from the oxycodone, Seth closed his eyes, said nothing.

Drummond's anger wouldn't let him slow down. "I ain't done with you. No goddamn way. I want you in my office next week ready to go to work. That's a goddamn order."

Seth opened his right eye. "You remind me of a drill sergeant I had a hundred years ago."

Drummond stood motionless, frozen to the floor. Profanity exploded in his brain.

"You son of a bitch. Seth. Next week, ready for duty. No one tells me no. Trust me. You're not good enough to be the first one." He stomped out of the recovery room. He left his coat on the bed.

***

An hour later, Sergeant Marcus said, "Excuse me, doctor." "I'm checking up on Sergeant Arnold Pappas. Is he going to be okay?"

"I'm sorry," Doctor Bryce said. "He was deceased on arrival."

"Oh, how terrible," Marcus said with the best expression of anguish he could muster. "He was such an excellent officer. He'll be missed."

***

Charged with distributing drugs for the Halcon Cartel from Chicago to Ohio, Carlos Torres watched her. Studied her.

She was on a killing mission.

Stepping out of the Mercedes-Benz limousine into the shadows of an abandoned warehouse in Cicero, Illinois, her spiked-heel platform shoes anchored themselves to the concrete floor. She had to be tall, he thought. North side of six foot with the shoes. Her olive complexion and curled-black hair caressed her shoulders signaling her Hispanic heritage. Dark-brown, cold eyes complemented her intense red lipstick. A provocative mini-skirt accentuated a svelte figure.

A Walther P22 semi-automatic pistol with an AAC Element Suppressor hung in her right hand. An assassin, unequal to any other.

Angel.

Her hair shined when she stepped away from the car into the lights. Heels clicked on the floor. The cool air in the warehouse chilled him, but the car window remained down. Carlos wanted to watch her do her best work—the sound of death.

"This won't take long, Carlos," she said.

He'd heard the stories. Her exploits spread from one hacienda to another, making her a legend among the Mexican drug lords. Ordered by Manuel Robles, who led the Halcon Cartel, she'd tracked a Bulgarian drug lord halfway around the world before killing him in Puerto Varas, Chile. He kidnapped and enslaved young Mexican girls including a member of Manuel's family.

The distinctive ring of a Spanish guitar on Carlos' cell phone broke the silence in the cavernous warehouse.

"Problem?" Angel asked. Problems surfaced when Carlos' phone rang.

Carlos listened to the message. "Sergeant Marcus from Hillsdale. Captain Boyd Turner lost the shipment."

"The shipment was worth a half of a million dollars."

"Dammit, I know that," Carlos said.

"What happened?"

"For Christ sake's, Angel, I just got the call. Something about a raid."

"Manuel will be angry with you."

"Dammit, Angel. Give it a rest."

Angel raised her eyebrows, tilted her head. "Touchy."

Goddamn bitch

Intuition kept Carlos alive during his forty-two years. He sensed when he was in danger and when he was safe. He murdered his enemies before they could kill him. He hid when the DEA searched for him. Carlos realized being Manuel's closest cousin wasn't enough to save him. Manuel would decide someday the lost shipments made him a liability. He'd order Angel to kill him.

The problem had an easy solution. He'd kill her before she killed him. How he didn't know. But she needed to be dead. No other option. His gut told him she could turn on him like a wounded Wolverine.

Such a waste of a beautiful woman.

Carlos' driver Garcia leaned down into the open limousine, handed him a second cell phone. The phone was for personal calls—sex.

"The masseuse is on the line," Garcia said.

"I don't have time now."

"Make time," Angel said. She always enjoyed the sex after the massage.

Angel shivered in the cold, empty warehouse. It was time to finish her business. A middle-aged, naked man, beaten, stood in front of her with the aid of Carlos' bodyguard, Cesar. The man whimpered.

"Stand him up straight," Angel said.

Tobias Ruiz's eyes were puffed closed from the beating and his broken ribs made breathing difficult. Blood from his crushed nose covered his chest. Tobias gave up fighting to live. Death would be the release of pain. She imagined he heard the click of her heels when she approached and smelled her distinctive perfume.

"Angel."

"Yes, Tobias, it is me, Angel," she purred. "Can you open your eyes?"

Tobias said nothing. Most of his teeth were broken from the beating.

"Can you feel my warm fingers, Tobias?" Angel touched a spot on his left cheek free of blood.

Tobias said nothing.

"Nod, Tobias, if you can feel my fingers."

Tobias nodded.

"Tobias, I have caught you several times staring at my body. Do you want to see my beautiful naked breasts before you die?"

Tobias shook his head, struggled to open his eyes. One eye half-opened. It looked glazed over, milky. Angel sensed he had fantasized about her breasts for a long time.

"Tobias, can you stand on your own feet?"

Tobias struggled to plant his feet.

"Stand on your own two feet, Tobias, and I will show you my breasts." Angel motioned Cesar to step away. Tobias collapsed. Angel squatted down. "Tobias, you cannot die like a dog. You must stand up."

She motioned for Cesar to help him. Head hanging down, Tobias weaved back and forth when Cesar stepped away.

"Tobias! Look at me."

He raised his head, opened one eye again. This time she saw his vision was clear. He held his gaze on Angel's breasts.

"You know, Tobias, you must die. You stole from us."

Blood dribbled out of his mouth.

"Do you want me to pray for your widow and three children?"

Tobias nodded.

"Do you want to see my breasts now, Tobias?"

Tobias grunted.

Angel unbuttoned the top button of her silk blouse revealing the cleavage of her breasts.

Tobias looked up, struggled to focus on the swell of her breasts. Angel shot him in the chest. She leaned over his crumpled body, shot him twice in the left ear. The CCI Stringer 22LR hollow-point bullets reduced his brain to mush.

Returning to the limousine, Carlos said, "You enjoyed killing him."

"Death is never enjoyable."

"You're good at your work, Angel."

"Yes, I am and never forget it."

Carlos felt a tickling sensation on the back of his neck.

"Carlos, you must handle the Boyd problem. Manuel does not like problems and losing shipments."

"For Christ's sakes, I'll take care of it." For an instant, Carlos dropped the thought of killing her. He'd settle for hitting her— hard. But that wouldn't work either. One blow on her beautiful face would be a painful death sentence. "You know, sometimes

I wonder if you are working for Manuel or me."

Angel lied. "Only you, my darling. Only you."

Chapter 3

Exhausted, Major Hunter Billingsley, Kansas City Police Department, stepped out of the patrol car, muttered, "Jesus Christ." He had just left Ivanhoe Park after an earlier stop at Oak Park. "This is unreal."

Standing next to the open window of the patrol car, Detective Harrison Weber said, "Yes, sir. They're in the car."

Halfway down the block of E 39th Street, Billingsley saw people in their front yards looking at the sea of blue and red lights in the intersection. "Any witnesses?"

"Haven't found any."

"Let's see what you have."

The new red Cadillac XTS imbedded itself into the brick wall of a building, leaving a shower of bricks on the hood and caving in the windshield. Bullet holes began at the front tire on the driver's side, advanced to the trunk. Peering into the car, the major saw the driver and passenger were unrecognizable from the multiple gunshot wounds to the head.

Unable to arrest a yawn he stood up. "Do we know them, Weber?"

"The car belongs to Chano Velasquez. That's him behind the wheel. Know the tattoo on his arm. Don't know the passenger."

"What's the building the car hit?"

"Bail bonding."

"Has someone called them?"

"I called them."

Billingsley shook his head to ward off an advancing yawn. Finished, he said, "Any collateral damage?"

"Some rounds hit the first gray house across the street. No one was hurt."

"Good. Had to be an ambush. How did it happen?"

It was Detective Weber's turn to yawn. Unlike the Major Billingsley, he'd never made it to bed. The desk sergeant called him while he still was brushing his teeth. "Found casings in the empty lot across the street. They're behind those dirt mounds. Forty-five caliber. Shooter fired a full magazine. We should know more about the gun soon. Has to be an inside job. The shooter had to know Chano would be driving down the street at this hour."

"You work narcotics, Weber. Is this the same as the others?"

"Same. Chano and the two in Ivanhoe Park are Los Guerreros' drug dealers. You saw the one in Oak Park. They shot him in the face with a shotgun. I think I know him from the tattoos. He's also Los Guerreros."

Billingsley leaned against the driver's door. "Son of a bitch. Five in one night. We've got us a drug war, Weber."

"Yes, sir. Big time."

***

Hesitation.

An assassin's worst nightmare.

It gave the target time to slip out of the crosshairs of a scope or for the enemies to encircle the shooter. To stay alive, Angel had disciplined herself to make an immediate response to any threat. Hesitating once is an invitation to do it a second time. The second time could be fatal.

Despite her discipline, Angel changed when she arrived in Chicago. She discovered she lingered before calling Manuel. First, had to check her makeup or drink another cup of coffee. She wasn't aware of what she was doing until one day she caught herself staring at the phone. She didn't want to make the call. It puzzled her. She couldn't allow any hesitation to enter into her life. Why had it become a problem? The answer was opaque.

Perhaps it was because Manuel was in love with her. The thought of Manuel being in love with anyone amused her. His definition of love allowed him to continue having sex with the beautiful young women at the villa. Angel was little troubled at Manuel's promiscuous habits. She suffered the same affliction. Unlike Manuel, she used sex to gain information and discover the vulnerabilities of her enemies. Carlos was her latest conquest.

No, Manuel's love for her was not the author of her hesitancy, something else. He told her he wanted her beside him when he expanded his drug empire. She could help to destroy the other cartels and capture the American drug trade. A simple, safe plan. She would no longer be the huntress or the hunted. When she left for Chicago, Manuel told her to assess Carlos' usefulness distributing drugs. It would be her last mission before joining him to expand his empire.

Manuel's decision left Angel unsettled, anxious.

Why?

The door closed and locked to ensure privacy, Angel leaned against the bathroom vanity. She convinced herself to make the call while Carlos slept in the nearby bedroom.

"I want to speak to Manuel."

"Yes of course," a young woman said. "One moment please."

Angel examined her nails, brushed away some errant hair on her face. The woman, naked, entered Manuel's bedroom, waved the phone at him. Manuel ordered another young mistress off of him and out of his bed. He grabbed the phone, flipped his hand for both women to leave the room.

Satisfied he was alone with the door closed, Manuel said, "I have missed the press of your breasts against me."

"And I have missed our loins becoming one."

"What is it you have for me, my sweet Angel?"

"The *policía* have seized another one of Carlos' shipments."

"Not acceptable," Manuel said, making a backrest of pillows against the headboard. "There must be payment for the loss."

"Of course. I am prepared to take whatever course of action necessary to please you."

Scratching the stubble on his chin, he said, "This is the third time this year Carlos has lost a shipment. We must receive payment for his stupidity."

"Shall he be sanctioned?"

"Perhaps. I must reflect on the matter. He is my blood."

Carlos snorted in the bedroom,

"Wait. . . he may be awake" Listening, she was satisfied Carlos was still asleep. "I shall wait for your decision." Angel was bored with Carlos. She didn't give any thought to if he should live or die. She wanted to leave Chicago. The cold weather disagreed with her.

"Los Guerreros Cartel has attacked us in Kansas. You must come to the villa. "

"I will be on the first available flight."

"You will consume me with your passion?"

"Of course," Angel said.

Brushing away a sudden itch on the back of her neck, Angel stared at herself in the mirror. Her face, still red from Carlos' stiff, thick beard, would require extra time to repair with make-up. Satisfied with her examination, she reflected on her conversation with Manuel. Would she be satisfied remaining at Manuel's side? Would helping him expand his drug empire give her the same rush as hunting a new target? Or, having a target turn on her, and she became the hunted? Was her life as an assassin fulfilling or was a change required?

The unanswered questions gave her the feeling the bathroom walls were closing in on her. With little sound, she unlocked the door, retreated to the sliding glass doors overlooking the patio and the Chicago Loop in the distance. The glass door to the Park Homes Condominium was cold to her touch, confirming winter still had a grip on spring. She brushed aside the hair in her eyes, watched the morning sun struggle to show itself from a bank of thick clouds.

The view held her attention for a moment before her mind wandered back to the memory of sitting again in the last pew in the sanctuary of the Parroquia de San Diego de Alcala Church in the Mexican state of Michoacán. Her home, since she was three was the orphanage next to the church. The thought of sitting in the pew gave her the suggestion of another smile, almost a light chuckle. She sat for many hours in the back pew of the sanctuary. Instead of being engaged in thoughtful prayer to God, it was what the sisters had called it—punishment.

Angel's independent spirit refused to recognize time or discipline. She wanted to escape from the sisters watching her. Skipping prayer, she'd sneak out into the dirt courtyard to gaze at a flight of birds or ants scurrying to build their nest. Ignoring the dinner bell, she'd climb the dead tree with barren limbs bleaching in the sun. Having lost most of her early childhood memories of living at home, she wanted to gaze over the high adobe wall at the world that was strange and unknown to her. Her dream of escape did not include any thought of what she would do with her freedom.

The orphanage was unable to confine her. The sisters always knew the missing Angel was somewhere in the courtyard. Sister Angela Marie was harsh, grabbing Angel by the ear, dragging her back inside. The practice ended when nine- year old Angel slapped her hand away. Angel spent the following week confined to a small, stark room with a bed and Bible.

By the sisters' count, Angel had committed a host of transgressions against God's will, including being mindful she was a child of God and irreverent to the sisters' teachings and discipline. The last pew in the sanctuary always followed Angel's latest misstep. No remorse or resistance. Mindless boredom had ensnared her life. She existed. Nothing more. God and the sisters were agents of punishment, reining in her spirit that ached to be free.

Love had never been a part of the equation in Angel's life. It remained so until a hot summer day when she was again sitting in the pew. A sister said she had a visitor, and she must hurry to the Mother Superior's office. Her first visitor. She was anxious. She dreamed the sisters would release her before her eighteenth birthday. The visitor must have arrived to take her away.

A bowed, old man with a shaggy beard and uncombed hair stood in the office. Beside him was a girl several years younger than Angel. He said he was a neighbor of Angel's grandfather, and she was Angel's sister.

"No" Angel kicked a chair, fled from the room. Sitting in the dirt, leaning against the dead tree, the sisters ordered her inside.

Angel again said no and threw a handful of dirt against the adobe wall in protest. Fathered by a faceless man and expelled from the womb of a heartless woman, Angel's fate was to live alone, without hope or love. Her shriveled empty heart was incapable of accepting she'd had a grandfather or a sister.

Hours later, the sisters returned to the tree where Angel sat. The young girl, named Belicia, stood next to Mother Superior, who told Angel the old man's story. A widower, the grandfather, gave a home to Angel and Belicia when his daughter died. There weren't any other relatives to care for the children. He was poor and could only feed one of the children. It was difficult for him to cope with Angel's three-year-old independent spirit. He placed her in the orphanage and kept Belicia at home. After his death, the neighbor, who was in ill health and had no interest in the girl, decided to place fifteen-year-old Belicia in the orphanage.

Angel couldn't remember her mother. She did have a faint memory of someone in her life. The memory of who it was never revealed itself to her. The Mother Superior left, leaving Angel and Belicia alone. Like two wild animals, they circled each other. They tried to ignore each other, but the small orphanage made it difficult. One day, the sisters told Angel to sit in the pew for refusing to pray before a meal. On the same bench was Belicia, waiting out her punishment for cursing a sister who sent her to her room. Within hours, Angel and Belicia dropped all reservations, became sisters of the heart.

The adobe walls were high surrounding the orphanage making escape impossible. The daughter of a peddler who sold vegetables to the church agreed to help the two sisters and threw a rope over the wall. Soon Angel and Belicia were free and hid in a field in the next village. They were frightened the authorities would find them. Angel was ten months away from being released on her eighteenth birthday.

Life was hard. They survived by picking vegetables and living in abandoned adobe huts with dirt floors. The future? None. Just existence and being together. Belicia was attractive, with budding breasts and inexperienced on how to respond to men who leered at her. Angel, toughened by years of punishment and being alone, did her best to protect her sister. Several times she waved a butcher knife to ward off men who approached Belicia.

Angel failed.

She found Belicia's body in a field, raped and murdered. The killer, a ranch overseer, fled to escape punishment.

Angel began her quest to avenge the death of Belicia. First, to the killer's home. Next were visits to neighboring fields. No one saw him. Angel survived stealing food from gardens and money from the drunken soldiers who slept outside the homes of the local village whores. She'd taken a revolver from one of the soldiers and carried it in a tattered cloth bag.

The days turned into weeks. She wouldn't quit. Ranchers sympathized with her but didn't know where the killer was hiding. They told her the man was a coward and knew Angel was hunting him.

Four months later, Angel found him in a field working. She'd shot him in the leg to stop him when he tried to run. The man begged her for his life. Angel spit in his face and shot him in the groin.

A local drug lord was aware of Angel's search and hired her to track down the killer of his brother. Another drug lord learned of her exploits, and Angel's reputation grew. Manuel was next to hear of her exploits. She joined the cartel, became a legend. Men feared her. No one had managed to escape from her.

The howling wind interrupted her reflective thoughts standing at the cold glass door. She wondered, was she ready for her life to change? Would joining Manuel's efforts to expand his empire replace the thrill of the hunt? The answers eluded her.

***

Seeing Sergeant Porter standing in the doorway of his office, Captain Drummond slammed the papers on the desk. "Goddammit!"

Three officers looked up from their desks in the adjacent squad room.

Glaring through the window separating his office from his men, Drummond waved his finger in a threatening gesture, yelled through the open door, "Eyes on your desk, gentlemen or by God I'll have you stand in front of my desk!"

The men returned to their reports. Their ears remained tuned to what would come next.

Raising his hands, Porter said, "Sir, I'm just the messenger. Drug Enforcement Agency is in the lobby."

Drummond anchored his hands onto the edge of the desk. "Porter, I know you're the goddamn messenger. How many DEA are in the outer office?"

"One, sir."

"Son of a bitch." Drummond's second outburst.

"Shall I send him in?"

"Yes, send the sorry bastard in."

Standing at six-feet- five, Special Agent Quinton Templeton filled Drummond's doorway. Despite his thick chest and long arms, the blue suit fit him. In the years he knew Quinton, Drummond never saw him with any excess body fat. Quinton kept the same physical conditioning he had playing professional football.

"You have a loud voice, Drummond." Quinton chuckled, filling the chair opposite the desk.

"You heard?"

"Every word you spoke to Porter from the lobby." Quinton crossed his legs, scooted down to be more comfortable.

"Good. Now you know my position on the issue. What in the goddamn hell is the DEA doing in my office?" They were friends though neither would acknowledge their relationship.

"The death of Sergeant Pappas is interesting."

"Is the DEA going to stay out of my face so I can do my job?"

Quinton said, "Let me lay it out for you."

"Goddammit."

"No, Drummond, you'll like it."

Pushing his chair back, Drummond crossed his short legs, loosened his tie. "I'm listening."

"The Los Guerreros Cartel at the warehouse is mine. Clear?"

Drummond hated to surrender jurisdiction in any case. Quinton didn't give him a choice. "Clear."

"Drummond, I've known you for years. You're an honest cop. You have a dirty department. Clean it up, or I'll clean it up for you. Fair?"

"Fair," Drummond smiled. It was a warm smile reserved for those people he admired. "Thanks, Quinton. It's going to be messy. I'll need you on my flank."

"I'm the senior agent in Chicago. I can keep the FBI and us out. Just don't take forever doing it."

"Understand."

Checking his watch, Quinton chuckled. "I have exactly seven minutes. Now tell me about the wife and kids."

***

The two drivers pulled up next to each other, rolled down their windows at the abandoned Chevron station.

Hard, cold eyes signaled Sergeant Marcus' mood. "The son of a bitch selling drugs on Powell Boulevard?"

Turning off his engine, Escobar said, "Yeah?"

"Name is Max. Want you to set an example. You know what to do."

Escobar shrugged. "He has whores with him."

"Jesus Christ, Escobar. No witnesses." Sergeant Marcus raised his eyebrows in scorn. "You have a problem understanding 'no witnesses?'" He had little use for Escobar, who often complained and demanded more money.

Marcus started his engine while a dispatcher on the radio sent two units out on a suspicious person call. Turning down the radio, he said, "Boyd been talkin' to you?"

"Been a while."

"Good. I want to know if he does. I'm the new boss. You answer to me now, understand?"

"*Entiendo*," Escobar Padilla grunted, flipped his cigarette.

***

"Thanks, Kat. Appreciate." Seth said as he laid the crutches in the back seat, dropped into the passenger seat. Kat parked the car under the expansive roof canopy at the hospital entrance.

"How long am I going to have to haul your dumb ass around?"

Seth said nothing.

Police Officer Kat MacKenna was going to have to work for it. After chasing the perps, Seth was her quest in life. She'd tease, berate, or give him her best killer smile to squeeze out a response from him. Forget about making him laugh. She'd never caught him with happy, silly thoughts.

"Dammit! We have car problems."

"What's wrong?"

"Car won't start until you give me, at least, a suggestion of a smile."

Seth shook his head in mock disapproval. "You're not going to give up, are you, Kat?"

"Nope."

Seth gave her the best one he had to offer. Kat remained underwhelmed.

She slapped him on the arm. "Maybe it will be enough to go around the block."

Seth gave her shoulder an affectionate squeeze. They shared the age of thirty-four, but Kat was his polar opposite. So much of Billie Spencer in her. Sassy, with a bit of an in your face attitude and a burst of unrestrained, infectious laughter. She, like Billie, told him she wasn't going to give up on him. She had decided they were going to be friends and he had to deal with it.

He told himself he already had a friend, Billie. He didn't need another one. He was wrong, later admitted it. She proved to be the best tonic to help him spit out the last of the bile taste of Allison. And she wasn't as one offensive trucker called her, "An eight or nine dumb-ass blonde."

Instead, she was a happy-go-lucky Irish girl who was a petite five-three. Her bright blue eyes, and hint of rose in her cheeks, complemented her strawberry-blonde hair. A stranger would have been surprised the beautiful girl with a happy face carried a gun, called herself a third-generation cop. An expansive imagination could not have fathomed she also had served with the army's military police in Iraq. Even more surprising, her brown belt in Brazilian Jiu-Jitsu matched the toughest bad guy on the streets. Those who challenged her realized their error in judgment. They ended up on the ground, cuffed, with her knee pressed hard against their neck. A Phi Beta Kappa graduate from college, she'd finished second in the overall ranking in her police academy class. Seth was number one.

Kat surprised everyone.

They tried it, but sex interfered with their friendship. It didn't take for Seth. Kat became a friend. Friends carried expectations about sharing, spending time together. Lovers dreamed there might be a future for them together. Kat fell in love with him. He felt its presence, saw it in her eyes. Whatever the future held for him, falling in love again was not part of it. He had loved Allison and in return, she'd given him years of bitterness.

Knowing he was no longer capable of maintaining a relationship, it surprised him Kat loved him. He was aware of his social shortcomings, offered no apology. Like most everything else, Seth didn't give a damn. He was Seth. A person could accept or ignore him but don't ask him to change. Any change was his decision to make. He enjoyed Kat's friendship. She was good for him but not as a lover. She'd become an anchor. He wanted to be free.

Whatever the hell that meant.

Kat maneuvered around a driver who had backed up to park his car. "Are we going dancing tonight?"

"You're trying to make me smile again."

Kat shrugged. "Sorry. Don't know what came over me."

The comment generated a small chuckle.

"Nice sound, Seth. Very nice."

"Only one I'm going to give you."

"Works for me. How's the leg?"

Scratching, Seth said, "Itches."

"Looks like hell."

The bullet ran a shallow trench on the outside of his right leg from the thigh to midway down the calf. The doctor wanted the wound wrapped with dressing for a week to avoid any infection before performing surgery to repair the damage and suturing the wound. He said Seth needed two to three months of physical therapy before returning to duty. Seth gave himself a couple of weeks.

"You have a sexy leg," Kat said, as she turned north on Parkway Drive East.

"At least, it wasn't my butt."

Kat looked amused. "Where are we going?"

Rubbing his beard stubble, Seth said, "Take me home for a minute before we see my dad."

Chapter 4

Seth slept on the ride home. Sleep was fleeting for him during the night. Pain and a thin mattress were a deadly combination. At each red light, Kat studied his face.

Seth.

She loved him.

Why? She sometimes wondered. He didn't talk much. She seldom knew what he was thinking. Still, outside of her family, he was the first man who had overwhelmed her. Somehow, he was larger than life. She honored and respected him. Respected him for his long years of military service and for his integrity. Seth was a principled man.

She continued to stare when the light changed. The driver behind honked his horn and raised his fist when he passed her on the four-lane street. Ignoring him, Kat brushed her hand against Seth's arm. Where would she be if he never entered into her life the first morning of training at the police academy? Unlike the other cadets who'd stepped into the auditorium laughing and joking, she watched Seth stop at the doorway to the large room. Standing alone, Kat realized later his eyes searched the room for hidden places. Places where cover could save his life. She imagined the ingrained habit kept him alive in Iraq and Afghanistan.

Weeks later, she remembered him waiting his turn on the

running track. The morning air was cold, but he'd tossed his sweatshirt into a heap in the infield. She'd noticed how his hard, flat stomach complemented the pectoral muscles in his broad chest. The size of his biceps even surprised the instructors when he bench-pressed three hundred pounds.

Shorter than many, Seth stopped a couple of inches shy of six feet with legs wrapped in thick-muscled thighs and calves. They carried him with a speed few matched when bursting from one place to another. The instructor sniggered when Kat yelled encouragement watching Seth pass all the cadets in the five-mile endurance run.

Despite his impressive appearance, it was his eyes and face that arrested Kat's attention. His blue eyes darted from one image to another, encompassing everything before him. A blank canvas, his square face with a broad chin and cheekbones never offered a suggestion of an expression. She imagined his emotionless face left his enemies confused on what to expect from him. She harbored the thought several terrorists made the fatal error of trying to read his mind.

She believed his blonde high and tight haircut announced he was a warrior who walked with the best the world had to offer.

Minutes later, passing through the center of town, Kat, out of longing, reached up to touch his cheek when the driver ahead stopped. Flattening the brakes, they slammed hard against the locked seat belts. Seth woke up with a start, his eyes searching for the cause of the sudden stop.

***

"Sorry, Seth. A car pulled out in front of the driver ahead of us."

Seth grunted, sat up in the seat. "Must have fallen asleep."

"You snored."

"I don't snore."

"Whatever," she said before traffic resumed. Ten minutes later, she turned onto Seth's street.

"Want a beer?"

"Touch early," Kat said. "Still morning."

"What are you? A wuss?"

"You say the most romantic things."

Lips closed, Seth curled his lips up imitating a smile. "Come on."

Turning off the ignition in the driveway, Seth grabbed the crutches, charged toward the house.

"Slow down, John Wayne. You're going to fall over. Then I'll have to decide if I want to pick you up."

Seth ignored her, continued his charge toward the porch. Without a signal, he stopped in mid-stride, pulled his left crutch up to balance himself.

"What?" Kat said.

Seth said nothing, studied the house as if he was seeing it for the first time.

The small, vintage single-story 1940's house was home. Chipped paint on the outside walls showed time was not kind. The paint on the porch boards had faded into oblivion years ago while a front porch window remained cracked from an over-exuberant paperboy. Brown mush covered much of the roof. A few maple leaves sticking up from the choked gutters identified themselves.

"Seth. What is it? What happened?" Kat wrapped her arm around Seth. The look in his eyes told her he was in a different place.

"Kelly," Seth whispered. His best friend in high school, they sat for hours listening to Kelly's dad, Tony, tell his stories. A former Marine Force Recon, he'd served in a covert special-ops group, losing both of his legs in the battle at Hué during the Tet Offensive in Vietnam.

Graduating from high school, Seth never looked back at his life at home after he enlisted in the Marines. Twelve years later found Marine Corps Staff Sergeant Seth Collins leading a special-operations team in Helmand Province, Afghanistan. He was on his way to achieving his goal of becoming a gunnery sergeant when a phone call changed everything.

The doctors told Seth they had moved his dad to a nursing home after he suffered a debilitating stroke. He became the best possible father to Seth. Given a hardship discharge from his beloved Marine Corps, Seth returned home. His father was there for him when his mother left. Now it was his time to be there for him.

Almost three years had passed following his discharge from the Marines. The first year he cared for his father and paid the bills. The last two years he'd spent being a cop. Dad was growing weaker. When he died, there'd be nothing left for Seth in Hillsdale. He'd sell the house if anyone wanted it, or give it to the fire department for a practice burn.

"Seth," Kat said.

"Yeah." Seth returned to the present moment.

***

"It's cold in here," Kat said when she entered the house.

Seth spent the next minutes turning on the furnace and closed a bedroom window. He couldn't remove the musty smell. He dropped a Glock 30S into a shoulder holster. Seth felt naked without a gun. Popping two beers, he joined Kat at the kitchen table. She kept her coat on to ward off the chill.

"How's Dad?" she asked.

Sitting in a chair with his right leg stretched, Seth said, "Not good. Slipping some."

"Sorry."

Seth played with his beer, turning it around with his fingers. "He used to pray every night when I was a kid. First, it was for Mom. . .then me. . .then whatever. He's had a sad life. You'd think his God would have given him a better deck."

Arms folded, beer in hand, Kat asked, "What's going to happen to the house?"

"Sell it if it doesn't fall first."

"What are you talking about?" Kat threw out her arms. "This is your home."

The word "home" was unexpected, hitting a sensitive nerve, unsettling him. Seth examined the beer can, glanced at her. She realized he was mulling over an answer. Finally, he said. "This house was never a home for me. After Mom left, it was just a place for Dad and me to hang out."

"Sad."

Seth re-examined the beer can.

The next question was hard. Kat feared she wouldn't like the answer. Still, she needed to know. "What's going to happen to Seth?"

Seth shrugged. "Hit the road, I guess. Nothin' holding me here."

Kat lost it in an instant. She slammed the can down, erupting beer across the table. "Nothing? What the hell are you saying? What about me, Seth? Am I nothing? Is that what you think?"

"Jesus Christ, Kat. Slow down. You're as bad as Drummond."

"Now what the hell does that mean? Did you quit on him too?"

"Never mind."

"What do you mean never mind? Drummond asked for your help, and you told him to go screw himself. That's what the hell you did."

"Dammit, Kat. You're starting to piss me off."

Kat swept an open bag of chips off the table. "Good. Great. How does it feel, bastard? What the goddamn hell is going on with you? You're just going to go away, leave everyone behind? Is that the new Seth?"

"Dad's dying. What the hell is left when he's gone?"

"Me. Seth." She threw a second sack of chips hitting him in the chest. "I'm still here. I'm your friend, remember? I used to be your lover till you got a hair up your butt. People don't walk out on friends, Seth. They tough it out. What's next? You're gonna walk out on Billie?"

"Dammit, Kat. That's a cheap shot. Leave Billie out of it."

"The hell I will. Billie and I are the only two friends you have in the whole goddamn world. But that ain't good enough for you. No sir, you want to jump on your horse and ride out of Dodge. Leave us behind. Hell, you don't need us. We're just a royal pain in the butt."

Kat jumped up from the kitchen table, kicked her chair over and marched to the window, her feet crunching chips on the floor. She stared hard at the world outside, saw nothing. The anger was gone. The broken heart was in control. The floodgate of tears opened.

"You son of a bitch, Seth. You goddamn son of a bitch." She hugged herself to strangle the sobbing.

Seth hobbled up behind her, wrapped his powerful arms

around her. The sobbing stopped. The only sound was Kat's crushed, broken heart.

"You hurt me, Seth. You hurt me bad," she said.

Seth said, with a tenderness seldom heard, "I'm sorry, Kat. I'm sorry I hurt you." He kissed the top of her head. "Please forgive me."

"Seth. I know I'm not supposed to love you. Sorry. Can't help it." She buried herself in his arms.

He stroked her hair. "Kat, I love you but not the way you want me to."

"Do you at least like me?" Kat said, with the first hint of humor in her voice.

"Nah," Seth said.

"Don't like you either. . . can we start over?"

"Good plan. Let's go see Dad," Seth said.

"Could use another hug before we leave."

"Me too, Kat."

***

Seldom escaping from his lips were the foreign words, "Thank you." Examining Elena's efforts, Captain Boyd Turner mumbled approval. Time was short. Given his semblance of approval, she hurried to complete the decorations in their home. Everything must be perfect. Their daughter Alyssa was coming home to celebrate her recent graduation with magna cum laude honors from Ohio State. She'd earned a Bachelor of Science degree majoring in Molecular Environmental Biology and now worked in a medical clinic in Columbus.

Boyd would have none of the effort to prepare for the party. He'd reserve his energy and gaiety for the moment Alyssa returned home. She, unlike any other, made him happy.

Pouring himself a cup of coffee, he returned to the living room, watched Elena. He'd decided years ago their marriage was a mistake. The biggest one he made. And permanent. The Catholic Church and Alyssa glued them together. Divorce was not an option—only tolerance.

The daughter of a captain in the police department, Elena was Boyd's ticket for a quick ride up the promotion ladder and filling his pocket with a never-ending supply of confiscated drug money. Elena's overprotective father made the initial courtship difficult. Suspicious of anyone showing an interest in his daughter, he questioned Boyd's integrity and character. Remembering earlier times with other women and their worried fathers, Boyd turned on the charm. A chameleon at heart, he became what interested Elena's father the most, an honest, courteous, and respectful suitor. It worked and four months later, Elena accepted his proposal.

Marriage soon followed. The honeymoon was short-lived. His lust for money overshadowed the fact he and Elena were two different people. Boyd loved sex while she accepted her martial responsibilities without enthusiasm or initiative. He enjoyed the nightlife. Elena hated the loud music and crush of humanity. The home was a place for Boyd to sleep and a sanctuary for Elena.

What made matters worse in the early years of their marriage were the weekly dinners with Elena's parents and the cross-examination by her father. He wanted assurance Boyd was a dutiful husband.

Alyssa, born two years after the wedding, changed everything. At the expense of any affection for Elena, Boyd found someone to love. Alyssa was the first to receive his attention when he came home, the last when he left. The dream of quick money never left him, but Alyssa anchored his heart.

Their marriage tumbled into a level of tolerance and indifference. The cross examinations ended with the death of Elena's father. So too did the charade of a happy marriage. Estranged, they spoke when necessary. Elena had Alyssa before and after school. Boyd was with her in the evenings. Neither one smothered her. The time of day determined who would be with her. Elena accepted living her life without the love of a husband. She had Alyssa. She'd never agree to a divorce and break her daughter's heart.

Alyssa decided to change the rules. A seven-year-old child wasn't immune from the chill of a loveless marriage. She asked one evening at dinner, "What's the matter, Daddy? Don't you love Mommy?" Their selfishness at ignoring Alyssa's emotional needs devastated them. They became a happy Mom and Dad when Alyssa was in the room. The charade ended when she left.

Boyd returned to the kitchen, placed his coffee cup in the sink. Enough of Elena. There were other problems. Serious problems. Like last night, the worst night. Sometime before sunset, Carlos would call him to set up a meeting to discuss the loss of the ten kilos of coke. Carlos killed men for lesser offenses.

***

Jarred from a sound sleep by the incessant ringing of the cell phone, Carlos Torres managed to open one eye to a narrow slit. He saw an unfocused image walk past the open bedroom door to answer the phone. Covering his head with his arms, he heard her talking, but she muffled her words.

Angel. Bitch. Why in the hell did I ever open the door that day and let her enter?

But he had opened the door. Manuel told him of her pending arrival to monitor changes in the distribution of drugs to the three states.

Introductions were absent when they met. He learned later she introduced herself to no one. She brushed passed him for a quick examination of the condominium. Three men followed her with a mountain of luggage. She finally spoke, ordering him to remove his clothes from the master into the smaller bedroom.

Carlos was surprised she was so young for being such a legend as an assassin. Had to be in her mid-thirties, he thought. He believed legends were people, larger than life, who died heroic deaths performing Herculean deeds.

Such a strange woman.

She killed her enemies and saved the lives of innocents. A drug dealer in Denver told him Angel saved the life of a police officer. Assassins from another cartel had ambushed her. Caught in the crossfire, she pulled a wounded police officer to safety. The story puzzled Carlos. Why would anyone save the life of a cop?

Such a confusing woman.

She'd ordered him to her bed. He should have realized Manuel Robles wanted Angel to discover all of his secrets.

The telephone call continued. Goddammit, woman. Don't you ever shut up?

A throbbing scotch headache also added to his sour mood.

Bitch.

"Bitch" was in the inner circle of his vocabulary. Women served him. Angel needed a beating to remind her he was in control.

Unable to remain in bed, he slipped on a robe, examined himself in the bathroom mirror.

Despite his disheveled appearance, God had sculpted him into a masterpiece of masculine art. He stood an even six foot with a thick chest and powerful arms and legs. Short, black, naturally curly hair highlighted his square face. Thick, straight eyebrows dropping at the corners of his eyes complemented his pencil- thin mustache anchored to a manicured scruff beard. He intimidated men with his commanding presence. Women stepped back in fear. It was time he took his life back.

Angel was a woman. No goddamn legend.

***

Standing in the bedroom, Angel said, "That was Manuel on the phone. He is not pleased with you." She pulled the sash on her gown tighter to cover the cleavage of her breasts. "Sleeping late after spending the night with the masseuse is disrespectful to Manuel. You should have called him early this morning and reported your stupid blunder. There isn't any excuse for your offense. You live because Manuel allows you to live."

Carlos' face, flushed red with anger.

"Listen, you goddamn bitch. I make the decision when to call Manuel. You are just a whore he sent to please me. I could kill you now, and your memory wouldn't trigger a thought in his mind. You'll goddamn do what I want when I want. Don't you call Manuel without my approval. Are we clear, bitch?"

Angel looked at him with complete boredom, disdain. He had no value to her. Reaching into her purse on a table, she pulled out a 9mm Model 809 Taurus pistol, released the safety, cocked the hammer. She aimed the gun at his forehead. "I will kill you if you disrespect me again or threaten me."

Carlos saw death in her eyes. The same when she killed Tobias Ruiz.

He raised his hands in defense. "I have misspoken. I welcome your wisdom to correct this most unfortunate circumstance."

He wanted to gag on his words. He wanted to strangle her even more.

Angel lowered the pistol, reset the safety and hammer, put it back into the purse. "Manuel has called for me. There is trouble in Kansas City. I leave this afternoon. You will honor my wishes and wait until I return before settling the Hillsdale problem. Now, I want to forget this most disagreeable moment between us." She gave him a smile. It was empty without emotion. She cooed, "I will be anxious for my return and the thrust of you into me."

She decided they would no longer have sex. In or out of bed, Carlos was a dog in heat. Others mastered gentler techniques leaving her breathless and satisfied. Still, she enjoyed taunting him with the promise of sex. His frustration would give her joy. He was such a fool.

***

Bored, Sergeant Marcus asked, "You okay?"

Boyd's chest heaved, and he gripped the edge of his office desk. He struggled to suck in air. "I don't know. It's hard to breathe."

"Want me to call an ambulance?" Marcus didn't move or offer assistance.

Sucking in gobs of air, Boyd said, "No. I'm fine. Just give me a minute to catch my breath."

Feeling better, breathing easier, Boyd asked, "Have you heard from Carlos?"

"No. Not a good sign, Boyd."

"We'll be okay."

Marcus knew better. Wished Boyd would drop dead. It

would make his life much easier. His persistent problem remained. How could he kill a police captain and get away with it?

Murder hadn't always been on his mind. He'd wanted to be a good cop like his retired neighbor who lived three doors down the street. Coming home after high school, Marcus spent hours sitting on his neighbor's porch listening to his stories while the old man rocked back and forth in his chair. Working out of the 77th Street Division in South Central Los Angeles, the neighbor told stories of gang warfare, murders and police officers hiding to escape death during riots. No question in Marcus' mind. Being a cop was the right decision.

His record at the policy academy was not stellar nor was it dismal. Just an average cadet who turned out to be an average police officer. After three rejections from the Promotions Board during his ten years of service, Marcus received his promotion to senior patrol officer. The promotion was his second mistake. The first one was much worse.

Marcus and Stella told each other they were in love. Marriage was a catastrophic error in judgment. Coming from a single-parent household with little income, Stella didn't disclose she also loved money and a lifestyle she had never experienced. Her nagging about Marcus' inadequate salary to care for his family reached a crisis level when their second daughter was born. The nagging of not enough money to feed the family became more intense when the third daughter joined the family. A senior patrol officer's take-home pay fell far short of Stella's expectations.

He discovered two solutions to solve his problem. The first were prostitutes for relief from a nagging wife, and the second, an extortion racket for more money for the family. The extortion started when a bar owner complained to him about being threatened by a neighborhood street gang.

Having already served two prison terms, the gang leader backed off after Marcus threatened him with arrest for extortion. A third conviction would have tagged him a habitual criminal, sentencing him to life in prison. Freed from the gang's threat, the bar owner agreed to pay the monthly extortion payment to Marcus in return for protection from other threats. Soon, one bar became two until there were many. Then his prostitutes paid for protection from their pimps.

Happy with more money to spend on herself and the three girls, Stella showed no interest in the source of the extra money.

The bright spot in Marcus' life was his three teenage daughters. He worked hard at being a loving, attentive father. His struggle was convincing them they lived in a happy home. Seldom agreeing on anything, Marcus and Stella managed to hide their marital discord from the girls.

For two years Marcus extorted small amounts of money from the bar owners and prostitutes. Fifty dollars drew fewer complaints than a hundred but greed soon took over. He was weary of chump-change extortion.

At first, Marcus was terrified Boyd would arrest him for his shakedown scheme when he invited him for a drink. Boyd proved to be Marcus' salvation.

"Work for me," Boyd said, "and you'll never have another financial worry. There is more work than I can handle selling drugs. I could use your help. Don't work for me and I'll fire your ass for accepting kickbacks." Branded with a felony record, Boyd assured him he'd never work again. The choice was easy. Marcus joined Boyd to help sell drugs.

Money.

More than Marcus could spend without attracting the attention of law enforcement and IRS. He knew his limitations. Money laundering was not his strongest suit. He was smart enough to hide most of the money from Stella, knowing her spending habits would grow exponentially, alerting the IRS.

Despite having so much money, Marcus was not satisfied. He wanted control. All of it. Boyd was in the way. He observed the slow degeneration of Boyd's physical and mental capacity in the past two years. Boyd had gained copious amounts of weight, and his heavy drinking impaired his judgment. Someday, Boyd would make a serious miscalculation resulting in both of their arrests.

To save himself, Marcus had no choice. Boyd must die. Otherwise, he would never quit. Enraging him to the point of a fatal heart attack was the preferred method. Murder was on the table if Boyd didn't die first from a heart attack.

Chapter 5

Two rats.

They had a choice. Hide in the filthy abandoned furniture warehouse and stay alive. Or, be caught on the Kansas City streets and murdered before nightfall. It was an easy decision to make. Strangers to the area, cartel assassins Tejano and Gustavo Delgado remained sprawled on the floor waiting for news to help their escape. News could also be terrifying. Where was Angel? Would she come to kill them?

Traveling from Los Angeles, Tejano was the best assassin in the Los Guerreros Cartel. But his skill paled in the shadow of Angel. Known throughout the drug world, she was the most feared. No one escaped her relentless pursuit.

The brothers' mission was to kill a large number of Halcon drug dealers. The stakes were high for both cartels. A successful attack would give Los Guerreros assurance on stealing territory from Halcon's drug trafficking distribution. Fail, and they'd have to hunt for new territory.

Tejano saw his younger brother asleep on the floor in the sunlight beaming through a broken window. Unlike his own, no imperfections on Gustavo's handsome face. He wanted Gustavo's perfection never to change. It depressed him every time he touched his cheek. The hideous scar. Gustavo must never bear a scar from the slash of a stiletto.

An ambush in a nightclub restroom left Tejano with a scar from cheekbone to chin. The ambush also left the two attackers with their throats slit. Tejano was never the same. Women turned away or thought him less than whole. Money forced them to overlook his ugliness, and men died when they fixated or commented it.

Waking up, Gustavo said, "Did I do good, Tejano?"

"I'm proud of you, Gustavo. You hit the Cadillac with all thirty rounds. One day you will step into my shoes. Everyone will fear you."

"I can never replace you. You are the best."

"Yes," Tejano lied. "I am the best."

"I'm hungry. How much longer do we have to wait?"

"Anytime, baby brother. She said she'd be here." Gustavo had turned eighteen three days earlier.

Despite his youth, murder was easy for Gustavo. It never left him with any residual thoughts of remorse. When he was eight, his thirst for murder began as he watched his older gang friends beat an informant to death. Quitting the sixth grade, he'd sold drugs on the street, hustled whores for pimps. At the age of fourteen, during his initiation into a gang, he murdered an old man sleeping in a park. The following year, he added three more victims. One of them was a young mother with two children who'd refused to surrender her car to him.

"What's her name?" Gustavo asked.

"Ariella Cervantes."

"Is she Cidro's sister?" Cidro Molina was in charge of the West Coast operations for the Los Guerreros Cartel. He was second in command to Salvador Serafin, who headed the cartel and was hiding somewhere in the Sierra Madre Mountains near Ciudad Madera in the Mexican state of Chihuahua.

"She's his niece. Cidro sent her here a year ago to spy on the Halcon Cartel."

Gustavo rolled over, rubbed the sleep out of his eyes. He grinned at Tejano. "I liked shooting them in the head last night. Seein' all of their brains fly out."

***

Tejano heard it. Two pounding knocks on the side door.

"Dammit, hurry," Ariella said from outside the door. "They're after me."

Grabbing their guns and backpacks, Tejano and Gustavo stumbled through the darkness out onto Highland Avenue. Ariella slid in behind the wheel. "Gustavo, in the back. Tejano, I want you in the front."

"What the hell is going on?" Tejano asked.

"They know I set them up."

Doors closed, tires spinning, she turned west onto E 31st Street headed toward Interstate 70.

Focused on her driving, nineteen-year-old Ariella's face was hard without any trace of humanity. Her flat eyes darted from one side of the street to the other in search of cops and Halcon spotters. Thin straight lips didn't give any hint of happiness, and her tousled hair could have used a brush. Her exposed cleavage flaunted sizable breasts, her equalizer to offset her plainness.

"What happened?" Tejano said.

"My boyfriend, Chano Velasquez was in the Cadillac. I knew they'd realize I was the one who knew where Chano would be last night. I parked a block away from my apartment and watched. Two carloads of Halcon assassins pulled up at dawn. Didn't think they'd finger me so soon. I drove off and hid behind a church for four hours. Thought they would become tired of searching for me. Which one of you is the fastest at stealing a car?"

"I am," Gustavo said.

"Good. There's a post office up ahead. We'll steal a postal worker's car."

"Where are we going?" Tejano asked.

"Lawrence. Less than an hour west of here. I called my uncle, Salvador. He's sending a plane for us. The pilot will call when he's ready. Fly us to the compound in LA."

"Is Salvador pleased?"

"Yeah."

"What's the fallout?"

"It's not good, Tejano. Saw Nemesio early this morning before Halcon picked up on me. He runs the Kansas City operation for Halcon. Told me he didn't know if LA, Miami, or New York killed the dealers. He called Manuel in Mexico to have Angel kill whoever attacked them."

Ariella saw it, so did Gustavo. The sudden expression of fear on Tejano's face.

"You scared, Tejano?" Gustavo asked.

"No,"

Angel terrified Tejano.

***

Seth was quiet. His mood somber on the ride over to the Greenbrier nursing home with Kat. He admonished himself again for his thoughtless words breaking Kat's heart. Why was it so damn hard to talk to a woman? He never struggled with men. He said what needed saying. If it pissed them off, so be it. Kat was different. What in the hell was he going to do about Kat? An answer refused to surface.

Frustrated with himself and concerned about his dad, Seth didn't offer any warmth when he greeted the heavyset, nursing home administrator Martha Ainsworth.

"Hello, Martha."

"Seth." Having met Kat earlier, Martha said. "Kat," and gave her a light hug. Kat's hug was as perfunctory as Seth's smile. Her sad face revealed Seth's attempt to repair the damage from their fight had failed.

Martha saw the hurt. "You kids okay?"

Removing her coat, Kat lied. "We're fine." The temperature in the nursing home was set at seventy-two degrees to satisfy the residents' complaints. Seth didn't make any effort to remove his coat. Afghanistan taught him heat tolerance.

Lifting up from his crutches, he asked, "How's Dad?"

Martha leaned back against the counter in a futile effort to remove some of the copious weight off her feet. "Seth, I'm not going to lie to you. It's not good. Not good at all."

"What's happened?"

"The doctor thinks the night you were shot your father had another mini-stroke."

"Kat must have called you?"

"Yes."

Seth released his grip on a crutch, touched Kat's arm. "Thanks, Kat. Appreciate."

Kat removed his arm, looked away, bit her lip.

Ignoring the rebuff, he asked, "Tell me about Dad?"

"I'm sorry, but his mind is almost gone. It happened all of a sudden. The stroke must have done it. He keeps asking when Cheryl is coming."

"His ex-wife." Seth hadn't called her mom since the day she

left. He couldn't remember calling her anything. She was just an angry memory seldom crossing his mind.

"Be prepared, Seth. Every five minutes he asks when he is going home."

"Damn," Seth asked the question he wanted to avoid. "Does the doctor have any sense of how much longer we'll have him?"

"I'm sorry Seth. Your dad doesn't have much time. Have you made arrangements?"

"Yeah."

"Martha brushed a strand of hair from her face. "His friend Ethel died yesterday."

"She was a sweet lady. I liked her."

Laying a report into a basket on the counter, she said "Ninety-seven. She lived a full life." She pointed at Seth. "You warm with your coat on?"

"I'm okay."

"Seth, I'll wait here," Kat said. Her eyes searched for a place to sit.

"No, I want you with me. You are as much family as anyone."

Kat bit her lip, kept her arms hanging. Seth sensed she wanted to reach out, touch him.

Stepping into the room, Seth saw a curtain dividing the room with his father occupying the space next to the window. Lifting his crutches, he stepped past an old, obese man who was asleep. Standing at the curtain, crutches back in place, he looked at his dad staring at the ceiling without any expression. The bed sheets showed little protrusion from the mattress. Raymond's body had collapsed into itself. The sunlight on his face revealed the stubble of a beard and hollow cheeks. Seth saw more scalp showing through his dad's uncombed hair.

Despite his stoic face, Seth's clenched jaw revealed his pain. He was losing his dad. The last anchor in his life.

"Hi, Dad," Seth said with a soft voice seldom heard.

Raymond looked at the man standing next to his bed. Studying Seth, his face revealed the struggle to remember if he knew him. At last, recognition lit up his eyes. The answer escaped from the darkness of his mind. He whispered, "Son."

Seth gave his best smile. "Dad, you look like they're taking good care of you."

Puzzlement returned to Raymond's face. "When is Cheryl coming?"

Seth's throat tightened. "Soon, Dad. She'll be here soon."

"Oh. . .when am I going home? I want to go home."

"Dad, I want you to come home."

Raymond saw the crutches. Puzzled, he said, "Did you hurt yourself playing football?"

"Yes, Dad."

"Oh." Pointing at Kat, he asked, "Who's she?"

"Kat. Dad, you remember Kat MacKenna. Kat, come here. Say hello to Dad."

"Hello, Raymond."

"No, I don't know who she is." Raymond's voice was weak requiring concentration to understand his words. He looked at Kat. "Do you know when Cheryl is coming?"

"Soon, Mr. Collins. Soon."

Seth and Kat exchanged glances. She touched his shoulder. Her pain was real. She loved Raymond too.

"Dad, do you want me to bring you some licorice?" Seth asked.

"Do I like licorice?"

"It's your favorite."

"Oh. When is the next football game?"

"Pretty quick, Dad. Coach says we need more practice before we play again."

"Oh." Confused, Raymond returned his gaze to the ceiling.

Seth stepped back, "I have to go, Dad. I'll be back tomorrow. Okay?"

"Will you bring Cheryl with you?"

"Yes, Dad."

"You'll take me home?"

Seth kissed his dad's forehead. "Sure, Dad. I love you."

"Remember, you promised," Raymond said with all of his strength.

Stepping outside into the hallway, Seth said, "He won't remember anything about today. I'll be lucky if he remembers me."

Kat slipped inside the crutches, hugged Seth for a long moment. Tears pooled in the corners of her eyes—his were moist also. Seth didn't make any effort to pull away. Kat MacKenna was a friend. He wanted her with him.

He stared down the hallway above Kat's head. "God, I love him, Kat. And dammit to hell—I'm losing him."

***

A dump was Sergeant Marcus' assessment of the bar where Captain Boyd Turner hung out. Standing outside on the sidewalk under the protruding Paddy's Bar sign, he decided his assessment required modification. A forgettable dump. The outside brick walls were blacker with dirt than red. The two windows flanking the entrance were opaque from years of grime. Marcus decided one of the first things he would change when he was in control was the selection of a different bar to run the drug operation.

Stepping inside, he was overwhelmed with the stench of stale tobacco smoke mixed with beer. The kind of stench that stuck to a person's clothing. A drunk slept in a chair next to the pool table. Boyd sat in a far, dark corner, two empty shot glasses on the table. He'd drunk his lunch. Marcus was pleased Boyd appeared lifeless. You son of a bitch. Maybe I'm lucky, and you're dead.

Boyd opened his eyes when Marcus walked up to the table.

Marcus said, "Dammit! We have a problem, and you're already smashed."

Boyd surprised Marcus. He straightened up from his slouch, eyes alert. Marcus had expected him to be in a stupor.

"Back off, Marcus. Don't piss me off."

"Whatever."

Boyd slapped his closed fist onto the table. "Damn you, Marcus. I'm still your captain. By God in hell, you're going to show me some respect."

Marcus lowered his voice to avoid a nearby whore and her trick from hearing their conversation. "Boyd, I don't have the time or energy to fight with you. We just lost a half a million. Carlos wants his money back. There's not much money in the evidence room. Our only option is to come up with the money ourselves. I don't want Carlos on our ass."

Boyd settled down in his chair, drink in hand, head resting in an open palm. "We won't lose it, Marcus. Trust me. Carlos needs us—he knows it. We've been in tougher jams. We'll find a way out of this one. What about this Seth guy? Is he going to be a problem?"

"I don't know. Might order Escobar to take care of him."

"Where's Coleman and King?" Boyd asked.

"Back at the station waiting for me."

A year earlier, Narcotics Detectives Frank Coleman and Logan King joined Boyd and Marcus. Charged with security, they were responsible for hiding the drugs from Federal Drug Enforcement Agents and overseeing their distribution.

"Have you talked to Carlos?" Marcus asked.

Boyd finished his drink. "I called him this morning. Some guy said he was busy. He'd call me back."

Marcus called Carlos within minutes after the seizure of the drugs. "Angel called back later, said she would arrange a meet."

"Not good, Boyd."

Signaling for another drink, Boyd said, "We'll be okay. You worry too much, Marcus."

"How much money do you have?"

"I don't know," Boyd said. "Must be about three-quarters of a million. Why?"

"I have about the same. We'll split it."

"Split what?"

"We'll each give Carlos a half a million. He'll double his money. Maybe it's enough."

"That's Alyssa's money."

"Tell that to Angel."

***

Stepping outside through the front door of the police department, Marcus said, "Coleman, King, wait up," Coleman and King stood silent while they waited for Marcus.

"Step over here for a minute," Marcus said, indicating an area away from the front steps.

"What do you want, Marcus?" King said, without any suggestion of respect for Marcus' superior rank.

"King, I want you to find out everything on Seth."

"What's to find out? Son of a bitch is a goddamn bull. Fought in the war, stops bullets with his teeth. Don't think I left anything out."

"Drop the attitude, King. And include Kat."

"Whatever."

Marcus paused while two patrol officers left the station, passed them on the steps. He waited until they opened the doors of their squad cars. "Coleman. Seth has a father in a nursing home. Find him. Pay him a visit. I want Seth to know we found his dad. He'll back off."

"It'll piss him off," Coleman said.

"Do it. That's an order."

***

Manuel's chest heaved as he sucked in air. He was exhausted. Movement was impossible. "I can't breathe. I shall die."

"I have pleased you," Angel purred, pressing her breasts against him.

"You have killed me two times. . .no, three times over."

"And I shall never walk again."

She stroked Manuel's hair while he kissed the naked young girl lying beside him. "Tell me, my sweet Angel. Did Dulcea satisfy you?"

"Yes. You must reward her for her skills."

"Dulcea," he said, "You must go now, my precious flower. I'll be anxious for you to lie beside me again." Manuel kissed her a final time. Dulcea walked out of the room.

"Now, my sweet Angel, let's retire to the balcony and drink our coffee." Slipping on matching Béliveau silk robes, they lounged on the terrace in the rising heat of the morning sun somewhere in the mountains of Sierra de Tamaulipas, Mexico.

Manuel's Mediterranean heritage gave him a long slender face with a narrow nose, olive skin and a crown of thick, curly, black hair. He refused to wear sunglasses to shield his brown eyes from the sun. The robe exposed the thickness of the black hair on his chest.

On either side of them, thirty feet away stood two men carrying Israeli Uzi-Pro submachine guns. A severe beating would follow if either man glanced at Manuel or Angel.

The flowery pleasantries were over. Time to talk about the two most paramount words in Manuel's vocabulary—money and control.

"What happened in Hillsdale?" he asked.

Sipping her coffee, Angel crossed her legs exposing much of her thighs. "A *policía* stumbled onto our transfer. He killed both couriers. Boyd's man was old. He died of a heart attack."

"It is inexcusable for Boyd to send an old man to receive a shipment. I must eliminate him."

"Agreed," Angel said, struggling to control her long hair in the morning breeze.

"Is there a replacement?"

"Yes. A man named Marcus." She pulled her hair back into a ponytail, slipped on an elastic band.

"Is he *policía?*"

"Yes."

"Take the measure of the man. Is he worthy of our trust?"

Angel said, "I shall do as you order."

"I must be made whole for my loss."

"It will be done."

"Is the *policía* who broke up the sale becoming a problem?" Manuel asked. He set his empty cup on the saucer.

"Yes, I believe he will become a problem."

"What is his name?"

"Seth Collins," Angel said. "He must die. I will see to it."

Manuel signaled for more coffee. "Excellent."

"My informants tell me," Angel said, " the DEA is investigating Chicago. Maybe Kansas City. We have problems in Hillsdale. Seth's superior is a captain named Roscoe Drummond. He is most troublesome. If it is necessary, I will kill him, too."

"What is your recommendation on what we should do with Carlos?"

Resting her elbow on the arm of the chair, she touched her face. "He disrespected you, Manuel, with the lateness of his call about the lost drug shipment. There must be punishment for the offense."

"I agree. Carlos has been with me from the beginning. He is my cousin. My mother raised us. I shall consider if he should die. I will let you know of my decision. Now about Kansas City," he said. Dulcea filled his cup.

"Do you want me to go there?"

"No. I trust Nemesio in handling the Kansas City operation. I am sending him extra help to protect our investment."

"Did the assassin Tejano hit them?"

"Yes. A cook named Larunda is our informant inside Cidro's Los Caballeros compound in LA. She said Tejano and his brother Gustavo were the shooters. Ariella gave them inside help. She, Tejano, and Gustavo are hiding out in the Los Angeles compound. I want you to attack the compound. Kill all on sight."

"It will be done. Do you want me to kill Cidro?"

"No. His attack on Kansas City does not warrant his death. Such an attack would escalate into a drug war neither one of us wants. He is in Mexico with Salvador, who runs the Los Guer-reros Cartel. Angel, I want you safe. I trust you above anyone. I must know you will return to me."

"I will be safe. And I will return to your bed."

***

Ankles crossed, leaning against a treadmill, in Bowerman's Gym, Kat asked, "Want me to answer your phone?"

Sweating on the bench press, Seth grunted, "Yeah. Thank you." Thank you were foreign words to Seth. For years, his cryptic speech ordered men what to do—when to do it. It worked in combat. It failed with Kat. Their fight hurt her.

After Allison, Seth's solution to an argument was simple. "Screw it," and he'd walked out of the person's life. He didn't need their grief—it was his solution to everyone.

Not this time.

Not with Kat.

Like Billie, she somehow managed to slip inside his encased heart. He didn't want to lose her friendship. His problem was he didn't know how to fix it. He'd apologized. Trying to be pleasant should also have helped. Kat's angry expression told him he'd failed. He realized her promise she'd drive him around until his leg healed was the only reason she stayed with him.

"This is Kat."

"Drummond. Seth available?"

"Rambo is on the bench press sweatin' like a stuck pig."

"Get his butt to the reservoir at noon."

"Seth," Kat yelled. "Drummond wants to see you."

"Ask him if it's about our conversation in the hospital?"

"I heard him," Drummond said. "Tell him yes."

Yelling again, Kat said, "Drummond said yes."

"Tell him the answer is still no."

"I heard him, Kat," Drummond said, anger boiling up in his voice. "You tell Seth he's still a cop, and I'm still his commanding officer. That's a direct order. Move his butt down here, or I'll suspend him without pay. Try paying the mortgage with that."

Kat looked at the phone and Seth. Threw a towel at him. Wished it was a barbell. With disgust on her face, she said, "He'll be there."

"You too, Kat. Want your butt down here."

"Couldn't keep me away."

"Thanks. . . Kat?"

"Yeah."

"You have my permission to kick his ass if that's what's needed."

"Plan on it."

Pointing the phone at Seth, she warned, "Don't even think about blowing the captain off."

Setting the bar on the barbell rack, Seth sat up, wiped his face with the towel Kat threw at him.

"You're a cop, Seth. Start acting like one."

"You want to fight again? Is that what you want to do, Kat?"

"No, I want you to do what's right. The captain needs help. Give it to him."

Seth saw the anger in her face. The disappointment in her eyes. Too much. He turned away. He walked to the laundry bin, stared at its contents. How could he explain it to Kat so she'd grasp why he said no? How could anyone comprehend?

Billie understood. Like Billie, he'd witnessed death a thousand times. They'd spit, whooped and roared at death. Twice they hid from it. But death was a consumptive force. Too much, and the mind slipped into madness. Only a monster had an insatiable appetite for death.

No more.

Enough was enough.

The killing had to stop.

Fighting someone else's battle was over. Fighting for the politicians in Washington was bullshit. Serious bullshit. All the men who died fighting the president's goddamn politically correct war. Seth felt his heart constrict. Rage raced through his body. He had to pull away, or the demons plaguing Billie would drive him mad too.

Rest. That was what he needed. Above all else, mind-numbing rest. A way to end the nightmares. The scream of an AK47 7.62 x 39mm bullet tearing into the dirt, inches from his face. An RPG obliterating the sunlight, deafening his ears. The dead corporal at his feet. The baby he'd never hold. The wife he'd never kiss. All of it. The terrifying black nightmares robbing him of the will to live.

"What's it going to be, Seth?"

He leaned against a counter. "I'll see the captain, but you have to understand, Kat, there's nothing left inside. The fight's all gone."

"Baby steps, Seth. Little baby steps. Listen to the captain. Hear what he has to say. Then make a decision. Fair?"

Seth studied Kat's face. "Fair."

The first one she gave him since their fight. A smile. Warm, open. "Now take a shower, Rambo. You stink.

Chapter 6

Settling into the passenger seat, Seth said, "Have to make a call."

"Billie?" Kat asked as she backed out of the parking space at the gym.

"Yeah. Gonna see him this weekend." He dialed the number as he watched a perky young woman holding a gym bag step out of her car.

"Seth?" Billie Spencer's wife said.

He heard the anxiety in her voice. "Mollie, you okay?"

"I've been better."

"Sorry. How's Billie?"

Sniffling, Mollie said, "No change. . .maybe a bit worse. I don't know. It's hard to tell. Excuse me." She blew her nose.

"Are the kids okay?"

"No, Seth. They're not okay. They're scared something is going to happen to their daddy."

Mollie told someone she was all right, became silent. Regaining her composure, she said, "Billie is sleeping now. Sleep doesn't happen often. I'll tell him you called. Still flying on Saturday?"

Kat drove out onto the street.

"Yeah. Should be at the house about eleven. Stay with Billie.

I'll catch a cab."

"Oh, God," Mollie said, sucking in air. "Billie is so look-ing forward to you coming. You know, Seth, you're his the best medicine."

"Tell him I love him."

"I will. God, hurry, Seth. Billie wants to see you real bad."

"I'll be there Saturday, Mollie. Love you."

"Love you, too, Seth. Bye."

Five minutes passed without a sound. Kat drove while Seth stared at the buildings along the streets. Saw nothing. His eyes were red, wet with tears. Billie was worse—broken. He told Seth he couldn't escape from the endless parade of dead faces marching through his mind. The shame of being alive because someone else died. His family had moved on while he remained trapped in the hell of his former life.

Seth knew Billie's pain. He lived with the same pain every day. But unlike Billie, there remained a strong will to live. He was aware there were peace and a chance to become alive again if he could escape from his surroundings and people.

"Billie any better?" Kat asked. Seth shook his head, rubbed his leg to satisfy an itch. "No, the depression sounds worse."

"How many times did you two serve together?"

"Two deployments—Iraq and Afghanistan."

"Next time I go to mass," Kat said, "I'll pray for him."

"Thanks, Kat. He's a good man. The best. Goddamn, I don't want to lose him."

"It's good you're going."

"I just hope I'm not too late. Goddammit to hell, Billie nev-er asked for any of this. All he did was follow orders from that asshole president. Look what it got him."

"I'm sorry, Seth."

Seth rubbed his nose, wiped his eyes to restore his vision. "Me too, Kat. Sorry, you had to hear that."

"I'm not. It means you're still alive. You have Billie. You're not the lone wolf you think you are."

"Whatever. Let's go see Drummond."

***

Driving up alongside Escobar Padilla and Miguel Diaz in the Lindell Garden Apartments parking lot, Gilberto Nunez leaned out the window. "Sorry, I'm late, Escobar. What's up?"

"Marcus wants us to pay a visit to Max. He's in apartment seven."

"He's the one you warned before?" Gilberto asked.

"Yeah. He and the two whores are selling again. Marcus wants us to set an example."

"All three in the apartment?"

"No," Escobar said. "One of the whores is in jail. Rolled a trick. Where are they hiding, Miguel?"

"Upstairs. Front one on the left."

Escobar leaned against his car, studied the apartment building. Satisfied, he said, "No lights. I say their sorry asses are still in bed."

"Escobar," Gilberto warned. "It's daylight. Too dangerous now."

Escobar brushed him off. "Nothing to worry about. Max will expect a hit at night. We're okay. Marcus will cover for us. You two ready?"

Miguel pointed his head at the apartment and Gilberto fired an imaginary gun with his fingers. It would be a good day. Murder was their business.

"Let's do it," Escobar said. "Miguel, stay with the cars. Gilberto, cover me."

Approaching the apartment building, Escobar and Gilberto saw an old man step out of his apartment next to the stairs. Bursting through some Weigela shrubs lining the sidewalk to the building, Escobar slammed the old man against the wall. The man opened his mouth to scream. Too late. Escobar jammed A FNX-45 tactical pistol with a SilencerCo .45 Osprey suppressor under his chin.

"If you want to live, old man, nod your head."

Terrified, the old man froze.

"What's it going to be?"

The man nodded his head.

"You never saw me, right?"

The old man's hands shook.

"Now get out of my face."

The man disappeared back into his apartment.

Gilberto sprinted up the stairs, stopping short at the top of the landing in front of apartment seven. Escobar followed behind at a slower pace. Two years earlier, a 12 gauge shotgun blast left him with a limp in the left leg.

"He has to have a chain on the door," Escobar said. "Ready?"

"Yeah."

"Let's do it."

Escobar stepped back. He was useless at kicking in doors. His slight build didn't help either. Gilberto, fatter and taller, charged the door, ripping the chain out of the casing, smashing the door open. Sitting on the sofa smoking a cigarette, Max reached for the Glock on the coffee table when Escobar shot him in the stomach. A young woman screamed from another room. Gilberto picked up the Glock, kicked Max to the floor.

Gripping the pistol in his right hand and resting the gun in his left palm, Escobar raised the gun to eye level, entered the bathroom. A young girl in her twenties with red hair was naked in the shower.

"Please, mister," she begged. "Don't shoot me. I won't tell anyone. I promise."

"Close your eyes and you'll live."

Her arms were shaking. She tried to cover her breasts and crotch. "Do you promise?"

"I promise. Now close your eyes."

She closed her eyes, and Escobar shot her twice in the breasts. She fell backward and slid down the shower wall. The water, turning red, sprayed down into her dead eyes.

Escobar returned to Max, lying on his back next to the couch. Gilberto kicked the coffee table away.

"Shoot his ass and let's get the hell out of here," Gilberto said.

Escobar ignored him, looked down at Max's face, still blue from the beating he gave him two weeks earlier. Max pressed his stomach to slow down the bleeding. Moaning, he said. "You didn't have to kill her…she was pregnant."

"Shut the hell up. I warned you to stop selling."

Moaning in pain, Max tried to press harder to halt the bleeding. Escobar shot him in the face.

***

"Where is he?" Kat said.

"Drive around back," Seth suggested.

They saw the unmarked car parked behind the partially buried, concrete water reservoir. "There he is," Kat said. "Hey, Porter is with Drummond."

"Porter?"

Kat waved Seth off with her hand. "Never mind."

She parked her car while Captain Drummond and Sergeant Porter leaned against the car waiting for them. Handshakes exchanged, Drummond said, "No crutches?"

"Threw them away," Seth said. "Pain in the butt."

"The leg's better?"

"Stitches will be out in a couple of days. Be back to normal in no time."

Kat said, "Rambo thinks he knows more than the doctor. He had some bleeding in the gym."

Drummond ignored Kat's comment. "Seth, I've been yelling at you a lot, don't like it."

Easing the tension between them, Seth said, "Hell, you yell all the time."

"True. Let's say I'm turning over a new leaf. Just hear me out. Think about what I am going to tell you. Then give me your decision. Fair?"

"Fair."

"What's up, Drummond?" Seth asked.

"My friend Quinton from DEA paid me a visit. Only federal son of a bitch worth his salt. He's going after the Los Guerreros Cartel. They're the ones who shot you. Quinton said our department was dirty. Like I didn't know. Told me to clean it up or he'd do it. I have an opinion on that subject. Been a cop for twenty-three years. Nineteen of them in Hillsdale. No goddamn feds are going to clean up my department. That's my job. Quinton won't give me much time. That's why I wanted to meet with you two. Didn't want to do it at the station. Too many ears. Seth, Kat, I could use your help."

"My family has been cops forever. Tell us what you want?"

"Thanks, Kat. I appreciate it. You and Seth are my two best

officers in the patrol division. You're smart. You get the job done. I don't have to clean up any mess."

Embarrassed, Kat said, "Thank you."

"Seth?" Drummond asked. "How about you?"

"I'm still here."

"Can't ask for more than that. Okay, here's what I know. Boyd's dirty. He's dealing drugs. There's no other explanation for his dismal arrest record. His whole division is either on the take or incompetent. It needs a total house cleaning. Boyd can't be doing this alone. He's not that smart. His heart attack has slowed him down. Someone else is now the brains of their organization. I think it's Marcus. Police Chief Wendell Bateman has to be in on it too. Hasn't done squat to clean up the narcotics division. The only explanation is Boyd giving him kickbacks. Seth, have I said anything you didn't already know?"

"Not much. Do my best to avoid narcotics detectives on the street. Don't trust them. They tell me they're taking over. Next day, the bad guy is still on the street. Don't know much about Boyd or Bateman. Marcus reminds me of a snake with those long arms and legs."

"Kat, any surprises?"

"Seth covered it. I try to handle the problems on the street without bringing in narcotics."

"What goddamn pisses me off," Drummond said, "is I can't prove any of it. That's where you two come in. I want you to help me prove it."

Seth leaned against Kat's car, folded his arms. He respected Drummond's integrity and leadership. Drummond reminded him of his commanding officers in the Marine Corps. Principled men dedicated to serving and accomplish the mission. Seth knew if he said yes to Drummond now, it would never stop.

Then what? Would there be a chance for him to escape the spiral trapping Billie? Would there be any hope to heal, find release from his demons? To be alive again?

"I told you, Drummond, I'd listen. I'm sorry. I haven't changed my mind. Kat's a tough, smart officer. She can do the job for you. You don't need me."

Drummond leaned away from the car, stared at Seth. "You know what really pisses me off, Seth, is sometimes I can't hear a damn thing. I didn't catch a word you said. You told me you'd listen. I'm haven't finished by a long shot. Do we have an understanding?"

Seth rubbed his cheek, refolded his arms. Said nothing. He wondered how many times he'd heard those words from Drummond, "Do we have an understanding?"

"Kat, where are you?"

"I'm in."

"Thanks, Kat. Porter is going to fill you and Seth in on how we're going to set it up. Porter."

Energetic, with a perennial smile, Porter was unusually sober. "Seth, you're on disability. You're the easy one. I don't have to explain your absence at the station. Find out what in the hell is going on. Quinton knows it's going to be messy. Try to clean up your mess, so you only make the back page of the paper and the eleven-o'clock news. There aren't any boundaries. Go where the evidence leads you. Stay safe. They'll try to kill you when they discover you're on to them. Questions?"

No response.

"Good. Seth, Drummond is going to place you on suspension with pay. You'll lose your law enforcement authority. The record will show the suspension is necessary to evaluate your medical condition and determine when you will be fit to return to duty. Miranda rights are out the window. Understand?"

"Affirmative."

"You agree with the suspension?"

"Still listening."

"Kat, you'll remain in uniform with a patrol car during your shift. Your assignment is Seth. Give him whatever he wants. I know you will be working with him during periods when you are not on duty. Don't tell me what you're doing for Christ sakes, and don't let them catch you doing it. Are we clear?"

"Yes."

"Seth is not authorized to enter the station. Keep him outside. I don't want Captain Boyd or Sergeant Marcus to see him. Kat, you will have unlimited access to any records to assist you in the job. Tell me what you can't find, and I'll bring it to you. I don't expect to receive daily reports. Keep me posted when I need to know something. Questions?"

"No," Kat said.

"Sir, have I left anything out?"

"No, Porter," Drummond said "Now, where to start? That's an easy question. We had a double murder an hour ago. Both victims had a drug record. It's messy. While I was waiting for you, I received a phone call. An eight-year-old boy told an officer he saw a man leave the apartment with a long gun in his hand. Had to be a suppressor. He said the man was Hispanic, thin, with a limp in his left leg. The boy's mother later denied he saw anything. There goes our witness. The description fits Escobar to a tee. Some of my patrol officers have observed Boyd and Escobar together. I'll send you copies of the reports when they are available. One last point. You two are my best officers. Stay safe. You're worth more than a dirty department. Seth, I understand you're out of town this weekend?"

"Leave tomorrow morning. New York. Back Sunday afternoon."

"Porter, any last words?"

"Just to echo the Captain's words. Stay safe. And Kat, don't do anything stupid."

Seth saw it. A small suggestion of a smile on Kat's face.

Drummond was pleased he'd given his best shot to keep Seth on the force. "Think about it, Seth. Let me know your answer when you come back from New York."

Seth nodded acknowledgment.

Returning to the car, Seth said, "What the hell was that all about?"

Kat waited until Drummond and Porter drove off. "What are you talking about?"

"Kat, don't do anything stupid."

Kat blushed. "He said it to both of us."

"The hell he did. He said it to you. Kat has a boyfriend."

Kat shrugged, opened the door. "He's no goddamn boyfriend. He's just horny."

"Whatever. He's also unmarried." Returning to the city, Seth was surprised Porter was attracted to Kat. Somehow he'd missed catching the signals. It also pleased him. Porter was a perfect choice for Kat. Bringing them together was a free ticket to hit the road.

***

"That son of a bitch can wait," Captain Boyd Turner said when told Police Chief Bateman ordered him to report to his office. Boyd left for a two-hour coffee and whiskey break. Needing a cover for his drug operation, he discovered four years ago the chief had an appetite for teenage whores. With a hidden camcorder, he caught Bateman snorting cocaine in bed with an underage girl. The rest was easy. The chief began accepting kickbacks. Boyd had the cover he needed.

Two hours later, Boyd said, "What the hell did you call me in here for?"

"Close the goddamn door, Boyd, and show me some respect. I can still fire you."

Smirking, Boyd said, "And I can have you killed, so we're even." He closed the office door.

The chief, with his bulbous nose, double chin, matched Boyd's copious gut. His short breath and raspy voice were his rewards for years of chain smoking. Lack of sunlight and exercise made him appear older than sixty-four years.

"I want my money now!"

"And I want Miss America naked in my bed," Boyd said, stopping at the desk. He never sat in the chief's office. It signaled his deference that Bateman was superior in rank. "Don't you order me around again."

"One damn minute, Boyd. I—"

"Shut up, Bateman. We took a big hit. Your cut is five thousand, and I've had it with you bitchin' about money."

Leaning into the chief with hands on the desk, Boyd said, "Be careful. You are seriously starting to piss me off. Don't push it. Now, is there anything I've said that needs clarification?"

Not a sound.

"Dammit, I asked you a question."

Boyd watched the chief sit back in his chair. Massaged his neck under the shirt collar. "No."

"Good!"

***

Awareness. Instant response. More important than sleep. A valuable lesson Seth learned in combat. It served him again when his hand was on the receiver after the first ring of the phone.

Mind alert from a sound sleep, he said, "Yeah?"

"Oh, dear God," the woman cried. "I can't find him, Seth. I can't find my Billie. He's gone. The car's gone."

Seth bolted upright in the bed. His mind exploded in panic. Oh dear Mother of God. Goddamn you, Billie. . .what the hell did you do? Seth yelled above her crying. "Mollie!"

The sobbing softened. "Oh, Seth. . .I'm scared. He was so sad today. Just sat next to a tree. He was back there again, calling out their names."

"Mollie." Seth caught himself yelling again. Goddammit, Seth. Calm your jets. Speaking softer to hide his dread, Seth asked, "Mollie, just relax. It's me, Seth. I'm here. I'll help you. Are the police searching for him?"

Mollie remained silent.

Seth jumped out of his bed. Had to move. Where? Why? He didn't know. A crazy thought. Maybe if he moved, he'd find Billie. He realized he was walking in circles at the end of the bed when he heard Mollie say, "Yes. . .my sister called them. Oh, Seth. . .what if I lose him? What if he never comes home?" The sobbing exploded again.

With the cell phone speaker on, Seth waved his hands to interrupt. "Mollie."

"Yes."

"I'm on the first flight out of here. I should be at your house by midmorning."

"Oh, please hurry. Maybe you can save him."

"Want to talk for a minute?"

"I can't. The kids are all crying and upset. My sister is on the

90

way over. I have to go."

"Mollie, I love you."

"I love you, too, Seth. Help me. Help me save my Billie."

Wide awake, Seth sensed he wasn't alone. It surprised him. Dammit to hell, who's in the room? He saw him in the far corner, outside of the light from the nightstand lamp. Marine Staff Sergeant Billie Williams in full combat gear, holding an M4A1 in the ready position, grinning.

He loved Billie's mischievous, silly grin.

You son of a bitch.

Seth stepped forward one small step. Not enough to disturb anything. He wanted to touch Billie. Tell him he loved him as a brother. Another step.

Billie disappeared.

"Goddammit!" Something was wrong. Seth couldn't see. Tears pooled in his eyes along with a crushing sense of doom. Billie was AWOL. Maybe dead. Oh, sweet Jesus. What the hell have you done, Billie? What the goddamn hell have you gone and done?

Silence.

You better not be dead, Billie. No, sir. I wanna see your face. Crush you in my arms 'cause I love you, and you're alive.

Seth couldn't do it. Remain standing in place. He had to move. Eyes wiped clear, he abandoned the bedroom, started pacing. From the kitchen to the living room. What was out of place? A stupid question. No sense of orderliness. What the hell? Anything needing to be tossed found a home on a chair or the table. Sometimes the floor. It didn't matter. Dad was in the nursing home. Seth didn't give a damn.

The fridge. What the hell was in the goddamn fridge?

Question answered, beer in hand, he leaned back against the

kitchen counter with its stained linoleum. Eyes registered noth-ing. Seth asked the question again for the four-hundredth time. Why you, Billie? Why did I love you above all the others?

The answer. For the first time, Seth saw the answer written in big letters. Why had Billie such a strangle hold on him? Why he loved him like the brother he never had?

Billie was the only one who loved me back.

Chapter 7

Standing away from the throng of people rushing down the Detroit Metropolitan Airport concourse, Seth leaned against the wall, answered his cell. "Mollie?"

"Seth?"

"Who's this?"

"It's Audrey," she said, crying. "Mollie's sister. I'm using her phone."

Goddammit. Don't tell me?

Struggling with her words, Audrey said, "The police found him this morning in a park. Oh, Seth. . .Billie. . .he shot himself."

"Oh Mother of God!"

"Seth." Audrey heard Seth's choking, gulping in air. "Seth. . .I can't hear you."

"Sorry." Seth searched the concourse. Goddamn, where can I go?

"Jesus Christ," he muttered. A woman stopped, looked at Seth with concern. A man scolded her for staring, pulled her away.

He saw it across the corridor. "Audrey, give me a second. It's hard to hear." Wiping his eyes, he started to work his way across the crowded walkway. He bumped a man who cursed him while a woman, seeing the pain on his face, pulled away to let him pass. He reached a seat at an empty gate. "I'm back." Scratched the itch in his leg

"I've heard Billie mention you. He loved you."

"I loved him. Can I talk to Mollie?"

"She's with Mom, Dad, and the minister."

Seth inhaled deeply. "Okay, Audrey. Give me a second. Don't hang up." Sucking on his lips, he pushed his way back across the swarm of people to the Flight Departure Board. "Audrey, I'm at the departure board. Let me think. . .Ah. . . My flight's on time. Should board in twenty minutes. I'm trying to figure this out. It's a direct flight, two hours. I'll take a cab. Audrey. . .tell Mollie I'll be there by eleven."

"I will. Seth."

"Yeah."

"Mollie's been asking for you. Hurry."

Seth sagged when he dropped his phone into his pocket. They were gone, all of them.

"Goddamn you, Billie!" he said through gritted teeth.

Billie Spencer was dead.

***

It happened on DEA Quinton Templeton's watch. And everything changed.

Garcia was driving Angel home to her condominium after she'd flown in from Mexico on a Gulfstream G150 business jet. Traveling on the inside lane of East Randolph Street, Garcia pushed down the turn signal in preparation for a left turn onto N Field Blvd and Angel's residence on E Benton Place. Oblivious to traffic, Angel was on the phone thanking Manuel for the comfort of her return flight home when a siren behind them exploded in sound. A black, unmarked, Chicago police car lit up with red-and-blue lights. Startled, Angel dropped the phone while Garcia forced the Mercedes-Benz S-Class stretch limousine over the curb onto the grated steel plates in the median strip. Glancing out the window, when the police car accelerated past them, Angel saw two men parked in a vehicle on the other side of the street. The driver, who was watching her with binoculars, dropped the glasses out of sight. Angel didn't have any doubt. The two men inside the black Chevrolet Suburban with U.S. government license plates were Drug Enforcement agents. Picking up the phone, she said to Manuel, *"Policía."*

DEA had her and Carlos under surveillance. No other explanation made any sense. With a plan in place to avoid DEA monitoring their phone calls, Angel ordered Garcia to retrieve the disposable phones and the portable cell phone voice changer hidden in a garage storage locker.

The coded phones identified each dealer, eliminating the use of names. Calls were limited to ten seconds using the voice changer. Driving around in the city, the caller discarded the phone in a public place after completing the call. Angel was surprised how much she could say in ten seconds.

***

"Angel made us, sir," an agent said in the Suburban on North Dearborn Parkway.

"Dammit," Quinton said.

"Sorry, sir."

"What happened?"

The agent said Angel spotted them when a police car lit up and hit the siren.

"Okay, we'll work around it," Quinton said. "Pull back some of the mobile surveillance on Angel but don't lose her.

She's their enforcer. She'll think we dropped her. Who knows? Maybe she'll screw up, make a slip-up. Besides, I want Carlos. He's the one running the show."

***

"Thanks, Mom," Mollie said, holding the cup of hot coffee with both hands. Mollie and Seth were sitting in a postage stamp of a backyard under a London planetree that continued its diminished struggle to survive. Mollie had recovered some from the initial shock of Billie's death. Living for months with Billie's worsening depression had toughened her heart to the possibility she might lose him.

"How about you, Seth?" Mollie's mother, Joan Freeborn said. "Cup of coffee?"

"Yes, please. Thank you, ma'am."

"Don't tell me. Just like Billie, black?"

"Don't want to pollute it."

Joan tried to force a smile at the lame joke. She rejoined two children standing on the back porch and disappeared into the house.

Setting the coffee on a small cast-iron leaf table, Mollie removed the photograph from her Bible, handed it to Seth. "What does it mean, Seth? Billie used to sit under this tree with this picture in his lap. Sometimes he'd cry."

The picture was of eight men standing together in the Syrian Desert in Iraq. Seth was surprised to see the picture again. He'd lost his copy. He held the photograph in his hand, returned to the desert. The day was hot, but every day was hot. And the wind. Did the damn wind ever stop blowing sand?

Warriors. Everyone. Standing together, invincible. Filled with bravery. "Ooh-rah" competed with the wail of the wind.

They all agreed. The history books would record this fateful day. The terrorists didn't have any chance.

Seth's throat tightened, eyes moistened. Billie stood in the middle of them grinning like a Cheshire cat. The picture followed the deployment of the 2nd Battalion of the 5th Marines to Ramadi, Iraq.

Mollie folded her arms, hugged herself. "You're holding the picture like Billie did. I can remember him doing it."

"We were all sergeants. Proud to be assigned to the most decorated battalion in Marine Corps history. We called ourselves the Iron Mike Squad. We were going to kick some serious butt."

Seth had to pause. Unable to speak, he struggled to focus. Forcing himself, he pointed to two Marines in the photograph. "They were killed a month later. There were three of us left during our last deployment to Afghanistan. The third member was Takahashi. He was one damn, fine Marine. We lost him six weeks before his rotation home. Billie took Takahashi's death hard. They grew up just twelve miles from each other. They were tight."

"He talked about Takahashi almost every time he held the picture."

"Did he tell you Takahashi saved his life during their first deployment to Afghanistan?"

"No," Mollie said, "but I believe it. Billie never did say his name without becoming choked up." She rubbed her eyes in a futile attempt to stop the tears running down her cheeks.

She paused for a minute, another piece of Billie was leaving her. "I have something for you, Seth." She pulled a letter out of the Bible. "Billie wrote it about three months ago. We both knew it was a goodbye letter. He said he wanted you to have it if something happened to him."

"Mind if I read it tonight?"

"I thought you would want to be alone."

"Thanks." He slipped the small letter in his shirt pocket. He couldn't continue. The tears wouldn't stop. Mollie wrapped her arms around him, held him tight while they cried together. A long moment. The two of them in the back yard under the London planetree.

A nearby truck with a loud muffler broke the silence of the moment. Mollie said, "Take the photograph, too, Seth. Billie would want you to have it."

Seth added the photograph to the letter.

The tears continued to run from Mollie's eyes. Searching the gray sky failed to give her any relief. Rubbing the tears off her cheeks, she said, "You know what hurts the most, Seth? I knew it my heart. I was going to lose him. I could never take away the depression that sucked all of the life out of him. I loved him so much. . .Not a damn thing I could do to save him."

Seth wrapped his arm around her. "You know what hurts me the most?

"What?"

"Billie was the only brother I had."

***

"Where in the hell have you been?" Disgusted, Marcus joined Boyd, who was sitting at a table in Paddy's Bar with a shot glass in his hand.

"You bastard. You think you can just walk in here and start yelling at me? No goddamn way." Boyd waved his hand, knocking over the shot glass. It bounced off his shoe, the whiskey splattering his nylon sock.

"Back table in the corner," Marcus said. "We'll finish this."

"No, goddammit. We'll finish it here. What in the hell is your problem?"

"I've been trying to call you for two hours," Marcus said. "Two hours. We have serious problems, and you've been sitting here drunk."

Boyd slapped the table. "That's it, Marcus. It's over. I want your letter of resignation on my desk first thing in the morning."

"Oh, what a brilliant statement. Must have taken you all day to come up with that one."

"Don't you think of interrupting me. I'm not finished by a long shot. I—"

The bartender rushed up to the table. "If I even think there's gonna be any more trouble, I'll throw both of you out of here. Do we understand each other?"

They looked at the angry bartender, his bulging biceps, knew they met their match.

Alone again, Marcus lowered his voice. "In case you forgot, Carlos could shoot our ass. We got problems, Boyd. We need a plan."

Boyd's face was red with anger. No one disrespected him. No one. Marcus worked for him, not the other way around. And not for long either. Narcotics Detective Frank Coleman, now he was different. He could work with Coleman. Kill Marcus and everything would return to normal. He'd be the boss. No disputes. First, he had to kill Marcus.

Satisfied with his plan, Boyd said, "Carlos is not going to shoot our ass. He can't afford to lose us. We're good for him. Now get the hell out of my face. And I want your resignation."

"When hell freezes over. I can burn you, Boyd. I can burn you straight to hell."

***

A minute later, Sergeant Marcus stood on the sidewalk in front of the bar. A plan had surfaced in his mind. A simple plan. One he should have thought of a long time ago.

***

Seth returned to the Econo Lodge at the Newark International Airport. Tossed the carry-on onto the bed. He was oblivious to the roar of jets swallowed into the darkness of midnight.

Good-bye had always been part of the job. One moment they were his comrades, the next unrecognizable from the bomb blast. It was that way since his first firefight. It remained until he left the battlefield for the final time. Death was just another part of the workday. No time for tears or reflection. He had to keep his head down, or he'd become unrecognizable too.

Maybe it was because he was older. No longer invincible. Just mortal. Subject to death. Or maybe Billie was the one who had unlocked his heart. Whatever, it was a terrible night. A good-bye night. The letter was Billie's last words he'd read. Tomorrow, Billie would be a memory.

There'd never be any new words.

Seth held the letter like a jeweler held a diamond. He'd seen the hand of death too many times. Tonight was Billie's turn. Eyes clouded, filled with tears, he unfolded the letter.

> *They're all gone, Seth. Cooper, Byrne, Pod-laski, Santos, Johnson, Takahashi. I see their dead faces every day. I'm so sorry to do this to Mollie and the kids, but I'm no good for them. They need someone who is alive and can love them. I've been*

dead for a long time. Please watch over Mollie. Cover her flanks. I love you, Seth.

Semper Fi.

Billie

***

Their faces never registered in Seth's mind nor could he tell anything about them. They were just people. Hundreds of them scurrying down the terminal walkway while a loudspeaker announced flight schedules. Paying attention, he would have seen the old couple strolling down the corridor creating a serious roadblock for passengers trying to make the last call. Grandpa must have told Grandma they should arrive three hours early to catch their flight to coo over their newest grandchild. Or the heartbroken wife with her new baby, telling her soldier husband good-bye. Maybe, never hello again.

He missed all of it, sitting alone in a darkened gate. But he wasn't alone. Billie was still with him all night.

Soon Billie would be gone, retreating to the back corners of his mind. Then it would be over. All of it. There wouldn't be anyone to ratify his twelve years of service in the Marine Corps. No one to share the special memories captured during his six combat deployments. Those terrifying two days and night, in Musa Qala, Afghanistan. The brand-new, dumb-ass second lieutenant who didn't know shit from Shinola. Three days later, earned a silver star. Lived to tell about it.

Who was here now who would want to hear those stories? Or understand the emotions of escaping certain death. The faces. All the dead faces. Outstanding men. Everyone a warrior.

Someone needed to tell their stories.

Goddammit, Seth. Don't let them fade away.

Seth was suffocating from memories, but reality refused to release its grip. It kept kicking him in the head.

Okay, smartass. You want to cut and run? Fine. What about Kat? You taking Kat with you? Give her a lifetime of "Hurry up" and "Let's go?" When she says, "Where?" you say, "I don't know." Come on, Seth. That's no goddamn life for Kat.

She should have someone to love her. Give her babies. She doesn't need your sorry ass. So how are you going to tell her without breaking her heart? I don't know. Maybe Porter will love her. That would be one way.

Oh, that's brilliant. You just solved the Kat problem. Outstanding. Now, where are you going to go? Are you going over there? Or over here? Or maybe you're going somewhere else. Good plan, Seth.

What the hell? There ain't no one who gives a shit about you anyway.

True.

God, you're a piece of work.

Memories. So damn many memories. They buried him. The day he took off his Marine Corps uniform for the last time. The pain he would never wear it again. He was a Marine—a lifer—a lifetime marriage. And he was good at what he did—an icon with the new, young Marines. He knew it, accepted it without comment. He'd have given his life in a heartbeat to keep his young Marines alive.

The last day in combat. Why did it have to be so ugly? They were on patrol in search of a Taliban leader. Seth's mood was black. An RPG had killed two members of his team earlier in the day. They never found the leader. Two men died in a futile mission.

The patrol was set to end at 2200 hours. Seth, knelt on the ground, studied the faces of each of the ten surviving members of the joint Alpha-Bravo team. There wouldn't be any more young Marines looking in awe at his dust-covered, sweat-streaked face. Nor would there be terror-stricken, young Marines hoping Seth would keep them alive. He wanted to hug each one, tell them he loved them. Keep every one of them alive—send them home whole in body and spirit. He failed twice that morning.

The next morning he showered, put on a clean uniform, flew to Germany. He left his young Marines behind. Seth couldn't brush their faces away. Who would step up now, shield them from death?

Drowning in memories, Seth was unaware of the man walking down the corridor with a young girl. He was a big man, standing six-foot-five on a two-hundred-fifty-pound African-American frame. His back was ramrod straight. He appeared to be in his mid-forties with solid muscle, and the overhead lights reflected on his bald head.

No, Seth didn't spot the man with the suggestion of a limp in his left leg. But the man saw Seth and his thousand-yard stare. The man found them everywhere. They sat alone away from lights. The-high-and-tight haircut and taut, compact muscles were their signatures. Their faces etched with pain, anger. He saw all of it in Seth.

"Mehah. Sweetheart, I'll meet you at the kiosk in ten minutes. I won't let you out of my eyesight." He peeled away from his daughter.

Seth sensed movement, saw a big man stop in front of him. The man said, "Semper Fi, bro. I was there, too." He lifted Seth up, gathered him into his massive arms.

The words spilled out of Seth's mouth. "I couldn't save him. Called him most every day, I still couldn't save his ass."

"I couldn't save a lot of them either," the man said. "It still tears my gut, but you have to move past it, bro. Your buddy would want you to live. You owe it to him to live."

The man released his hold on Seth, extended his hand. "Moses Remington. How much time before your flight?"

"Some." Seth shook his hand, felt Moses' tight grip. "Seth. . .Seth Collins."

"Unit?" Moses asked.

"3rd Special Operations Battalion. Yours?"

"1st Battalion, 6th Marines."

Releasing his hand grip, Moses asked, "Home?"

"Ohio…Hillsdale."

"New York City. Daughter was in Florida with her grandmother. You work?"

"Policeman. City." Dropping his carry-on bag onto a seat, Seth said, "That's about to change."

Missing Seth's comment on change, Moses said surprised, "Well, I'll be damned. I was a cop. Not long. My folks weren't too thrilled."

"What happened?" Seth asked, dropping his jacket into his bag.

"Went to college. Majored in business. Was going into Dad's steel business. Didn't pan out. Dad sold his interest in the business, retired. Mom had a weak heart. Wanted to be where it was warm."

"Sorry."

"Thanks," Moses said. "It worked out okay. Mom lived another twenty-one years."

"Dad still alive?"

Finding his daughter waiting at the kiosk. Moses raised two fingers. "Lost him about four years ago. Life was empty for him without Mom. Couldn't make it. He just wanted to be with her. He used to take me shooting when I was a kid. He loved guns. The bigger, the better. I seldom missed the bull's-eye. Dad left the steel business. So, why not be a police officer? They had guns. Lousy decision. Had to arrest drug dealers. Hated those bastards."

"Amen."

"Knew two kids in high school who died of drug overdoses. The girl was a math whiz. Had a helluva life ahead of her. I wanted to kill the dealer. Can't handle people who prey on kids. Sell them drugs. Turn young girls into prostitutes—that kind of people are a goddamn air thief."

"What's on the plate now?"

"Have myself a little business. Call it GRYB."

Seth's solemn face reflected the reverence he had for the four initials. "Green, red, yellow and blue. The four landing beaches at Iwo Jima."

"It's sacred ground. Been there, Seth?"

"Once."

"Two times for me. Today, I gather intel on foreign countries for my business clients. They decide if they want to set up shop in the country. Keeps me busy. Lots of travel. Cost me a marriage." Rubbing his left thigh, Moses said, "Leg's bothering me. Time to sit, talk for a minute?"

"Sure." Seth noticed Moses's prosthetic left leg when they sat down.

Continuing to rub his thigh, Moses said, "Lost it above the knee in Garmsir. Not much left of it. Pisses me off. Can't move like I used to. I can bench press three hundred pounds, and I run like an old woman. Have to hire people to do my bidding when I have to move around. It's like I'm a goddamn invalid."

"Can appreciate how you feel." Seth saw the introspection on Moses' face. Needed to change the subject. "Been to Garm-sir. Lost one damn fine major there. You a gunny?"

"Yeah. You?"

"Staff Sergeant."

"Saw you rub your leg, Seth. Touch of blood on those khaki pants. You okay?"

"Scratch."

"Had some of those," Moses said. "Hurt like hell. Itches too."

"Yeah. And then some."

"Your friend. Suicide?"

"Yeah. There were eight of us. He and I were the only ones left."

"How's the widow?"

"Mollie? Not good. She tried so damn hard to save him. He was her life."

"I can help her."

"How?" Seth felt his throat constrict. Was that going to happen every time he thought about Billie Spencer? Would there be a time when the thought of Billie made him happy?

Moses explained he'd formed an organization called The Brotherhood. The members were former combat Marines and some widows. They're a support group to help other Marines readjust to civilian life. He added there were seventy-five members in his group with most of them living around in and around New York City.

"Seth, four other groups are being formed across the nation. We can't save them all, but at least, we can save some of them."

"I wish to hell Billie had known about you."

"Me too. I know we could have helped him."

Seth grunted acknowledgment. Wiped the tears in his eyes.

"The group is not just for moral support."

Seth had an idea of what Moses was about to tell him. The sniffling stopped. "I can only imagine," he said with a trace of humor. "What else?"

"We've sent out members to provide whatever assistance is required, including security.

"Security?"

"Sure. Why not? Sometimes, a former Marine finds himself in a situation where they may want help to protect their families or need a weapon. Our people provide the support. Hell, if I had to, I could form up a fully armed combat platoon in twenty-four hours to kick some serious butt."

"Feds must love you."

"They'd be pissed if they knew what I've done or what I can get my hands on. Let me say no more."

Seth liked what he heard. His contempt for the president and Congress included the Department of Defense.

"Want you to join the group, Seth. You'd be our first police officer. Want Mollie to join, too. I have three widows who can help her."

"Sounds good." They exchanged phone numbers including Mollie's number.

Moses held Seth's hands. "I know your pain, Seth. God knows, I know your pain. Time for a quick story?"

"Sure."

"We were on patrol looking for a Taliban leader. Stopped at a small village called Karatoo. Maybe a dozen compounds. Hell, Seth, you've seen a million of 'um."

"And then some."

I met a young girl. Name was Alasah. Checked it out later. It means purity. Had her baby with her. A girl. . . Goddammit, Seth. I can see her as plain as day." Moses stopped to recover from the pain in his words. Looked at his daughter standing at the kiosk. Seth saw the young girl staring back at her father. Seth thought she had to know how the war had scarred him.

"Sorry, Seth."

"Don't be. You had Alasah. I had Billie. So, what happened?"

Moses never heard Seth. He'd left and returned to Karatoo. Looking at Seth and seeing Alasah, he said, "She was wearing a bright, gold-colored dress with a swirling skirt. The wind fluttered her baggy trousers. She was such a frail girl. Pretty. Had a long face with the saddest blue eyes. She was terrified. The Taliban threatened to kill her and her family if her grandfather talked to us. Begged me for help. Kept saying 'Mrasta ze'. Help me."

"Coming back from patrol, we heard the shooting in the village. The Taliban ran away before we made it back. Alasah and her baby were dead. Stood them up against a wall and shot her. Killed four other women too. The irony is the grandfather didn't say spit to the captain.

"Goddamn, I couldn't save her, Seth. Just a kid and they shot her. Of all of the faces, hers is the one that won't leave me. Wakes me up at night. Haunts me during the day.

Moses returned and looked at Seth. "I know. I was under orders. On patrol. Had to get the job done. Wife said nothing I could have done. Didn't help a goddamn bit. She didn't see the terror on the girl's face. It was like Alasah knew she was going to die.

"Made a pact with myself. Swore I'd never walk away again

if someone asked me for help. Seth, your pain for Billie may never go away. But you can share it. You can share it with me. I'm a hell of a good listener."

Seth relaxed, inhaled deeply. His cheeks were streaked with tears. Finally someone who understood and gave a shit. Seth said, "Stand up you ugly ol' bear."

Moses chortled.

They hugged. Tight, hard.

"Got a flight to catch," Seth said.

"I'll call you in a couple, Seth. Semper Fi, bro."

"Semper Fi."

Chapter 8

"Something happened. I called you last night, Martha, but your daughter told me you were out for the evening. I didn't leave a message." Melanie Bryce was an aide at the nursing home. Martha instructed her to report any event out of the ordinary.

"What happened?"

"A man called earlier in the day. He said he was a detective with the police department doing a routine investigation. He asked if Raymond Collins resided at the retirement center. I told him yes. Last night he came in and showed me his badge. He mumbled his name, wouldn't give me his card. He said it wasn't necessary. He asked for Raymond's room number. I gave it to him. Did I screw up giving him Raymond's room number?"

"No," Martha said. "You should always cooperate with the police. What happened next?"

"He was gone for just a minute and then came back asking if Raymond was in front or behind the curtain. I told him he was behind the curtain, and I would be happy to introduce him. He said Raymond was asleep, and he would come back another time. I checked on Raymond after the detective left. He was wide-awake in his bed with the television on."

"Thank you for calling me, Melanie. You followed procedures. I'll call Seth."

***

Habits. Easily acquired. Hard to break. Punctuality was the cornerstone of Seth's career with the Marine Corps. It was a painful lesson he had learned in boot camp. The habit failed him when he tried to wash the blood spot off his loose-fitting pants. He made it worse. He arrived for the last call with the attendant's hand on the breezeway doorknob. He paused at the doorway into the plane, covered the blood spot with his jacket. His leg itched. He wanted to stop, scratch it.

"Sir," the Delta Air Lines flight attendant said, motioning for him to enter.

"Yes, ma'am." Seth turned right toward his window seat in the first-class section of the Boeing-Airbus A319-100 aircraft.

It was impossible for Seth to ignore the beautiful woman who occupied the aisle seat. She was slender with shoulder-length, lustrous black hair. Contrasted against her alabaster skin were startling, bright-blue eyes. She wore a white silk blouse with a paisley scarf and a black pencil skirt. Many of the women Seth saw earlier in the terminal wore mismatched outfits or sweatshirts, jeans, and open-toed sandals.

"Excuse me, ma'am," Seth said, moving past her to his window seat.

The woman gave a polite smile.

Fastening his seat belt, he said, "My compliments to you, ma'am."

Seth, who had closed his eyes, perplexed the woman. She was accustomed to men making passes at her. At the age of thirty-four, she had acquired at least a dozen responses to discourage their advances. He'd complimented her, closed his eyes, ignored her. She had never experienced such an approach from a man. Watching him out of the corner of her eye, she concluded he was exhausted but not sleeping. His eyes opened during take-off. Who was this strange man who confused her?

There must be a further explanation for what he'd said. She was surprised it was important to know what he thought when he complimented her.

"Excuse me," she said. "You confuse me. I appreciate the compliment, but I don't understand."

Seth opened his eyes. "You are beautiful, and you dress like an elegant lady. Obviously, you are one. It's unusual to see."

Surprised, she said, "Thank you."

Seth turned his gaze back to the magazines in the pouch in front of him and closed his eyes again. He didn't make any effort to adjust his position to fall asleep.

She continued to watch him. There had to be a story behind this brooding man who didn't smile. The haircut, his muscular build. The military bearing. Who are you? She wanted to talk to him, to know his story. He would be in her life for such a short period.

"Thank you," she said, again.

"You're welcome."

"No. Not for the kind compliment but your service to our country. It must have been hard for you."

Seth remained motionless, staring at the seat cushion in front of him. A glance out the window told him the sky was blue. All he needed to know.

She saw the pain on his face. Allowing a minute of silence to pass between them, she continued, "You don't talk much."

"Hard to talk to a lady. Not much experience."

Ignoring his comment, she said, "Hello. I'm Pamela Brighton."

"Seth." They shook hands.

Pamela was confused Seth failed to disclose his last name. Why? There had to be a reason. Such a strange man. Different. But in a good way. Pamela decided not to press for the last name. She said she was traveling to pick up her daughter Dusty at her husband's parents farm in Wisconsin. She didn't reveal her mother lived with her and Dusty in a penthouse on Central Park South in New York City.

"Daughter ride horses?"

With a bright smile, Pamela said, "Yes, every day, sunrise to sunset. Wants to be a veterinarian someday and take care of them."

"Nice. No ring. Husband?" Seth was unable to overcome a lifetime habit of speaking bluntly with few words.

"Widow. Lost my husband to a drug overdose." Pamela was stunned. Embarrassed, a flush of heat crept across her face. She told Seth a secret only a handful of people knew. It was her deepest secret. Without any hesitation, she said it. Why? What power did this man have over her? Who was this man? The questions didn't have any answers.

"Sorry."

"Me too." The secret was out. She had to finish it. "He had it all and threw it away."

Seth said nothing.

This strange man struggled with words—there were so few of them. She had to know more. "I saw you in the terminal. A big black man was hugging you."

"A new friend."

"Military?"

"Yes. Name is Moses Remington. Strange name."

113

Pamela wanted to remember the name. It could be important later.

Seth didn't offer any information about himself other than his first name. The brooding man had secrets. He wasn't danger-ous. She sensed he was hurt, without love.

Their conversation for the remainder of the flight consist-ed of Seth asking and Pamela answering questions. He was an enigma at the end of the trip. Still, she was pleased he'd shown a genuine interest in her life.

A wave of sadness engulfed her as Seth stood up when the pilot stopped at the gate in Detroit. In an instant, he would be out of her life forever. She felt the loss. He was different from any man she had ever met. The draw to him was intense in her heart. She wanted to make him laugh and feel alive again. To touch him and give him joy.

"It was my pleasure, ma'am," Seth said and disappeared into the crowd.

Pamela would have cried if she had allowed herself.

***

Seth caught a momentary glimpse of Pamela through the crowd of passengers. She stood up, watched him. Their eyes locked. She appeared pensive, he thought. Maybe even sad. She was untouchable for the likes of him. Never loved a lady. Wouldn't know how.

"Sir," the flight attendant said. Seth was still fixated on Pa-mela, blocking the exit. He didn't want the moment to end.

Stepping into the breezeway, it happened. The memory of Allison returned, hitting him with full force. Goddamn, bitch of a whore. You couldn't even stay in the same building with Pamela, much less the same room. Seth's mood was black when he entered the concourse walkway.

Allison did that to him every time.

Enough of that goddamn whore. Enough. Time for Dad.

Turning his phone back on, he saw a voice mail message from Martha Ainsworth at the nursing home. An older woman crashed into him when he stopped to listen to the message.

"Goddammit, mister," the woman said.

"Sorry, ma'am." Seth escaped to the side. He wanted to react to the woman who continued to scowl at him while she rearranged her coat. Must have been a former truck driver or lady wrestler.

Calling the number, Seth said, "Martha, tell me Dad's okay."

"Seth, your dad's fine. The reason I called is he had a visitor."

An alarm exploded in his head. All auxiliary thoughts of Billie and Pamela evaporated. Muscles tightened—jaw set. He and Kat were Dad's only visitors.

"It was a policeman," Seth said.

"Yes. How did you know?"

"Never mind. What happened?"

Martha explained what Melanie said to her.

"Did she describe him?"

"Yes," she said. "He was tall and thin, maybe in his thirties. Handsome too."

"What color was his hair?"

"Black."

"Narcotics Detective Frank Coleman," Seth muttered.

"What did you say?"

"I know him. Martha, I want Dad moved before sundown."

"I can't do that. Not without you signing a release first."

"Do it, Martha. I'll sign later. He's in danger. Don't tell anyone where you move him. And I mean anyone."

Gone. All of it.

Any thought about what in the hell to do with Kat. The sudden surge of sadness when he saw Pamela for the last time. Boyd crossed the line when he declared war by targeting his dad. Seth was comfortable with war. He knew how to stay alive. Kill the enemy. Boyd was the enemy. There would be only one outcome.

***

"You're late," Angel said.

"New distributor in Dayton met me here in the city. Took longer than expected." Carlos Torres pushed off his shoes in the condominium, collapsed into a recliner. "How about a martini?" he asked.

Returning with the drink, Angel said, "Did she have a name?"

"Who?"

"The girl you were with this afternoon."

"No. No name. Just young and beautiful." The sex had exhausted him. Still, he managed a sly grin. "The dealer gave her to me as a token of his appreciation. It would have been inhospitable of me to refuse. Is this a problem?"

"No."

"Then what is the problem?"

Angel sat on the couch, placed her drink on the end table. "There are three problems, Carlos. Two of them are minor issues between you and me, and one is serious."

"What's the serious problem?"

"No," Angel said in a laconic voice. She crossed her legs, exposing most of her thighs, taunting him with her body. "First the little problems. Manuel has decided to let you live. At least for a little while. I wanted to kill you for your incompetence in losing the shipment. It is perhaps best you do not upset me. I may forget Manuel's instructions."

Angel's brittle smile grew broader gazing at Carlos. She loved words, inserting them like a surgeon into the mind of her adversary. "Now, my sweet pet, you could kill me while I sleep. It would be such an easy thing to do. But trust me, Manuel would take days to kill you. Not a happy thought."

"Bitch."

"Maybe. Second, I will no longer lie in your bed. You disgust me. You are a boorish brute. You should sleep with bitch dogs." Angel smiled. It was a dangerous smile suggesting death. "Right now, you want to strangle me with your bare hands, don't you?"

Carlos smashed his martini glass against the fireplace.

"Well, do it. I don't have any strength. I cannot defend myself."

He remained frozen in place. His face consumed with hate.

"Can't do it?"

"Trust me, bitch, not tonight, but you're good as dead already."

"Oh, my pet, you forget one thing."

"What?"

"I will kill you first."

Exhausted from the sex and taunts from Angel, Carlos sank back into the recliner. "This is getting us nowhere. What's the serious problem?"

"We're under surveillance."

Eyes alert, Carlos asked, "Who?"

"Policía."

"DEA?"

"Yes."

The tension dropped between them. They spent the next hour implementing their security procedures to defend themselves from the surveillance.

Chapter 9

Half-asleep from eating too many baby back ribs for lunch, Captain Drummond sat up in his desk chair, squinted at his cell phone. "Yeah, Seth."

"I'm in."

Chapter 10

Sergeant Porter stuck his head into Captain Drummond's office, "Sorry, sir. Line one."

Half-asleep from a long night investigating a gang shooting, Drummond settled in for a quick nap at his desk. "Tell them I'm out of the office."

"Sir, it's Quinton."

Drummond stared at the blinking light wishing it would go away. It kept blinking. Dropping his feet onto the floor and drinking the last of his cold coffee, he lifted the receiver. "Yeah," he said.

"My, aren't we happy today," Quinton yelled above the noise of the dual aircraft engines.

"Short night," Drummond sighed.

"We need a meet."

"Am I going to be happy?" Drummond asked, pointed his finger at Porter and the coffee cup.

"Drummond, you're always happy to see me."

"Yeah, right. When?"

"When my plane lands," Quinton said.

"What the hell?"

"I'm about an hour out. Assemble your team. I'll call when I land. Find us a nice quiet place."

"What's up, Quinton?"

"My gut's talking to me. You need to know about it."

"Appreciate the heads up."

"Who knows, Drummond, we may end up as friends."

"God forbid." Hanging up, he yelled at Porter standing at the door, "Find Seth and Kat. Have them meet us at the Hillsdale Water Reservoir in an hour. And dammit, I told you to bring me some more goddamn coffee."

***

Hidden behind one of three large water tanks, DEA Special Agent Quinton Templeton stepped out of the rental car, stretched and looked at the expansive Ohio countryside. Shaking his legs, he hoped he could restore circulation, kill the numbness. He hated airplanes, most cars. His muscular build on a six-five frame made traveling difficult, uncomfortable.

Surveying the foothills and farms, he said, "Like your office, Drummond."

"I don't know, Quinton. Kinda small."

Gazing at the water tank, Quinton said, "Could stand some paint."

They both sniggered. Despite their polar opposite viewpoint of federal versus local, they both knew they'd passed the point of being adversaries and were friends. Part of their friendship was professing they weren't friends.

"You feeling better, Drummond?"

"Yeah. Coffee is my salvation. Quinton, before we start, I want to introduce the team."

Focused on the two men and one woman next to Drummond's car, Quinton waved. "Good-looking team."

"Thanks. Sergeant Jeff Porter and I have our hands full trying to hold the department together. Police Officers Seth Collins and Kat MacKenna are making it happen in the field. Kat is one damn fine officer. Her family has been cops since the pilgrims. She served with the military police in Iraq."

Kat said, "Before the pilgrims, Drummond."

"Of course, how could I have missed that?"

"Good humor," Quinton said. "We're going to need some of that before we're through."

Drummond continued. "Seth was a lifer in the Marines until his family called him home. He had twelve years under his belt and multiple tours in Iraq and Afghanistan. He's your point when Hillsdale is on your radar."

Exchanging handshakes, Quinton said, "So Seth, you, me, and Kat will be working together?"

Seth dropped his hands. "Yes, sir."

"Call me Quinton. I played pro football for three years, and you were a Marine. Kat, your family, has been cops since Moses. Hell of a combination."

Seth said nothing. Kat smiled.

Quinton said, "The silent type, huh, Seth?"

Expressionless, Seth said, "Unless something needs to be said."

"Nothing wrong with brevity. Brevity is good."

"Quinton," Drummond said. "Let's move on. You came here to give us some bad news."

"Now why would you say that?"

"Experience," Drummond said.

"Can't argue with experience. Gentleman and Kat, I'm afraid Drummond's right. We are expecting a turf war between two rival drug cartels. Hillsdale is in the center of the battleground. What I am about to tell you is what we know, not what we can prove in court. What we're doing now is building our case."

"What do you want us to do?" Kat asked.

"Stay alive. It's going to be rough."

"Reasonable position," Seth said.

Quinton leaned against the rental car, folded his arms, crossed his legs. Kat copied Quinton's movements while Seth remained flatfooted. Habit taught him uncrossing his legs was cumbersome when he started running to or from someone.

"Talk to us, Quinton," Drummond said.

"The director of DEA has appointed me to head up a task force to go after the cartels. The Mexican cartels have carved up the United States into their individual territories. There's a bunch of them centered in the major cities. Right now, we're focused on two of them—Los Guerreros and Halcon Cartels. The FBI has pulled back, let us take the lead.

"The Los Guerreros Cartel is on the West Coast. Their leader is Salvador Serafin. He's hiding out in the mountains somewhere in western Mexico. Their territory is California, Oregon, Washington, and Idaho. His chief lieutenant is Cidro Molina in LA.

"Salvador has a problem. He's ambitious, wants more territory. The cartels in Phoenix and Denver are blocking him from moving east. They're too tough for him to muscle his way in. He sent five men to Alamogordo to explore gaining a foothold. The Phoenix cartel executed them. So, he decided to leapfrog over Phoenix and Denver, move into the Halcon's Midwest territory. Manuel Robles, who's hiding out in the mountains in eastern Mexico, runs the Halcon Cartel. The cartel is unique because they have two separate territories. The first is centered in Kansas City, goes northward through the Dakotas to the Canadian border. The second one is Illinois, Indiana, and Ohio. Carlos Torres runs the second one. His base is Chicago."

"What's between Halcon's two territories?" Seth asked.

"A cartel based in Detroit. Manuel and Detroit have traded potshots at each other. Nothing serious. Salvador decided to test the waters, attacked Manuel in Kansas City, killing five drug dealers. He wanted to know Manuel's reaction to the attack and if he had a chance to gain a foothold. His assassins Tejano Delgado and his younger brother, Gustavo, were the shooters. The attack failed. Manuel is too organized in Kansas City.

"Now we think Salvador is studying Manuel's second territory. He may have better luck with Chicago. Carlos in Chicago is weaker than Kansas City. He's lost three major shipments including, Seth, the one you stumbled onto at the warehouse. Carlos is in trouble with Manuel. The proof is Manuel sent his assassin Angel to check out replacing Carlos. We'll know their decision if Carlos turns up dead. I'll say more about Angel in a minute.

"Manuel has five drug centers in Ohio. Columbus, Cincinnati, Toledo, Akron and Hillsdale. Hillsdale was set up as an experiment. They tried using dirty cops and city officials to run a drug operation. Your mayor and three council members are dirty. The district attorney is ineffective and should retire. Two people who can help turn Hillsdale around. The city manager and Penny Majors in the DA's office.

"Seth, the drug delivery you busted up may be the loose pebble that starts a landslide. I think using cops to run a drug operation is a failure. They don't have the culture and discipline the other drug dealers have. Greed and ambition are their downfalls.

"I have two wild cards. The first is Angel. We don't know

her last name. God, I sometimes wonder if she has one. She's Manuel's assassin. There isn't anyone better. The worst error in judgment for an agent to make is underestimating her. Angel is smart as hell and cunning as a damn fox. She doesn't make a move without planning it first. The lady has no fear. What really pisses me off is surveillance has lost her. She's disappeared. It's damn frustrating.

"We've spent most of our energies chasing the drug dealers, haven't spent much time on her. Right now, she is doing our work by killing other drug dealers. We'll deal with her later.

"Salvador hit Manuel in Kansas City. Manuel is using Angel to attack Salvador. Tit for tat. Salvador has two major bases in Southern California. A drug distribution center somewhere in San Diego and Cidro's compound in LA. We think she's going to hit the distribution center. We have surveillance on the compound and discovered Manuel is doing the same. There are too many guards in the compound. She's going to hit San Diego.

"Now the war begins. It's Salvador's turn. He has to retaliate, kill Carlos and Angel. Carlos is an easy target. Angel will be Salvador's problem. Angel has to save Manuel's operation in Hillsdale. She has to kill you, Seth, Kat and the rest of the dirty cops before Manuel can bring in new people.

"While Angel is cleaning up Hillsdale, Manuel has an Achilles' heel. Hillsdale is in turmoil. Salvador has an opening. He'll send in his assassin, Tejano, to kill Angel. I've had dealings with Salvador. He's from the scorched-earth policy. Blow it up, burn it up, shoot it up. Hell, every local, state and federal will be crawling all over each other in Hillsdale. When everyone leaves, Salvador slips back in, sets up shop. Now he'll have a firm foothold on the Ohio drug trade.

"Drummond, I said I have two wild cards. The second is the

ATF. They like to do their own thing. Trust me. Cooperation is not their strong suit. They may decide to play in Hillsdale and the hell with us and the FBI."

"Can't you complain to your boss?" Drummond asked.

Shaking his head, Quinton said, "Their boss is the Attorney General. He's also our boss. He appointed the director of ATF. They're buddies. Go way back. The director and the president are pals. "

"Not good news," Drummond said.

"Seth and Kat, I will deny what I am about to tell you. Disappear if ATF shows up. Do your work where they will never find you. They won't have any problem throwing your butts in jail for obstruction. Clear?"

"Clear," Seth said.

"Folks, I have to run. Drummond, say hello to the wife."

"Will do."

"She's still putting up with you, huh?"

"At least through the week."

The two men hugged each other.

Quinton whispered into Drummond's ear, "Stay safe, my friend."

"Back at you."

Chapter 11

An old man with a shopping cart stopped, watched him step out of the car in front of the Blue Parrot Bar. "Seth, did you find out anything out about Angus?"

"Tommy," Seth said, locking the car.

The old man wobbled on bowed legs, and a hunched back toward the car. He'd spent too many years on the rodeo bull rider circuit. The two little front wheels on the cart wobbled in step with the man. Seth shook the man's gnarled, dirty hands with the black fingernails.

"Sorry, Tommy. Judge gave Angus seventy-five days for shoplifting. You going to be okay till they release him?"

Tommy Lewis and Angus Backus had pooled their meager skills and possessions to survive on the streets long before Seth became a police officer. An ex-railroad cop, Tommy's eyes, and ears were still good. He was Seth's best informant.

"I hope so, Seth. Kinda hungry."

"Go in the alley, wait at the kitchen door. I'll have Mike bring you some food." Seth had strong feelings for Tommy. Except for Angus, Seth was his only friend. He was the one who put food in his belly, money in his jeans. He told Tommy when he found a safe, dry place for him to sleep.

Tommy reminded Seth of another lost soul, and the sadness

he'd left behind. The pain in Marine Sergeant Brandon Wythe's eyes. It was a cold October day when Wythe and Seth hunkered down in a wadi in Afghanistan trying to escape from a sniper. The sergeant told Seth about his twin sisters who'd died in a car wreck. Wythe's father never recovered. Died a derelict. Tommy was someone's father. He'd never die alone. Not when Seth was nearby.

"Need any money, Tommy?"

"A twenty and I are good friends."

Giving him the money, Seth said, "Enjoy your beer."

"Thanks again."

"I'm looking for a young Hispanic with a limp in his left leg. Want to see him before he sees me."

Caressing his dirty gray beard, Tommy said, "I know him. Names Escobar Padilla. He's real mean. I'll ask around. Somebody has to know where he's holed up."

"Stay warm, Tommy."

Waving his hand limping away, Tommy said, "You're the best, Seth. God bless."

A blue neon parrot anchored to the outside brick wall made the entrance to the bar unique in the Elgin District. Inside, it was no different than any other rundown bar across the planet. The bar extended the length of the room on the left side with assorted tables and chairs on the right. A pool table with a single light in the back right corner. The kitchen and restrooms occupied the other side. The stench of stale beer and cigarettes impregnated into the paint on the walls and chair cushions. The bartender was the tipping point for Seth deciding it was his kind of bar.

Mike was an ex-Marine who served two deployments in Iraq, including the second battle of Fallujah. They'd both fought in the Jolan District, never met. Their simple greeting was always the same. A fist bump.

"The usual, Seth?" Mike asked.

"Yeah." Seth had a serious affliction for chicken fried steak. "Tommy is in the alley. Could stand some chow. Put it on my tab."

"Appreciate you taking care of him."

"He's hungry."

"On it."

Kat was waiting for him at a table.

Still standing at the table, Seth asked, "Are we better, Kat?"

Kat glanced up from her beer, pursed her lips, said nothing.

Seth waited for an answer while Kat kicked an empty chair from the table. "Sit your ass down. And no, Seth, I don't know if we are any better. I know I don't hate you anymore. Right now, I'm trying to like you again."

"Don't want to lose you, Kat," Seth said.

"Quit trying to sweet talk me. Order your goddamn beer."

"How's your mom?"

The question brightened up Kat's face. "She's fine. Irish mothers worry when they haven't heard from their baby daughter in a week."

"God, you must have a billion relatives."

Kat smiled. First one in a while. "Irish and Catholic," she said. "Deadly combination. We rent the college football field for Thanksgiving dinner."

"How come you didn't invite me?"

"You're too scary. Frighten the babies."

Mike set a beer before Seth.

"What's in your head about Drummond?" Seth asked.

Kat spent a moment reflecting on her answer. "Taking on a cartel. Scary. Chasing dirty cops. Love it. Hate dirty cops. The independence. . .being my own boss is beautiful. How about you?"

"Same. Right now, they don't know we're on to them. Want to change that, get in their face. Have them screw up. Then we got 'em."

Playing with her beer mug, Kat asked, "What's your plan?"

Speaking in a staccato rhythm, Seth said, "I have Tommy looking for Escobar. He could use your help. Shouldn't last long. Tommy doesn't forget a face. When we find him, I want you to ride Escobar. Uniform, black and white. Do ID checks but be careful doing it. Have lots of people around you. He's a viper. Make him so pissed he goes to his boss. That's the plan. Who's the boss? Captain Boyd, or Sergeant Marcus. Want the personnel files on Chief Bateman, Captain Boyd, and Sergeant Marcus. Anyone else you think is dirty. You have a couple of retired cops in your family. Have them stay with your folks. Escobar can be squirrely."

"Good idea. What are you going to do?"

"PSYOPS."

"Psychological operations?"

"Yeah. I'll find something in the files. Let them know I know. Rattle their cage."

***

Kat yelled into her cell phone. "Seth! I spotted Escobar."

"Where?"

"Jack's Liquor. Fourth and Taylor. I'm turning around."

"Call for backup."

Lit up, sirens screaming, two backup black and white patrol cars raced toward Kat while she did a U-turn on Taylor. Spotting Escobar jumping into the passenger side of a beat up Dodge

Charger, Kat slammed on the brakes, stopped a foot short of the trunk of the Charger. Jumping out, she stood behind the open door, leveled her Glock 22 service pistol at the driver.

"Driver, both hands on the steering wheel, now!"

Guns drawn, two other officers joined her, their weapons leveled at the occupants.

In her loudest voice, Kat said, "Passenger, hands on the dash." Escobar didn't move.

Kat covered the driver while an officer opened the door, threw Escobar to the ground. "The officer told you to put your hands on the dash." A second officer moved up to cover.

"Driver! Open the door with your left hand," Kat said. "Keep your right hand on the steering wheel." Crying hysterically, the girl complied. "Driver, now step out of the car, walk backward to the sound of my voice."

The girl was walking backward when a third police cruiser pulled up.

"Cuff her," Kat said and raced around to the two officers who were wrestling with Escobar on the ground. She jumped into the fray, pressing her knee into his neck.

"I gotta em cuffed," an officer said.

Escobar cried out in pain.

"He's cuffed," another officer said.

Pulling Escobar up to his feet, Kat pushed him against the car. "Escobar, you're charged with resisting arrest and suspicion of murder."

"You're dead, bitch."

"You are also charged with threatening a police officer. And if you keep it up, you'll be charged with pissing me off."

***

Three hours later, lounging with Seth against an unmarked car in the back parking lot at the John F. Kennedy Middle School, Drummond said, "Excellent work, Kat. We have one thoroughly pissed Escobar sitting in isolation at the county jail."

Standing with her hands in the back pockets of her jeans, Kat said, "I still want to charge him with pissing me off."

"I bet you do. Can't think of a more serious offense. Seth, you're running the show. What's next?"

"Escobar's pissed. Want him back on the street. Can't just release him. He'd smell that a mile away."

"Seth, we have to drop the murder charge," Kat said, "Can't fly. No witnesses."

"Agreed. We can keep the resisting and threatening charges. Have either of you worked with Deputy DA Penny Majors?"

"Nope," Kat said.

"She's one of the good guys," Drummond said. "I can work with her. Why her?"

"Drummond, she's been helpful to me a couple of times. Escobar is going to be arraigned in the morning, right?"

"Yep," Drummond said as he rubbed his eyes. The long days were catching up with him.

"Captain, can you see her tonight? Have her assigned to the case? Tell her everything. Why we want him back on the street. Maybe she can get low bail on him. Have Sergeant Porter follow him. Escobar knows Kat."

"Works for me, Seth. I'll call her."

***

Following a hug and pat on the back, Cidro Molina said, "Salvador, I apologize for my absence. You are a man of many responsibilities. I am appreciative of your hospitality and the time you have given to me."

With a broad smile, Salvador Serafin said, "It is true there are many demands for my attention." Seven years earlier, Salvador had murdered his way into control of the Los Guerreros Cartel. Your visit pleases me, my dearest friend. May I serve you a drink?"

"Yes. Thank you for your kindness."

A naked young woman, standing nearby, left to pick up a drink. Salvador had many beautiful, young women who gave him pleasure and service.

"You wish Elvita to return to your bed?"

"Yes," Cidro said. "She is an artist at satisfying a man's needs."

"She is one of my favorites. I am pleased you will enjoy her. Come. Let us sit on the terrace and enjoy the evening breeze." The covered terrace with an antique patterned travertine floor and Tuscan pergola columns overlooked an infinity pool. The mansion was somewhere in the Mountains of Sierra Madre, Mexico.

The woman returned with drinks, retreated to her position twenty feet away next to a tiled Mexican wall fountain.

They fell silent, enjoyed their drinks and being together again. They watched three naked women swimming in the pool.

Tasting his drink, Cidro said, "We have shared many years together."

Salvador pointed his finger at Cidro. "Ah, since we were children playing in the streets of Morelos. But my friend, I must break from the serenity of the moment. I have news for you, Cidro. It is not unexpected."

"What have you heard?" Cidro said, with sudden interest.

"Dulcea keeps me informed on what is happening in Manuel's Halcon compound. She has learned Angel is being dispatched to attack your compound in Los Angeles."

"Your news confirms the rumors I have heard," Cidro said.

"Angel is the best." Gazing at the pine-oak forest covering the mountains, he said, "It continues to be a distressful thought that I once refused to accept her services in our organization. A foolish miscalculation of mine. . .but. . .such is the history of the past." Returning his attention to Cidro, he said, "Are you prepared for her, my friend?"

"Yes. Following the rumors we received, I've recruited more men to repel her attack."

"She must not succeed," Salvador said.

"She will not. That is my pledge to you."

***

Showing her irritation, Penny Majors wiped her hands on a kitchen towel. "Captain Drummond, you do know what time it is?"

Standing on her front porch, Drummond said, "Sorry. Bit chilly outside. Can I come in for just a second?"

Penny checked her watch. "My daughter goes to bed in exactly twelve minutes. That's how much time you have."

"Thanks. Could use a favor."

"As usual."

Rubbing the brim of his worn, stained Stetson hat, Drummond said, "Can I tell you a story?"

A child yelled from another room.

"Excuse me." Penny returned a minute later. "My daughter thinks it's time to watch TV. Make it quick, Drummond."

"I have a dirty department."

"I know that. Know the players. My problem is I don't have

the evidence."

"I want to clean it up."

"Good for you."

"Will you help me?"

"Drummond, I've always liked you." Still irritated, she said, "Tell me what you want."

Drummond explained his plan on returning Escobar back to the street.

"You've got it. Now go away. My daughter needs her mother."

Drummond opened the door, stepped out onto the porch. Adjusting his hat, he saw her smile.

"Call me anytime, Drummond. I'm on your side," and closed the door.

***

Tightening the sash on his robe, Carlos studied her. The early morning found her dressed for the day, purse in hand. She had summoned him from a sound sleep, an egregious insult. He must find a plan, accelerate its implementation. Angel had to die.

"Why the hell did you wake me up at this hour?" The morning sun shined through the condominium sliding glass door, highlighting the anger on his face.

Bored with the question, Angel said, "Cesar and Garcia are now mine. Find a new bodyguard and driver. I am also going to need the maid Pedra."

Nostrils flared, Carlos charged, stopping short of Angel. "No goddamn way! Cesar and Garcia have been with me for years. You don't make the decision just to take them."

Angel shrugged, with a thin smile. "I can and I did. Do you want to complain to Manuel?"

Nostrils flared, Carlos snarled, "Bitch."

"True."

"Why in the hell do you need them?"

"Manuel has dispatched me to Los Angeles. They will assist me."

Carlos planted his hands on his hips. "Doing what?"

"Did Manuel disclose his plan to you?"

Silence.

Angel smiled. A sardonic smile spoke volumes of her contempt for him. "I thought not. Why should he waste his time explaining himself to you? You have no need to know his plan."

Carlos' neck cords popped as his face flushed hot revealing the depth of his anger. He balled his fist to hit her.

"What, you want to break my neck so early in the morning?"

Angel pulled a Glock 43 handgun out of her purse, aimed it at Carlos' chest. "If I even think your arm is going to move, I will kill you where you stand."

Carlos lowered his arm, opened his fist. "I'm going to enjoy killing you," he said.

Angel smirked. "Go make yourself useful," and left the room.

***

Sitting in the corner away from the regulars at the nearby tables, Marcus asked King, "What did you find out about Kat?"

Lighting a cigarette, Narcotics Detective Logan King said, "She comes from a long line of cops. Third generation. Her dad and two uncles were cops. They've worked Vegas, Pittsburg and Oklahoma City."

Marcus took a sip of his drink, loosened his tie. He hated ties.

Taking a deep drag, King said, "She graduated just behind Seth in her class. He was first. She's into some kind of kung fu thing. Phi Beta Kappa. She's a tough, smart cop. Here're her and Seth's addresses. That's about it."

"Thanks. You're a good cop, King. Enjoy working with you."

"What do you want now?"

Hand over his heart, Marcus said, "What the hell are you talking about?"

"I know you, Marcus. Remember, I work with you."

"There is something you can do for me. But let's enjoy our drink first. How's your girlfriend, King?"

"Good."

"Expensive?"

"That too," King said.

Earlier, Marcus made it a point to learn King's background. He needed his help to wrestle control from Boyd. Fed up with numerous girlfriends, Marcus discovered King's wife left him two years ago. It was months since he had visited his two daughters who lived in Sacramento.

Seven months ago, King arrested his current girlfriend for the possession of cocaine. She spent the night with him instead of the county jail. One night led to others. Soon he was paying her rent in an expensive condominium. It was a continuous struggle for him to pay for her clothes, spa and beauty salon appointments.

"What do you think, King?"

Eyeing the Templer's barmaid bent over at a nearby table serving drinks, King said, "About what?"

"Us. We make a good team, don't you think?"

"Yeah. It's alright."

"You know, it's kinda sad. Things are always changin'."

King crushed his half-smoked cigarette. "Where are you taking me?"

"Our working together. What's going to happen to us if something happens to Boyd? I worry about his health."

"He doesn't look good."

"Heaven forbid," Marcus said. He gave his best expression of concern. It was unconvincing. "What's going to happen if he doesn't make it?"

"English, Marcus. English."

"King, we're just having a drink, visiting. Don't be so suspicious. I'm just sayin' I like working with you. You're smart. Now Detective Coleman spends all his time fussing about his appearance. But not you. You're the one who's going places. I like that about you. Nothing wrong about being ambitious."

"What's this have to do with Boyd?"

A young couple moved in, sat two tables from them. Marcus lowered his voice. "Simple, Boyd's sick. I don't think he has much time left. I intend to take over when he's gone. I need someone who is smart, ambitious, and wants a promotion. There is a hell of a lot of money waiting for him."

"You're talking about me instead of Coleman?"

"Yeah. I want you to join me."

"More money?"

"More money than your girlfriend can spend. Hell, you could have a dozen girl toys."

"But only after Boyd is gone. He could live another five years."

Marcus finished his drink. "Yeah, that's a problem, isn't it? Boyd is going to die. It's just a question of when. In the meantime, you're scratching around trying to find more money."

Despite the young couple nearby, King leaned back raising the front legs of the chair off the floor. He said, "You're talking about murder."

"No," Marcus countered. "I'd prefer calling it an acceleration of the inevitable."

"Sounds better."

"I think so."

"Still murder," King said. He paused for a minute, studied Marcus. He also looked at the cocktail waitress who'd checked him out earlier. King remembered the smell of her perfume. He dropped the chair back onto the floor. "Gonna cost you, Marcus."

Marcus grunted. "Figured that. How much?"

"A hundred thousand."

"Sounds reasonable. You're in."

Later, watching King talking to the barmaid, Marcus placed the call. Time for the second part of his plan.

"Elena, I apologize for disturbing you at this late hour," he said.

"It's fine. I was reading."

Marcus heard Elena close her book. "Is Boyd home? An important matter has come up." Marcus knew the answer before he asked the question. An earlier call confirmed Boyd was at Paddy's Bar.

Setting the book down on the end table, she said, "No, he hasn't been around. Do you want to leave a message?"

"No. I'll keep searching for him. Thank you."

"I'll tell him—"

"Perhaps it's good I have you on the line, Elena. Can I have a minute of your time?"

In a confused voice, she said, "Yes."

"Elena, I'm worried about Boyd's health. I know you feel the same." Marcus hoped his voice was convincing.

Silence. Elena Turner considered her answer.

"Yes," she said.

Marcus and Elena lied to each other.

"Elena. The work and stress of his job are hard on his health. I know there must be something I can do here at work to make it easier for him. I want to have Boyd around for a long time. He's my friend. I know you share the same sentiment. If you're available, I would like to have lunch with you tomorrow. You know, compare notes on what we can do to help Boyd."

"Alyssa is coming home this weekend. We are having a party for her."

"I know. Boyd invited me. I promise I won't take much of your time."

"I don't know if Boyd would want me to have lunch with you."

"Elena, we're doing this for Boyd's benefit. How can that be wrong?"

Elena paused. Marcus was pleased. It wouldn't take much to seduce her. Marcus heard the rustle of fabric. Elena had moved.

"If you're going put it that way, okay. Where and when?"

"How about Isabella's Italian Restaurant on West Forty-Fifth Street at eleven-thirty?"

"I know the place. I'll see you tomorrow."

"Thank you, Elena."

His plan was working. Soon there would be changes. Big changes.

***

Later in the day, King waited until the last remaining police officer washed his hands at the station and left the restroom.

Washing his hands, Marcus asked, "What's the urgency? You pulled me from a meeting."

"Something's up," King said. "Just checked the status board. They changed Seth from disability leave to suspended. There isn't any reason for the change unless he's moving around and Drummond wants it a secret."

"Alert Coleman and the rest. Pull back until we find Seth."

"Including distribution?"

"No. Keep dealer and street sales. I don't want any new shipments until we find Seth. I'll tell Boyd, and that goes for you too, King. Don't contact anyone. Scope out Boyd. Make sure he keeps his mouth shut."

"I'm on it." Leaning against the washbasin, legs and arms crossed, King said, "Marcus, there's more. The patrol swing shift has pulled Officer MacKenna."

"Where did they put Kat?"

"Nothing on the duty board. She's still wearing blues, has a black and white."

"She's a floater. That's what the hell she is. Seth's eyes into the department. I'd say our boy Seth has himself a partner."

***

The laws of nature were constant. For every action, an equal reaction. For every life, death. For every strong point—a weak point.

Seth knew Police Chief Bateman was the vulnerable link in Boyd's drug operation. He had surrendered his command authority to Boyd, Drummond and the lieutenant in charge of the administrative services division. Seldom found in squad meetings, he appeared timid and weak before patrol-shift-change meetings. Door always closed, trivia consumed most of his day. A calendar, displaying his retirement date, hung on the wall in his office.

The chief was Boyd's Achilles' heel. Like a chain of dominos on edge, knock over Bateman and Boyd was next. Psychological operations were an essential element for the Marines in Iraq and Afghanistan. It worked for Seth there. It could work for him in Hillsdale.

The e-mail in his laptop was perfect. The chief's personnel file was helpful. One final review, a soft touch on the send button, and the house of cards would begin to fall.

> *Hello, Chief. Thought I'd make your day. United States Code, Title 18, Part 1, Chapter 96, Section 1962 (a), RICO Act, says it shall be unlawful for any person who has received, directly or indirectly, from a pattern of racketeering activity. Interesting, don't you think? There's more. A guilty verdict isn't pretty. Up to 20 years in federal prison on each count, a fine up to $25,000 and forfeiture of all properties gained thru the violation. Heavy stuff, Chief. You should have thought about it a little while longer before taking money from Boyd. Now I'm going to tell everyone what you did. Bet your three children will be proud of you. Especially your son who's a cop in LA. I can imagine your wife's joy when they take her house away and leave her homeless. We'll talk later.*

> *Seth.*

He hit the send button.

Chief Wendell Bateman pushed back from his office desk, terrified at the e-mail he had received from Seth. He felt a gigantic wave was about to hurl him to the broken rocks on the shore.

It was over. All of it.

The money he'd hidden for his fake death and escape to the Caribbean was worthless. His dream of a tropical island filled with nubile young girls with white breasts against bronze skin evaporated in the heat of his panic.

He peered again at the e-mail. How could he explain to his son Jason and the twin girls when they saw him handcuffed? Would they turn away in shame? What could he do to temper his wife's anger and rage?

Nothing. There weren't any words to comfort his family. One option remained.

Run.

***

"Kat, is Seth there?" Drummond said.

"Tarzan is screwing up his leg on the treadmill."

"Does he ever relax?"

"Not as long as I've known him."

"Want to talk to him, now."

"Seth!" Kat said above the sound of Seth's grunting. "Drummond's on the phone."

Turning off the treadmill, Seth rubbed away a spot of blood below his shorts, grabbed the phone. "Yeah?"

"What did you do to the chief?"

"Sent him an e-mail. Why?"

"I saw him come out of his office screaming for Boyd and

Marcus. They've been in his office for over an hour."

Wiping his chest with a towel, Seth said, "Outstanding. Boyd's turn is next."

Chapter 12

Seth was amazed. "God. You ate those pancakes like you hadn't eaten in a month."

"I was hungry," Kat said. "Was that Drummond on the phone?"

"Yeah. Escobar's out."

"Great. Now let's see where he goes."

"Talk to me, Kat. What do have you on Boyd?"

"Have everything you wanted including his e-mail," Kat said before finishing the last of her IHOP scrambled eggs. "It's on your laptop."

"What about the daughter?" Seth slid across the vinyl-up-holstered booth, rested his back against the wall.

"The daughter's name is Alyssa Turner. I called her moth-er, Elena. Said I was from the local *Hillsdale Tribune*. Told her we were doing a feature story on college graduates. She said Alyssa's working at the Ohio State University Wexner Medical Center. She e-mailed me a picture. I told the medical center the same story. Have her shift and lunch schedule."

"Good job. Now who do we know in Columbus?"

Finishing the last of her coffee, Kat said, "Have a cousin who's a cop."

"Is there anyone in your family who isn't a cop?"

Kat's eyes sparkled. "Mom."

"I'm surprised."

"Thought you would be."

Each day the relationship had improved between them. Kat began to smile more and tease while Seth was more sensitive to her moods.

"Do me a favor, Kat," Seth said while signaling the waitress with a raised coffee cup. "It would help to have a photo of Alyssa eating lunch at the center."

"How soon?"

"Yesterday."

"See what I can do."

"Thanks. I don't have to tell you to be careful, do I?"

"No," Kat said. Threw her napkin at him. "Do I have to remind you I'm a big girl? I can take care of myself."

***

"Captain, Escobar Padilla is out," Sergeant Porter said on his cell phone. "Just posted bail."

Entering the hallway toward the restroom, Drummond said, "Where is he now?"

"He's sitting on a bench in the park across the street from the county jail. Has to be waiting for someone."

"Where are you?"

Porter moved to the side of the building to avoid Escobar spotting him. "I'm at the coffee kiosk in front of the courthouse."

"I'm sending Alexander and Stephen to help you. They'll be there in a second."

"Good."

"Stay loose on the tail."

"Will do."

"At some point, Escobar's going to suspect a tail and run. Be prepared, Porter. Try and give me a heads-up when you think he's going to do it. I'm going to find you some help."

"Thanks."

"Stay safe, Porter."

"It's part of the plan."

"Goddammit," Drummond said an hour later, knocking over his half-empty, morning cup of coffee. "Someone bring me some paper towels. Now!" Two officers jumped up, saw the spilled coffee through the open door. One officer slapped the other one on the shoulder and sprinted for paper towels in the restroom.

Stepping away from his desk, Drummond stretched the phone cord to its length. "Quinton, thanks for returning my call."

"Always a pleasure, Drummond. Read about your double homicide at the Lindell Garden Apartments Two drug dealers. One was a girl in the shower. Are you on it?"

"Chasing the perp as we speak."

"Good. Message said you wanted something."

"Can you give me a chopper on standby? The perp we're chasing wants to play hide and seek."

"One chopper coming up."

"When?"

"Does now work for you, Drummond."

"Thanks, Quinton. Owe you one."

"Yeah, you do."

Drummond set the phone on the receiver. "Where's my god-damn towels?"

***

Throwing the candy wrapper into the wastebasket, Sergeant Marcus picked up the phone. "Marcus here."

Cesar said, "We will meet you soon at a day, time and place of our selection. Be available. We expect payment with interest for our loss. You will be alone. My employer is angry with you."

Marcus glanced around to see if anyone heard the conversation. The nearest police officer was three desks away on the telephone. Despite the threat, Marcus was pleased with the call. Carlos knew who was in charge of the Hillsdale drug operation.

"Seen Boyd?" Marcus said to a patrolman who entered the squad room.

"In the head."

Marcus was happy. Carlos hadn't given him much time to handle the Boyd problem. Still, his plan was working.

Washing his hands, Captain Boyd Turner looked up in the mirror when Marcus entered. A patrol officer was next to Boyd. "Leave us," Boyd said. The officer hurried out the door.

"I apologize," Marcus said.

"Where's your letter of resignation?"

"I didn't write it. I was way out of line yesterday. My wife is leaving me, and my girlfriend and I had a big fight. Too much on my plate. I'm sorry."

"You pissed me off." Boyd reached for a paper towel. Water splashed onto his white shirt.

"Boyd, you're the boss. I don't have any problem with that."

Discarding the towel, Boyd said, "Damn your hide. Don't forget it."

"I won't."

"Good."

Leaning against the basin counter, Boyd asked, "Have you heard from Carlos?"

"No. You?"

"No. We should have heard two, three days ago. Something's wrong."

Marcus said, "I got an idea how to make Carlos happy. Let's meet at Paddy's later and I'll tell you about it."

Seeing Boyd an hour later sitting in his office reading, Marcus stopped at King's desk. "How do you find anything here?" Stacks of reports and files covered the top of his desk.

"If I can't find it, I don't have to work on it."

"I'm meeting Boyd at Paddy's. I want you there."

"Okay. What's it about?" King said, returning a file to a desk drawer.

"Just sit and listen. Play along with whatever I say."

***

Boyd was proud of the smile he gave Marcus earlier. It hid his anger. Marcus was a threat to his leadership. Their partnership ran its course. Dammit, where in the hell was Escobar? Marcus needed to be dead.

***

"Porter. What have you got?" Drummond said.

For an hour, Porter watched Escobar visiting with four men. "Sir, right now, he's leaning against a car with a bunch of guys at El Tigre Bar. I recognize Miguel Diaz and Gilberto Nunez. The other two I don't know. He's being smart. Sending out cars into the neighborhood searching for a tail."

"Where are you?"

"I'm in a vacant office. They haven't spotted me."

"I don't think I want to know how you entered into a vacant office. How fast can you move?"

"Just step out the door. Car's at the curb."

"Where are Alexander and Stephen?"

"Parked a mile away. They should be okay. Captain, he's going to start driving around. I can smell it."

"Chopper is on standby. I'll send them in. Stay loose, Porter. Not too close. Let the chopper do its job."

Turning left through a yellow light five minutes later, Porter said, "He's moving, sir."

"Where are you?"

"Nine hundred block of West Geneva. I'm about a block behind him. Traffic is heavy. I may lose him. Alexander and Stephen are right behind me."

Returning the report to the file, Captain Drummond asked, "Chopper in the air?"

"Yes, sir. Eighty-nine hundred feet. Boyd or Marcus will never see him. Pilot says he has a hell of a picture with his FLIR SC8000 infrared camera. Frequency is 125.25 megahertz if you want to listen in."

"What's Escobar doing?"

"Right now he's wandering around trying to find a tail. When he's happy, he'll stop, meet our mystery guest."

Signaling for two patrol officers to enter his office, Drummond said, "Let me know the instant he stops."

Pulling to the curb a minute later, Porter said, "Captain, he's stopped."

"Just a second," Drummond said. Sending away the two patrol officers in his office, he returned to his desk. "Where?"

"Harris Supermarket. Sumpter and Mission. It's vacant."

Running his finger on the map spread out on his desk, Drummond said, "Got it. What's he doing?"

"He's parked in the back in the shade, The pilot thinks he went inside with two unidentified subjects. My guess it's Miguel and Gilberto. Chopper is on standby."

"Excellent. What's your position?"

"I'm south of the market." Porter said. "Albertson is north. We're facing each other. Got them blocked."

"Alert Albertson and the same for you. Marcus or Boyd will be in an unmarked squad car. Watch your back."

"Will do. I think—" Porter saw the car, ducked out of view. "Captain, I have an unmarked coming up in my rearview mirror."

"For Christ's sakes, don't let him see you."

"I'm kissing the center console. He's coming up fast . . .just passed me." Sitting up, Porter said, "I can see him now. Sweet damn, he turned into the market. Going around back."

"Outstanding."

Picking up his Unity XG-100P portable radio, Porter said, "Helo 124. Have you found him?"

"Affirmative," the pilot said. "He's parked next to the other car. Door opened. Okay, now he is out of the car. He's alone. Can't see his face."

"Description?" Porter said, checking the rear view mirror for any other unmarked police cars.

"Tall and skinny."

"Marcus," Drummond and Porter said.

***

Vacant for years, Marcus saw the clouds through the holes in the roof of the supermarket building. Picking his way through years of trash discarded by vagrants, he motioned Escobar to join him at a broken out window with more light. The afternoon breeze sweeping in failed to dissipate the stench of urine and feces.

"Goddamn, this place stinks," Marcus said.

Miguel and Gilberto stood away smoking. The smell of marijuana was a welcome relief from the stench.

"No one will find us here," Escobar said. "I want money."

Marcus pulled a wad out of his coat pocket. "Here's five hundred. Make it last through the weekend."

Escobar threw his hands up. "Jesus Christ, man, what's your problem? I've got expenses. I need twice that."

"Dammit, Escobar. Money's tight till the next shipment."

Escobar flipped his cigarette. "I want a thousand on Monday."

Overdosed with his constant bitching and attitude, Marcus decided Escobar was a liability. Boyd's enforcer for a year, he knew Escobar was good at keeping the street-drug dealers in line. The double murder of the two dealers at the Lindell Apartments would make them fear him even more. But Marcus wanted a new enforcer when he gained control. One who kept his mouth shut. Followed orders.

"I'll try," Marcus said.

"No. A thousand, Monday."

"Okay." You son of a bitch. "A thousand on Monday. Hear from Boyd?"

"He called, left a message. He wants a meet."

"Keep me posted."

Escobar shrugged.

"Have a job for you." Marcus wrinkled his nose. The smell of the stench returned when Miguel and Gilberto quit smoking, left the building.

"Who?"

"Seth."

"Good. That bastard has been in my face a couple of times.

What about the bitch he hangs out with?"

"Kat MacKenna." Marcus shrugged his shoulders. "No, too much heat. We'll do her later."

"Gonna cost you seventy-five thousand."

"Fifty."

"Seventy-five or you can go to hell."

"Seventy-five," Marcus said. He settled on the solution to the Escobar problem. He'd personally kill him. Enjoy doing it.

***

Marcus hoped the ambiance of Isabella's Italian Restaurant would soften Elena into a relaxed, pleasant mood. It should also help he changed clothes after leaving the supermarket. The Mediterranean terracotta tiles and hand-hewn ceiling beams complemented the plank tables with red gingham tablecloths. He even selected a private table behind the Tuscan Limestone fireplace.

His plan was a nonstarter.

Unsmiling, her greeting was cold with a flat "Hello." She remained silent, wary when Marcus thanked her for joining him for lunch. Small talk couldn't dislodge a response from her. Seeing Elena was uncomfortable, suspicious. Marcus gave up, became quiet.

Caressing the stem of her water glass, she finally said, "Are you comfortable lying to me?"

"What?" Marcus arched his eyebrows.

"I asked you if you were comfortable lying to me?"

Jolted by Elena's accusation, Marcus' mind raced for a response. Satisfied he had an answer, he said. "I apologize if you have misinterpreted my intentions. I asked you here to talk about Boyd. I'm concerned about him. We're both worried about him."

"Excuse me, Marcus. I have been around my husband much

too long. That's bullshit. I've noticed how you gawk at my breasts. You want to sleep with me."

Thinking he had masked his intentions, his mind went blank on how to counter Elena's comment. She spoke the truth.

"What's wrong, Marcus? Can't lie your way out of it?"

Moving his spoon closer to the knife, looking at Elena, he asked, "Have I offended you?"

"No. Perhaps you have even complimented me. It has been a long time since a man desired me."

"You are a beautiful woman."

Elena waited while the waiter placed bread sticks on the table. Marcus waved him away when he offered them menus. Waiting until he disappeared around the fireplace, Elena said, "You are lying to me again, Marcus. I am attractive, but I am not beautiful. I have blonde hair—men like that. My complexion is fair, and I'm not fat. I'm still young, forty-three. I'm like millions of other women. You are attracted to me because I have full, firm breasts you want to fondle." Elena slid back into her chair, waiting for Marcus' response.

"Okay, Elena, I want to sleep with you."

"I like it when you're honest with me. I have lived with Boyd's lies for almost all of the time we have been married. Trust me, Marcus, I'll leave now if you lie to me again. Do we understand each other?"

"Yes. If you knew my intentions, why did you join me for lunch?"

She tilted her head, looked at Marcus, "Curiosity. I was curious about how you would ask me to sleep with you. Maybe I was flattered a man wanted me."

"Elena, you are a surprising, perceptive woman. Trust me. I am not lying to you. You're different from any other woman I have known. You even scare me. You may be out of my league."

"Thank you, but the answer is no. I will not sleep with you. I've thought about having an affair for a long time. I believe Boyd would kill me if I did. He'd kill me and get away with it because he's a cop."

"Perhaps you're right."

"There is no perhaps about it. And I could never face Alyssa if I was unfaithful."

"I forgot about Alyssa. Guess that makes me pretty selfish."

"True. You are a selfish man. You sleep with other women instead of your wife. I've known that about you for a long time. I'm not bothered by it."

"You know me too well."

"Perhaps I know you better than you know yourself."

"May I see you again?"

"Yes, you may see me again. But as a friend, Marcus."

"Same time, same place next Tuesday?"

"Yes."

Smiling, Marcus was a happy man on the way back to the police station. His plan was working. Time to implement the next phase.

***

"Garcia, why the hesitation?" Angel said. "I have issued an order. You work for me now."

Sitting on the couch in the expansive living room with a Spanish Mediterranean motif, Cesar and Pedra shared Garcia's fear of Angel. Her frame of mind was unreadable.

"I will follow your order, *señorita*," Garcia said. Struggling to find the appropriate words, he added, "*Señor* Carlos has been my boss for many years. I do not wish to offend him."

"Are you telling me you want me to bring in Carlos to approve my order?"

Coughing to alleviate his sudden fear, Garcia said, "No, *señorita*."

"Garcia, do you wish to offend me?" Garcia shook his head. "Any of you?"

They were terrified. She was an assassin. An assassin who killed without remorse. They couldn't remember when Carlos had murdered anyone. They feared Angel more.

"Speak!"

"I believe," Garcia said in an apologetic tone, "I speak for the three of us. It is our honor to serve you. Our loyalty will remain with you. *Señor* Carlos must know of our decision."

"He knows!" Angel snapped. Agitation replaced her hidden mood.

They were pleased. Angel and Carlos had settled the matter between them. They sank back into the couch, comfortable their decision would save them from anguish, perhaps death.

Angel studied each of their faces. Cesar squirmed at the examination while Garcia coughed again. Pedra pulled away from the couch cushion, anxious.

Angel suggested a smile. Her pause served its purpose of preparing the scene for her announcement.

"Carlos plans on killing me."

Stunned, they froze in place. Soon they could witness murder.

"I must know his every move. You must never allow me to be surprised. If I die, Carlos will kill all of you. Do you want to die?"

Reeling back into the couch, they said, "No."

Angel relaxed. "Good. You please me with your loyalty. Listen to my words. Manuel has given me much work to do. I want each of you to help me. Garcia, you will travel to Los Angeles. Manuel has directed me to attack the compound of the Los Guerreros Cartel. You will study the grounds to assist me in my attack. Your contact is the Los Guerreros cook, Larunda. I must know who is staying in the house and the location of all of the guards. I will give you the address and a list of the weapons and supplies for the attack. See Segundo Ayala on East Eighty-Fifth Street. He will give you everything. You leave immediately."

"*Sí, señorita*. I will learn every detail."

"Cesar, you will go to the market. Call Sergeant Marcus of the Hillsdale Police Department. He must think Carlos wants to meet him. I will select the day, time, and place later. Tell him he is to remain available for our call at all times. Express our deep anger at his stupidity in losing the shipment. He shall repay our loss with interest. I will give you a list of dealers in Hillsdale. Identify who can be trusted to remain loyal to us. I must know this man Marcus like he were my own. Do you understand the importance of my instructions?"

"*Sí, señorita.*"

"You will drive me to Hillsdale. I will give you further instructions later."

"*Sí, señorita.*"

"Pedra." Pedra quit playing with her hair, dropped her hands to her legs. "You will accompany me to the theater tonight. I will give you a list of items I want you to carry for me. Do any of you have questions?"

"No, *señorita.*"

"Cesar and Garcia. You shall leave me now. Pedra, you will sit with me in the kitchen."

Angel terrified Pedra. Now she must sit with her. Pedra was

shocked when Angel smiled at her.

"*Sí, señorita.*" Angel never smiled at her.

"Relax, Pedra. I do not know you. I want to change that."

"*Sí, señorita.*"

"Pedra, can I pour you a cup of coffee?"

Pedra was wary, unsure of herself. Angel wanted something. What did she have that Angel wanted? Nothing. "*Si, señorita.* Thank you." She knew Angel would have been offended if she had said no.

Coffee poured, Angel stirred the cream into her coffee. "Pedra, you must understand when I tell you to do something, you will do it. When I tell you to answer a question, you must answer it. You know these truths, don't you?"

"*Sí, señorita.*"

"Carlos has raped you?"

Playing with her coffee cup, Pedra stopped. How should she answer the question? Carlos would beat her if she said yes. Angel would kill her if she said no.

Angel reached for Pedra's hand. "Don't be afraid. You are safe with me. Answer my question."

"*Sí, señorita.*"

"He's raped you often?"

"*Sí, señorita* . . one or two times a week. . .sometimes more."

"I will not permit it to happen again. You will tell me if he tries it again."

"*Sí, señorita.*"

Angel pushed her coffee cup away. "I have visited with Garcia and Cesar. They know of your life. They tell me your grandmother tried to raise you after your parents abandoned you. You belonged to a gang. You've been in prison for burglary."

Pedra didn't respond.

"Am I speaking the truth?"

"Sí, señorita."

"Have you used drugs?"

"A little. Drugs scare me. My sister died of a drug overdose when she was fourteen. I saw her die."

"I am sorry for the loss of your sister."

"Thank you."

Angel folded her hands on the table, studied Pedra's face. "Tell me, Pedra. Have you ever killed anyone?"

Pedra arched her eyebrows.

"Answer me, Pedra," Angel said in a sudden loud voice.

"No one must know."

"What happened?"

"A man dragged me into an alley and tried to rape me. I hit his head against a brick wall. . .then I stabbed him."

"Did you feel bad about killing him?"

"No."

"Would you kill again if I ordered it?"

"Oh, *señorita*," Pedra said with anguish. "Please don't order me to kill again. Please."

"Pedra, I will always protect you. You will be safe with me, and no one will rape you again. We are women. It is different with us than it is with Garcia or Cesar. You can be helpful to me. Do what a man could never do. Pedra, if you help me, I will give you beautiful clothes to wear and money to spend. You will never be a maid again. I am offering this life to you. Do you want it?"

"Oh, *Sí señorita*," Pedra said without hesitation. "I want it."

"I am going to Los Angeles to attack my enemies. They are now your enemies. Do you understand what I have said to you?"

"Sí, señorita. I understand."

"I have plans for my attack. I will want you with me to help kill my enemies, your enemies. Will you do as I order?"

Pedra studied Angel and her promise of a life she never knew. Apprehensive, she bit her lip. *"Sí, señorita,* I will do as you order."

***

Pressed against the brick wall to escape the rain, Captain Boyd Turner was at the back of the narrow alley separating the two abandoned storefront buildings. The narrow roof overhang did little to shield him from the evening rain. Stepping into the glow of the street lamps, he tossed the empty pint whiskey bottle into a dumpster and said, "Over here, Escobar." Ignoring the rain, Escobar kicked a can as he sauntered up to Boyd.

"Need money, Escobar?" Boyd asked. He'd smoked one of his occasional cigars, leaving him with a raspy voice and irritated throat.

Escobar kicked the can for the final time. "Yeah. A thousand will help me through the weekend."

Boyd pulled out ten one-hundred bills from his wallet. "Not much left till the next shipment."

Counting the money, Escobar said, "I gotta have more next week."

"See what I can do."

"You wanted a meet?" Escobar said.

"Have a job for you."

"Who?"

Coughing, Boyd said, "Marcus."

Escobar whistled in surprise. "Expensive."

"I'll give you a hundred thousand."

"A hundred thousand, huh. I can handle that."

"Make like it was an accident. Run him off the road or something."

"When?"

"Now," Boyd said, walked toward the street. Staggering, he brushed up against a dumpster before disappearing around the corner of the building. Escobar remained behind, wet from the rain.

Puzzled, he stopped on the sidewalk. Marcus promised him seventy-five thousand to kill Seth. Boyd promised him one hundred thousand to kill Marcus. It was easy to figure out he'd have to kill Seth before Marcus. But was there a way he could have Boyd pay him to kill Seth? How was that going to happen? Strapped with a fifth-grade education, Escobar never was good at solving problems. He'd have to think about it for a while. And Marcus wanted to know about his meeting with Boyd. What lie could he tell Marcus?

Chapter 13

Shaking his raincoat, Boyd glared at Marcus, "What the hell is King doing here?" The rain soaked his coat and shoes.

Narcotics Detective King scooted his chair back and planted his feet to stand up. "Screw you, Boyd."

Sitting at a nearby table, a burly man with a sleeveless shirt looked away from the basketball game on TV in Paddy's Bar. Scowling at Marcus, he said, "Goddammit. I'm trying to watch the game."

Marcus ignored the man. "King, Boyd, knock it off. Both of you. Sit down."

The water continued to drip off Boyd's overcoat.

Pulling Boyd's chair out, Marcus said, "Boyd, it's important. We need to talk."

Boyd said, "King, I want your goddamn butt in my office first thing tomorrow."

King grunted. "Whatever."

Boyd threw his overcoat, on a chair at the next empty table, signaled for his usual drink. He struggled to breathe.

"I asked King down here," Marcus said, "because I have a solution to the Carlos problem."

"What?"

Marcus reached down to the floor, picked up a large leather

bag, wet from the rain, set it on the table.

"What's that?" Boyd said.

"My ticket to staying alive. There's five hundred thousand in the bag. King is going to deliver the money to Carlos. Call it a gift to make up for the shipment Drummond seized."

"Why don't you go yourself?"

"What, let Carlos take the money, then kill me? No, thank you. Carlos hasn't met King. He hasn't any reason to kill him. King can come back, tell us if Carlos is happy. I'll know if we're going to stay alive."

"That doesn't make sense," Boyd said. "Carlos lost five hundred, and you give five hundred back to him. He'll want more."

"Right. Remember, Boyd. We've talked about it. I want your five hundred thousand. One million should make Carlos happy."

"You want me to give you five hundred thousand?"

"Yeah. King can come by your house about ten in the morning, catch the noon flight to Chicago."

Boyd pushed back into his chair. "You trust King with a million dollars?"

"You son of a bitch," King said, slamming his fist on the table.

The burly man stood up, marched to the table, glared at King. "You don't want to piss me off the third time."

Tilting his head, King raised his hands in an apology. "Sorry, won't happen again."

"Bastards," the man said to the woman with a purple streak in her hair sitting next to him, a large bruise on her neck.

Glaring, his eyes cold, Marcus leaned into Boyd. "Goddammit, that was uncalled for. King has been with us for a long time. Now, you apologize, or I'll have King tell Carlos you refused to pay a damn dime."

Trapped, Boyd had placed himself into a box. Carlos would kill him if he skipped the payment for the loss of drugs. King might kill him for failing to apologize. He'd made a blunder. A serious one.

Rubbing his hands, Boyd shrugged. "Sorry, King."

King relaxed his clenched fists. Grunted. Said nothing.

***

The agent stood motionless. Only his eyes moved. He was good, better than good. The actors at the Marjorie Penhammer Theatre lost any awareness of him standing backstage observing the audience. He was just another object they had to move around to enter and leave the stage. He started watching her when she first sat down in the center section, the fifth row back.

Angel.

The audience sat in rapt silence, watching the intense drama on the stage. Unlike Pedra, who sat next to her with a bag in her lap, Angel ignored the performance. Instead, she was looking for the man who followed her into the theater. Never saw his face. Just sensed the movement of him coming closer to her at the bar. She knew who he was. Drug Enforcement Agency. No other explanation worked.

The first survival lesson for any assassin was to be aware of their surroundings. In a sea of harmless faces, the assassin had to decipher which face belonged to the enemy. The second lesson was short.

Kill or be killed.

During the intermission, the agent followed Angel to the bar. She wore a black sheath dress with fake diamonds around her neck and wrist. Red lipstick accentuated her olive-toned face. Pedra, still clutching her bag, stood at Angel's side. They waited to enter the women's lounge.

The agent was professional, but his eyes betrayed him. Standing away from the lounge, Angel caught his eyes watching her when he moved for a better view. He even looked like an agent. Non-descriptive face, plain dark suit. The suggestion of a slight bulge in his left breast pocket. She had never seen him before.

Mistake. Big One.

Angel found him. Now he had a face. Her plan had a better chance to succeed if he was unaware she'd made him.

Time to disappear.

The agent watched Angel enter the lounge. He never saw her leave nor did he notice the woman who left the restroom with an older woman.

Angel had covered her long black hair with a short auburn wig and changed into an elegant pinstriped pantsuit with kitten heels. Her face, highlighted with tortoise shell rectangular glasses and neutral-colored lipstick, didn't hold any interest for him. In minutes, Pedra had aged into the older-looking woman.

The agent continued to search for the woman in the black sheath dress. The one with diamonds around her neck. Meanwhile, Angel slipped out of a side door into a taxi.

The next morning in Munster, Indiana, Angel turned away from the window above the pool and patio, She asked, "Cesar, what have you found?" Two hours earlier, Angel told him to search the area surrounding the Hampton Inn for any suspicious vehicles or drug enforcement agents.

"I have traveled every road many times around the motel. There is no one," he said.

"Cesar. I am pleased with your service to me. Have you prepared the rental car?"

"*Sí, señorita.*"

"The *policía* must not discover the purpose of my visit to Hillsdale."

"*Sí, señorita.*"

"Excellent. You must leave me now. I have much to consider. Take my luggage with you."

***

Frightened when she opened the door, Olivia said, "What in the hell is the gun doing on the desk?" Despite being married to the police chief, she hated guns. Bateman always tried to hide them from her.

"Dammit, Olivia, I've told you a million times to knock before you come into the den. I could be doing police work."

"What's going on, Wendell? You came home yesterday morning like you'd seen a ghost. I tried to talk to you about it, and you won't say a word. Every five minutes you're peering out the window like you're expecting someone. This morning you hardly said hello to our daughters when they came over for breakfast. They wanted to know why you were upset. Now I find a gun on your desk. You know I hate guns."

"Goddammit, Olivia. I have stuff on my mind."

"Good God, Wendell," she said, panicked. "You're not going to use the gun, are you?"

"For Christ's sakes, no."

"Then give me the gun."

"I can't do that."

"Why? Did someone threaten you?"

Bateman stared at her. "Yeah, Olivia. Someone threatened me."

Sitting in the corner, close to four loud teenagers, Sergeant Marcus picked up his cell phone. "You have the money?"

"Yeah," King said as he waved at police officers on patrol in a black and white "It's in the trunk of my car."

Marcus watched the two loud teenage girls leave for the restroom. "Count it?"

"Christ, Marcus. I just picked it up."

"How's Boyd?"

"Pissed."

"Screw him." Sticking a potato chip in his mouth, Marcus asked, "Where are you now?"

"Parked two blocks from Boyd's house."

"I'm at a Subway in the seven hundred block of Market. Meet me here."

***

Standing in front of the brick fireplace in the vaulted-ceiling living room with his arm wrapped around Elena's shoulders, Boyd said, "Does everyone have their glasses filled?" The crowd raised their glasses in acknowledgment. Standing several feet away from Boyd, Alyssa's eyes were moist from all the love surrounding her.

"Elena and I would like to propose a toast to our beautiful daughter, Alyssa for her achievement in receiving a Bachelor of Science degree at Ohio State."

Crowded with mostly Alyssa's friends in the great room, they let out a loud roar of approval. Unlike her parents, Alyssa was vivacious and gregarious with many close friends.

The few older adults in the room were neighbors and acquaintances of Boyd and Elena. Boyd didn't have any friends while Elena had several who shared lunch or an afternoon with her. Her friends loathed Boyd and left whenever he returned home. They were aware of his drunken, brutish ways.

Boyd reached out, pulled Alyssa to him, kissed her cheek. The initial congratulations completed, Boyd continued, "I want you folks to know Alyssa graduated with academic honors. She has a three-point-eight grade point average." More hollering. "This fall, she's off to Stanford University's School of Medicine to study neurosurgery specializing in cancers of the brain and spine. Your mother and I are so proud of you, sweetheart for your accomplishment. To Alyssa!"

Glasses raised, the crowd yelled, "To Alyssa."

Before the group began to sip the champagne, Alyssa raised her glass. "I would like to propose a toast" The crowd stopped, fell silent. Petite, unable to peer over the heads, she said, "I would like to thank you, Mom. You have always been there for me. When I was upset or discouraged at school, I'd call home, and you'd give me advice and encouragement. It was always better after I called. I hope I can be a good mom someday." The guests whooped and hollered for Elena.

"And, Daddy. You're the best cop in the world. Always helping people, catching the bad guys, making us all safe. You're the best father. I love you." The crowd remained polite with little clapping.

"To Mom and Dad!"

The crowd swarmed around her, her boyfriend Jacob first in line. Everyone talked at once expressing their love and congratulations.

Marcus, standing away from the crowd, saw Boyd remove his arm from around Elena and moved across the room. Marcus caught Elena's eye. She was watching him. He was proud of himself. He figured she'd be in his bed within a month. Elena could wait. Time to push his plan along.

Stepping away from the crowd to the hallway entrance leading to the bedrooms, Marcus said, "Boyd, have a minute?"

"Not a good time." The sight of Marcus erased Boyd's jovial mood.

Marcus ignored the brush-off. "How do you keep it away from Alyssa? She doesn't have a clue."

"I work hard at it every day so she'll never know. I'll kill any son of a bitch who has other plans. My daughter is gonna receive the finest education in the world and not owe a single goddamn dime in student loans."

"Sounds great. Boyd, need a minute of your time."

"What about?"

"Carlos didn't take the money," Marcus said, looking at Alyssa's roommate's ass as she entered the kitchen.

"What the hell? What happened?"

"One of Carlos' people told King the timing wasn't right. He'd be in touch. The guy asked if we added a gratuity on top of the million. King said no. The man said, 'big mistake,' and hung up."

"Okay, what's next?"

Marcus stole another glance at Elena. She had turned sideways. He liked the silhouette of her full breasts. "We wait. Figure we might hear again on Tuesday."

"Why Tuesday?"

"Just a guess."

"Goddammit, Marcus. All I have left is a couple hundred thousand."

"Me too."

"Where's the money?"

"King has it hidden." The money was at the bottom of Marcus' closet in his apartment.

"The money better be safe, or you're in deep shit. Are we clear on that?"

"Clear." Marcus wanted to move up the date on killing Boyd, But he knew haste made for bad planning. Bad planning earned a gurney in the gas chamber.

***

Sitting in the back seat of the Lincoln MKS limousine, Angel asked, "Your informants have told you Marcus is in the apartment at this hour?"

"*Sí*," Cesar replied.

"You know what to do. It is important no one sees me."

Cesar stepped out of the car, entered the Broadmoor Manor lobby. A moment later, the concierge sat on a toilet seat in a nearby restroom. He had three crisp one hundred dollar bills in his pants pocket.

Entering the lobby of the former hotel, Angel stopped, examined it for hidden threats. Finding none, she studied the vestibule's décor. The room remained unchanged from the roar of the 1920's. Angel's quick examination revealed three original art deco, crystal chandeliers hanging on black chains. The light fixtures arranged in a triangle illuminated an eclectic mix of faded red velvet cushions on wooden chairs. Added to the mix were two well-worn Chesterfield sofas.

Enough. She had wasted valuable time. Serious business at hand. Angel's stiletto heels clicked on the charcoal gray granite floor interspersed with smoky veins of white and black. Her black leather miniskirt held tight against her silky-toned legs.

The overhead light reflected on her long black hair wrapped into a French twist. Removing her black cashmere wrap coat, she draped it over her forearm and extended her arm. Cesar stepped up, gathered the coat into his arms. Her white silk blouse with a boat neckline, kimono sleeves, popped against her black skirt. Angel's elegant appearance was her signature of an assassin at work.

She studied every minute detail of the location. There couldn't be any surprises. Where to place each step. How to open the door. The dark recesses of a hallway. The quickest escape route. Which weapon to use. So much to know to stay alive.

So much.

Angel smiled. It would be a good night. She was the matadora again in the bullring. She had survived each of the bull's thundering charges and slashing horns. Now it was time to slay the *Toro de Lidia*.

Cesar held the elevator door open when Angel stopped in place.

A sudden thought crossed her mind. Surprised her. Such an elementary question. One that struck at the core of her being. She had one life. Where would it lead her? How would she spend it?

What did she want above all else? Was it control and power? Kill Carlos, become the best at selling drugs across the states. Was that what she wanted for herself?

She'd be like no other, invincible. A shadow escaping through the police net. Manuel would step back in awe. The police would roar in frustration. Awash in luxury, all of her needs would be satisfied.

Angel. The best there would be.

Or would the tedium of selling drugs suffocate her?

Stepping into the elevator, it rose up, engulfing her. A rush of adrenaline. Danger. Maybe death. In the next minutes, surprise and the enemy's fear would keep her alive. Failure and she'd never see another morning sun.

The rush of hunting a new target? Or the target turning on her, and she became the hunted? Would the thrill be greater than selling drugs?

She saw them all around her, heard their chants to join them in their dance. They wore headdresses of eagle feathers, carried a wooden blade weapon called the Macuahuitl. They were the Cuāuhocēlōtl. The ancient Aztec Jaguar Warriors. She felt their touch pulling her into their circle.

Angel had received her calling.

She was a Cuāuhocēlōtl, who must be set free to pursue her destiny of destroying the evil that preyed on the defenseless.

Manuel must know of her decision.

Her step was more purposeful. Her imagined life selling drugs evaporated. She saw the clarity of her destiny. She was at peace.

Standing at the door to apartment 302, Cesar returned the coat to Angel while he faced his first obstacle, the deadbolt. Removing a tension wrench from a pants pocket, he inserted it into the lock and turned. Next was the pick lifting the five pins. The deadbolt retreated into the lock mechanism. The door chain was the last roadblock. With the door opened, he wrapped a rubber band around the chain, anchored it to the door handle. The chain dropped with little sound when he closed the door.

Standing inside the living room, Angel accepted a stainless steel Beretta 92FS Inox pistol Cesar had removed from his shoulder holster. Adding an AAC M9-SD suppressor from his coat pocket, Angel snapped it onto the barrel, entered the living room. She heard a man breathing through the open door into the bedroom. Cesar laid Angel's coat down on a chair, waited for instructions.

The time was now.

She turned on the light, saw a naked man and woman sleeping on their stomachs, sprawled on top of the covers. The woman had an arm and leg wrapped across the man. Angel fired a single 115gr FMJ bullet into the four-inch space between their heads. The pillow exploded into a shower of feathers.

"What the goddamn hell?" Marcus cried out. His body jerked, almost dropping him to the floor. Thrashing, covered in feathers, he rubbed his eyes, spit feathers out of his mouth. He threw the woman off, sat up on the edge of the bed. Marcus spit more feathers, starred at the Beretta aimed at his forehead, He slapped the plain-looking woman's butt. "Get up, bitch."

Feathers matted her hair like snow. The woman sat up, her mouth opened to scream when Cesar slapped his hand over it. Angel was pleased. In less than ten seconds, the situation was under control. She was in command.

"Who in the hell are you?" Marcus said.

"My name is not of your concern. What is important is whether I decide to let you live or not."

Marcus rubbed and squeezed the back of his neck.

Angel signaled Cesar to lift the woman up, stand her next to the bed. Knees buckled, whimpering, she stood like a rag doll. Cesar stood behind her, clasping his hands around her wrists like handcuffs Angel walked up to the terrified woman, tapped her chin with her pistol silencer.

"Open your mouth," Angel said.

The terrified woman's lips remained sealed. Her face frozen in fear.

"Open your mouth, or I will kill you."

The woman opened her mouth. Angel inserted the silencer, resting it on her tongue.

"You see where my right index finger is resting?"

Wide-eyed, the woman stared at her finger resting on the trigger.

"If you scream, I will shoot you. Nod your head if you understand me."

The woman nodded.

"Marvelous. You learn so quickly."

Unable to move, Marcus stared in disbelief. The woman was going to blow the top of his girlfriend's head off.

"Cesar, step around here so she can see you."

The woman's eyes were wide open, unblinking when Cesar stood before her.

"Listen to me. I will say this once. If you say anything to anyone about what happened here tonight, this man will come back and slit your throat. Do you understand me?"

The woman nodded again.

"Good. We have an understanding. Cesar put her in the living room. . .and find her some clothes. She looks better with clothes on. Tell her she is dead if I hear her moving."

With cold eyes, Angel turned her attention to Marcus. "Put some clothes on too. You are a repulsive man."

Marcus paused, surprised at what she had said to him.

Kicking his sprawled clothes on the floor, Angel waved the gun at him. "I will not be distressed if I have to kill you."

Unzipped pants on and a crumpled dress shirt held together with two buttons, Marcus sat on the edge of the bed.

Glancing at the large bag on the chair, Angel asked, "Is that the money?"

"Are you with Carlos?"

"I don't recall coming here to answer your questions." Angel fired another round into the bed, missing his left leg by an inch.

"Jesus Christ, lady!" Marcus jumped sideways, hitting his head on the wall.

"You will address me as ma'am."

"Yes. . .ma'am."

"It is not wise to disrespect me."

"Yes, ma'am."

"Cesar, come in here and pick up this bag."

Watching Cesar remove the bag, Angel asked, "Will I be pleased with what's in there?"

"There's a million dollars in there. . .ma'am."

"I suppose I will have to accept the money. Hillsdale displeases me. Clean it up, or I will come back and kill you."

"Does that mean I am in charge. . .ma'am?" Marcus asked.

Angel fired another round between his legs, Marcus yelled again. He didn't jump.

"You were told there would be no more questions. The next time I will not miss."

Angel retreated to the door, turned back. "You are such a pathetic, disgusting man. I wonder if I am wasting my time with you."

Terrified, Marcus watched her leave, the Beretta hanging from her right hand.

"Angel."

***

Such a brilliant plan. One of his best. But he made a mistake. A stupid oversight. Angel could kill him because of it. Garcia forgot to ask the neighbor if Manuel Robles' spy, Larunda, the

175

cook at the Los Guerreros Los Angeles compound had any pets.

Frozen in place, one foot ahead of the other, he saw a confusing outline highlighted by a streetlight coming through a window behind it. Neither he nor the creature standing in the bedroom doorway moved. Something had to happen to end the standoff. Garcia hoped he knew the answer. He knelt down, extended his arms, making a soft clicking sound. The Havanese dog advanced to have his neck scratched. Larunda continued to snore in the bedroom.

Garcia reset his baseball cap. Angel didn't have any reason to kill him.

He stood for a long moment at the door while studying the layout of the room. The streetlight revealed the woman's expansive girth sleeping in the center of the double bed. The pushed up covers would have made a challenging mountain for the Havanese to climb. Excluding the dog, Garcia knew everything he needed to know about her. The neighbor was helpful when Garcia said he was an undercover police officer investigating a recent series of break-ins at the Lookout Hill Condominium complex including Larunda's apartment. The badge Angel gave him passed the quick examination by the neighbor.

One disturbing fact remained. Larunda's employer gave her a gun to defend herself. Somewhere around, under, or beside her was the gun. Taking one-step at a time, pausing, he advanced to the bed. What the hell? He stepped on an overturn loafer shoe, almost losing his balance and crashing onto the bed. Regaining his balance, he crept up to the head of the bed.

Dammit. Where in the hell is her mouth? A short examination gave him satisfactory results. She was facing away from him, her mouth above the covers. Avoiding the shoe, he walked around the bed, looked at her. Her mouth was open. He saw her nose twitch when she breathed.

Garcia slapped his right hand over her mouth, gripped her right shoulder, pressed his body against her. She surprised him with her unusual strength as she twisted and squirmed to escape his clutches. She tried to bite him. "I'm a friend. Manuel and Angel have sent me." He repeated himself until she became exhausted, quit moving.

"Larunda, I'm a friend. I will not hurt you."

She rolled over. "What do you want?"

Garcia explained Angel's request for the location of the guards. Thirty minutes later, he petted the dog, left with the information. Larunda remained in bed with a wad of hundred dollar bills in her hand.

Chapter 14

Parked inside the empty hanger at the Deer Valley Airport in Phoenix. Cidro Molina stepped out of the coolness of the air-conditioned Chrysler 300 stretch limousine. He watched the twin-engine Beechcraft King Air 350i taxi up to park. The pilot switched off the right and left magneto switches. The propellers came to a stop as the port rear passenger door opened. Impeccably dressed, Tejano Delgado stepped down into the bright sunshine. Wearing casual clothes was a personal affront when Cidro summoned a visitor. Approaching seventy, Cidro was a courtly gentleman steeped in the traditions of honor and respect. Still, violence remained close at hand. When angered, he ordered the beheading of his enemies.

Stepping into the cavernous hanger, Tejano walked into Cidro's outstretched arms. The men hugged, kissed each other on both cheeks before they retreated to a small table with two chairs. The table, covered with a Belvivere linen tablecloth and a lead crystal vase with a single, long-stemmed red rose, set up away from the limousine. A beautiful young woman in a tight wrapped, silk dress stood away from the table. The woman stepped forward following Cidro's flick of his hand. Picking up the silver carafe, she poured the full-bodied Columbian coffee into two bone china cups. He thanked her when she stepped away.

Returning his cup to the saucer, Cidro said, "It is the finest Columbian coffee. I hope it pleases you, Tejano."

"My palate is honored to receive such a hearty flavor. Thank you for your gracious hospitality." Tejano stole a quick glance at the young woman who touched her hair, looked at him. Tejano had to pay women to ignore his scar, have sex with him.

"Thank you for meeting me, Tejano. The day requires much work. Today, three men will die for betraying me."

"They should die a terrible death."

"Such distasteful discussion for an early hour," Cidro said. "Does our hostess please you?"

"She is beautiful. My compliments to you for your exquisite taste in women."

Raising his coffee cup to the beautiful mistress, Cidro said, "Of all of them, she is my favorite. I shall give her to you when there is time. You will enjoy the taste of her fruits."

Tejano smiled with anticipation. "I look forward to the time I may receive her into my bed."

"Tejano, we have much to discuss and little time. What is your report?"

Returning his cup to the saucer, Tejano said, "A man is watching us. We have seen him in the surrounding hills. I have allowed him to live. Our plan is for him to report to Angel the compound is impregnable, and she will withdraw."

"Excellent. What are your plans if she does attack?"

"We have reinforced the guards surrounding the compound. They have many weapons and are skilled to repel any attack. They are honored to serve you and will die to defend you."

"Their deaths will bring honor to their families," Cidro said. "I expect you to defend my honor and the compound. It is a heavy responsibility. You must not fail."

"I will not allow Angel to dishonor you by defeating us on the field of battle."

"I am pleased with your loyalty. Now tell me, how is my niece?"

"Ariella wishes to leave the compound. I told her it was your decision when she may leave."

"I will see her and tell her what she will do. I am staying at the Sanctuary Camelback Mountain Resort to rest from my visit with Salvador Serafin. I shall return to the compound on Friday. You will prepare my welcome." Cidro retrieved a walking stick leaning against the table.

"You have honored me," Tejano said. "You have given me this important responsibility. I have prepared a special gift for you. There are three of them. They are beautiful and are anxious to please you."

"Thank you for your gifts. I shall anticipate the pleasure they will give me. I am pleased with your report on your preparations for a possible attack by Angel. Now, you must return to the compound. I impress upon you again. You must not fail."

"Cidro, I will serve you with my life."

"As it should be," Cidro replied with a wave of his hand.

***

Wearing her police uniform, Kat muttered, "Damn early, Seth."

Taking off his coat, sliding into the IHOP booth, Seth said, "Day's half over."

"Yeah, right. God, I hate happy people before noon." She signaled the waitress for more coffee. "The Marines taught you some bad habits."

"Works for me."

"How's the leg, Rambo?"

"Still itches."

Seth made a point of smiling more, and Kat responded in kind. Their relationship revealed some healing despite Kat's broken heart.

"How's Dad?"

"We're losing him. Not much time left."

"Wish I could make it better."

"Thanks, Kat."

Pulling it out of her briefcase, she reached over, handed it to Seth. "Here's the picture you wanted."

A summer intern at the hospital, the picture showed Alyssa eating lunch in the cafeteria at the Wexner Medical Center.

"Your cousin moves fast."

"I'm his favorite."

"Is there anyone who doesn't think you're their favorite?"

"Nope. Never happen. What did you say to Boyd?"

Seth pulled out a piece of paper from his coat, unfolded it. Clearing his throat, he said, "Alyssa is such an attractive girl. You must love her very much. I wonder where she lives."

"Beautiful. Put your name on it?"

"Of course. You know it's going to be ugly real fast when we send this."

"I'm not worried," Kat said. "You shouldn't either. Hell, you have the best partner in the world."

"Is that what you are?"

Using his smartphone, Seth took a picture of the photograph, attached it to the e-mail.

"Can I have the honors?" Kat asked.

"Go for it."

Kat set her coffee down, hit the send button

***

Less than two minutes later, Captain Boyd Turner threw Drummond's office door open so hard, it slammed against the wall, shattering the glass door. "Where in the goddamn living hell is Seth?"

Captain Drummond and the two police officers in the room reached for their weapons before they realized it was Boyd.

"Out!" Drummond said to the two officers. The officers scurried to the squad room.

"Goddamn you, Drummond, where is that son of a bitch?"

The squad room chatter stopped. Telephone calls cut short. All eyes settled on Boyd.

"I asked you a question. He threatened Alyssa. Where is he?"

Drummond jumped out of his chair, slammed his hand hard on the desk. Glaring, he said, "You in the squad room. Every goddamn one of you. Eyes on your desk and get back to work. I'll suspend anyone I catch looking my way."

Enraged, Drummond continued. "As for you, Boyd, one more outburst, and I'll arrest you for disorderly conduct. If you think I'm bluffing, try me. You want Seth. You find him."

Boyd gulped for air, glared at Drummond. "This ain't over, Drummond. No one threatens my Alyssa."

Struggling to control his anger, Drummond walked around his desk, stopped a foot short of Boyd. Before Boyd was able to react to the sudden face off, Drummond said, spit flying from his mouth, "You're dirty, Boyd, I'm taking you down."

Storming out of Drummond's office, Boyd said, "Marcus, my office now!"

Marcus rushed into Boyd's office, closed the door behind him. "What the hell is going on?"

Still choking with rage, Boyd said, "Seth sent me an e-mail threatening Alyssa. Where's Escobar?"

"Careful, Boyd. Don't do something stupid."

"I asked you where in the hell is Escobar? I didn't ask for a goddamn lecture."

"Don't know." Marcus knew Escobar stayed overnight at a whore's apartment. He also knew the address.

"Well, find him."

"No can do. Have a date with an attorney. Dumb-ass wife wants a divorce."

"Screw it. I'll find him myself."

Marcus left the office pleased. A perfect morning. Boyd was one-step removed from dropping dead of a heart attack, saving him a hundred thousand dollars.

***

Standing outside the hotel, Seth raised the cell phone to his ear. "Can you talk like a whore?"

Turning the corner at Jackson and Walnut, Kat pulled to the curb. "What in the hell are you talking about?"

"I want you to call Detective Frank Coleman. Have him go to room 204 at the Edison Hotel at six." Seth paid for the single.

"What do you want me to say?"

"Sex, baby, sex. You'll figure something out."

"Where will you be?"

"Where do you think?"

"Why did I ask?"

***

Pushed aside by a fat man in search of hamburger, Cesar retreated to the pork chops in Dominick's supermarket in Chicago.

"Garcia, report."

"It's doable. They're expecting us. Found an opening."

"Excellent."

"They've made me."

Cesar brushed off the concern with a flippant, "You're still alive. Acceptable."

"There's a complication. Two men are watching the compound."

"Who are they?"

"*Policía.*"

"We'll deal with it," Cesar said. "Angel wants you to finish the surveillance."

"When?"

"Tomorrow."

"*Sí,*" Garcia said.

Cesar hung up, left the disposable phone on the pork chops. A shopper picked it up before Cesar left the meat department. The call lasted twenty seconds. Perfect. Angel would be pleased with his report.

He returned to the condominium and recapped his conversation with Garcia.

"I am satisfied," Angel said. "I am anxious to know their vulnerability."

"They will be expecting us.".

"I am not surprised. It is the only target available. I am pleased they are aware of our plans."

Cesar shook his head. "I do not understand."

"To defeat an enemy expecting us is the greatest victory. Is there any doubt we will not succeed?"

"No, *señorita*."

"That is good. You must never doubt me. I am bringing Pedra onto our team. One day she will be a valued member. You must teach her."

"I am pleased to hear the news, *señorita*. I will teach her all that I know."

"I expect nothing less from you. You will make the necessary arrangements for Pedra and me to travel to Los Angeles tomorrow. You will leave this afternoon. I want your independent assessment of the compound. We will attack on Thursday. Do you have any questions?"

"No, *señorita*. You have explained everything."

"You are dismissed. Pedra, I will receive you now."

Pedra returned from the bedroom brushing aside an errant strand of hair. She appeared nervous

"Pedra, you have followed my instructions?".

"*Sí, señorita.*"

Angel directed her focus to the coffee maker. "Your cousin knows what I expect from her?"

"*Sí, señorita.*"

Coffee cup in hand, Angel leaned back against the granite countertop. "Excellent. Your other two cousins know their assignments?"

"*Sí, señorita.*"

"You must learn, Pedra, to check all the details. Assume nothing. The car is fast, and the tank is full?"

Pedra remained nervous. "*Sí, señorita.*"

"You have done well on your first assignment."

Pedra responded with a quick smile. Angel was aware she remained guarded in her presence.

"I am pleased with you, Pedra. Now leave me. You must

check my list again on what I want you to pack in your suitcase."

"*Sí, señorita.*"

Angel was satisfied with her plan. The DEA was such an insignificant matter. They could not match her skill when she set her mind to escape from the twenty-four hour surveillance of the condominium.

***

Escobar was confused. With a rudimentary education in arithmetic, he struggled to understand how much money he stood to gain. Who would he murder first? Marcus offered him seventy-five thousand to kill Seth. Boyd offered him one-hundred-thousand to murder Marcus. Now Boyd promised him one-hundred-thousand to murder Seth. Escobar hated math.

"When can you do it?" Boyd asked.

"Now."

"Good." Boyd left, leaving Escobar standing next to several boxes of liquor. Tearing one open, he stole two bottles of Evan Williams's bourbon whiskey from Paddy's Bar storeroom. Who was he going to kill first, Seth or Marcus?

***

Edison Hotel room 204. Nothing more or less than tens of thousands of other cheap hotels. A carpet runner down the center of the dark, narrow hallway. The exposed wood floor on either side black with grime. Glass ball ceiling fixtures with burned out light bulbs. Walls decorated with graffiti. A box spring bed sagged from too much sexual gratification. A thin brown rug left bare feet dirty. A small table with mismatched chairs. A fitting place for Narcotics Detective Frank Coleman. It is where he did his best work.

Most of his snitches were whores. He was handsome with blue eyes and curly black hair cut close to the side of the head. Essential tools in the pursuit of sex.

The whores learned fast. Compliment his appearance and there'd be a twenty spot waiting for them on the nightstand. They never mentioned his narcissistic personality.

Coleman didn't have a clue who the whore was that called him on the phone. She'd given him a name which meant nothing. Names were never necessary. Faces and the size of their breasts were the measurements he considered. The whore purred, asked him to come over. She would reward him if he helped her survive on the streets. Coleman was happy. A good call. He always enjoyed variety.

He wished she had picked a better place. What the hell, it didn't matter. Sex was sex. The ending was always the same. The door to the room ratified the décor of the hotel. The number four was missing. No problem. Just a whore on the other side. Forget knocking.

Opening the door, one foot inside, someone lifted him up, threw him across the room into a chair and the wall. The armchair disintegrated. Lifted up again, his head exploded in pain when a fist slammed into his nose, crushing the cartilage. Mouth filled with blood, it was hard to spit. He slumped to the floor. Maybe it was over.

It wasn't.

Seth continued his message and picked Coleman up a third time. A closed flat fist pounded his left kidney, sending a stabbing pain throughout his body. He spit blood across the wall.

He tried to scream, to beg him to stop. His mouth wouldn't work. He couldn't breathe. His lungs starved for oxygen. He was going to die. He slumped to the floor again, prayed for death. His prayers were unanswered.

Jerked up by his hair, a voice yelled in his ear, "Look at me, you son of a bitch."

He'd heard that voice before, but the face and voice wouldn't come together. Coleman struggled to focus. He had to know who was beating him to death. He saw the hazy outline of his executioner.

"Seth," he whispered, spitting blood out of his mouth.

"You called on my father, didn't say hello."

Coleman tried to speak—mouth wouldn't open. He bit his tongue.

"You think you know pain? Wait till the next time you call on my dad." Seth slammed Coleman's head hard on the floor, stepped out of the room.

***

Two hours later Detective King said. "Jesus Christ, he looks like a truck hit him." Coleman had slipped into unconsciousness."

"Coleman told me earlier it was Seth who beat him," Marcus said.

"God. . .he could have killed him."

"Seth is sending us a message to leave his dad alone."

They stepped out into the hospital hallway. Checking no one was nearby, King said, "The hell with Seth. He needs to be dead."

"Already have Escobar on it."

"Good. Can we kill both Boyd and Seth?"

"We don't have any choice." Marcus pointed toward a left turn in the hallway to reach the elevator.

"What did the doctor tell you?" King said.

"Coleman has a hairline skull fracture, crushed nose, bruised kidney."

"Goddamn, animal. I want to waste Seth myself."

"Forget it, King. You have enough on your plate with Boyd tomorrow."

***

Stepping in from the balcony and his examination of the traffic below on E Benton Place, Carlos Torres said, "You make an excellent martini."

"Thank you," Angel said, sitting on the sofa with her drink. Carlos joined her, dropping into a chair across from the couch. She refused to change despite wearing her wool, Herringbone patterned Gucci dress all day. She didn't want Carlos to have any illusions she was interested in returning to his bed. Those days were over.

Carlos removed his sports coat, unfastened the top two buttons of his shirt. His thick chest hair filled the gap of the open shirt. Angel was aware he was engaged in a mating dance with her.

She crossed her legs, taunting him with her exposed thighs. Rested her elbow on the arm of the sofa. She didn't have any interest in fighting with Carlos again about killing each other. She'd have that argument another time. She was tired, a long day. The next few days would be even longer. What she wanted was a mellow evening for a change. Perhaps, she thought, it might be a good night to practice being civil to Carlos.

"Is Drug Enforcement still following you?" Angel asked.

"Like glue. If I stand up, I can see their two cars now."

"Hard to do business."

"Manuel is sending in someone to help while they're playing games."

Angel removed the pins in her hair and shook her head to release the hair from the tight bun. "Do you know who is coming?"

"No. I haven't seen Garcia around, and now Cesar is gone. What's up?"

"Manuel has given me a job. Pedra and I are leaving tomorrow."

"Stay safe."

"Why would you care?"

"I want to kill you myself," Carlos said with a smile.

"That's impossible."

"Why?"

"You'll already be dead."

They both laughed. Angel was pleased. They'd had a reasonable, civil conversation. Perhaps even a pleasant one.

***

Returning from the bedroom in their suite at the Breckenshire House, Victoria said, "You seem so far away, Pamela. Did the trip wear you out?"

"No, Mother. Just resting, watching the birds in the sanctuary and pond. A storm is coming." She gazed out of a twelve-foot high penthouse window at the panoramic view of the south end of Central Park in New York City. The darkness of the approaching storm clouds highlighted the intensity of the new green leaves on the trees. She watched people on the street rushing to find shelter from the fast-approaching storm. Her twelve-year-old daughter Dusty had returned to watch television in her bedroom.

Slipping on a La Perla Ricamato long robe and lace gown, Victoria rejoined Pamela, who sat on the oatmeal-textured sofa in the great room. Setting aside an eggplant colored pillow, Victoria said, "Pamela Brighton. I'm your mother. You don't get off that easy. What's on your mind?"

Pamela squeezed her mother's hand. "I've met someone. . .a man."

"Oh, that sounds exciting." Victoria clasped her hands in anticipation. "Where did you meet him? At the Spanish ambassador's cocktail party last week?"

"No, Mother. On the flight to pick up Dusty."

"Tell me about him." Victoria hoped her daughter would fall in love again after she lost her husband two years ago.

Pamela picked up the pillow, pressed it to her breasts. "That's just it. I don't know anything about him. I know he called himself Seth, and I started missing him the moment he left the plane."

"I don't understand." Terms of endearment were never a strong suit in Victoria's vocabulary.

"I don't either. We had a one-way conversation the whole flight. He asked questions, and I answered them. He seemed so sad and alone. My heart reached out to him."

"Surely, you must know something about him? At least something?"

Pamela sighed. Seth had remained with her from the moment he disappeared out of her life. "He's been in the military. I sensed he saw some terrible things. He's short and muscular with powerful arms. What impressed me the most was when he complimented me on my appearance. It was so real, soft and gentle."

Dismissing the thought of her daughter meeting a stranger

on a plane, Victoria said, "Pamela, it's nice you met someone, but you'll never see him again. You should think about the men here in the city. You know, Joshua Powell is interested in you. He is wealthy and influential on Wall Street."

The thought of Joshua Powell made Pamela chuckle. "Mother, he is twenty years older than me. I'd have to have a doctor along on the honeymoon to take care of all of his ailments."

"Pamela," Victoria scolded. "Remember, you are a lady.."

Pamela brushed the hair from her face, dropped her gaze to the pillow. "I saw Seth meet someone at the airport. He told me his name was Moses Remington. I think he lives here in the city. I can't find a listing for him. I'm thinking of hiring a detective to find him."

Surprised, Victoria said, "Pamela, are you sure?"

"Mother, I've never been so sure of anything in my life. I need to see Seth again."

Chapter 15

Sergeant Marcus wiped the sweat off the bridge of his nose. Planning a murder did that to him. Nervous. Eyes darted from one potential hiding place to another. Could Seth be watching him? Satisfied he was alone, he whispered into his cell phone, "Where are you?"

Relaxed, King leaned back in the driver's seat. "I'm just down the street from Boyd's house."

"For Christ sakes, don't tell me you're in an unmarked car?"

"Cool your jets, Marcus. I'm in my car."

"Good. Let me know the instant you're in the house. I—"

Sitting up straight, King interrupted. "Hold it. Elena is coming out of the house. Her car's in the driveway. . .she opened the car door. . .she's behind the wheel. . .door still open."

"Goddammit, don't let her see you."

"Jesus Christ, shut up. Wait a minute. Elena's out of the car. . .now she's standing on the front porch."

"What the hell is she doing?"

"You want me to go up there and ask her?"

"Oh, that was funny, King. Real funny."

"Screw you, Marcus. Hold on, hold on. She's going back to the car. . .now she's inside. The car is backing out. Marcus, you have yourself a luncheon date."

"Goddamn bitch. She better show up. Call me, King when you find the safe. That's where Boyd will go when he comes to the house."

Marcus drove four miles, parked in the handicap zone at Isabella's Italian Restaurant. He tossed the Police Vehicle on Official Business card on the dash. Marcus had a short wait before seeing Elena's car waiting for a string of cars to pass before making a left turn into the lot. He tapped the steering wheel in frustration.

"Come on, Come on. Answer the goddamn phone." Marcus had called Paddy's Bar.

"Yeah."

"Is Boyd there?"

"Yeah. He's drinking his lunch. Wanna talk to him?"

"No. I'll catch him later. Thanks."

Smiling, Marcus stuffed the cell phone into his pocket when Elena Turner stepped out of her car. Everything was perfect. Boyd was drunk, and King wouldn't have any problems. Better still, Elena was ripe for the picking.

Marcus touched her elbow. "Elena, it's good to see you again."

"Marcus," she said with a cold voice.

"Elena, is something wrong?" Marcus was worried some unforeseen event had happened, and his plan was out the window. "What have I done to upset you?"

"I almost didn't come today. Even got out of the car and stood on the porch."

"What's wrong?"

"I'm scared, Marcus."

Blocking an angry driver trying to park, Marcus ushered Elena to the patio in front of the restaurant. Gnarled grapes vines twisted around the pergola. Elena waited until an old woman with a walker and her husband left the restaurant.

"I'm married to a man who is capable of murdering me if I have an affair. Trust me, Marcus, you're not worth it. But you're available, which makes up for most of your shortcomings. No, I still will not sleep with you. And yes, this may be our last luncheon. I have to think whether you're worth the risk or not."

"Can we talk about it inside? It's cool out here." The brisk wind ushered in dark clouds promising more rain.

"Alright. But I'm not going to spend much time with you. Just a glass of wine."

Marcus panicked. He didn't know how much time Elena would give him. How fast it would take Boyd to go back to the house. Hiding his anxiousness, he said, "At least we'll spend some time together."

"Be careful what you say to me today. Don't give me false hope or promises my life will change. Don't lie to me. Now, do you still want to go inside?"

"Yes."

"Then I suggest we do. If it is available, I'd like to sit at the table behind the fireplace."

Marcus wasn't worried about Elena's threat on lying to her. He'd tell her the perfect lie. Undetectable. Poor Elena, she was clueless. She wouldn't know a lie if it bit her in the ass. He wondered how long he would keep her around after he had sex with her. Not long he figured. Still, she had beautiful, full breasts, slim hips. That said something about her.

Wine poured, it was time for Marcus to go to work.

"You're smiling, Elena. That's nice."

"Why not? I'm not sharing a glass of wine with Boyd. That's worth something. Make no mistake, Marcus. Your faults outweigh your assets, but you have shown an interest in me, and that's flattering. So yes, I have something to smile about."

"You've made me a happy man."

"I would caution you, Marcus, about telling me lies. I want to finish my glass of wine."

Marcus' cell phone rang.

"Go ahead, Marcus. Answer the phone. Boyd's phone rings all the time."

"Elena, we've been investigating a drug cartel operation in Hillsdale for three months. We received notice this morning the case may be breaking our way. I'm expecting several calls. Will you accept my apologies for any interruptions?"

"Of course."

"Excuse me." Stepping away from the table, he said, "King."

"Yeah. Found the safe. It's upstairs in his bedroom. Son of a bitch had it in a closet. Hid it behind a pocket door. Goddamn, safe is bigger than a tank. Has a couple of locks on it."

"Do you have the kitchen pans?"

"Yeah."

"Great. I'm going to call Boyd."

Marcus smiled at Elena who politely nodded. Dumb-ass bitch. He held up one finger indicating one more phone call. She raised her open hand, accepted his message. Marcus practiced several times being out of breath before he made the call. Boyd picked up on the third ring.

"Boyd."

"Oh, thank God, I have been trying to find you."

"Marcus, what the hell do you want?"

Marcus sucked in several times to signal he was terrified. "Carlos is in town."

"What are you talking about?"

"Carlos just called King. He's in town, wants his money now. He's asking for an extra twenty-five thousand to cover his travel expenses."

"Jesus Christ!" Boyd said.

"I'm on the way home now to pick up twelve thousand five hundred. You do the same. Carlos wants to meet in thirty minutes. He'll tell King where. Can you do it?"

"Goddammit. Who does Carlos think he is?"

"Boyd, I want to stay alive, so do you. Call me when you have the money."

"Son of a bitch. I'll do it."

Marcus disconnected, returned to the table. "False alarm."

Elena's face relaxed. "Marcus, perhaps I can be persuaded to stay a while longer."

***

"Love your culinary tastes, Kat," Drummond said. He tried to guess the number of calories in the bacon burger and fries on his plate.

"What's not to like? Burger Palace is my favorite place to eat."

"Sorry, Captain. I'm with Kat on this one," Seth said. He wrapped his mouth around the triple cheeseburger.

"I'm on a diet, guys. All I can have for dinner after this is crackers and water."

"Love saltine crackers," Seth retorted. "Tell me about Boyd. Anything else happen after he lost it in your office yesterday?"

"Saw him for a second this morning. You rang his bell. He's still in a rage. He's going to do something stupid. Then he's ours."

"That makes my day." Seth tried to wrap his mouth around

another bite of the cheeseburger. Most of it fell onto the plate.

"Also, saw Detective Coleman. It's going to take him weeks to recover. He's not happy."

"What did you say to him?" Kat asked.

"Told him I was going to arrest his ass when it was finished. He said he wanted to see me when he felt better. My gut tells me he's gonna turn on Boyd and Marcus."

"Love it. What's next, Seth?" Kat asked.

"Chief Bateman. He's their weakest link."

"I agree," Drummond said. "Do me a favor, Seth. I'd like to be there when you pay him a courtesy call."

***

King heard each of Boyd's heavy steps plodding up the stairs. His labored breathing broke the silence of the house when he stopped at the stairway landing to catch his breath. King counted each step in the stairway, fourteen. Seven to the landing, seven more to the second-floor hallway. Hiding to the right at the top of the stairs, King waited in a darkened three-foot hallway leading to the master bedroom. His back pressed against the wall, he tried to disappear.

Boyd announced his continued climb with four more labored steps. Another rest stop. More heavy breathing. Rested, he slapped the oak railing to propel himself up the remaining three. Then another stop at the top of the landing with more heavy breathing. Boyd turned his head to focus on the master-bedroom door when he saw the person standing in the hallway with something in each hand.

Their eyes met. Startled, shaking his head to focus, Boyd said, "King."

It was the last word he spoke.

It happened in an instant. King raised up the two cast iron skillets, slammed them together. The house erupted in an explosion of sound, startling Boyd, who grabbed at his chest, yelling out in pain.

King was surprised at what happened next. So easy. He dropped the pans, shoved before Boyd could raise his hands to defend himself from falling backward.

"Aaaahh," Boyd cried out, somersaulted down the stairs and crashed through the railing. He dropped eight feet to the hallway floor. Returning the pans to the kitchen, King saw Captain Boyd Turner lying on his back, open eyes staring empty, neck twisted. A circle of blood crowned his head. King said nothing, thought little when he drove away.

***

Boyd remained in the hallway while a countless number of picture flashes illuminated the dark corridor. Captain Drummond and Sergeant Porter used the spotless kitchen as their command center. Alyssa said she was on her way.

Remaining stoic, without tears, Elena entered the laundry room, shut the door, made the call. The police ignored the utility room in their investigation. Marcus used her. Knew it. Her grim face reflected her visceral anger.

"Marcus, The police are here. Boyd is dead. Of course, you already knew that."

"Elena—"

"Shut up, Marcus. I don't have any patience for you or your lies. You had lunch with me today so you could have Boyd murdered. Everything you have said to me has been a lie. You're a lie. I'll, at least, give you this much credit."

"What?"

"I'm not sorry he's dead. Alyssa will believe I am."

"Elena, it doesn't have to end this way between us. Can't we talk about it?"

"What? So I can hear more of your lies? No, I'm not going to do that. . .I'll tell you what I am going to do. Someday, when this is all over, I'm going to sleep with a man. Trust me. It will never be you. I can do so much better."

Marcus felt the sweat on the bridge of his nose. Elena could voice her suspicions. Maybe she should be dead, too.

***

Asked to be left alone with his pensive mood, Drummond propped his feet up on the foot-high windowsill behind his desk. Boyd was dead. The loss of a human life was tragic, even if the victim had contributed to their death. Boyd's funeral would be small with little police presence. Drummond would attend to offer comfort to Elena and Alyssa.

His remorse was the stain of dirty cops Boyd left on the department's image. It would take months before he could purge the corruption and restore respect to the police department.

***

Angel knew the secret.

What Chicago witnesses did at the scene of a crime. They kept their mouths shut, eyes closed. Never saw the suspect. It was safer that way.

"Car? Nah, I never saw a car."

Money helped too. Lots of it. It worked at the Amelia Menard Hair Salon. Satisfied with the several hundred dollar bills in their hands, the four women in the shampoo-and-styling chairs and the five employees didn't see Angel or Pedra peering out the salon window.

"Pedra, are your three cousins ready?"

"*Sí, señorita.*"

"You will not fail me?"

"No, *señorita.*"

"Issue the command, Pedra."

"*Sí, señorita.*" Pedra inhaled deeply, pushing her small breasts out. Her first mission. It must be perfect. Angel must congratulate her. She placed the phone to her ear.

"Now."

The three cousins picked up on their cue. A young woman with dyed purple hair left a doorway at a nearby payday loan office, began walking towards the black car. A handbag hung on her right shoulder with a red Macy's shopping bag in her left hand. Matching brown tape held the cut shoulder strap together on the empty bag.

Another cousin stepped out of the same doorway, followed the girl, ten paces behind. He was small with thin legs. Few could catch him when he started running.

The girl with the shoulder bag saw the two men in the black car watching the beauty salon. They ignored her. Approaching the car, she raised up the Macy's bag, trying to find a better grip. The signal. The cousin behind her began running. The timing was perfect. The cousin grabbed the handbag strap, tore it off, knocking the girl to the ground. He raced down the street, disappeared into a crowd. A third cousin, parked in a car three spaces behind the agents, pulled out of the parking space, began to move up to the black car. The girl on the ground jumped up, screamed at the two men in the black car to help her.

"You okay, girl?" the DEA agent said when he rolled down

the passenger window. The girl pulled out a can of pepper spray from the Macy's bag, blinding the two men with the spray. She dropped the can and ran while the third cousin pulled up to the salon. Angel and Pedra rushed out of the salon, jumped into the car, disappeared into traffic.

The remainder of the trip to Los Angeles was uneventful. To escape detection at O'Hare International Airport, they drove west seventy-five miles to Koritz Field in Rochelle. A chartered Cessna Citation Sovereign jet flew them on the three and one-half hour flight to San Diego. Angel and Pedra vanished into a suite at the Los Angeles Omni Hotel, California Plaza, following a limousine ride from San Diego. It was time to visit the reservoir.

An hour after their arrival, Chicago DEA agents gave up their search to find Angel.

***

"Nice body, Seth said."

"Aaaah." Chief Bateman's hand hit his drink, spilling it on the table and his crotch. The yell startled the dancer who reached down to remove her g string. Sneering, she said, "Son of a bitch," and continued her uninspired routine.

"Sorry, Chief," Seth said. He and Drummond stepped out from behind Bateman joining him at the small round table at the Gentleman's Delight Strip Club.

"Little field work, huh?" Drummond asked. "Like to look at naked young women?"

"Shh," warned a young man with a thick black beard, sitting three tables away.

Ignoring the warning, Bateman asked in a panicked voice, "What are you two doing here?" His hand knocked off his baseball cap when he rubbed his forehead. He wore it low over his eyes to escape recognition.

Seth was unclear if Bateman wanted to clean up the spilled drink or order another one. The naked, blonde dancer, picked up her discarded clothes, flipped her middle index finger at Bateman's table. Left the half-circle stage.

Ignoring the dancer, Seth retrieved the chief's hat. "We're just checking up on you, Bateman. Wanted to make sure you were doing okay. See if there is anything we can do for you."

Trying to avoid drawing attention to himself, Bateman said, "Goddammit, leave me alone." The bearded man glared. A second man, sitting with a young woman in thick makeup and large breasts spilling out of her dress, swore.

The new dancer, with a bored expression, stepped away from the pole, waited for a dozen patrons to quiet down. Ignoring the dancer, Seth fixed his eyes on the bouncer with a ring of fat hanging over his belt. The bouncer stepped out from behind the bar, glared over his bulbous, broken nose.

Lifting his chin in contempt, Drummond said, "You better calm down, Bateman. Creating a disturbance in a strip club can get you arrested. Bad for your image." Despite a short night and long day, Drummond reveled in Bateman's discomfort.

Bateman apologized to a woman at the next table while Seth watched the bouncer hurry to their table. "Knock it off, or you're all out of here."

Hating bouncers who beat members of his unit in bars around the world, Seth said, "Oh, the big bad wolf has come to our door." He knew bouncers beat up the weak, cowered away from the strong.

Seeing Seth's biceps up close, the bouncer retreated. The bored dancer completed her abbreviated routine, left with two five-dollar bills.

"Bateman, look at me," Seth said.

Lips sucked in, wide-eyed, the chief saw Seth's angry face. Bateman's life was over.

"Captain Drummond is going to talk to you about tomorrow morning and the press conference you're going to have at nine. You better listen to him."

Studying his shoes, Bateman started crying.

"Captain, I believe you have the floor."

"Thank you, Seth. Bateman, you make me want to puke. You're a disgrace to the uniform. Men died wearing that uniform—then there's you."

Bateman cried harder.

"Look at me, you son of a bitch, or I'll throttle you on the spot."

Bateman glanced up, returned his gaze to the floor. The new dancer and music stopped. All eyes were on the one table where a broken old man was crying.

Lowering his voice, Drummond said, "You have two options, Bateman. First one. Tomorrow morning at nine, you'll have a press conference to announce your resignation. When you finish, the state police are going to arrest you for every crime they can think of. Then they'll haul your ass off to the county jail in handcuffs."

Bateman was stunned. He rubbed his legs. He searched the nearby patrons and the dancer for relief from the two men who sat at his table. Seeing impassive faces, he said, "I have money."

Drummond ignored him. "The second option is to be in my office at eight in the morning, tell us everything you know about Boyd, Marcus, and their little scheme. You're still going to resign and go to jail in handcuffs. I promise the arrest will be private so the twins won't see it on TV."

"I have lots of money," Bateman pleaded again. "You can have all of it. I'll resign and go away. Please, I'm begging you. Don't do this to the twins. It'll kill them."

"Eight in the morning, Bateman. My office. And so help me God, I'll strip you naked if you come in wearing your uniform."

Without speaking, Seth and Drummond watched a broken, old man shuffle out of the club. The man cried without restraint, his baseball cap askew. Bateman clipped two cars driving out of the parking lot.

***

Hidden deep in Woodland State Park on a remote road was Bateman's secret place. Here he'd brought all the whores. Young and pretty—old and worn-out. So many faces. He struggled to remember all of them—any of them. Still, it didn't matter. Such a special place. Maybe here he should die, surrounded by all the memories of satisfied lust.

He tried countless times. Couldn't pull the trigger. He removed the SIG Sauer P220 handgun, laid it on his lap. The barrel pointed away from his body toward his leg. His finger rested on the trigger.

He was an hour past the tears and panic. His mind was numb. One plan of escape after another passed through his mind. One kept returning for further consideration. His wife always left the house for an early morning stroll through the neighborhood. He'd have time to unlock the garage door, grab the inconspicuous packing boxes filled with money.

Now for the twins—how in the hell could he explain his disappearance to them? It would have to be something to do with amnesia. That would work. Be gone for a couple of months, then remember his identity. A rough idea, but he could work out the details, make it perfect. No scandal. And he'd never go to jail.

He would have survived the night if he saw it approach.

But he didn't.

Sensing he wasn't alone, he saw the face of a deer touching its nose to the car window. Startled, he jumped back, the reflex in his finger squeezing the trigger. The .45 APC full metal jacket bullet blew out the femoral artery in his left leg. Unable to stop the bleeding, he tried to start the car. All strength left him. He remembered the twins — saw them admiring him with their blue eyes.

Then his heart stopped.

***

Perfect.

Minutes short of midnight, Cahuenga Boulevard East in Los Angeles was empty. Stopping for an instant at the pre-selected, two-story, stucco house with a red tile roof, Angel and Pedra jumped out of the car. Cesar remained inside, studying the near-by houses for movement.

No lights were turned on or shades opened.

Angel's plan was simple. Garcia reported the previous evening he'd seen two men hiding on the hill observing the Los Guerreros compound. What he didn't know was the men had spotted him, radioed the information to their headquarters.

Garcia also said Cidro's compound defenders made an error in preparing their defenses against an attack. Angel wanted to observe the error for herself. First, she needed to distract the men on the hill before finding a hiding place.

They threw their duffel bags over their shoulders, jogged thirty yards south. Stopped, Angel studied the hill below Hollywood Reservoir.

"This way, Pedra." She sprinted over a fifty-foot-high, dirt berm, dropped to avoid becoming a silhouetted target. The only sound was Cesar driving away to cross Pilgrimage Bridge on the way to his new position.

An outcropping of rock shielded them. Two men were above them on the hill, hiding in the eclectic mix of pine and deciduous trees observing the compound. Like Chicago, they had to be DEA agents.

Pedra spent several hours earlier in the evening training for the mission. Angel's closed-fist signal sprung her into action. She joined Angel in slipping on L-3 GPNVG-18 goggles. Adjusting the fit, she clipped on a Motorola PRC-153 Integrated Intra-Squad Radio to her web-pack harness and hooked up her headset. She signaled her radio was working when Angel blew into her microphone. They settled down for a ten-minute wait while Cesar drove to his new position.

"Cesar, have you reached your destination?" His position was a dirt parking lot on Weidlake Drive next to the closed gate entrance at the top of the reservoir.

"*Sí.*"

"I'll tell you when to move."

Angel's plan called for ten minutes to search and find the men hiding on the hill. Any longer would raise the chances of a sentry below spotting them with night vision goggles. Ten minutes to consider the fatal consequences of being discovered first. Ten minutes. A blink of an eye. A single breath. There were times when Angel remained motionless for hours until the target moved into the crosshairs.

Such a beautiful night. She broke away to study the blackness surrounding her. Clean. Pristine. The garbage strewn across the hillside disappeared. She saw a rabbit scurry for the safety of a chaparral. She liked little creatures. The kind that ran away from her. She was terrified of snarling guard dogs who wanted to tear her leg off. Several times, she'd shot them to escape.

She felt it, searching for the DEA agents, who listened for the snap of a twig underfoot or searched for a human silhouette in the faint moonlight. Her body filled with adrenaline. She was at the apex of her life. Every muscle poised for movement. All senses tuned in for instant response to being detected and escaping death.

She was home, where she always wanted to be. No one expected her or could see her. She was a ghost that spit out death, then vanished. It would always be like that for her. Her life's purpose was the next mission. Tracking the target. Moving to escape. Surviving the impossible.

Angel said, "Cesar. Are you with Garcia?"

"*Sí.*"

"Pedra. Ready to move?"

"*Sí, señorita.*"

"Follow me."

Spotting no thermal imaging of the two DEA agents, they jumped up, raced to the first objective. A rocky bluff, jutting up fifteen yards. They veered to the right, dropped where the outcropping sloped down to three feet.

With a view of the hill above them, Angel said, "Garcia, execute. Cesar, prepare to evacuate."

"*Sí.* Garcia is moving through the trees on the hillside," Cesar said. "The car is in position to leave when Garcia returns."

"Pedra, Garcia is moving on the hillside. The two men will spot him and start following him. Then we can go up and find a hiding place. Search the left flank to see if the two men are moving. I have the right."

Angel picked up the thermal image of Garcia moving through the brush and trees below Mulholland Dam.

Garcia walked among the trees, jogged through the open spaces. Twice he stopped as if searching for hiding places.

"Pedra, anything?"

"No."

"Nothing on the right flank."

"Wait," Pedra said.

"Where?"

"Just a second. . . *Sí* . . . there they are. Next to the dam. They're moving down to Garcia."

"Garcia, you've been spotted. Excellent. We have found their hiding place. Evacuate to the car. Deliberate pace. I want them to keep tracking you so we can come up the hill without being detected."

"*Sí*."

"Pedra, follow me." Crossing a trail, they charged up the hill around the chaparral into the trees. The two men continued to follow Garcia signaling to Angel they'd avoided detection. Above the location of the two men's hiding place, Angel found a shallow swale surrounded by trees. She had an unobstructed view of the compound and the agents. It would be their home for the next nine hours while they observed the Los Guerreros defenders positions.

Chapter 16

Sergeant Porter ignored the written-in-stone rule about knocking before entering Drummond's office. Seeing him on the phone, he said, "Need some time."

Scowling, Drummond covered the mouthpiece. "Dammit, are you blind, Porter? I'm on the phone."

"Now, Captain."

Drummond said, "Call you back," and disconnected. "This better be good, Porter. I'm in a shitty mood. And where in the hell is Bateman?"

"Dead."

Stunned, Drummond said, "What?" He removed his finger too fast from the coffee cup, spilling coffee onto a mugshot. "Goddammit." He wiped coffee off of the photograph. Didn't help much. "What the hell do you mean he's dead?"

"Park ranger found him this morning at Woodland Park."

"Oh, Jesus Christ. Suicide?"

"Hell of a way to commit suicide. Shot himself in the leg. Bled out."

Drummond slapped his desk, spilled more coffee, kicked back his chair, "Goddammit, that's not what I wanted to hear. He's supposed to be standing in my office."

"Sorry, Captain."

Drummond couldn't sit. Impossible. His mind raced from one image to another. Standing didn't help either as he combed his thinning hair with his fingers. Looking out the window to gather his thoughts wasn't much better.

First, Captain Boyd Turner and now Chief Wendell Bateman. Drummond didn't have any sympathy for Boyd's death. He was a dirty cop from the day he pinned on a badge. Bateman was different. Drummond remembered when Bateman was once a good cop and respected him. He hated him for surrendering to corruption, staining the department. He felt the anguish Bateman's twin daughters would suffer when they learned what their father had done. Drummond always liked the girls' cheerful attitudes.

Clearing his throat to capture Drummond's attention, Porter said, "Sir, What do you want me to do?"

Captain Drummond left the window and parked his thoughts on Bateman and his daughters. Standing at his desk, he said, "What do I want you to do?" Drummond rubbed his chin, thought about it. "The first thing I want you to do is to keep your goddamn nose clean. God help your ass if you ever turn dirty." Drummond attempted a smile to dilute his threat.

"Not a problem, sir."

"Good. Didn't expect there'd be one. Now listen up. First, call Seth and Kat. Set it up on the speakerphone. Want to talk to them yesterday. Call the city manager. Tell him what happened, have him on standby. I'll go to his office after I brief Seth and Kat. Get ahold of Special Agent Quinton. Gonna need him for a conference call in the city manager's office. Now move your ass, Porter. You're already wasting too much time."

Porter couldn't remember seeing the captain so energized. It reminded him of his first day in boot camp. He moved his ass.

***

"Congratulations, Sir," Seth said. "Police chief. Outstanding." The city manager appointed Captain Roscoe Drummond to be the police chief following Bateman's death. The manager commented the appointment was permanent.

"Thanks, Seth," Drummond said. "Kat with you?"

"Yes, sir."

"Put yourself on speaker. I have time to say this once. Here's what I know. Marcus and King are outside of my office now. I'm going to suspend them pending an investigation. Detective Coleman too. I can't clean the department until I cut out the cancer. Penny Majors from the DA will be in my office to add some muscle. She'll lead the investigation.

"Quinton told me he smells ATF coming to town. Nothing definite. If it happens, I have to play in their sandbox. I won't like it, but I don't have any choice. That means you are on your own. I can't support you. Kat, I'm going to suspend you. I'll make something up. You didn't shine your goddamn shoes, whatever. I want you free of the department to work with Seth."

"Yes, sir," Kat said, surprised.

"Porter is going to head up the Narcotics Division. He doesn't know a damn thing about drugs, but he's one helluva of a fine cop and a quick learner. The Narcotics Division is in shambles. Finding out who's salvageable in the division is going to keep Porter busy. The street dealers will also keep him busy.

"What I want from you two is to find out who's running the show here in town. Is Marcus in charge now or is Carlos bringing in new people? For Christ sake, watch out for Angel. If you need to contact me for any reason, do it through Porter. Questions?"

"Are Marcus and King under surveillance?" Seth asked.

"Will be. Coleman, no. He ain't going anywhere. Stay safe. Later."

***

"Good morning. Ziegler Investigation and Security Services. How may I help you?"

"Good morning. I'm Pamela Brighton. I would like to speak to Larry Ziegler if he is available."

"One moment please."

"Thank you." Pamela signaled she needed two minutes. The secretary left with her papers while Pamela enjoyed the explosion of sunlight coming through her office window.

Seth was on her mind for much of the night and morning. Her search for him would prove futile, or he'd say no to seeing her again. Whatever the outcome, she had to try. Her heart demanded it.

"Pamela, good to hear from you," a robust voice said. "How's my favorite girl this morning?"

"I'm doing well, Larry. Thank you. Mom, Dusty and I are excited to be your houseguests this weekend."

"Susan is thrilled you're coming," Larry said with continued enthusiasm. "She should be rested up when you arrive."

"What happened?" Pamela asked.

"She spent a week with the grandkids."

Smiling. Pamela said, "That explains everything. Larry, I need a favor."

"What can I do to help you?"

"I saw a man on Monday when I flew to pick up Dusty. He's a friend of a friend. His name is Moses Remington. He is a tall black man in his mid-forties who I hope lives here in the city.

I think he was in the service. I would like to see him. Can you help me find him?"

"I'll have something for you this weekend. Be sure and tell your mother and Dusty hello."

"I will. Thanks for your help. Love to Susan. Goodbye."

***

Angel whispered into the microphone. The DEA agents were forty-five yards below them "Garcia, has there been any change in their position?" Avoiding detection, Garcia returned earlier to the hillside to keep watch on the two agents. Having completed her surveillance of the compound, Angel was prepared to leave.

"No. The men remain in the same place. They are lazy and don't move around."

"Are you still above them?"

"*Sí.*"

Brushing at a fly on her cheek, Angel said, "Cesar, where are you?"

"On Weidlake Drive. Thirty seconds from the parking lot."

"Both of you, on my mark, set your watches to twelve forty-five. Five. . . four. . . three. . . two. . . one. Mark. Garcia. Evacuate your position. Hug the dam until you get to the car."

"I'm moving."

"Cesar. Not one second early or late to rendezvous. No one must see you."

"I'll be there."

"Pedra. Are both bags loaded?"

"*Sí.*"

"Now, follow me. Do not make a sound and anger me."

"I will not displease you."

Watching Marcus drop his lanky frame into a chair away from the front door at Teddie's Bar and Grill, King asked, "What did Carlos say?"

"We're in business," Sergeant Marcus said, stretching his legs.

"When?"

"Soon."

"What the hell do you mean?" King said.

"I asked if the delivery was scheduled. He said yes, hung up. Someone must have tapped his phone."

Motioning with his head, King said, "Did you see anything outside when you came in?"

"They're still there. Both cars."

Drummond had ordered four uniformed officers in two cars to follow them.

"We have to lose them."

"King quit your goddamn fussing. I'm taking care of things. You know my butt is in a sling too."

"Sorry."

"Escobar is finding us cars, guns, and a place to stay. We're gonna meet him in an hour. It shouldn't be a problem to ditch our friends outside."

"Escobar still have a contract on Seth?"

"Tonight."

"Good." Detective King removed his tie, stuffed it into his coat pocket. Ties suffocated him. He felt sweat running down his armpits. "Goddammit, Marcus, what the hell are we going to do?"

"We stay smart. We have the money to buy the shipment.

We can sell the merchandise in one or two nights. Then get the hell out of Dodge. There has to be a Caribbean island with our name on it."

"Damn, sounds good. What about Coleman? He isn't in any shape to travel."

"Yeah, it's a problem, isn't it? You should say hello."

"Coleman? Christ, we've worked together for six years."

"Do you want to go to jail?"

"Son of a bitch."

"Say hello," Marcus said.

***

"You know, Mom," Kat said, "I don't like chicken and dumplings."

"Is that why," Linda MacKenna replied, "you just had your second helping, and you'll beg me to let you have the leftovers?"

"Caught you, sweetheart," Ron said.

"Dad, am I that obvious?"

Ron snickered. "And then some."

"You can have the chicken and dumplings," Kat's sister Angie said, "but you can't have the apple pie. That's mine."

Linda chuckled at her two daughter's game of dividing the food. What she didn't tell them was she made an extra apple pie and a second pot of chicken and dumplings.

"Nothing's changed," Linda said to Ron. "Our daughters are still fighting over the leftovers."

"Maybe," Ron laughed. "We shouldn't invite them over for dinner anymore."

"No way," Angie said. The doorbell rang.

"Expecting someone, Dad?" Kat asked.

"No. Linda, you expecting anyone?"

"No, sweetheart. See who's at the door. I'm going to get more salad."

"Okay." Ron returned a minute later. "Kat, it's for you. Porter."

"What the hell?"

Meeting Kat at the front door, Porter said, "Sorry to bother you while you're eating dinner."

"Don't worry about it. Is it Marcus?"

"Yes. I want your dad here, too."

"Dad."

Joining Kat and Porter, Ron said, "What is it, sweetheart?"

"Porter wants to talk to us." Greetings exchanged, Kat continued. "What's happened?"

"Sergeant Marcus and Detective King have disappeared. We lost them in the Hillsdale Shopping Mall. I'm worried they're going to come after you and Seth."

"I'm a cop, Porter. Remember?"

"Not good enough, Kat. Sir, Kat is in real danger. I'll worry when she's not with Seth."

"Jesus Christ. Porter, I'll call her two uncles. We all used to be cops."

"Great."

"Dammit, Dad. I can take care of myself."

"Not on this one," Ron said. "No damn way. So deal with it."

"Your dad's right, Kat. You need to listen to him."

"Oh shut up, Porter. Did you call Seth?"

"Yes."

"You could have just called me."

Porter blushed. Kat picked up on his motive.

Sensing he was the third person in the room, Ron excused

himself and returned to the dining room.

Watching Ron walk away, Porter said, "I have to know your safe, Kat."

"Are you being horny again?"

"It's a hell of a lot more than that."

"Porter, you need to know I'm in love with someone else."

"And I'm in love with you. I don't intend to let Seth beat me out on this one."

"You're impossible. Move your butt into the dining room. You're having dinner with us. I'll be there in a minute."

Despite Porter's words of caution, Kat wanted fresh air. Wearing a coat, she hugged herself to ward off the evening chill. Sitting on the porch swing with her legs drawn up, Kat examined her dilemma. She loved Seth and a part of her always would. It perplexed her how to fall out of love with someone. She couldn't continue to love Seth without love in return. She was confused where it left her. Porter added to her confusion. How did he fit into the mess? She knew Porter had a bright future ahead of him in law enforcement. He'd be an easy man to love, but Seth tugged at her heart.

Without any solution, she returned to the dinner table. Focused on her father, she felt the presence of Porter sitting next to her. It surprised her. She was comfortable, happy with the seating arrangement.

Several hours later, parked at the curb in front of her apartment on Belmont Street, Kat examined her finger poised to tap his name on her phone. Seth. In the time she knew him, his words were few, and he revealed little about himself. Now he said he was leaving—alone. She loved him. Her explanation was simple.

He was Seth.

Unlike anyone else. Not much of reason, but logic and love were sometimes strangers.

Her mind raced with the knowledge the call could seal her fate that Seth would never love her. Still, she had to make it. She stared at the phone, closed her eyes, tapped his name.

"Seth. . .just checking. . .how's your dad?"

"He's slipping fast, Kat. He didn't know me or recognize my voice when I stopped by."

"I'm sorry."

"He's ready," Seth said with a sigh. "Wants to go."

"Is there anything I can do?"

"No. Did Porter call you?"

"He was at the house earlier."

"Where are you now, Kat?"

"I'm parked in front of my apartment. Had to pick up a couple of items. Dad won't let me stay at the apartment until this blows over."

"Your dad is a good man. Listen to him."

"God, now don't you start on me."

"Just listen to your dad, and I won't have to kick your butt."

"Like that's going to happen," she said.

The light moment passed into an awkward silence. Time for words. Kat's heart needed to express.

"What?" Seth said, in response to the silence between them.

"Seth?"

"I'm still here, Kat. What is it?"

"Can we talk?"

"About what?"

"Us," she said.

Us. Such a microscopic word, yet so powerful. And such a defining word. The summary of the relationship between a man

219

and woman. Was there an "us" between Seth and Kat? Would there ever be an "us" between them? Would they become lovers again or remain friends? Why did the question demand an answer at such an awkward moment? Unexplainable. Or was it? Porter told her he loved her. She'd dismissed it as a testosterone overdose. But it was much more. Porter's attraction to her wasn't a surprise. She had sensed it for a long time. How did it fit with her love for Seth? Was Porter an interference or a replacement? She didn't know. She needed to find out.

"Seth. I want to talk about you leaving after your dad is gone."

"We've talked about it, Kat."

"I want to visit some more. Can we?" she said, tears running down her cheeks unchecked. She tried to speak without choking on her words.

"Sure."

"I don't want you to go."

"Know that."

"Will you take me with you, Seth?"

"I'm sorry, Kat. I can't do that to you. You have a family. They don't have any interest in you skipping from town to town, country to country. And I couldn't handle you begging me to stop and rest. Or your sadness because you don't have a home or children. Kat, I've been bouncing from one place to another. It's all I know. Dad's leaving. It's time for me to go."

"I can't change your mind?" she asked.

"Kat. . .I lost Billie. You're the only one I have left. I don't want to lose you somewhere on the road. I don't want you to turn on me and hate me for the life I've given you. You deserve better. I'm not leaving you, Kat. You and I still have a lot of days ahead of us."

"I love you, Seth."

"I love you, Kat. I just wish I could love you back the way you want. I can't. Allison sucked out all of the love I had inside of me. I don't know how to love anymore. Kat, I'm sorry."

Kat watched a dog run across the street. She couldn't tell if it was small or big. Studied the steering wheel without seeing it. She said, "Right now, I think I hate you."

"Not sure?"

"You're a royal pain in the butt."

"Now that's my Kat. That's the girl I love. Give me a smile."

"No." She wiped the tears away. "Go to hell."

"Kat."

Tears spent, mascara ruined, she said, "You won't see it."

"I have magic eyes."

Kat gave a quick, thin smile. "That's all you get," took a breath to slow the beating of her racing heart. She reached over, searched for a tissue in her purse. She was going to need a lot of them. "What are you doing now?"

"Going to eat at the Blue Parrot. Then go Marcus hunting."

"Call me when you finish dinner. I'll help you."

Seth chuckled. "Yeah, right. Catch you in the morning, Kat."

Kat liked it when she made Seth laugh, even when it was a suggestion of one. Call ended, Kat's vision returned to the street. She thought Seth would remain with her for much of the night—she was wrong. Porter was the one who lingered with her when she went to bed. What in the hell was she going to do about him?

221

Chapter 17

Seth had a problem.

Not a serious problem but still, a problem.

Three men across the street from the Blue Parrot Bar wanted to kill him.

He'd first noticed them when he glanced out the front window of the bar on the way to the restroom. Parked across the street, sixty meters south of the front door of the pub was a dirty blue Chevrolet SUV with multiple dents, two cracked windows. Eight parked cars were in front of the SUV, two behind. The vehicle's exhaust plume rose up in the chilly nighttime air.

Ambush—not a good one.

Seth knew all about good ambushes. The scary ones, like the afternoon at an abandoned school compound near Marjah, Afghanistan. Caught by surprise, Seth, and his patrol dashed for cover inside the compound while Kalashnikov PKM machine guns and RPG's pounded them. The route of escape was an open, treeless field behind them. Leg blown off by a mine, Seth held the head of a dying young Marine and new father, while he radioed for a nearby patrol to rescue them.

A good ambush was secret. The victim never realized their mistake until ensnared in the web. Then death loomed up, wrapped its arms around the hapless victim.

The three men in the SUV hadn't bothered to hide their intentions.

One final glance on the way back to his table told Seth everything. The driver and passenger were in the front seat while the third man in the backseat had the window down. The front seat passenger would be the spotter identifying the location of the target and any approaching police cars. The passenger in the back would be the shooter with an automatic rifle to ensure the victim was hit multiple times.

Seth nursed his beer, considered his options. Escape was either out the front or side door into the alley. Each firing .45 caliber APC cartridges, the Glock 21SF pistol with thirteen rounds was tucked inside his belt and the ten round Glock 30 Gen4 was in his pocket, The two pistols, along with an extra magazine for each handgun, gave him sufficient firepower to defend himself. Awareness of the pending attack gave him the element of surprise. Experience told him a fourth man was involved.

The shooter wasn't stupid. He'd have someone hiding in the alley with a cell phone in the event Seth tried to escape through the side door. The alleyway stopped at a high cyclone fence twenty meters beyond the kitchen door. Seth would have to run twenty-five meters to the street. The man hiding in the alley would have an easy shot at Seth's back.

An unappealing option.

Seth often joined his friend Mark, owner of the Blue Parrot Bar when Mark needed a break from bartending to smoke a cigarette in the alley. Standing outside the door on the landing. Seth's eyes never rested while they traded stories about their kickass life in Iraq and Afghanistan. Listening to Mark, Seth's ingrained habit had him studying every detail of the alleyway.

Combat taught him frequenting a place like the Blue Parrot

could make it easy for his enemies to find him. Knowing how to escape from the bar would help keep him alive. A dumpster was on the left side of the landing. Across the narrow alley, an empty, two-story brick warehouse. Recessed into the building next to the cyclone fence was an eighteen-foot square receiving dock with a double shutter-rolling door perpendicular to the alley. The receiving dock and the space between the dumpster and the wall were the only hiding places in the alley.

Distraction was the best weapon to attack the enemy. Seth's distraction sat at the bar waiting for her next trick. Jessie, a big-breasted, happy whore with a blond wig, displayed her wares with a deep V-neck blouse.

"Jessie, can I buy you a drink?" Seth said.

"Of course."

Pointing at her empty glass, he signaled Mark.

"Jessie, you got five minutes?"

She roared with a belly laugh, startling three men at a nearby table. "Seth, the ladies tell me you're good. You're not that good."

Seth laid a fifty-dollar bill on the counter.

"Hey, baby. If you want to taste Jessie's delights, it's gonna cost you a hundred and fifty."

Seth explained what he needed. Jessie agreed fifty dollars was adequate compensation. She waited for the signal from Seth.

"Mark, there's an ambush across the street. Keep everyone inside. Lock the door if you have to."

"Want some help?"

"It's not your fight."

Mark said nothing. Didn't have to. Seth knew the answer. Mark would have his back. That's what Marines did.

Seeing the signal, Jessie told Mark she was going for a cigarette. "Be sure and save my stool and drink," she said. Un-
buttoning the second button to her blouse in the kitchen, she
stepped out onto the landing in the alley. Her breasts became
the bait. Seth was behind her. He remained in the kitchen, standing to the right of the door. He knew the fourth man would be
watching Jessie from his hiding place.

Stepping into the alley, lighting a cigarette, Jessie took several deep drags before looking up and down the alley. She knew
the man in the doorway was watching her. Acting as if she was
alone, she pulled down her pants, scratched her ass. Added a
moan of relief for effect. She never wore underwear when she
was working. Too much time dressing—undressing. Keeping it
simple made more time available for sex. More money.

The man in the doorway, Montrel Rector, grinned at the unexpected sight and hid his gun inside his belt under the coat.
Pressing his cell phone against his coat for silence, he stepped
out and followed Jessie. She pulled up her pants, sucked on the
cigarette, and moved toward the street.

"Hey, baby," the man said. "Wait up."

Jessie turned, giving him her best, startled expression. She
had a host of expressions in her repertoire. Surprise was her best
one. Good for business. "You scared me."

"You have a beautiful ass."

"You saw that? Why you naughty boy. You shoulda closed
your eyes."

Montrel walked past the kitchen door toward Jessie, who
had stopped. He continued to have the cell phone pressed against
his coat. Slipping out the door, Seth jumped over the railing,
dropped down behind the dumpster. He sprinted undetected to
the warehouse receiving dock.

"I'm on a job," the man said. "Where will I find you when I finish?"

"Around."

"I'll find ya, baby."

Jessie returned to the front of the bar. She buttoned the second button of her blouse before opening the door. Fastest fifty bucks she'd made in a long time.

Walking back to his hiding place, Seth heard Montrel talking on his cell phone.

"Relax, Escobar. It's just a whore havin' a smoke."

Escobar Padilla. Seth wasn't surprised. He'd be the shooter in the backseat.

Stepping back into the receiving dock, Montrel never saw Seth or the blow swinging at his head.

Seth slammed his right fist hard alongside Montrel's right temple. Grabbed the phone out of his hand. Wrapping his arm around his waist, Seth dumped him into the corner. Placing the phone on the ground, he covered it with Montrel's baseball cap to silence any noise. He pulled the gun out from behind Montel's belt, removed the magazine and threw it and the gun into the dumpster.

Seth emptied his mind of Kat, Drummond, and his father. Even Pamela walked away.

God dammit, Seth, get it together. There's killing to be done.

The admonishment failed. He hadn't placed the pieces of his life back together—not even close. Leaving the Marjah district in Helmand Providence, Afghanistan for the last time, he'd thought it was finished.

The killing.

He'd had a lifetime of it. All those empty faces of men who'd died trying to kill him. The young boy he'd shot in the Keshawar

226

Village, Afghanistan, when he tried to throw a grenade at him. The teenager he'd killed in Al Kut, Iraq, when she tried to detonate her suicide vest.

The sticky sweat that bathed him when their curses woke him up. The dead, blown-apart bodies strewn across the landscape. God, would it ever end? Would he have rest, peace? Or would his hell end like Billie's?

Self-inflicted.

Pressing the grip on the Glock 21SF returned Seth to reality, restored clarity in his mind. His demons left. He was back in Afghanistan. The enemy wanted to kill him. Not going to happen. He'd kill them first.

Moving without conscious thought, he stepped out onto the sidewalk. Locking his hands around the Glock, he fired three quick rounds into the windshield below the rearview mirror. Bullet fragments tore through the roof and rear window. The driver Miguel Diaz and front seat passenger Gilberto Nunez dove for cover.

Escobar saw Seth run across the street, disappear between a Honda Accord and a Jeep Wrangler. He pulled the AK-47 away from the left rear window while Miguel and Gilberto continued to hide behind and under the dashboard. Bobbing his head, Escobar raised up in search of a firing position to skip a bullet off the street and under the jeep, hitting Seth. It wouldn't work. He was sitting up too high. Frustrated, in eight terrifying seconds, he emptied the thirty-round magazine in Seth's direction, blowing a foot-wide hole in the windshield.

Hugging the ground, Seth tried to disappear. The exploding, popping sound of 7.62x39mm bullets cracked all around him before ricocheting off cars with a whining sound into the night. The memory of the terrifying August night came back with a vengeance. The heavy incoming fire. Ricocheting bullets and RPGs left him the sole survivor of the patrol outside of Shewan, Afghanistan.

Slapping a new magazine into the rifle, Escobar looked down at Miguel hiding under the steering wheel howling in pain. He had a deep gash on his forehead. Gilberto remained squeezed down between the seat and dashboard.

Escobar jammed the rifle muzzle hard into their shoulders "Get the goddamn hell up."

Miguel and Gilberto started to move when Seth raised up, fired three more rounds into the vehicle. One bullet smashed into Gilberto's headrest missing Escobar's stomach by two inches.

"Seth, you son of a bitch!"

Despite being exposed, he rose up, slapped Miguel and Gilberto harder with the rifle. "You sacks of shit."

Yelping in pain, they rose up, waving their guns in search of a target.

Escobar fired a short burst. "You're dead, Seth!"

"Where the hell is he?" Miguel asked.

"You dumb sack of shit. On our side of the street between the yellow Honda and blue Jeep."

Miguel and Gilberto each emptied a magazine through the windshield to convince Escobar they were in the firefight.

The bullets missed by four feet. Seth didn't move or make a sound. Combat was a great teacher. Bullet ballistics told him when to duck. And Escobar's yelling spoke volumes to Seth. The ambush failed. They were losing the fight.

"Miguel, out of the car. Come up on him from the left." Miguel had little choice. Seth would shoot him if he stepped out of the car. Escobar would kill him if he stayed. He jumped out, hugged the left front tire.

"I can't see," Miguel said, wiping the blood out of his eyes.

"You pussy. Shut up. Gilberto, you're with me."

Escobar and Gilberto slithered out of the car onto the sidewalk. Gilberto moved sideways to let Escobar crawl past him.

Seth knew what to expect. He was dead if he continued to lie on the pavement. He jammed the Glock under his belt. Using his left foot, he raised it up over the bumper onto the rear trunk of the Honda, grabbed the grille guard of the Jeep with both hands. Pushing his left foot against the Honda, he pulled his body up off the pavement. Escobar fired a burst under the Jeep skipping rounds where Seth had vacated. Seth gave his best scream of pain. It worked with Julio at the warehouse—maybe it could work again.

"Miguel, move up, finish that son of a bitch off."

Rising, Miguel wiped the blood off his face with his coat sleeve before taking two bullets in the chest. A man raised up from behind a parked car across the street, fired a Sig Sauer P226. Miguel died without a sound.

His back to the street, Seth didn't see who shot behind him. No need. He had his back covered.

"What the hell?" Escobar said.

"Got the son of a bitch," a voice said. "Seth, watch it. Hostiles left flank."

Mark.

Beautiful Mark.

"Copy."

Seth dropped to the pavement, fired two rounds under the jeep, skipping them on the sidewalk.

"Oh, God, my ankle!" One of Seth's rounds blew out Gilberto's ankle.

Escobar rose up, fired a short burst at Seth. Dropping to the sidewalk he wiggled backward, leaving Gilberto and retreated behind the SUV.

Gilberto fired three times at Seth. The intense pain in his ankle destroyed his aim. He was going to die. Knew it. Maybe he could kill Seth first.

Maybe.

He ejected the empty magazine, struggled to retrieve a new one out of his coat pocket. Seth leaned out away from the jeep, shot the prone Gilberto in the head, burying bullet fragments into the base of his brain. The second round tore through his left shoulder, destroying Gilberto's lung. Eyes half open, a pool of blood circled Gilberto's head.

Seeing Seth move up into a squatting firing position, Mark fired three more rounds, advanced to the cover of the next car.

Mark was closing in on Escobar. Escobar knew it.

In a second, Mark would have a clear shot at him. He fired a longer burst at Mark, who fell to the pavement, bullets spitting over his head. The intersection wasn't far behind, thirty feet.

Not far.

He could make it. With Mark on the pavement and Seth behind the jeep, dead or wounded, he had a chance. He fired a short burst at Seth and Mark, ran for the intersection. Despite his deformed leg, he moved with surprising speed. Any slower—he'd be dead.

Slapping in another magazine, he stopped twenty feet short of the intersection, emptied the magazine at both of them. Running onto a side street, he disappeared into the night. Seth and Mark stood up, assumed a firing position.

Seth raced to the corner. On the sidewalk, the empty AK-47. Escobar was gone. He heard the scream of sirens moving closer to him.

"Mark, you okay?"

"Affirmative."

"Give me your gun. They'll trace it."

Seth wasn't worried his name would be flagged as the owner of the Glock 21SF. Billie gave the gun to him as a gift. The gun wasn't listed on the federal NFA registry or listed on the FBI's national database of stolen guns. He never questioned Billie on where he'd picked it up.

"Mark, move your butt back into the bar. I don't want them to see you out here. Owe you one."

"Love you, bro. Semper Fi," and raced back into the bar.

"Semper Fi." Running to his car parked across the street from the SUV, Seth disappeared before the first police car screeched to a stop at Miguel's body.

Time to move. Kat was the next target.

***

"Goddammit, Porter." Police Chief Drummond wasn't happy. Every reporter throughout the state and Fox News wanted an exclusive report on the "horrific gun battle" the previous evening in Hillsdale, Ohio, leaving two men dead without any suspects. Quinton's call alerting him the ATF was on their way added to his cranky disposition.

"They're in the building," Porter said.

"ATF?"

"Yeah."

"How many?"

"Two."

"Have my secretary head them off. Make them wait. Tell the sons of bitches I'm in a meeting. I'll catch them in a minute."

"You got it, Chief."

Chief.

Damn, that word has a ring to it.

Drummond imagined the word would be his favorite. He dreamed of becoming chief for as long as he'd been a cop. People would remember Police Chief Roscoe Drummond. He was the chief who made the Hillsdale Police Department the model of professionalism. But enough of dreams. ATF was outside. If he kept them waiting, he'd have two pissed-off agents.

Hell of a plan.

Hillsdale was his town. He was in charge. Want to play in my sandbox? Then by God, you'll play by my rules.

Drummond spent the next five minutes on the phone reviewing the weekend plans with his wife. First, was their daughter's ballet recital on Saturday night followed by the family barbecue on Sunday. Then the matter of the garbage. He forgot to haul it to the curb in the rain. "Husbands don't treat their wives like that," was his wife's final remark.

Fox News wanted an interview. ATF was outside his office, and his wife was pissed. It had the makings of an outstanding day.

Drummond said to his secretary through the opened door." Send them in. Have Porter stand by."

He glared when the two ATF agents entered into his office. The two men glared back. The room was thick with attitude. The police chief was a buffoon. The ATF agents were assholes.

"Chief Drummond?" the taller agent said in a toneless voice.

"That's what the nameplate said the last time I saw it."

The man ignored the curt reply. "My name is Nicholas Barringer, special agent in charge of the Columbus Field Division of the Bureau of Alcohol, Tobacco, Firearms and Explosives."

"Mouthful." Drummond was bored with the introduction.

"What do you say we knock off the bullshit, Chief? With me is special agent Edwin Garner. Agent Garner will head up our investigation in Hillsdale. We are assuming jurisdiction on all matters relating to the deaths of Police Captain Boyd Turner, Chief Wendell Bateman, and Sergeant Arnold Pappas. We are also assuming jurisdiction of the investigation regarding the shootout at the Atlas Warehouse and the Blue Parrot Bar. The evidence shows there were violation of federal laws.

"We also have identified Patrolman Seth Collins as a person of interest. We want his complete personnel file and for you to order him to report to your office now. We have reason to believe the warehouse incident was a cover-up by Patrolman Collins to hide his involvement in the sale and distribution of drugs here in Hillsdale."

Drummond lost it.

In an instant.

He jumped up out of his chair, slammed his fist on the desk. His face red, jaw set, he said, "You goddamn son of a bitch. How dare you come into my office and accuse Officer Collins of being involved in the sale of drugs."

"Watch your language, Chief. I'll charge you with obstruction of our investigation."

"Oh God, I'm terrified." He scurried away from his desk, stopped within spitting distance of Barringer's face. Drummond's voice became louder, spit sprayed from his mouth. "The Hillsdale Police Department will cooperate fully with your goddamn investigation. Provide you with whatever information you want. Your assumption of jurisdiction does not require me to like it. This is my town. I have a department reeking with corruption, and I have a handle on cleaning it up. I don't need some goddamn federal son of a bitch idiot telling me what to do. Now

233

let me tell you how I'm going to play. We will arrest you or any of your agents if there is interference with any lawful duty performed by one of my officers. That includes any violation of a city ordinance. So help me God, we'll throw your sorry excuse in jail for jaywalking. Let the judge decide the issue of federal versus local jurisdiction."

Raw with anger, Barringer said, "Now let me tell you how I'm going to play. The United States Code on Obstruction of Justice is a comprehensive document. If necessary, we'll exercise its provisions against you or any of your officers interfering with our investigation. Do we have an understanding?"

"If you're finished, get the goddamn hell out of my office."

"You're on notice, you son of a bitch," Barringer said and left, Special Agent Garner lingered. "Use to be a police chief myself. Understand," and hurried to catch up with Barringer.

"Porter, move your ass in here now!"

"Yes, sir."

"Goddammit, Porter. I hate the federal government."

"What about Quinton, sir?"

"Only Christian in the bunch. ATF thinks Seth is dirty."

"Jesus Christ."

"Find him first, Porter, or I swear to God, you're on parking meter patrol until you retire—no until you die from old age."

***

"Is your room any better?" Sergeant Marcus asked.

"No. Worse," King decided. The twelve-room, single story Sahara Motel on the edge of town had a single street lamp to illuminate the parking lot. The stark room, with a spring mattress double bed and threadbare carpet, didn't have any table or chairs. The bathroom sink and shower were dirty, stained from years of use and hard water. Such amenities were unnecessary for the whores and tricks who frequented the motel.

Removing his jacket, throwing it on the bed, Detective King said, "You sure the owner will cover for us?"

"A thousand a week. You can count on it. She hasn't seen us in months."

"What did Escobar say?"

Marcus shook his head. "Montrel went to the emergency room with a concussion. Miguel and Gilberto are dead."

"Dammit. What's next?"

"Pay Coleman a visit this morning. We can't afford for him to turn on us and do a plea bargain to escape jail time."

"Oh, Christ."

"Do it, King."

"Okay, Okay. Then what happens?"

"Simple," Marcus said. "Seth is going to be tough to find. We have to draw him out so Escobar can kill him for sure. Kat and his dad are his two weaknesses. Mess with either one of them and Seth comes flying out of his hiding place. Coleman told me the room number where Seth's father was staying. My girlfriend checked it out. His nametag wasn't on the door. Seth moved him. That leaves Kat."

"What about her?"

"I'm going to kill her."

***

The sun highlighted the pain on his face. Sitting back in a recliner next to the window, Coleman said, "God, I'm glad to see you, King. I'm going nuts sitting here alone in this apartment."

"Sorry for the delay in stopping by," King said, sitting on the couch next to the recliner. "How are you feeling?"

235

"Awful. I can't breathe through my nose. It hurts to piss, and I've got a headache that won't quit."

"What does the doctor say?"

Coleman momentarily closed his eyes in a vain effort to will away the pain of his headache. He had to wait another hour for his next Amitriptyline pill. Grimacing, he said, "I'm going into surgery next Tuesday for my nose. At least, I'll be able to breathe again. Doctor says it will take two or three surgeries to rebuild my nose. In ten days to two weeks, the headaches and kidney pain should be gone.."

"Great. How long before you return to duty?"

"Probably a month."

"We need to get you back, Coleman. You're the best partner I ever had."

"It's been fun. The ladies miss me?"

"Every single one," King laughed. "I can't stay long. I'll come back tonight and bring you some dinner."

"Chinese. You know that's my favorite."

"Yeah, right. Anything I can get you before I leave?"

"Could you draw the shades? Sun hurts my eyes. And I need my headache medicine on the nightstand."

"Be happy to."

King went into the bedroom, taking a moment to put it together. Ignoring the headache medicine, he walked up behind Coleman.

"Did you find it, King?"

"Yeah." King raised up the Beretta 92A1 with a YHM Wraith XL Q.D. suppressor and fired a single 9mm FMJ bullet into the back of Narcotics Detective Frank Coleman's brain.

"Sorry, partner. Shit happens."

Chapter 18

Standing behind the CarBeKleen Car Wash, away from Mill Street, Porter said, "Seth, you look like a train wreck. Sleep in your car?"

"Yeah." Seth rubbed his bloodshot eyes, stroked the stubble on his face, leaned against Porter's car. "Stopped by the house. Picked up an overnight bag and more ammo. Didn't want to stay and greet visitors. Kat, how are you?"

Standing next to Porter, wearing her favorite jeans and Ohio State sweatshirt, she said, "I'm okay." She tucked in her chin, looked away.

To alleviate the tension, Porter said, "Seth, I have a spare bedroom in the condo. You can crash there. Feds won't expect it. What else do you want?"

"Thanks. Could use a car."

"Leave your car here. I'll have someone hide it. My brother-in-law is working in Europe for a couple of months. The wife and kids are with him. You can use his. I have some news, Seth."

"What?"

"Got a call coming over. Coleman's dead. Sister just found him shot in the back of the head, execution-style."

"Marcus."

"That's what I figure."

Kat continued to stand close to Porter.

Seth said, "Worried about you, Kat."

"Don't be." Her stoic expression announced Seth's concern was not well-received. His efforts to ease her heartache failed.

Seth ignored her mood. "When do your uncles arrive?"

"They spent the night at the house."

"Good. I want your dad or uncles with you at all times."

"I don't need you to tell me what to do."

"Dammit, Kat, a pissed off attitude isn't going to save you from Marcus." Seth felt his frustration with her. Being pissed at him was acceptable but not to the extent of placing herself in unnecessary danger. "Marcus is after you. Dad is in hiding. You're not. They can find you at either your apartment or your dad's house. That makes you the target to draw me out. Porter, I want you on her like glue. They'll hit her at night."

"Not a problem," Sergeant Porter said with a smile.

"Don't you get horny on me, Porter."

Seth picked up the budding chemistry between Kat and Porter. He ignored it. Kat's life was on the line. "Porter, was Montrel Rector arrested last night?"

"No. Nothing to charge him with. Medics transported him to the ER for a concussion. He's on the street now."

"I want to see his record."

"I'll leave it on the kitchen table. What are you going to do?"

"Find Escobar, Marcus, and King. Want to say hello."

***

The Facilities Maintenance Services Garage at the Hollywood Reservoir is a one-story cement-block building with a green, metal corrugated roof. Located at the base of the dam in the southwest corner, years of wind-blown dust stained the cement blocks to the color of the surrounding soil. Hidden from the service road and the top of the dam, Pedra parked under a stand of Bishop pine trees.

It was what Angel expected when she watched them pile out of the Ford Econoline cargo van with no rear or side windows. Cesar, Garcia, and Pedra looked around, anxious. Fear was in their eyes. Death was a real possibility.

"Faster, faster," Angel said. "You've used up fifteen seconds. Too much time. Too much. Form a line. I must examine your clothing."

Unlike the others, Pedra was wearing blue coveralls with the City of Los Angeles embroidered above the left breast pocket.

"Pedra, remove the handgun from your bag in the van. Stand by. Check for a round in the chamber and screw the suppressor on tight. Count your grenades. I must know when you have finished."

Pedra stepped away while Angel read the sign painted on the side of the cargo van, Los Angeles Public Services. The block letters appeared official. She selected a perfect name. A yellow emergency beacon light highlighted its appearance of being an official government vehicle.

Turning her attention to Cesar and Garcia, her eyes swept over their Crye G 3 MultiCam Arid pants and shirts. They raised their legs several times to assure they had sufficient flexibility to squat or run. Angel mirrored Cesar and Garcia's apparel.

"My gun is ready, and a round is in the chamber," Pedra said. "I have six grenades."

"Excellent." Another glance at Angel's Hammacher Schlemmer watch. She had to make up thirty seconds.

A quick glance confirmed they had double-knotted the laces on their LALO Recon running shoes. Tripping on an untied shoelace could result in failure of the mission or death.

Ninety seconds had passed. Twenty seconds slow.

"Gear up."

Angel, together with Garcia and Cesar, pulled out their canvas bags. With hours of practice behind them, they moved with precision motion. First, was the Blackhawk S.T.R.I.K.E. Tactical Armor Vests with ceramic plates along with cummer-bunds with pockets for the rifle and pistol magazines. Next, they dropped HK MK 24 MOD O combat assault pistols with laser lights and ACC Ti-RANT 45S suppressors into thigh holsters. Cesar retrieved a HK 416 A5 carbine with an 11inch barrel from his bag while Angel and Garcia carried HK MP 7 submachine guns. Each suppressed weapon had a carrying sling.

Added to the mix were Camouflage Boonie Hats, Motorola, model 3.5, SRX 2200 combat radios, Daniel Winkler fixed-blade knives and two 308-1 napalm grenades along with M18 violet smoke grenades.

Another glance. Back on schedule.

Cesar and Garcia slung their rifles over their shoulders while Angel kept hers in the ready position. The remaining weapons were two Barrett M 98B tactical sniper rifles with ACC Titan suppressors for the initial attack. Angel motioned for them to move in closer.

"Too slow, Garcia. You must move faster, or you will die today."

"I will move faster."

"Round in each of your weapons?"

"*Sí,*" Garcia and Cesar said.

"And ski masks?"

Another acknowledgment. They each carried a full-face, knit ski mask.

"Cesar, you have the bolt cutters, rope, hoods, and cuffs?"

"*Sí.*"

"Excellent. We have ninety seconds left before the attack begins. Listen to my words. Are you frightened?"

They stammered for an answer.

"Remember, it is not wise to lie to me."

"*Sí,*" were their answers.

"It is good you are fearful. It will keep you alive. You have my promise to each of you. Do what I command of you in the time I will give you. Do this for me and you will live to see the sunset."

Their faces showed relief. Angel would not permit them to die.

Again, she examined each of them. Costing tens of thousands of dollars, they had the vehicles, equipment, and weapons she selected, and Garcia purchased from a South Central Los Angeles arms dealer. A quick check showed the radios were working.

"Gather before me. The enemy expects our attack at night. They think we are cowards and hide in the dark. They do not expect us when the sun is full. Many are sleeping. Others are full of food, unable to move. You know, I speak the truth."

They stood silent in rapt attention.

"Remember, we are Aztec Jaguar Warriors, the Cuāuhocēlōtl. The Gods of the night sky. Our enemies shall flee in terror. Are you ready to serve me?"

Pedra and Garcia turned to Cesar for a decision. They accepted his leadership to speak for them. "*Sí,*" Cesar said. "We are ready."

"Move out, Pedra. You have ten minutes to reach your staging area. Drive with care. Do not fail me."

Traveling two miles up the Hollywood Reservoir frontage road, Pedra passed the Upper Hollywood Reservoir to a locked gate at the intersection with Lake Hollywood Drive. Seldom used, she wasn't worried she'd meet a service vehicle on the road. Cesar picked the lock earlier in the day, replacing it with a lock combination she memorized.

She had ten seconds to spare when she left the gate. Now the challenge. Reaching the staging area required twisting through a neighborhood on Lake Hollywood Drive before making a left turn onto Barham Boulevard. Minutes later, headed southwest, Pedra made a left turn onto Cahuenga Boulevard East.

Then it happened.

She wasn't going to make it. A wreck. She felt the sweat on the palms of her hands. Waving her fake identification card at a nearby police officer, she said a water line ruptured on San Marco Drive. The patrolman waved her through. Angel would be proud of her ingenuity when she told her what had happened.

Now the hard part—crawling up San Marco Drive. Turning left onto Cahuenga Terrace and a quick right, Pedra started the slow crawl up the narrow twisting road.

"*Muevense, pendejo*,"she swore at a lumber truck blocking the road. "*Chigao!*"

Less than two minutes.

Leaning out the window, she yelled at the driver. "Emergency." The driver glared, blew her off with his hand. He drained his water bottle before pulling into a driveway. He pressed his hand hard on the horn when she passed.

Seconds later, the staging area was in sight. She had fifteen seconds to spare. A hundred yards away, two men were living out the last minutes of their life.

Angel sensed Pedra's relief when she received her report. Time to move. Garcia and Cesar sweated in the bulky clothing and body armor.

"Follow me," Angel said. "It is time to kill our enemies."

Three minutes to run two hundred yards from the west corner of the Hollywood Reservoir's Mulholland Dam to the staging area.

Without making a sound.

Doable, despite the brush and trash strewn across the terrain.

First, was the matter of a chain-link gate between them and the launch of the attack. The gate was at the entrance to a narrow dirt utility road around the base of the dam. Sloping from the utility road to the terrain below were stands of Bishop pines mixed with an occasional Valley oak. Sprinkled between the trees were small clearings.

Using the bolt cutters, Cesar made quick work of cutting out the center of the gate before discarding the cutters into the brush. Passing through the gate, Angel stopped for a brief moment to gaze down through a clearing in the trees to the compound below.

Surrounded by hills and the nearby Hollywood Reservoir, is the three-acre, walled Los Guerreros compound built on top of a hill. Away from curious neighbors, the property sloped up from the street entrance to the villa. It dropped away from the driveway into a shallow ravine parallel to the wall on the left side of the compound.

The Mediterranean-style two-story home, with rose-tinted stucco walls and red ceramic roof tiles, had two wings extending out from the central house at a forty-five-degree angles creating an expansive half circle. Roman arches over the doors and windows accentuated the ornamental ironwork on the balcony jutting over the entrance to the house.

A reproduction of the Roman Piazza Campitelli fountain highlighted the courtyard in front of the house. Surrounding the fountain were terra cotta pavers in a Herringbone pattern. The large fountain dominated the view of visitors driving up to the villa on the cobblestone driveway. A short distance away on the right side of the house is a six-car garage built in the same Mediterranean style.

Scattered across the grounds were eucalyptus trees, fan, and triangle palms separating Aztec sandstone rock features.

A glance at her watch told her it was time to move. Pointing to her feet, Garcia and Cesar received the message. They carefully placed each footstep without making any sound.

She heard them before seeing them. Two elderly tourists above them on the top of the dam. They stood on the southwest rim for a panoramic view of Los Angeles. Pointing, Angel ducked into a recess in the face of the dam before the two tourists peered down at the dirt road below. Cesar and Garcia pressed against her in the narrow space.

Dammit.

Two minutes and five seconds to reach the objective and they stood motionless. For three minutes and fifteen seconds, Angel listened to the couple babble about the beauty of the city.

Seventy seconds behind. Dammit, dammit, dammit.

The voices faded away. Angel signaled, and they moved ahead seventy-five yards.

Voices. Faint. The enemy.

Angel pointed, and Garcia and Cesar nodded. They each pulled the ski masks over their heads followed by Cesar removing the bags, cuffs, hoods and rope from his pants pockets.

Sweeping her left forefinger across her mouth, Angel ordered silence. Pointing, Garcia and Cesar advanced twenty yards through the trees to a small clearing. Cesar stopped once in mid-stride to avoid breaking a fallen branch with his foot. Satisfied he'd been careful, they moved down the slope while Angel listened to one DEA agent report into his radio.

"Everything is quiet. There isn't any sign of Angel. Los Guerreros on patrol below us. We'll call in again at fourteen hundred hours unless we spot something sooner. Out."

The agent asked his partner, "What time do you want us to come over Saturday?"

"The barbecue starts at two. Come at one. Kids can swim. We'll have a beer before everyone shows up."

"Sounds good."

Stupid fools, Angel decided. They bantered about cookout recipes while their enemy squatted like ghosts behind them. Rising, she began her slow advance toward them. Planning each step, she avoided the litter and small dried tree branches. Nine yards away, she froze. One agent turned his head as if he heard a sound. Instead, he scratched his neck. Still undetected, to avoid a scattering of branches, she stepped around two trees. Standing at the edge of the clearing, she was a ghost. A silent ghost.

Anxious the Los Guerreros patrol below might hear her, she said in a low voice, "If you even think of turning your head around to look at me, I will kill you. Remain motionless and you will live."

The men froze.

"Angel," one of the men said.

Dropping her left arm twice to signal advance, Garcia and Cesar hurried forward without a sound, to begin their work while Angel timed them. Garcia duct-taped the agents' mouths, slipping a black cotton bag over their heads while Cesar hand-cuffed their hands and feet. Pulling up the drawstring on the bottom of each bag over their heads, Garcia tied them off while Cesar arched the two men's backs and tied a rope from the ankle chains to the handcuffs. A second rope looped around the hand-cuff chains, was tied off to a tree The men would remain im-mobile and silent until other agents checked up on them several hours later. They pitched their ski masks into the brush along with the agents' Rock River Arms LAR-15 ATH carbines.

Ninety seconds to secure the two agents. Still seventy sec-onds behind.

Mierda.

Angel danced the Steiner 7x50rc M50rc Commander Mil-itary Binoculars between the two guards on patrol below and a third guard leaning against a wall on the eastern balcony of the villa. A wrought-iron railing protected the imposing balcony with cushioned chairs and umbrellas. The balcony guard's eyes were closed. He was alone.

Perfect.

With rifles slung over their shoulders and barrels pointed to the ground, the two perimeter guards continued their casual stroll around the compound. Garcia was right. There were not enough perimeter guards, and they hadn't received any surveil-lance training.

On Angel's hand signal, Garcia picked up his sniper rifle and moved forty-five yards southwest to a small clearing concealed by a berm. Angel and Cesar advanced twenty yards and sighted in on the two men patrolling outside the compound walls.

Resting the bipod on the berm, Garcia lifted the lens caps and sighted in on the guard on the balcony. The arms dealer assured them he zeroed-in all of the weapons.

"In position, target acquired," he said.

The guards began moving toward Cesar and Angel.

"Cesar left target."

Cesar sighted on the guard with his sniper rifle while Angel did the same with Cesar's carbine. A hundred and ten yards.

"Cesar, ready?"

"*Sí.*"

"Garcia, Cesar. On the count of three, fire one round. Do not miss. One. . .two. . .three, fire."

The rifles spit and three men fell dead, their heads blown open.

"Move, move, move. Pedra, execute."

They ran hard, dodging rocks and debris on their one hundred and forty yard sprint to the eastern compound wall. The weight of their equipment and the sweat in their eyes, made it difficult to dodge rocks, brush, and debris. Cesar stumbled several times but managed to remain on his feet. They slammed against the ten-foot high compound wall. Scrambling to the southeast corner, they pressed against the wall to avoid discovery by the two guards at the driveway gate on the south side of the compound.

Time.

"Damn," Angel said, tapping Cesar and Garcia on the shoulder. "We're twenty-five seconds to the good." Frozen in place was their only option. Time for Pedra to act.

Pedra was terrified. Angel had ordered her to kill two men. Could she kill again? Not once but two times? What would Angel do if she failed? Silly question. Pedra knew Angel's response. Her dream of a better life would vanish when Angel's bullet entered her brain. No, she would not fail. She would stand tall, filled with pride when Angel praised her skills, valued her service.

Parked on the southwest side of the gated entrance to the compound, perpendicular to the street, was a new, metallic blue Mercedes sedan. She saw the two men watch her when she drove up alongside their car.

Thrusting her small breasts out, she arched her back rubbing her spine, as if seeking relief. The driver, impressed with her efforts, rolled down his window.

"Whatcha want?" the middle-aged man, with long black hair and a curved mustache, asked.

"I'm with the water department," Pedra said. "There's a broken water line on Holly Drive. We must find who does not have water."

She was shaking. Sweating too. She pinched her left leg to keep it from bouncing on the floorboard. She needed to regain control, be nonchalant.

It worked.

"We have water. Beat it."

"May I talk to the owner to sign my paper? I must alert them?"

"The owner's gone, and I ain't gonna sign any report. Now get the hell out of here."

"Please help me, *Señor*. My boss is very mean. Can you sign my paper so he will know I talked to you?"

"All right, give me the goddamn report," the man said.

Pedra pulled out the suppressed MK 24 assault pistol, shot both men in the forehead. Reaching under the jumpsuit, she pulled out the headset microphone. "Done."

"Move it, Pedra."

Pedra opened the door and threw up before driving away.

Picked up by Pedra at the southeast corner of the compound, Angel saw it when her team jumped out of the cargo van at the entrance gate.

They moved without any wasted motion.

Practice, more practice, and still more practice created fluid motion. Smeared with blood, Garcia and Cesar dumped the second guard's body into the trunk. Pedra completed duct taping the bomb to the latch locking the two driveway gate panels together. The gate was below the sight line of the two guards standing at the front door.

Three minutes were gone. One left. They could do it. Better still, Pedra gave them three extra minutes. Angel was happy. She wanted to hug Pedra. Instead, she examined the bomb to ensure it would work. Taped to a thick piece of cardboard, was a cell phone wired to two AA batteries with a blasting cap buried in a one-quarter brick of C4 plastic explosive. There weren't any loose wires. The ten-foot gate, anchored to large stone pillars, was massive and the wrought iron appeared impregnable to Angel's touch. Centered on the left swing gate was a Spanish León coat of arms shield. She expected the gate would offer little resistance to the blast of the bomb.

"Pedra. Come to me. Hurry, Hurry."

Pedra came up from the other side of the cargo van, panting hard. Her first mission. Men died—she killed them.

"*Sí, señorita.*" She pressed her hand to her breast to slow down her breathing.

"Tell me again, where do you go from here?"

"I drive down Deep Dell Place and park this side of the doorway at six four seven five. It is a vacant lot for sale. I am to ignore the no parking sign and turn on the emergency light."

"And what do you do when I tell you 'mark?'"

"I will tell you when every thirty seconds has passed."
"You know, Pedra, I will die today if you fail me."
"I will not fail you."

Chapter 19

The seventy-yard sprint to the southwest corner of the compound left them breathless. Despite their heaving chests, they had three minutes to breach the wall and scramble to their firing positions. No time to rest or catch their breath. Garcia and Cesar set their sniper rifles on the ground and joined their hands to form a step. With her submachine gun slung over her back, Angel climbed onto Garcia's shoulders. Crouching with arms extended above her head, she leaped up, catching the inside lip of the wall cap with her fingertips. With Garcia giving her feet a push, Angel crawled over, dropped to the ground. Hugging the ground, she lay motionless. She was dead if the guards at the front door detected her.

Thirty seconds. All the time she had allotted. Thirty seconds to determine if the guards saw her scaling the wall.

The wait was an eternity. Finally, said in a soft voice, "Go."

Catching the folding grappling hook Cesar had thrown over the wall, Angel secured it around a tree trunk. Two minutes later, Garcia and Cesar were huddled beside her in the ravine. Angel studied the grounds for any changes from the aerial photographs she'd seen the previous day. The property was an even worse nightmare to defend than she had imagined.

The two front door guards couldn't see through the tops of

the eucalyptus trees to discover Angel's hiding space. The sentry's only hope to defend against a hidden invader were three Doberman Pinschers running free and silent on the property.

Two minutes down with six remaining before the attack. First, they had to silence the two guards at the front door. Using the shallow ravine to avoid detection, they crouched down and sprinted forward to a rock landscape feature. Shaded by three windmill palm trees, Angel knew their movements were difficult to observe from the porch. The sun failed to reflect off the two camouflaged sniper rifles when Garcia and Cesar sighted in on the guards. They waited while Angel shot the three dogs when they jumped into the ravine and charged them. The dogs were below the sight line of the guards.

One twenty-four on Angel's watch. Three minutes to wait before entering the house.

Too much time.

Someone from the house might see them. Sixty seconds to advance to the front door. Two minutes ahead of schedule.

Acceptable.

"Fire."

The two guards crumpled onto the porch tiles with little sound.

Abandoning the sniper rifles, Angel and her team sprinted forward toward the water fountain. Running, Angel saw him out of the corner of her eye. A bearded man standing in second-story window wearing a white towel around his corpulent stomach. He fell away in a splash of blood when Angel blew in the window with a short burst. The element of surprise was gone. Now it was a gun battle with an uncertain outcome.

"Now, Pedra, now! Mark."

An older fat man in one of the four cars lined up in a row beyond the courtyard attempted to jump out of the driver's seat and run away. His right knee caught on the steering wheel, freezing him in place. A burst from Cesar's carbine tore through the open door, killing the man before he had time to move his hand from the steering wheel.

Surprise lost, overwhelming firepower was Angel's remaining weapon. She and Cesar ejected their half-used magazines for full ones.

Garcia was on her left, Cesar on the right.

"Firing position."

Pressing the weapons into their shoulders, Angel threw open the thick, wooden door and screamed, "One. . .two. . .three. . .Angel." She spun in an 180-degree circle and back as she counted, emptying forty 4.6x30mm cartridges through the open door of the den on the left, down the center hallway to the family room and kitchen and the full length of the grand staircase on the right. In the den a man let out a whoosh of air, dropped. Cesar covered their rear flank and any target on the upstairs landing.

"Thirty seconds!" Pedra yelled above the explosion of gunfire.

"One. . .two. . .three. . .Garcia." Garcia repeated the sweep from the den to the staircase and back while Angel slapped in a new magazine. Two people cried out and collapsed at the end of the hallway in the kitchen.

The defenders were unable to return fire with Angel and Garcia's continuous firing.

"One. . .two. . .three. . .Angel." Empty brass shell casings flew in all directions, bouncing off and sliding on the white marble floor. The pungent smell of nitroglycerin filled the circular sandstone walled foyer.

"One minute!" Pedra yelled.

"Advance, advance," Angel screamed above the continuous gunfire. She moved toward the hallway entrance

"One. . .two. . .three. . .Garcia."

Someone from behind the corner of the upstairs landing stuck out an AR-15 semi-automatic rifle and fired three rounds right-handed. One bullet whistled over Angel's head while the recoil sent the remaining two into the large crystal chandelier showering Angel and Cesar with glass shards.

Cesar fired a quick burst into the wall at the corner. A woman cried out when a bullet ripped through the drywall and hit her. She fell forward onto the landing screaming in pain, holding her chest. A man reached out to pull her to safety. Cesar shot him in the head. The woman tumbled down the stair, eyes staring empty at Angel.

"One. . .two. . .three. . .Angel."

The wounded man in the den, his eyes covered with blood, moved to the doorway, fired a pistol at Angel. He missed. Cesar shot him in the chest.

"One. . .two. . .three. . .Garcia."

Four magazines left for each sub machine gun.

"One minute thirty seconds!" Pedra cried out.

They entered the four-foot-wide hallway with Garcia and Angel shoulder to shoulder while Cesar covered the rear. The left wall of the corridor separated it from a formal living room with the entryway into the parlor eight yards ahead of them. They dropped to the floor when someone fired a long burst through the wall ahead of them.

Lying on the floor, Angel signaled she'd attack the living room while Garcia and Cesar cleared out the kitchen and family room. The three of them would then attack the pool and backyard.

Hearing no sound, Pedra whispered, "Two minutes."

Another burst through the wall. The bullets were three feet above their heads.

They heard it when they crawled on the floor to the entrance of the parlor. Someone in the room slapped in a new magazine. Another sound, softer, like a magazine for a pistol.

Garcia held up two fingers. Angel nodded. There were two shooters in the room.

"Ready?" Angel said.

Cesar nodded. Tapped Garcia and pointed to the end of the hallway.

"Go," she said. She crawled into the room firing bursts back and forth. A man hiding behind a couch cried out, fell to the floor. Angel saw the second man's feet hiding behind a desk. She emptied the magazine. The man and his IWI TAVOR SAR full-automatic rifle fell away from the desk to the floor.

"Two minutes, thirty seconds!"

Angel heard a single round before sustained gunfire ripped through the patio doorway into the kitchen. She crawled to the kitchen and discovered the bodies of a teenage girl and an older woman. The older woman was wearing an apron, Larunda, the cook. A stray round hit her in the throat. The young girl, dressed in a bikini, bled from two stomach wounds. A third bullet shot her in the heart. Either Garcia or Cesar had shot the dying young woman to end her suffering. She was Cidro Molina's nineteen-year-old niece, Ariella Cervantes.

A third body of a young teenager sat on the floor in the corner leaning against the wall. His head dropped to his left shoulder. He'd tried to hide in the darkened corner. Angel recognized him, Tejano's younger brother Gustavo Delgado.

"Three minutes!"

255

Hiding behind a water fountain and a stone outdoor barbeque kitchen, Tejano and the remaining defenders stiffened their resistance shooting continuously into the house. Pinned down, Garcia and Cesar hugged the floor on the right side of the sliding door and breakfast bar. Behind them, Angel pressed herself to the floor as bullets tore into the kitchen above her head and down the hallway.

The attack was over. One or more of them would die if they continued.

"Pedra! Execute. Now! Now! Now!"

"Garcia. One napalm and one smoke on the patio. Withdraw. Cover fire."

Garcia pulled the pins on a napalm and a smoke grenade, tossing them through the blown-in patio door while Angel did the same in the family room. The defenders continued to shoot into the kitchen. Angel crawled back, tossed her remaining napalm and smoke grenades into the living room.

They would die in the hallway if they didn't escape fast enough. Bullets whistled over their heads while black, roiling clouds of smoke exploded out of the family room engulfing the kitchen and entrance into the hallway. Discarding their rifles, they wiggled, slid and pushed themselves backward into the foyer. In front of them, an intense wall of orange fire, smeared with black acid smoke, raced down the hallway.

Despite her eyes burning, her throat raw from choking and coughing, Angel yelled, "Cesar, one napalm and smoke on the upstairs landing. Each of you, one napalm and smoke on left and right outside side gates. Cover fire for Pedra from the water fountain in the courtyard."

They crawled out through the front door amid the acrid smoke, pushing glass shards aside with their Mechanix gloves.

Bullets continued to fly over their heads.

Pedra stopped the van fifty yards from the entrance gate. She didn't know what to expect other than it would be loud.

It was more, much more.

Glancing at the speed dial number of the cell phone taped to the bomb at the gate, she hit the send button. The gate disappeared in an angry ball of red flame. The left swing gate, blown out of the anchor pillar, somersaulted through the air before falling into the yard. Twisted up and away from the pillar, the right gate remained anchored.

Trained until each step became an ingrained habit, she raced up the driveway. Angel, Garcia, and Cesar were huddled behind the water fountain exchanging gunfire with two men in the left wing of the villa. Smoke was already coming out of the first-floor windows. Pedra ignored the gun battle and the fire at the two backyard gates. She had her assignment.

Driving behind Angel, she raced up to the adjacent six-car garage next to the house. She threw four napalm grenades through the glass garage windows and two under the four cars lined up next to the dead, fat man.

Side door open, she raced back to the fountain while Angel yelled, "Cover us."

Sticking her left hand out the window, pressing her breasts against the steering wheel, Pedra emptied her HK MK 24 ten-round magazine at the two men shooting from the window while Angel and the others dove into the van one on top of the other. Pedra jammed the accelerator and leaped forward down the driveway. Half in and out, Cesar wrapped his arm around Garcia's neck, pulling him in. Angel slammed the door.

"Change clothes. Hurry, hurry, hurry."

Pedra's last sight racing down the driveway onto Holly

Drive was the columns of black smoke rising up into the clear blue sky.

Modesty was out. Elbows were in.

Stripped to bra, panties and briefs, they struggled to open up their individual suit bags to put on clothes appropriate for airline travel. Dumped into a back corner of the van were the body armor, vest, weapons, and clothing. Pre-moistened towels and soap helped to clean their faces and hands. Angel changed into slacks, blouse, and a jacket. Kitten heels followed while the men slipped on slacks, sport shirts, jackets and loafers. Angel was able to apply a rudimentary application of makeup.

Careful to observe speed limits in the residential neighborhood, Pedra turned right off Holly Drive onto W Odin Street headed toward their escape on N Cahuenga Boulevard. Three hundred yards later, Pedra turned left and headed south on the four-lane boulevard. A right turn onto Franklin Avenue followed with another right turn onto Highland Avenue completed their escape. Turning left off Highland Avenue into a back parking lot at the Hollywood Hilton Garden Inn, Pedra saw four men with two Chevrolet Malibu cars waiting for them. No one spoke. Angel picked up her overnight bag from the cargo van, slid into the back seat of one of the cars.

Angel understood the Los Guerreros Cartel would realize she had attacked the compound. She was the only one with the skill to pull off such a daring daytime raid. A convoluted escape route would confuse their pursuers, giving them time to escape.

A chartered jet waited for Angel at the Long Beach Airport to transport her to San Diego for an overnight stay before embarking for Lincoln, Nebraska. Her planned destination, the General Mariano Escobedo International Airport in Monterrey, Mexico.

She had to give her report to Manuel at the Halcon compound.

Pedra discarded her coveralls, joined Garcia and Cesar for their return to Chicago. They each flew separate flights from Los Angeles International Airport, John Wayne Airport, and the LA/Ontario International Airport. Their trip would include multiple stops taking two days to complete their journey home. Cesar's flight took him to Dallas to wait for Angel's return trip from Mexico.

Two men drove an 18-wheel Freightliner Cascadia truck to San Diego with the cargo van inside a Fruehauf trailer. Fifteen thousand dollars assured Angel the cargo van, together with the weapons and all the other equipment would be shredded without the required record of destruction.

***

Despite the air-conditioned room, Tejano felt the sweat on his forehead. The two men standing behind him had fixed-blade knives in their hands. If ordered, they would slit his throat without thought.

Enraged, Cidro picked up a SIG P226 and jammed the SWR Trident 9 suppressor into Tejano's mouth, drawing blood. Unable to spit, Tejano gagged, tried to swallow.

"You have failed me! My beautiful niece, Ariella, lies in the rubble of my home, burned beyond recognition. Your stupid incompetence killed her."

Cidro withdrew the suppressor, spit into Tejano's face. "I shall kill you a little at a time. You will take all day to die."

"Angel killed my brother."

"I care nothing for your brother." He slapped Tejano.

"I can restore your honor, Cidro. I can avenge Ariella's death."

"You can give me nothing." He slapped Tejano again.

The Pierson Motel manager knocked on the door, demanded the yelling stop. One of the two men stepped out, threatened her. The woman didn't return.

"Give me men," Tejano said. "I will go to Chicago, kill Carlos. I will kill all of them and their families. When the *policía* leave, the territory will be yours. It will be your magnificent victory. I shall bring you the head of Angel impaled on a sword. You can spit on her dead face."

Cidro turned silent, stared into Tejano's eyes. Breaking away from his reflective gaze, he smiled. "I would enjoy spitting on her dead face."

Tejano wondered if he'd saved himself from being murdered.

Before Cidro could speak, Tejano continued, "I am the best assassin of all men. I can do what no other can do. Give me the chance to avenge the loss of your beautiful Ariella."

"Angel is the best. She defeated you."

"When I bring you her head, you will call me the best."

Cidro made a wide sweep with his arms. "See around you, Tejano. I stand in the squalor of this room. I am a rat living in filth. She destroyed my home. The *policía* are pursuing me. I must flee to Mexico. If you fail me again, I will kill you and your entire family. I will show no mercy. Your mother will suffer for days. Do you believe me?"

"*Sí.*"

"Then leave me before I listen to my heart and kill you."

***

Waking up from a two-hour nap in Sergeant Porter's Bellflower Condominium, Seth struggled with what to do first—eat or take a hot shower? The shower won and after shaving, the thought of a steak the size of Texas propelled him to dress in a rush. With his cell phone in one hand, car keys in the other, he was imagining the thickness of the steak when his cell phone rang.

"Did I catch you at a bad time, Seth?"

Surprised, Seth stared at the screen. "Moses."

"Have a minute for a new friend?"

"Hell, I have all day for you, Moses." Returning to the couch, Seth threw his coat over a chair, sat down. "What's up?"

"Been snooping."

Seth believed him. He figured intrigue was Moses' middle name. "Into what?" He settled back into the couch.

"You."

"Me?"

"Yeah, you. You learn to read people when you're a gunny. Who'll do just fine in combat. Who requires some watching. Which lieutenant was a danger to himself and the men, and the ones who don't need much coaching? Think I read you pretty good at the airport."

Seth chuckled. "Know about reading lieutenants. Helped a time or two to stay alive. What's on your mind, Moses?"

Moses Remington began the sales pitch he had practiced before calling. "Seth, I reviewed your service record book. I know. . . I'm not supposed to see it, but I do a lot of things I'm not supposed to do. I can get my hands on things that go boom and know what to do when I want to review someone's record. I've talked to three of your former commanding officers. You impressed the living hell out of them. Listening to them comment and reading your Navy Cross Citation impressed the hell out of me. Want you to come to New York City and work with me.

We'd be full partners, along with my friend Jonathan."

Seth was stunned. His mindset was to hit the road to wherever it would take him.

New York City.

He wondered if Pamela lived in the city.

Dammit, Seth, stop thinking about her. Seth looked at the stack of dirty dishes on the kitchen counter to remind himself Moses was on the phone.

Pamela would never call him.

"Kinda of busy at the moment," Seth said.

"Know that, too. We'll talk about that in a minute."

"You don't miss anything."

"I'm paid well not to miss anything."

"Partners, huh?" Returning to work with a steady job after quitting the police department was a new thought. Working with Moses was an interesting, attractive idea.

"We'd be three outlaws on the loose," Moses said. "You, me and Jonathan against the bad guys."

Moses' offer began to resonate. What the hell? Maybe working with Moses was a better idea than hitting the road. "Tell me some more about your business?"

"Like I told you, I gather intel on foreign governments for our business clients. Before my client invests millions of dollars, they want to know about the stability of the government, any problems they may encounter. Have to tell you, Seth, the state department isn't too happy with me. They spread bullshit—I spread the truth."

"You want me to be a spy?"

"Nope. That would be Jonathan's job."

Seth left the couch, started pacing in and out of the kitchen. "That's the third time you've mentioned his name. Who's Jonathan?"

"Jonathan is my best friend. He and I spent a pleasant for-ty-two minutes in a blown-out building close to the Ramadi Gov-ernment Center. Our hosts served us volumes of small arms fire and rocket-propelled grenades. Forty-two minutes was a long time to try and stay alive. When it was over, I knew Jonathan better than my wife, Ashlyn. We've become friends for life."

"Sounds like Billie and me."

"You know about my leg. Seth, I'm in my mid-forties and in great shape. If I, at least, had my left knee, I'd do better. But I don't. So, I have to hire people to do my running for me. I can't do fieldwork, move too slow. Hell, I'd be dead in five minutes. Pisses me to the bloody bone. So I hired Jonathan."

"You have Jonathan. What do you want me for?"

"I have an idea. It's a hell of a plan. I want to expand the business. Move into hostage rescue."

"What the hell are you talking about, Moses? That's SEAL's territory."

"Hell, there aren't enough Navy SEALS to even touch hos-tage rescue. They focus on the terrorist kidnappings. I'm talking about all the other kidnappings around the world. The ones you never hear about. Let me tell you, Seth. The bad guys are kidnapping company employees all the time for ransom. Their companies are paying big bucks to bring them back. That's your store. You have the skills and aptitude to do the job. It isn't the Marine Corps, but it's damn close. I don't have any interest in you telling me 'no.' So tell me, Staff Sergeant Seth Collins, in-terested?"

Seth was shocked Moses' five-minute sales pitch changed his plans. "Damn straight. I'm interested, Moses. Kinda of busy right now."

"I know about the dirty cops. What can I do to help you?"

"What don't you know?"

"Not much," Moses said. "Not much at all."

"Feds have frozen my bank accounts. Some money would help."

Moses fired back, "Done. How much longer before you're on board?"

"Shouldn't be more than a few days.

***

It should have aroused suspicion with the DEA and the ATF. It didn't.

Delta Air Lines, Flight DL 1906, departed from Los Angeles International Airport with a destination for Chicago. On board were three men who sat in separate seats. Never acknowledged each other. Known to both federal agencies, two were brothers, Fidel and Saul Acosta, along with a friend. For years, the three murdered and sold drugs for the Los Guerreros Cartel.

The flight to Chicago was the first of four over a two-day period. When the final flight landed, twelve men assembled to listen to Tejano Delgado's plans to murder Carlos and attack the Halcon Cartel in Hillsdale.

Chapter 20

Maybe a year—not two. Cocaine was her demon. It'd kill her from either an overdose or a heart attack.

Nineteen. Damn shame. She deserved better.

Seth had arrested her several times for soliciting. Offered to help each time. She refused. Her addiction wouldn't allow her to escape her death spiral. Seeing her standing in the darkened entrance at Tobie's Pawn Shop made him angry. Her pimp had beaten her. Her bruised left eye remained shut. A deep cut split her lower lip. Seth saw a black-and-blue mark between the cleavage of her small breasts. He didn't have to ask for the name of the pimp. He already knew. The rap sheet identified him.

Montrel Rector.

"Hello, Lana. He beat you bad tonight."

"Yeah," she said, leaned over, spit blood out of her mouth. "Oh God, I hurt, Seth."

Seth wrapped his arm around her shoulder, pulled her up. She leaned her head into his shoulder. Blood dripped onto his coat. "Want me to pay him a visit?"

"No. He'll beat me worse."

"Not when I'm through with him."

"Please tell me you're gonna kill that son of a bitch?"

"Can't promise you that, Lana. I can promise you he'll never beat you again."

"Help me, Seth, please You've been nice to me. You're the only one." She wiped blood off her lips with the back of her hand.

"Where is he?"

"He told me he's staying in an apartment over a secondhand store on Hanson Street." She stopped. Bent over again, she spit more blood, coughed.

"Oh, Seth, I want to die. I hurt so bad."

"Not tonight, Lana. Tell me about the secondhand store?"

"That's where I'm supposed to take my money. It's across the street from a burned building."

Seth kept his arm wrapped around her shoulder. "Have a place to stay tonight?"

"No. They threw me out of where I was staying."

"How about I find you a room? Just sleep. No tricks till to-morrow."

Lana gaped at Seth. "You'd do that for me?"

"Come on, Lana. Let's go for a walk. I'm gonna have some paramedic friends of mine check you out. Then find you a nice room with clean sheets."

Lana cried when Seth wrapped his arm around her.

It took Seth fifteen minutes to reach the secondhand store. Waiting for the police to clear the street following a drive-by shooting at the intersection of Halsey and Parker ate up ten min-utes. Seth parked his car on Manfield Street and walked to the front store window of Ardmore's Secondhand Store.

He was not happy.

Two places to cover at once. Tough. A front entrance and a fire escape in back. And someone had turned the lights on and off inside the upstairs apartment.

Squeezed in between a narrow alley on the right and a one-story upholstery shop on the left, is an ancient two-story brick building. Heavy wrought-iron bars and a metal accordion security gate secured the store entrance with gang graffiti covering the front and alley sides of the building. Anchored in the six-foot space between the store and upholstery shop with an open wooden staircase leading to an upstairs apartment.

Studying the small parking lot in back solved one of Seth's problems. Adjacent buildings ringed the lot, forcing anyone fleeing down the fire escape to go through the alley to the street. Standing in front of the building, Seth could cover both exits.

Outstanding.

The apartment didn't belong to Escobar or Montrel. ATF would have torn it apart looking for Escobar. It had to belong to one of Montrel's whores. No other scenario fit. She would be on the street or her back working. Her head wouldn't hit a pillow to sleep until first light. So who was turning lights on and off? The girl was working. Montrel would be out hustling, stealing, selling drugs. One person left. Someone who couldn't afford the police spotting him on the streets.

Escobar Padilla.

Escobar was upstairs.

Seth had to guess on the layout of the apartment. He'd be dead if he were wrong. Still, he was satisfied he had it right. The front door opened into the living room overlooking the street. The postage-stamp-sized dining room and kitchen would be beyond the living room. There'd be a hallway between the living and dining rooms leading to the bathroom and bedroom. The bathroom would be on one side of the corridor with a broom closet on the other side. The exits to the fire escapes would be in the living room and bedroom. Escobar would be sitting on the couch in the living room. The exceptions would be trips to the bathroom or kitchen for another beer. The couch would be against the left wall facing the windows.

Escobar would have at least a pistol inside his belt, an automatic rifle next to him on the couch. He'd be hungry. Whatever he ate earlier couldn't sustain him at the midnight hour. Someone had to bring him food before he went to bed at dawn.

Now the wait.

Seth expected the girl or Montrel to show up within the hour with food. Escobar would have the front door locked. Whoever arrived would have to knock to gain entrance. Waiting in his car was out. Someone would spot him. One place left—the burned-out building across the street.

Once a mattress store, a fire had destroyed the rear of the building. Seth figured transients started it trying to stay warm. Saved from the fire, the front of the building was intact with the blown-out windows and door boarded up.

He stepped into the alley next to the building and tore the boards off a side door entrance. The building reeked with the smell of burned wood, singed mattresses and urine. With enough light from the streetlamp, Seth picked his way through the rubble to the front of the building.

An hour later, peering through the space between two boards in the window, Seth saw a car park in front of the secondhand store. The driver was smart, remaining motionless to study the street. A whore, oblivious to her surroundings, wouldn't have hesitated climbing the stairs. It had to be Montrel Rector.

Seth was right. Montrel stepped out, stood next to the car, holding a sack from McDonald's while he glanced up and down the street. A young woman, with large breasts more exposed than covered, joined him. Escobar had multiple appetites. Leading the woman by ten steps, Montrel raced up the stairs two steps at a time into the apartment. The whore followed him in and closed the door.

Food first. Sex second.

Seth gave Escobar ten minutes to eat, five minutes for whatever and five more minutes to get the woman into bed. That took care of Escobar. The best Montrel could hope for was seconds. He'd be sitting on the couch watching TV, waiting his turn. If Seth were lucky, he'd be high on drugs.

Twenty minutes later, Seth stood on the landing outside the solid door with an entry door lock and a deadbolt. He gambled the woman made a critical slip-up. She failed to set the deadbolt, or at best, only locked the entry door lock. The police weren't pursuing her so there wouldn't be any reason to turn the deadbolt. Escobar wouldn't have noticed because he was busy eating.

A reasonable gamble, kick in the door. If he was wrong, all he had to do was step sideways to avoid the fuselage of bullets tearing through the door. Unless Escobar was smart enough to fire through the wall on either side of the door.

Assumptions. Conjecture. Seth's life was on the line. Guessing wrong had a terminal ending.

Combat experience, especially in Iraq, taught Seth how to charge into a room and survive. With the Glock 30 Gen 4 in his left hand and the Glock 21 SF in the right, he raised up his left leg, slammed his foot hard to the left of the doorknob. The doorframe around the strike plate exploded in splinters when he dove inside. Crashing onto the floor, he fired four rounds to his left above the couch cushion and four through the doorway into the kitchen.

One round hit Montrel in the stomach, the second in the center of his chest. "Jesus Christ," Escobar yelled. His words were lost in the whore's screaming. Montrel's eyes registered shock, glazed over. Covered in blood, he remained sitting, his head dropped to his chest. Seth crawled past the hallway toward the empty kitchen when the woman screamed again. Escobar tossed her off the bed.

Escobar fired a short burst down the hallway, blew out a window. Seth recognized the sound. A Bushmaster AR-15 on full automatic. The woman continued to scream.

"Shut the hell up" Escobar shouted, followed by the dull sound of a rifle butt plate hitting bone.

The woman didn't scream again. Escobar fired another short burst down the hallway. Seth guessed he had about a dozen rounds left in the magazine. Between bursts, he heard Escobar thrashing in the darkened bedroom in search of his clothes.

"What's your problem, Escobar? Wanted to pay you a return visit. Now you want to shoot my ass? Not very neighborly."

Taunting confused the enemy on how to execute a counter-attack.

"Screw you," Escobar said and fired another burst up and down the hallway. The last burst tore up the floor at the living room entrance to the hallway. Seth was on the floor behind the dining room wall next to the hallway.

"Sorry about your friend Montrel," Seth said as he jumped up, fired three rounds and dropped to the floor. "He isn't feeling too good. Just sitting there—kinda quiet."

Escobar fired two rounds from a pistol. "You son of a bitch."

Pistol shots. He'd emptied the rifle magazine. Too dark to find another magazine.

Seth was winning the gunfight.

"Goddammit!" Escobar tripped over the whore sprawled on the floor.

Time was running out for both of them. Someone would re-port hearing gunshots with cops filling the street in minutes. No time left. Seth had to end it. He reached up, grabbing dirty dish-es off the dining room table, tossed them against the two lamps and ceiling fixtures. Seven plates and glasses later, fixtures and lamps destroyed, the streetlight reached to the edge of the hall-way.

Escobar fired three more rounds at the hallway entrance from the living room. A fatal mistake. Seth had crawled halfway down the hallway past where the Escobar's bullets hit the floor. He fired two rounds at the muzzle flash in the back of the bed-room next to the open door. A body collapsed, made no sound.

Escobar was dead.

Seth was a block away in his car when he heard the sirens at the apartment.

***

"What the hell are you doing?" Marcus asked on the phone.

"I'm shaving," King said. "Why?"

"Move your sorry ass over here now. We're on the news."

"Jesus Christ! I'm coming."

Detective King entered Marcus' motel room barefoot, wear-ing jeans and shaving cream.

"Sit down, King. The commercial is almost over."

"Good morning again. This is Abigail Stevens with the nine o'clock morning news here on Channel 10, KHIL-TV. Continu-ing with our lead story, Hillsdale was again the scene of another horrific gun battle last night as warring gangs fought for control of the drug trade here in northeast Ohio. Following a shootout two nights ago that left two people dead on Hillsdale streets, authorities reported finding three more bodies in an upstairs apartment. The apartment is located over a secondhand store on Hanson Street.

"Responding to reports of gunfire, police found the bodies of Escobar Padilla, Montrel Rector and Pia Lopez.

"Edwin Garner, Special Agent for the Bureau of Alcohol, Tobacco, Firearms and Explosives heads up the investigation into the two shootings. In an early-morning interview, Agent Garner said law enforcement authorities are searching for suspended police officer Seth Collins who is a suspect in the murders. Agent Garner said Seth Collins is attempting to wrestle control of the drug trade from two other suspended police officers, Sergeant Marcus Holman and Narcotics Detective Logan King. Agent Garner said all three men are extremely dangerous. Following the commercial break, we will show pictures of the three suspects and who to contact if anyone knows of their whereabouts."

Marcus turned off the TV. "Not one goddamn word, King. Not one. Go back, finish shaving and cover that god-awful body of yours. I need time to think. When I'm ready, I'll call you. Now get the hell out of here."

Two hours later Marcus summoned King.

"Jesus Christ," King said. "What the hell is going on?"

Marcus' grim face answered the question. "Sit down, King."

"That serious?"

"Yeah. That serious. Now, goddammit, sit down. We have to talk." King sat on the edge of the bed while Marcus paced. "I've been on the phone for the past couple of hours. Not good. The bitch of a manager in the front office now wants two thousand a week. She also watches TV. I should waste her for being greedy. I found out they're not sending us any more drug shipments. Called some of our dealers. A new shipment came on Thursday night. Carlos has a new crew doing the distribution. We're a liability to Carlos. We know too much."

"Son of a bitch." King's world had collapsed. All of it. He gambled with his life. Lost. Once a respected police officer, he'd thrown it all away for the dream of unlimited money and an island full of naked women and alcohol in the Caribbean. He'd be lucky to live out the next few days. He had to stand up. Go somewhere. Do something. Escape. Talk to somebody. Who would listen to him? Marcus? Jesus Christ. He threw his life away for Boyd and Marcus. How in the hell was he going to escape?

"How much money do we have?" King asked.

"What the hell do you mean how much money? There's forty-one thousand hidden in my garage. How much money do you have? Ten bucks?"

"You owe me a hundred thousand for Boyd."

"I don't have a hundred thousand."

"We're partners," King said. "Half of the forty-one thousand is mine."

"Help me kill Seth, half of it's yours."

"How do I know I can trust you?"

"How do I know I can trust you? King, we have to trust each other."

"Why Seth?"

"Cause he put us here," Marcus said. "Are you in?"

"Do I have a choice?"

"No."

"I'm in," King said. He didn't say he was going to kill Marcus when Seth was dead. Forty-one thousand was at least a start. "How do we do it?"

"Easy. Have a plan."

"I'm listening," King said. He picked up the rifle on the bed. Sighted it through the dirty window. "Thirty-ought-six, bolt-action Springfield with a scope. Nice."

"Dad gave it to me," Marcus said, wiping the last of the shaving cream off in the tiny bathroom. "He was the best thing in my life."

"Christ, Marcus, you have two kids." King laid the rifle on the bed. "Your mom is still alive."

"Mom's a drunk. God knows where she's at, and I have two snarly teenagers."

"Sorry. Have any trouble picking up the rifle at the house?"

"Damn wife changed the locks on me. Had to pick it. Broke her favorite vase when I left. That should piss her off."

"She still with her sister?"

"Yeah, and she can rot there for all I care."

"You have the money, right?" King asked.

"Yes, I have the goddamn money."

"Good. You said you have a plan. What is it?"

"Officer Kat MacKenna's our plan," Marcus said. He threw the towel on the floor, left the bathroom. "She's our ticket to draw Seth out of hiding, so we can kill that son of a bitch. I've been doing some checking. Kat's staying at her folks' place on Forest Lane."

***

Sitting at the table on the terrace overlooking the Sierra de Tamaulipas mountains, Angel was puzzled. Manuel asked her to dress and join him for coffee. He said her dress must be modest. She was unable to remember a previous time they didn't have sex after she had arrived. Was Manuel displeased with her sexual performance?

Unimaginable.

Despite never having a romantic relationship between them during their years together, their lust was boundless. At the end of their trysts, Manuel collapsed into a heap, begging for relief. "No," Angel thought, "sex was not the author of Manuel's troubled state." While drinking her coffee on the terrace, the guards with Israeli UZI PRO submachine guns stood nearby, studying the grounds and distant hills. Angel's option was to wait. Sipping her coffee, she joined the guards in studying the barren, rock infested mountains surrounding the villa.

Ten minutes later Manuel Robles, dressed in white slacks and a bronze polo shirt joined her. He and Angel both accepted coffee from the once naked attendant who now wore a gathered, light jersey dress.

"My apologies, my sweet Angel, for keeping you waiting."

"Your apology is accepted. It was not necessary."

"And my apologies for not inviting you to my bed last night."

"The hour was late when I arrived."

"The lateness of the hour was no excuse. I should have welcomed and loved you." Speaking more boisterous, he said, "You have given me a tremendous victory, Angel. My enemies are terrified. They know my sting is poisonous."

"I am pleased to have given you the gift of victory," Angel said, satisfied Manuel was not displeased with her sexual skills.

Signaling for more coffee, Manuel's serious countenance remained. "May I tell you a story?"

"Of course."

"Many years ago, I controlled the drug trade in Reynosa. Later, I made an error in judgment and joined the Halcon Cartel. Their leaders were old and timid. I was young, invincible. A group of us banded together, and we fought the old men. I committed my life to gaining control of the cartel. I didn't allow any distractions. Today I am Halcon.

"I hoped your attack would stop Los Guerreros. We traded attacks. Our fight was over. I was wrong. I have received many reports in the past hours they are moving to counterattack. Angel, we are engaged in a drug war. There can only be one survivor. Your beautiful body distracts me. That is why you slept alone last night and now wear modest apparel. I must not allow my passion to control me. I must be in total focus."

"I am here to serve you. There will not be any distractions."

"Excellent. I needed to hear your commitment. You are the tip of my spear. You will kill my enemies." Relieved their relationship had established new boundaries, he signaled the young woman to bring him a Louixs cigar.

Ignoring Manuel playing with the cigar and despite the looming drug war, Angel decided it was time to make her request. Hearing it, would he allow her to live or would she die before sunset? She didn't know.

Set me free, Manuel. Set me free.

Manuel said, "Your face is a window to your heart. What is the burden you carry?"

She had practiced the words many times, but her lips remained sealed. Speak, Angel, speak. Declare your heart.

Manuel pressed. "I must know what has distracted you from me."

Her words were solemn—her heart anxious. "I want to serve you, Manuel, and give you a final victory over your enemies. It will consume me in the days ahead. Then I want you to reward me with my freedom. Allow me to have my destiny and soar with the eagles."

Shocked, Manuel withdrew the cigar from his mouth, blew

out the smoke. "You wish to leave me after we win the final bat-tle? You belong to me. I have plans for you."

"Yes, I wish to leave you."

"I have never allowed anyone to leave me. I kill them first."

Angel didn't flinch at Manuel's words nor did her eyes sug-gest she would withdraw her request. Angel, with an intensi-ty seldom heard, said, "Manuel, I have served you with honor. Your heart knows I will never betray you. You are a warrior, and I am proud to walk with you. I too am a warrior, a Jaguar war-rior. The Cuāuhocēlōtl. You must give me the greatest gift I can receive—to live out my destiny."

Manuel stabbed the cigar into the ashtray. "Your destiny is to serve me."

"My destiny is to destroy the villainous tyrants persecuting the defenseless."

Manuel was stunned. Angel could turn against him, join his enemies.

Dropping the dramatic tone of her words, Angel reached across, touched his hand. "I will serve you with honor, Manu-el, and slay your enemies." Despite the danger she had placed herself in, she remained relaxed. I am the Cuāuhocēlōtl. I fear no one.

Manuel signaled for the young girl to replace his crushed cigar. Again, he played with it, considered her fate. Conflicted. Angel saw it in his eyes. She was aware he loved her as best he could love anyone. And she knew all of his secrets and vulner-abilities. Such information in the hands of his enemies would destroy him. Manuel had to worry if she would betray him? She sensed it would unsettle him if she lay dead at his feet.

Manuel scowl disappeared. He'd made a decision.

Forearms on the table, he leaned into Angel. "I was born

to wealthy parents, traveled the world, and was educated at the National Autonomous University of Mexico. You are unlike any other person I have met. I believe the Gods' transported you to the present from an ancient world unknown to me. There had to have been some oversight in the laws of nature to have allowed it to happen.

"You are a warrior equal to me. You have fought without fear, and your enemies have fled from you. You are the shield for the innocent. It is not my decision if you should live or die. It is the decision of the Gods' who have sent you to me.

"We must plan our attack. Do not fail me, my Angel. Then I will allow you to live and soar with the eagles."

***

"I thought I would find you out here on the patio," Larry Ziegler said.

"It's such a pretty day," Pamela said. "Must be in the mid-fifties. Sunshine, not much wind."

Larry looked at the thermometer next to the built-in barbeque at his Southampton, home. "Pamela, you're right on the button. Fifty-five. May I join you? I received a fax."

"Oh, please do." Pamela struggled to remain calm. "Tell me you found him."

Joining her at the table, Larry said, "Sure did. It took some doing. He likes his anonymity. There isn't any telephone listing or record of a residential address. We think his family is living a few blocks from you on West Sixty-Eighth Street. We have been unable to locate his residence."

Anxious, she returned her coffee cup to the saucer, careful to avoid spilling on her royal blue cardigan sweater. "Who is Moses Remington?"

"He was born and raised in Pittsburgh, Pennsylvania. He had a brother and a sister. His father was in the steel business and was rich and influential. One report said presidential candidates sought him out during campaigns."

"Moses has two daughters. The oldest daughter is Jabriella who is thirteen, Mehah is eleven. He doesn't have an extended family. All I found was one deceased uncle who made a fortune in energy. The uncle lived alone. He left everything to Moses and the brother and sister."

"I'm impressed, Larry. That is a very thorough report."

Pouring himself a cup of coffee, Larry said. "There's more, Pamela. The family has a long history of military service. Moses' grandfather was a Tuskegee Airman, and another uncle served with the Marines in Vietnam. He died during the Tet Offensive. Sister passed away a few years ago."

"His dad sold his interest in the steel business and moved to St. Croix. Moses became a police officer for about a year. Later he joined the Marines and served for eighteen years. He became a gunnery sergeant and served multiple tours in Iraq and Afghanistan. The Marines discharged him after he lost a leg in Afghanistan."

"He looked like a Marine when I saw him. Just like Se—my friend." Embarrassed she almost revealed Seth's name, Pamela said, "What does he do now?"

"That's the interesting part. He's involved in something. No one could tell us anything about what he's doing. All we found out was a name. GRYB, whatever that means."

"And you found me a phone number even though there's no listing?"

"Pamela Brighton, You have a seven-day-a-week phone number."

"Oh, Larry, I owe you big time."

"No, you don't. Seeing your happy face is payment enough. I don't know who you're searching for, but I hope you find him."

"Me too."

Chapter 21

"Faster," Angel said, passing a group of students strolling down the concourse at Dallas/Fort Worth International Airport. "We have much to discuss and a flight to catch."

"*Sí,*" Cesar said. He struggled to tote her luggage and carry-on around the students.

"There is an empty gate ahead of us on the left. Move ahead of me and make a path."

The crush of passengers in the concourse made it impossible for Cesar to be polite when he crossed over toward the gate. He apologized for jostling and separating passengers. Several glared and swore at him. Angel said nothing and looked at no one while following Cesar's path. Clearing the stream of passengers, they stood alone in the darkened gate.

"Here is my passport and driver's license from my flight. Destroy them before we leave."

"*Sí,*" Cesar said, handing her a new passport and driver's license.

"Garcia and Pedra have arrived safely and remain in the new apartment I have selected?"

"*Sí.* They are satisfied they're not under observation. They are anxious for your return and our next mission."

"And you?" Angel said.

"I have been here for three hours and have studied the faces of many people. No one knows I am here."

"Any problems getting through security?"

"No"

"Excellent, Cesar. The enemy remains close at hand. Are you ready to follow me again?"

"*Sí*. I am ready."

Waiting until the public address system finished its announcement of the last call to Seattle, Angel said, "Men will die."

"They are my enemies."

"Has Garcia assembled all of the weapons and equipment we will use in our next attack?"

"*Sí*. He told me late this afternoon the dealer has delivered all of the merchandise."

"Cesar, we have much work to do. Tejano is a day ahead of us. His heart burns with rage for the death of his brother at the compound. He is in Chicago to kill Carlos. If he fails, I will kill Carlos at a dinner I am hosting for him on Monday night. You will stand by if necessary to transport Carlos' body to the crematorium. You have been there before?"

Cesar nodded. "*Sí*, I know the place."

"Our informants tell us Tejano will leave Chicago for Hillsdale. I expect he will create much chaos for our dealers. We must kill him. I must also kill three additional targets. Two are former police officers who worked for us. I have met one of them, Marcus. Such a disgusting man. The other man is called King."

"Who is the third target?"

Angel paused. He would be her most difficult challenge requiring all of her skills. Trained by the finest teachers, he was a cunning warrior.

"What is his name?" Cesar asked again.

"Seth Collins."

***

Standing at her parents' window, Kat watched him sitting in the car. Porter. He'd told her he loved her. She believed him. She also thought she loved Seth. But Seth didn't return the affection. Never would. The Gods, or whoever determined one's fate, had decided Seth and Kat would be the best of friends—never lovers again. It was her destiny. Could she live with it? She didn't have any choice. And what about this Porter guy? Could she love him? He would love her forever and be as faithful as a priest is to his God. Yeah, maybe she could love him. He made her look forward to being with him. He also gave her joy.

She put the cell phone to her ear. "Are you just going to sit in the car all night and freeze your butt?"

"Yep."

"You're not going away are you?"

"Nope," Porter said. "Never."

"Let's not get horny now."

"It's in my genes."

"Check your genes, Porter. Ain't gonna happen."

"Yeah it is."

"What makes you so sure?"

Pointing up out of the window, Porter said, "It's written in the stars."

Kat rolled her eyes. "The stars? Porter, you're nuts."

"Over you, yeah."

"Enough of this nonsense. If I can't make you go away, you might as well come into the house and stay. You can sleep on the couch."

"I know where else I could sleep."

"In my parents' house?"

"Sorry."

"You'll be lucky if I let you sleep on the couch. Now move your butt in here."

Opening the car door, Porter said, "Yes, dear. I'm practicing what to say to you in our future life together."

"Now you're in the garage. Wanna try for the backyard?"

They both laughed. Porter stepped out of the vehicle while Marcus and King parked their cars two blocks away. Marcus settled into the back seat of King's car. He picked up the 30-06 Springfield rifle, laid it on his lap. King drove two more blocks and parked a block away from Kat's parents' house.

"You know what to do, King?"

"Yes, for Christ's sakes. I know what to do. You've told me enough times."

"Tell me once more. We can't afford to make a mistake."

"After you shoot Kat, I do a U-turn and drive you back to your car. You leave the rifle in the back seat of my car. I wait at the hospital emergency-room entrance, shoot Seth and come back to the motel. We divide the money up, and we're off to Florida."

"Good." Marcus checked the neighborhood again for cars or anyone outside. Satisfied they were alone, he rolled down the car window and sighted in on the front door of the MacKenna house. No obstructions. Rifle zeroed-in. Perfect shot.

***

Sitting at the dining room table with Linda and his two broth-ers, Conner, and Matt, Ron MacKenna saw it in Porter's eyes, heard it in his banter with Kat. The man loved his daughter. Kat appeared interested. Ron was a happy man. Porter seemed to be a good fit for the family.

"Another beer, Porter?"

"No, thanks, Ron. I'm good."

"How's the new chief coming along?"

"Not good. He has the ATF all over his butt. Not a happy man."

"I had that happen to me. I remember—"

"Dear," Linda said, returning with a berry cobbler. "Porter doesn't want to hear your stories. He has enough of his own."

Ron raised his finger. "Porter, when you're married, be sure your wife lets you tell your stories."

"Thanks. Good to know."

"Tell me, Porter. How's the new job?"

"I have two resignations on my desk. Working on trying to fire three more. Union is fighting me."

A block away, Marcus said, "Turn off the engine. She'll hear it." King switched off the engine. Waited.

Seconds later, Marcus said, "It's ringing. Come on, bitch, pick up the damn phone."

Kat pulled the phone out of her pocket. "Hello. Who's this?"

Marcus was startled at the abruptness of Kat answering her phone. He changed the tone of his voice.

"Hello?" Kat said again.

Rolling up the window to kill the sound of an approaching car, Marcus said, "Hello. My name is Jake Ruben. I am a nurse at the Eastland Memorial Hospital. We found your name in the personal effects of Seth Collins. He is in the emergency room. We're attempting to locate his next-of-kin."

Eyes wide open in shock Kat stared at the phone in disbelief.

"What?"

"There's been a shooting."

"Oh my God! He's alive?"

"Yes, ma'am, he's alive."

Marcus disconnected while Kat cried out, "Dad, Mom! Someone shot Seth. He's at the hospital."

"Oh, Jesus Christ!" Ron jumped out of his chair, spilled his coffee. He ran to the hall closet for his coat while Marcus rolled down the window and aimed at the front door.

Grabbing the keys on the table, Ron raced down the hallway. "Linda. Go to the next-door neighbors. Stay there until I come back."

"Call me when you hear anything, Linda said behind him."

Coat half on, keys in hand, Ron ran for the garage. "I'll call." Joining the others, he said, "Conner, Matt. My car. Porter, follow us."

"Affirmative," Porter said.

"Kat, your mom's car is in the way. Wait for me to back out. " He punched the garage door opener.

"I will. Hurry, Dad." Kat paced back and forth rubbing her left leg, muttering to no one. Tears flooded her eyes.

King watched the garage door begin its recess into the garage. "It's opening. See it?"

"Got it in the scope. Goddamn, you bitch. You better not be in the car already."

"Porter is in the driveway with two guys."

"God, I'd love to shoot that son of a bitch," Marcus said.

"Hot damn. Kat is walking out of the garage."

"Goddammit Porter, get the hell out of the way."

"Car's backing out. Hurry."

Marcus squeezed the trigger.

The night exploded with the sound of the rifle shot. "Aaaahh!" Kat collapsed on her back on the driveway.

Porter rushed up, dropped next to her. Screamed, "Kat!"

"Everybody on the goddamn ground, " Ron shouted.

"Oh my God!" Linda shrieked. "My baby, my baby."

"Dammit, Linda, on the ground. Matt, anything?"

"No, Son of a bitch is gone "

"Conner?"

"Negative."

Linda screamed in terror as she watched Ron run to the street, gun in hand.

Flailing her legs, kicking off a shoe, Kat pressed her hands to her chest. She jerked her head back and forth, eyes open, searching.

Then it was over.

Her body sagged like a rag doll tossed onto the driveway. Her arms, bathed in blood slid off her chest. Drool dropped out of her mouth.

Porter cupped her face. "Kat, he moaned."

They all heard it. Tires screaming a block away, white smoke erupting into the streetlight. Marcus slapped the back of King's car seat. "Move, move, move! Get the goddamn hell out of here."

"There's the shooter's car," Conner said, aiming his pistol. "Goddammit, he's turning 'round. I don't have a shot."

Porter put his hand over Kat's mouth. He felt the warmth on his hand when she exhaled and saw her Adam's apple move as she struggled to breathe. "Kat's still alive. Everybody back off." Fighting for control, he pulled out his cell phone, dialed 911. "Officer down. Five-nineteen Forest Lane. Need a bus. Move it!"

"Bus?" Linda's voice quavered.

Matt pulled her to her feet, away from Kat.

"Ambulance," Ron said, gathering Linda into his arms. Moaning, she tried to break away when she saw Porter cut open Kat's sweater with a pocketknife.

"Come on, sweetheart," Porter pleaded. "Don't leave me. Don't you even think of leaving me." He cut her bra strap, uncovered her left breast. The bullet wound was an inch above the swell of her breast.

Eyes half-opened, Kat whispered, "Porter."

"I'm right here, baby. I'm not leaving you."

"Who hit me?" she said in a soft whisper between gasps of exaggerated breathing, Porter struggled to understand.

"Don't talk, baby. Save your strength." He slapped his hand tight onto the open wound. Air sucked into a bullet wound could collapse the lung. Blood covered his hand, but he'd been a paramedic before joining the police department and knew what to do..

"Ron, find me a first aid kit. I need a dressing and petroleum jelly. Conner, Linda, find some blankets. Matt. You're with me. Take off your shirt. Help to stop the bleeding. Watch her breathing. Let me know if it becomes harder for her to breathe. I'll move my hand."

Porter was in charge of saving Kat's life until the ambulance arrived.

Returning from the garage, Ron shoved the kit at Porter."

Porter pulled out a large dressing, swabbed it with petroleum jelly and placed it over the gunshot wound.

"She closed her eyes," Matt said.

"She's okay, still breathing."

Linda and Conner returned with blankets.

"Cover her as best you can. She's in shock." Forehead bathed in sweat, Kat's face was pale.

"Matt, how's the pulse?"

"Weak."

"Come on, baby. Hang in there," Porter begged.

They all heard the screaming sirens. Then two black and whites almost abreast of each other. More behind. Doors open, they charged up the driveway shouting "Shooter?"

"Gone," Conner said.

"Sergeant Porter," the second officer said. "You okay? Want help?"

"Negative. Bus on its way?"

"Right behind me. Oh, Jesus Christ! It's Officer MacKenna. She alive?"

"Yes, and goddammit, she's gonna stay that way."

The ambulance rounded the corner, pulled into the driveway. Four paramedics rushed to Kat's aid. Porter slid away, letting go of Kat's hand.

Ron pulled him up into a bear hug. Porter started to cry.

"I can't lose her, Ron. I just can't."

***

Death.

It surrounded Seth, engulfed him, stalked him. Always close at hand, he lived with it every day in combat. It stole the life from the innocent. It was the weapon of choice for the terrorist. Never able to understand or explain, he managed to escape its random selection.

He wasn't naive. Death was a constant and, sometimes, even a relief. His mind lost and body used up, death would be a blessing for his dad. No more pain from Cheryl leaving him.

Death never played fair. Surrounded and outnumbered by his demons, Billie didn't have a chance of survival. Death closed his chapter, stopped the beating of his broken heart.

But Kat was a different story. Kat needed a life, surrounded by a husband's love, left speechless by children who called her "Mom."

Kat was dead.

Porter called, urged him to hurry. Seth's heart and mind were black with rage in his race to the hospital. Like the Wolverine, he'd become a killing machine. There wouldn't be mercy when he tracked Marcus and King. He'd rip the life out of their murderous hearts. Spit on their dead faces. Then he would grieve.

Tires screaming, his race to the hospital sent pedestrians and motorists scurrying to the safety of the curb. Seth slammed to a stop against the traffic flow in front of the hospital emergency room. Porter stood on the steps, waiting.

Something was wrong.

Something was beautifully wrong.

Porter was smiling and waving.

"Oh sweet, Jesus." Seth reached over, opened the car door. "Goddammit, Porter, you better tell me Kat's alive."

Running down the steps, tears in his eyes, Porter rushed his words. "She's alive, Seth. Our Kat is alive. I thought we'd lost her when I called you."

"She's going to make it, right?"

"You bet your sweet ass she's gonna make it. I have plans for that girl. Marcus shot her in the left lung. Lung didn't collapse. We were lucky. Lost a lot of blood. Doctor said it was good she's young and healthy."

"Surgery?"

"They're prepping her now. Bullet is still inside."

"I'm going to take down Marcus and King," Seth said. "Want in on it?"

Porter squatted at the open car door. "Goddamn right, I want in. But Kat's first. I'm not leaving her until I know she's okay."

"You have a severe case of Kat on the brain."

"And I'm not going to lose it, Seth."

"Better not, or I'll whip your butt. You're good for her, Porter. Just what she needs."

"Thanks. Have to go back. Make sure they're taking good care of my girl."

***

Detective King used up ten minutes to drive six city miles to Eastland Memorial Hospital. Not bad. Good timing. Finding an open parking space with a clear line of sight to the front door of the emergency room was even better. Everything else was in the toilet. Sweat bathed his hands, forehead. Several times, he'd wiped the sweat out of his eyes.

He crossed the line. Any hope of redemption or restoration to a life as a respected police officer was gone. Was Kat dead? He didn't know. Probably. Alive or dead made no difference. Sitting in the car was sufficient evidence. The jury foreperson would announce, "We find the defendant guilty."

Parole one day?

Never.

He was dead himself if he failed to kill Seth. At least, he could escape with Seth dead. Kill Marcus, and he was forty-one thousand dollars richer. Not much but, at least, a start.

"Goddammit." He threw the rifle into the back seat. The center console blocked him from assuming a firing position. It didn't matter. He'd qualified expert with his pistol at the firing range. Tonight would be a piece of cake—if he could see. Using his suit jacket, he wiped the sweat off his face, rubbed his hands hard on the suit pants until his hands were dry. Dammit to hell, King, pull it together. One more down before you kill Marcus.

He aimed at Seth's head, squeezed the trigger.

***

The first two bullets crashed through the driver's side window an inch to the left of Seth's head. Seth ducked down to the center console. Porter dropped to the pavement. The third bullet spit past them blowing out concrete fragments when it hit the wall above a ground floor window.

"Son of a bitch!" Porter said, dropping to the ground. He heard Seth's roar.

"Shit." Seth rubbed his face—saw blood on his hand.

King fired two more rounds, hitting the glass door of the emergency room.

Inside, two women shrieked, fell to the floor.

"Seth, you okay?" Porter asked.

"Affirmative."

"Where did it come from?"

Seth saw the bullet holes in the window and the windshield. "Left flank. Across the parking lot."

The women at the door were gone. Lights flashed on across the three floors of the emergency room wing.

The quiet of the night broke again, with screaming tires from somewhere in the parking lot. Seth rose up, his Glock 21 SF out from behind his belt, aimed at the shooter's car. Not a chance. The cars in the lot ruined any hope of taking a shot.

Watching the car turn right off Creekside onto Palmer Way, Seth saw the brake lights when the driver fishtailed into a parked car before regaining control. Speeding toward the emergency room driveway, the shooter fired two more shots through the passenger window in Seth's general direction. The bullets whistled into the night above Seth's car.

"He's moving fast."

"In the goddamn car, Porter."

"I'm trying."

"Move your ass. He's leaving us."

Porter dove into the passenger seat. "I'm in." The car was already moving. His shoe bounced off the driveway. Seth punched the Ford Escape down the forty yards to the street. Porter closed the door, buckled up.

"Hang on, Porter."

"Catch that son of a bitch."

"Field glasses on the back seat. Need a plate," Seth buried the throttle to the floor. The tires grabbed hold and the car leaped past the front door of the hospital.

"Damn, he's good," Seth said, topping sixty miles an hour "Porter, right or left?"

"Left for the freeway

Seth jammed the brakes. Hit a signpost.

"Sorry about your brother-in-law's car."

"Hell with the damn car. Drive."

"Whoever he is, he's a hell of a driver."

"That's King in the car," Porter said. "Has to be. Raced in college."

"Shit."

"Hard to read the plate."

"What the hell is he driving?" Seth asked.

"Chrysler 300."

"Dammit," Seth said. "I can't catch him."

"Got the first three, Five JK. Watch it, Seth. He's gonna turn right."

"Copy."

"Jesus Christ. He almost hit a van. Watch out. The van's losing it."

The van spun around twice, struck a parked car.

"You almost hit a car."

"Yeah, but I didn't," Seth floored the accelerator, powered out of a skid.

"Oww." Porter's eye hit the binocular . "Son of a bitch."

"Keep the goddamn glasses on him."

"I'm trying. I'm trying."

"Bastard is moving."

"Watch it, Seth. He ran a red light."

"Got it." Seth hit the brakes hard. Blew through the red light.

"Seventy-four."

"Two more."

"Know that."

"He's blowing another light, Seth."

"Where in the hell is he going? He's driving away from the freeway."

"Bastard is gonna try to lose you. Bingo. Five JKW Seven four three."

Seth hit the brakes, skidded to a stop.

"What happened?"

"Can't catch him. We have the plate. Wanna leave enough of you for Kat."

***

The light in the Sahara Motel room was on. Good. King wanted Marcus awake so he'd see the shock in his eyes when he killed him. Maybe Marcus would beg him. That would make it even better.

He reloaded his gun, assumed a firing position with both hands on the pistol. He knocked, waited. Just one more killing and he'd be home free.

"Who is it?" Marcus asked.

"It's King. Unlock the damn door."

"It's unlocked."

King reached down with his left hand, grabbed the knob. His pistol dropped an inch.

Pushing open the door, he saw death before he died. Sergeant Marcus, with a pillow wrapped around his pistol, fired two .45 caliber ACP hollow-point bullets into King's heart before he could raise his gun. Narcotics Detective Logan King was dead before his knees buckled.

Chapter 22

So where in the hell are Marcus and King?

Seth knew human nature, saw it countless times in combat. Safety was in numbers. Rarely, had one of his patrols been attacked by a single sniper.

Okay, smart guy. Where in the hell are those two bastards. They don't trust each other so that puts them together.

Seth watched Rita, a whore he knew and her trick leave the 7-Eleven store. He carried the beer. She had the chips. Dinner.

Has to be in Hillsdale. Out-of-town is too far away. Nah, those bastards are close. A friend's house? But who would want to be friends with those two sons of bitches? Christ, every cop on the planet wants their butt. So what hole did you two crawl into? Sure in hell ain't the Ritz.

A vagrant hotel was out. Hotels had one entrance. That wouldn't work.

Seth tugged at his nose, looked at the whore stepping up into a beat-up red pickup.

Where's the party, Rita? Hell, I bet you pay for the room by the minute.

Bingo. Hot damn.

Seth tapped the steering wheel, followed the pickup out of the parking lot, satisfied. He knew where to find Marcus and

King. A dump of a motel on the outskirts of town. Some place where no one gave a damn about a person's identity or why they were running.

Seth checked at least a dozen motels, prime candidates. Nothing. The Chrysler 300 with license number 5JKW743 had vanished. One place left. The Sahara Motel on Pullman Street.

Five minutes later, Seth drove into the motel parking lot, stopped, tapped the steering wheel again. Parked in front of room seventeen was a Chrysler 300 with license number 5JKW743 and a crushed left rear fender. The lights were off. Room sixteen was lit up. Seth parked four spaces away facing the street, drew his Glock.

The two rooms were in a separate building away from the darkened office. The manager skipped turning on the no vacancy sign. The message was clear. Don't knock on the door at four in the morning begging for a room.

Stopping short of room sixteen, the story of what happened was on the sidewalk. Scattered pieces of blood soaked pillow foam. A homemade suppressor. Someone is lying dead inside. Marcus or King? Who in the hell is it? Seth guessed right. He opened the door, found King lying on his back next to the bed, dead, staring at the ceiling. The blood and foam on the floor told the story. Marcus was standing next to the bathroom when he'd shot King entering the room. Dragging the body away from the door left the floor covered in blood. A hell of a way to end a life.

Seth decided it was time to piss someone off. He pounded on the office door several times.

"Police! Open the door, or I'll break it down, and you can freeze your ass for the rest of the night."

"Go to hell," a woman's raspy voice answered. "How do I know you're police? I have a gun. I'll shoot if you come in."

"Knock off the bullshit. Open the door, or I'll call the feds. Tell them you're harboring two federal fugitives."

Silence.

"What's it going to be? Open the door or I make the call."

A rotund, old woman with matted, gray-hair opened the door.

"Bastard."

"Registration cards for rooms sixteen and seventeen."

"I don't keep registration cards. It upsets my clients."

"Yeah, you do. How else are you going to find the people who give you bogus cards or trash the place?"

"Smart guy, huh?"

"The cards."

She rummaged through a box, pulled out two cards. "Now get the hell out of here."

"You might want to call someone to clean up the mess in room sixteen."

"Someone dead?"

"Yep."

"Goddammit. That's two in three weeks."

***

"You look like hell," Porter said the next morning. "Been to bed?"

"No," a weary Seth said. Pointing at a coffee cup, he signaled the waitress. Sat down in the booth in Elmer's Restaurant

"You need to crash."

"I'm on my way. You look like a mess too. Wrinkled pants and a coffee stain on your dress shirt. "

"Slept in a chair in Kat's room." Porter dumped his suit jacket in the corner, slid into the booth. "Where in the hell do they find those hospital chairs? Harder than a brick."

"Trust me. Better than sleeping on rocks. How's our girl?"

"Awake some. They have her all doped up. She's hurting. Let's me hold her hand, tried to smile at me. I'd say our girl is doing just fine."

"ATF still there?"

"Outside her door."

"She knows I'm close by?"

"Yeah," Porter said. "I've told her why you can't see her." Porter signaled for another round of coffee.

"How about the car?"

"Talked to my brother-in-law's insurance agent earlier this morning. We're covered. Vandalism. Told him what happened. He said vandalism worked for him."

"Good. Anything on Detective King?"

"Chief Drummond told me Marcus' prints were all over the room."

"Has he seen Kat?"

"Drummond? Yeah, he's been there at least a couple of times. He's insane with rage. City and county police departments for a hundred miles around have sent in officers to help him find Marcus. Drummond told ATF he'll throw them in jail if they got in his way. I think they believed him. They're still around, but they've backed off some. Drummond's worried to death about you. He said you're not authorized to get shot."

Seth laughed. "Love that man. The world could use more Drummonds. Thanks, Porter, for bringing me Marcus' personnel file."

"What are you searching for?"

Seth leafed through the file jacket. "Where in the hell he's hiding. Nothing on the motel registration cards. ATF seen this?"

"No," Porter said. "But it'll happen."

"I'll be damned. Guess what I found."

"What?"

"Marcus' list of beneficiaries. And guess who is number two?"

"I give up."

"He has a sister. Must live on a farm. If I were running, a farm would be one a hell of a place to go. Got barns and stuff. Good hiding places. Porter, when was the last time you were on a farm?"

"My grandpa had a farm."

"Impressive. I bet you don't even know what a chicken looks like. You're some kind of a farmer. You know what's unfortunate?"

"What?"

"The beneficiary list just fell out of the file into my pocket."

"Ain't that a goddamn shame? You can have the whole file if you want it."

"Nah. Too boring."

***

Carlos Torres remained anxious. He had received word Angel was at the O'Hare International Airport earlier with two men and a woman. His informants kept him posted of her whereabouts following the raid on the compound.

She was a cunning, dangerous assassin. His worst enemy. No question. Manuel had ordered her to kill him. Her return to Chicago proved he was right. He knew he was expendable after DEA forced him to step down from overseeing the drug distribution in the three states.

When she would try to kill him was not a mystery. It would

be during the dinner she planned for him on Monday night. The perfect opportunity. Knowing her plan gave him an advantage. He'd kill her first when she least expected it. The garage elevator when she returned from her trip. Manuel would never find him when he escaped to Brazil.

Enough of Angel. A more pleasurable thought to consider. Tomorrow, he'd pay a return visit to the Dayton dealer's personal whore. She was young and beautiful. A master at pleasing a man.

Twenty minutes away, the walls of Room 127 at the Motorcade Motel in Cicero began to close in on them. For more than an hour, Fidel and Saul Acosta waited in the small room with a broken TV. "Wait," they were told. "He will show up and identify who will be their next murder victim."

They'd never worked with him before but heard stories he'd killed men who angered him. The man's violent temper occupied much of their thoughts.

The door finally opened and the man entered the room. Tejano. He said nothing, studied Fidel and Saul.

Irritated at the long wait, Fidel said, "What's the job?

"The Dayton drug distributer called. He is displeased with the Halcon Cartel and wishes to join us. Carlos has agreed to meet his whore tomorrow. His bodyguard will complain of a sudden ailment and pull into the Pilot Travel Center on Market Street in North Lima. There won't be any survivors."

"Does that include the bodyguard?" Saul said.

"You dumb son of a bitch. What does no survivors mean?"

"I understand."

"Easy on my brother," Fidel warned.

"Don't even think of threatening me. I want terror at the

301

truck stop. Manuel and the Halcon Cartel must fear for their lives. Los Guerreros will have its revenge. Now, where is Kesara?"

"Room twelve," Fidel said.

"Bring her here. I want to see her. One last thing. If you fail me with Carlos, I will kill both of you."

Minutes later, Tejano said, "Kesara, I have a job for you."

"What can I do?"

"See me at eight in the morning. I'll give you a suitcase with money. Use one of our rental cars. Go to the Hillsdale barrio, find *a jefe* who you can trust. I want an empty warehouse that's been vacant for a while. I also have a shopping list of guns and equipment we'll need. Have him help you find someone to fill the list."

"Okay. Tejano. Do you want me to stay with you tonight?"

"Yeah."

The morning sun, a red ball in a naked blue sky beat its heat through the car windows. Carlos felt the beads of sweat on his forehead.

"Can I get off the goddamn floor now?" Carlos grumbled. His new bodyguard and the driver had been driving around for a half an hour hunting for DEA agents following them.

"There isn't anyone behind us," the bodyguard said. They spent twenty minutes on South Lake Shore Drive.

Carlos grunted, sat in the rear seat. Turning sideways, he stretched his legs trying to relieve the stiffness.

"Dammit, there isn't any room back here. What is this pile of shit?"

"It's a Ford, *señor*. My sister's car. I'm sorry if it displeases you. I thought it would be a good car to sneak out of the garage."

Carlos said nothing. His foul mood refused to allow him to say thank you. "How far is it to Dayton?"

"We should be there in less than five hours."

"Hurry up. I don't want to spend all day in this *pinche carro*."

"*Sí, señor.* We can only go the speed limit, señor. We can't afford to be stopped."

"Just don't keep me waiting."

"*Sí,* we will do our best," the bodyguard assured him.

***

"They should be here by now," Saul said. They had arrived an hour earlier at the travel plaza

"What time is it?" Fidel asked.

"It's just past one-thirty. Are we parked okay?"

"Little brother, quit worrying. You picked a good spot to park the car."

The one-acre plaza had truck-fueling pumps with parking on the north end, and passenger vehicle pumps on the south end. A McDonalds and travel center were next to the passenger pumps.

Fidel and Saul faced McDonalds with W Middletown Road behind them at the south end of the plaza. The restaurant was twenty yards ahead of them. Their planned escape called for driving past the restaurant onto Market Street to the Ohio Turnpike less than a mile away.

They checked their micro UZI PRO submachine guns were on full automatic and each of the magazines held twenty-five Parabellum rounds.

"It's ready," Fidel said.

"Now we wait."

Traveling on the turnpike a mile from the plaza, the bodyguard said. "Señor, I have to take a piss."

"*Pinche*," Carlos barked, "you just pissed a couple of hours ago. Forget it. Driver, keep going."

"*Señor,* I don't want to be disrespectful, I have to use the bathroom. There's a truck stop just up ahead. It will only take a minute."

"All right, but be quick about it. You keep me waiting, and I'll leave your ass."

"*Sí.*"

Pulling into the plaza, Carlos said, "This goddamn place is filthy."

"*Sí,*" the bodyguard said. "I'll just be gone a minute."

"Driver, pull up to the market," Carlos said. "I want something to drink. Move that damned old lady out of our way. Christ, it's gonna take her an hour to get the hell across the parking lot."

"*Sí,*" The driver said, honking the horn.

The startled woman jumped, and an old man hollered from the pumps. With the path clear, the driver pulled up to the market. Carlos stepped out of the car while the bodyguard struggled to untangle his arm from the seat belt.

Pointing, Saul said, "I see em. Blue car."

Turning on the ignition, Fidel said, "Get ready. You know what to do."

Fidel began driving toward the Ford. A rapid acceleration would have given Carlos time to draw out his gun. Twenty yards away. Carlos hadn't spotted them. Fifteen.

Saul pointed. "He's spotted us."

"Out, out, out." Fidel jumped out of the car, leveled his submachine gun.

"Ambush!" Carlos dropped to the pavement.

The bodyguard untangled his arm, stared at the attackers. Tejano told Fidel the bodyguard would be wearing a yellow shirt. Tejano assured the guard he would be safe.

Fidel fired a short burst at the driver who was trying to scramble over the center console while Saul fired a short burst into the bodyguard's chest.

Screams punctured the air between gunshots as people ducked behind cars or dropped to the ground. A young mother grabbed her daughter's hand, pulled her to the ground. Covering the child with her body, she begged the shooters, "Please, please, please."

Carlos could make it. He was still alive. He reached his hand up above the top of the trunk of the car, fired at the shooters. Jumping into a crouched position, Carlos sprinted to the sidewalk.

"*Pinche!* Move!" he said to the mother. Frozen in terror, she begged,

"Please don't kill us, mister." She twisted her body more to shield her daughter from the expected bullet.

Carlos kicked at her outstretched arm and sprinted around her toward the corner of the building. Throwing his arm back, he fired at his attackers. Fifteen feet and he'd be out of sight.

Six feet—still alive.

Fidel fired a long burst into Carlos' back.

Two minutes later Fidel and Saul drove onto the Ohio Turnpike headed northwest. Forty minutes later in Canfield, they picked up another car Tejano left for them. Back on the Ohio Turnpike, they continued toward Hillsdale.

***

Signaling his wife to turn down the television, Drummond

said, "Hello, Quinton, what's up?"

"Carlos was gunned down at an Ohio truck stop this afternoon."

"Son of a bitch. Hadn't heard." Drummond's wife frowned at her husband's swearing.

"I'm on a conference call now with the DEA Administrator, White House, ATF, AG's office and two U.S. senators. Having a drug war in the United States terrifies the White House and Congress. Our administrator is fighting to be the lead agency to stop the war. Intelligence is telling us the war is coming to Hillsdale. I want you and Barringer in your office tomorrow morning at eight. Tell Barringer there's been surprising developments in the case. ATF needs to be there. Whatever. Just have his butt in your office. Can you do it?"

"Done."

***

Waiting.

Hard for Seth.

The Marines taught him to hurry up and wait. Still, it was boring. The satisfaction was knowing Sergeant Marcus was in the farmhouse across the cornfield outside of Ravenna, Ohio. At least, his car was in front of the house. Parked in the middle of the field beyond the driveway was a large diesel tractor with dual rear wheels and an attached corn-seed-planting machine.

Seth wanted to smash the front door in, kill him on the spot. It would be a fitting end for having shot Kat. But he tempered the intensity of his hatred and passion for revenge. He had killed—never murdered. Justice demanded the arrest of Marcus. Suffer the shame of a public trial, life in prison.

There were other people in the house. From the information

Porter picked up, Marcus' invalid sister lived in the house along with a home-care aide. Two innocent people. No, he'd wait. At some point, Marcus would have to come outside.

Then his freedom would be lost.

Despite the waiting, Seth was comfortable parked behind a barn next to the cornfield. Across Peck Road was a small neighborhood grocery store with a public toilet that worked and two of four gas pumps that didn't work. He had access to food and a bathroom. Essential ingredients for a stakeout.

Strangers' curiosity could shut down a stakeout before it began. The elderly couple was confused why Seth wanted to park behind their barn. The old man running the store wanted to know why Seth kept coming back. Three curious people. The solution was simple. Seth said he was on a special mission to hunt down a gang of thieves who robbed elderly people living in farmhouses. They believed him. The couple promised him blankets and a fried chicken dinner.

Everything was good. The problem was waiting. When would Marcus leave the house? Seth got the answer to that question the next morning.

"Shit."

He hated falling asleep on a stakeout. Closing his eyes was acceptable while his senses remained alert. Sleeping four hours wasn't. Rubbing his eyes, he tried to focus on the farmhouse and Marcus' car. Too much of a blur. He had to take a leak and have the cold air slap his face. Moments later, he returned to the cold car, eyes clear, mind alert, body satisfied.

Hot damn.

Marcus' car hadn't moved. Someone had turned the lights on inside the house. Using his Nikon PROSTAFF 5 binoculars, he saw two people. A woman cooking breakfast and the other, a tall, thin man pacing between rooms.

Marcus.

Seth guessed right. Marcus would leave during the day when it would be less conspicuous than driving alone at night.

When are you going to leave, Marcus? Bet you want a big breakfast and traffic on the road. Eight-thirty tops. Yeah, you son of a bitch. You are going to leave at eight-thirty. Then I am going to hang your ass on a fence post.

***

Angel was standing at the Peninsula Hotel window peering down on E. Superior Street when Pedra announced she had a visitor. "It is Cesar, ma'am."

"He is permitted to enter." Angel waited for the sound of his footsteps to stop before stepping away from the window. "Cesar."

"I have received news," Cesar said. "It is most important."

"Carlos is dead."

"How did you know?"

"I have just received the information myself from a most confidential source. I know the mind of my enemy. He would want to kill Carlos on this day to exact his revenge. Tejano is blind with hate for the death of his brother Gustavo. His blindness is the weapon I will use to kill him. How did Carlos die?"

"Two men shot him at a truck stop near Lima, Ohio," Cesar said.

"An appropriate death." Angel returned her attention to the Chicago streets below. She said, "We leave tomorrow morning at nine for Hillsdale. Pedra?"

"*Sí?*"

"Tell Garcia we will use three automobiles. You and Garcia will travel to Hillsdale in separate cars with our weapons. Hide the weapons where they will be safe. Question our dealers. Learn what the street has to tell you. There will be many *policía*. You will return to me for the night. I will tell you where you will stay. Do not fail me."

"*Sí*, I will do as you have ordered."

"You and Garcia must be alert to avoid being stopped."

"*Sí, señorita.*"

"Cesar, you will be my driver. I am known by many. My enemies will expect me to stay in Hillsdale in the finest of accommodations. I shall deceive them all and stay nearby at the Motel 6 in Copley. You will arrange this for me."

"*Si.*"

"The two of you will leave me now. I have much to consider."

***

"Why in the hell are you here, Quinton?" Nicholas Barringer said the next morning.

"I'm your surprise. I'm taking back Hillsdale."

"No goddamn way."

Holding his hands up behind the desk, Drummond said, "Gentlemen, if you'll take your seats at the conference table, I'm sure Quinton will explain everything."

No one moved.

"Gentlemen, take your goddamn seats!"

Sitting at a small conference table, Barringer said, "Drummond, you in on this?"

"I don't know a damn thing. Quinton, what the hell is going on?"

"Gentlemen, I was on a conference call last night. I—"

"I'm scheduled for one at nine," Barringer said.

"With your director?"

"Yeah."

"Will you let me tell you what your director is going to say?"

"Dammit. Why in the hell wasn't I in on the call last night?"

"Barringer," DEA Special Agent Quinton Templeton said in a conciliatory voice. "I can't answer your question. White House set it up. I don't want a turf fight with you. The issue is too important. Agreed?"

Barringer glared at Quinton. Said nothing.

"Okay, Quinton," Drummond said. "What the hell is going on?"

Yawning to compensate for little sleep and an early flight from Chicago, Quinton said, "Sorry, short night. You all know we have a drug war going on in the United States. The Los Guerreros Cartel on the West Coast is trying to capture Halcon Cartel's Midwest territory. They've fought each other in Kansas City, Los Angeles and Lima, Ohio. The White House and Congress are scared shitless. The president's chief of staff announced the White House has taken the position the cartel turf wars do not take place in the U.S.

"DEA will be the lead agency. ATF will have a supporting but important role. The automatic weapons and explosive devices in the hands of the cartels is staggering. Where in the hell are they getting them? That's the ATF's job."

"Goddammit," Barringer said.

Quinton ignored Barringer. "The next battleground is expected to be here in Hillsdale. Intelligence tells us Los Guerreros' assassin Tejano Delgado is here with a dozen men. Their mission is to create as much terror and havoc as possible to flood the town with law enforcement. When we leave, they sneak back in, take over the city and have a foothold in Halcon's territory. Simple plan. Our job is to find and stop him.

"The other player is Halcon's assassin, a woman named Angel. From what we've learned, she attacked the Los Angeles compound with three people. It was a textbook military assault. Now she's coming to Hillsdale. She has to kill Tejano to save the town for Halcon. She'll also zero in on your team, Drummond. Kat is out of the picture, so that leaves Seth and maybe you.

"Angel is going to be the tough one to stop. She's the best any cartel has to offer. That's why we need to work together, gentlemen. Want to keep the citizens safe, the politicians happy. I can't think of a higher goal. Barringer, are you in?"

"Do I have a choice?" Barringer asked.

"No."

"Remember this, Quinton. Next one's mine. I don't give a shit what or where it is."

"We'll see."

The men stood up to leave.

"Drummond."

"Yeah, Quinton?"

"Seth's a free man."

"Appreciate that."

"Stay safe, my friend."

Drummond gave a thumbs-up. "Back at you, Quinton."

Chapter 23

The beginning of the end.

Stopping at his car, Marcus examined his surroundings. No strangers in sight. No surprises. Just another ordinary day. Satisfied he was alone, he backed his car away from the farmhouse to turn around and drive down the long rutted driveway. Two hundred yards and escape to an unknown future.

Seth watched him from the corner of the barn. Timing was everything. It would determine success or failure in capturing Marcus. Seth needed to block the driveway at the exact point when Marcus was halfway down the driveway. The point of no return. Too far for Marcus to back up to the house and escape capture.

Seth reasoned it would take Marcus twenty-five seconds to travel halfway to the entrance. Having practiced several times, Seth needed twenty-two seconds to reach the driveway from the barn. Simple plan. Wait for Marcus to finish turning around. Then take off for at a reasonable speed.

It worked. Seth had the driveway blocked with his car just when Marcus approached the halfway point. Stepping out of the car with his Glock 21 SF in hand, Seth watched for any hostile movement from the approaching car.

Trapped.

Marcus stopped, sat motionless staring at Seth.

Wet fog, almost a drizzle, engulfed them. It turned the field into a film of mud. Marcus turned on the windshield wipers to wipe away the mist.

Back and forth. Back and forth.

The only sound Seth heard standing in the empty road in the chilly morning air.

Marcus. What are you thinking? What are you going to do? You need cover. It's your best hope to fight back and escape. But where are you going to find cover in an open cornfield?

Son of a bitch.

The tractor. The tractor parked in the field a hundred meters away.

Marcus looked at the tractor. Seth saw the movement.

You're such a dumb shit, Marcus. So predictable. Patience, Seth. "Watch the car door, Seth. That son of a bitch is going to make a run for the tractor."

Marcus' best chance to escape was behind the tractor where he could fight back, maybe kill Seth.

Nah. That ain't gonna happen.

The tractor was Marcus' salvation and Seth's trump card. He'd seen Marcus often enough at the station. Marcus was lazy, one-step removed from being an alcoholic. Exercise was a foreign word to him.

Find a way to make him run, Seth. He'll wear out before he reaches the tractor. Yeah. And the sticky mud on his shoes should help to slow him down.

Movement. The reflection in the driver side window changed. Marcus pressed the door handle. Seth waited. Marcus had to be talking to himself, weighing his options, escape or capture. One other option. Dead.

More waiting. The door flew open, Seth ducked. Marcus reached his hand out, fired. The first round was close to Seth's head. The recoil on the Marcus' one-handed grip sent the remaining three rounds sailing into the clouds.

Okay, you bastard. What's next?

Seth had his answer. Wearing jeans and a white pullover sweater, Marcus jumped out, started running fast for the cover of the tractor. His fedora hat flew off, his black hair tousling as he ran.

Seth ran after him at a measured pace. His military boots helped to anchor his feet in the mud. He began closing the gap.

Fifty yards. Forty-five.

Seth knew Marcus would be lucky to make it to the tractor. He was running too hard, the mud on his leather shoes holding him back.

What are you going to do? Give up or turn around and make a fight out of it?

"You still have a long ways to go, Marcus. You'll never make it."

Marcus turned back, fired a round, the bullet hitting his car. Dumb shit.

Marcus eased up. Down to jogging.

"Give it up, Marcus. You're never going to make the tractor."

Marcus turned, fired two rounds. Not even close. At least, he missed his car. He sprinted but slowed down even more after ten yards. He still wasn't halfway. Seth kept moving. Saw the breath expunge from Marcus' lungs.

Making no effort to return fire, Seth held his Glock in his right hand while he maintained a thirty-yard distance. Marcus was down to a labored pace.

"You poor bastard. You're going have to crawl to make the tractor."

Another round fired. Marcus never glanced back. Just swung his arm back, fired. It was a miscalculation costing him his balance, sending him tumbling into the mud. Seth didn't try to catch up. Marcus' gun could have rounds in the magazine.

Covered in mud, Marcus tried to run again. He was down to plodding across the field. Nothing left. He stopped, bent over, tried to suck oxygen into his starved lungs.

Fifteen yards away Seth said, "Give it up, Marcus. It's over. Drop your gun. You'll never make the tractor."

Marcus said nothing, continued to suck in air. Lungs filled, he stood up.

"Don't make me shoot you, Marcus. I don't want you dead. Just drop the gun."

Marcus examined the gray sky, the mud covering the field. Seth wondered if he was taking a last look at the world surrounding him.

"Screw you." Marcus spun around and fired.

Seth shot him twice in the chest.

Sergeant Marcus Holman dropped to his knees, saw the blood, Seth standing in front of him. He tried to speak, but his mouth twisted into an odd shape.

He fell on his face into the mud.

***

Angel's question remained unanswered. Where are you, Tejano?

The almost six-hour car trip from Chicago to Copley, Ohio left Angel's muscles stiff, her mind blank. The shower helped after they arrived. A stroll in the pleasant afternoon would be even better therapy. Showered, dressed in fresh clothes, she told Cesar they should find a nearby park. Five miles later, they settled for a flat, easy trail in Sand Run Metro Park. They both carried Glock 42 pistols. Cesar remained several steps behind watching people instead of the offerings of nature.

There were few secrets in the drug world other than perhaps when a murder would happen. Information was the engine that kept Angel alive. Informants kept her informed on all matters surrounding her assignment. Knowing more than her enemy was her secret for staying alive.

She already knew part of the answer to the question. Tejano had Carlos murdered before traveling to Hillsdale with a group of assassins. A dozen or more could be in the group. Twelve was a significant number of people to hide. Motels and hotels were out. The *policía* would watch for them. Twelve people couldn't go unnoticed. Tejano also had to hide several cars.

A large building was the answer. A large building with big doors for automobiles. To avoid detection, it would have to be empty with a "For Sale" or "For Lease" sign. The building also had to be in Hillsdale to avoid traveling long distances to hide after the attack.

One type of building could hide people and cars.

A warehouse.

***

Angel waited until they exited from the car before finishing her cup of coffee. The Ospina Columbian coffee teased her palate with its rich taste and complex acidity.

Watching them walk past the Motel 6 Akron sign, she returned her cup and saucer to the kitchen. The sign confused her. Copley was the location of the motel.

"Garcia, Pedra. You have returned," Angel said. "It is good. I have secured your rooms here at the motel. You will stay with me tonight."

"Thank you, "*señorita,*" Pedra said.

"You must now listen to my words. They are important."

Garcia and Pedra joined Cesar in sitting on the edge of the bed while Angel remained standing.

"You must know of my plans. You must also know your future."

They were all solemn. Angel never discussed their future.

"Tejano will attack tomorrow night. His attacks are always in the darkest of night. He is a coward who crawls into a hole at first light. He wishes to kill many people and create much chaos. His plan is to destroy our organization in Hillsdale. After the federal *policía* leave, Los Guerreros will try to control Hillsdale and attack the remainder of our territory. We must protect that which is ours.

"I know him to be hiding in a warehouse. We must find it and destroy Tejano and his men before they launch their attack. One goal will remain following our victory. I must kill Seth. It is folly for him to try to hide from me. Seth wishes to destroy our organization in Hillsdale. He is a formidable fighter. I will destroy him. Do you have questions for me about what it is we will do tomorrow?"

They were silent. Each was more anxious about their future than the forthcoming battle.

"Garcia, Cesar, Pedra. I am proud to walk with you. We will continue our journey together when we have finished the last campaign. Manuel will release me from all further service. It is a great honor he has bestowed on me to be the master of my fate. We will travel the world and serve many masters in the time ahead of us. We will slay the evil men who plunder the wealth of others and enslave people. Terrorists who kill women and children at random will know our wrath. The destruction of evil is my destiny. Your destiny. Garcia, do you wish to walk with me?"

Garcia was unsettled Angel called him first. He wanted to answer after Cesar. Cesar spoke with wisdom. It would have been best to follow him, repeat his words.

"Garcia! I order you to speak."

"Will my sister and her children be protected and provided for?"

"They shall never know the pain of hunger or a future without hope."

"Thank you. I am proud to serve you."

"Cesar," Angel said, "You are the oldest with the most service on the field of battle. What say you?"

Cesar was anxious to respond. "I have received much respect and honor from those who know of my service to you. I wish for that to remain. I will continue to serve you."

"You are a trusted warrior. I honor you. Pedra, will you serve me?"

"May I speak freely, ma'am?"

"You may speak freely."

"You have promised me a future I wish to achieve. My life is rich and full for allowing me to be a part of that which is you. It is my honor to serve you."

"You have much to learn, Pedra. I will enjoy teaching you all I know. One day you will be feared by all men."

"Thank you, *señorita*."

"It is done."

The three of them stood up, smiling. Angel set their future.

They each embraced it.

"Now," Angel said, "We have much work to do. Pedra, go online and print me a complete list of warehouses for sale or lease in Hillsdale."

"*Sí, señorita.*"

"Garcia, I will receive your report now."

"We have visited with many of our dealers in the barrio. They have seen Tejano's men. There are many. They have bought much food, guns, and ammunition. They paid the *jefe* much money to hide them. No one knows where. The dealers have left the streets. They are afraid. There are *policía* every-where. Something is happening. It will be big."

"Did the people suspect you?"

"No, they were anxious to talk to me. I told the dealers and merchants I am from México and have much business to dis-cuss. Pedra was with me. I told them she is my personal whore. They said she is beautiful."

Pedra blushed.

"Garcia. I am pleased. You will now call your new dealer friends. Tell them I will fill their pockets with money. They are to call their customers who run businesses and wish to remain anonymous. I must have a plumbing and an electrical van, plus a real estate car available for our use at eight in the morning. All vehicles must also have a GPS. There must be coveralls and blank work orders on the seat of each van. If the *policía* stop you, have a work order for each warehouse. I also want property disclosure forms."

"*Sí.*"

"The weapons and equipment are secure?"

"*Sí.*"

"I am pleased. You have much work to do. See to it. Pedra,

have you completed your task?"

"The last of the list is being printed now."

"Cesar, Pedra, you may join me now. We have little time."

An hour later, they had the first part of the answer. Tejano had to be hiding in one of the forty-one remaining warehouses. Angel eliminated thirty-nine others for being unsuitable to conceal men and cars. Garcia and Cesar would remove more following a drive-by inspection. The vans would attract little attention from the police patrolling the city. Angel, posing as a real estate agent, would inspect the remaining candidates. She was confident her plan would discover Tejano's hiding place.

***

Seth heard her in the hallway.

"Stop it," Kat said through the opened door. "Don't make me laugh."

He also heard Captain Drummond's "Sorry," when he entered the room.

Captain Drummond and Sergeant Porter sat in chairs surrounding Kat, who was propped up in bed with an IV hooked up to the back of her hand.

She grinned, extended her other hand. "Look who showed up."

Seth squeezed her hand, kissed her on the cheek. "How's my girl?"

"Your girl is doing fine except for these two clowns who think this is a comedy show."

"When are you going home so you can start running my life again?"

"In a couple of days. Mom and Dad are already fussing about me coming back home for a while."

320

"They love you, Kat. Don't know why. You're ornery."

Kat pointed her finger at Seth. "Wait until I'm back on my feet."

"Porter. How do you put up with her?"

"Tough."

"Porter," Kat scolded. "You don't want to be on my bad side."

"You don't have any bad sides."

Kat blushed.

"How's your dad doing?" Drummond asked.

"Just came from the nursing home. He's gone. Sleeps most of the time or stares at the ceiling. I'll be surprised if he lasts out the week."

"Seth, I'm sorry."

"Thanks."

"You okay about Marcus?"

"Tried to talk him down. I didn't have any interest in shooting him. He didn't want any part of it. He wanted to go out his way."

"Sad waste of a life," Porter said.

"Yep."

"Coroner called me, Seth," Drummond said. "Wife refused to claim the body. An unmarked grave has Marcus' name on it, unless the sister claims him. Porter, you and I need to go back to work. We've wasted enough of the taxpayer's dime. Seth, stop by the office. Lots to talk about."

Seth tapped Drummond's shoulder, exchanged a fist bump with Porter.

The mood became emotional when Drummond and Porter left. Seth and Kat were closing a door between them. Kat's eyes were moist. A wave of sadness engulfed her.

"Hold my hand, Seth. Sit on the bed."

Seth felt a lump in his throat. A big part of him would always love Kat.

"Seth, you're saying good bye to me today, aren't you?"

Seth stroked her hand. "I have a job offer in New York."

"When do you leave?"

"When this business is over."

Kat refused to restrain her tears. "Will I see you again?"

"Kat. I'm not leaving you. You're a big part of my life, always will be. Just because I'm in New York doesn't mean I'm out of your life."

"You know I love you."

"A big part of me loves you too, but it isn't going to work out that way for you and me."

"I know inside you're right. It still hurts."

"Porter loves you."

Wiping her eyes with a tissue, she said, "I know that."

"He'll give you a good life."

"I know that, too. You'd have given me a better life."

Seth shook his head. "Not true, Kat. I'd give you a lonely life. I've spent too many years moving from here to there. It'd be tough to settle down."

"Porter is going to ask me to marry him. I know it."

"What are you going to say?"

Eyes cleared, Kat said, "I'm going to say yes. He's a good man. Maybe someday I will love him more than you."

"Can I dance with you at your wedding?"

"You better. I love you, Seth."

"I love you, Kat. I always will. And no, I will never walk out of your life."

"Will you stop by before you go?"

"Yes."

"Good. Now go away, Seth. I want to cry again."

***

Tejano had much to prove—much to lose.

For the first time in his life he'd been defeated. Cidro Molina told him to protect his niece, Ariella Cervantes. Tejano found her body, burned beyond recognition in the rubble of the villa. His younger brother Gustavo lay nearby.

He failed. Angel had defeated him. A woman.

Women didn't shame or defeat him. They served him with their bodies. He would restore his honor when he met Angel within days if not hours. His rage would terrify her. Rising from the dust and smoke surrounding him, he would find Angel at his feet. She would honor him for his strength and cunning, crown him the most feared of all men. She would beg him for her life, relief from her wounds. The vision was clearer now. He saw men gather around to follow him. Angel's cries for mercy would escape his ears when he drew out his sword.

Dreams. But only dreams. He must return to the business at hand and examine the warehouse he had selected. Sunland Chemical Corporation, Industrial Lubricants Warehouse # 12. He imagined the large letters painted on the side of the building ratified the overwhelming victory he would achieve.

***

Sitting at a window overlooking Madison Square Park, Moses pulled his chair closer to the table. "I've met your mother."

"I'm surprised," Pamela Brighton said, placing her Mulberry Bayswater leather bag at her feet. "When was that?"

"Couple of years ago at a breast cancer benefit."

"Mother is a generous supporter."

"I lost my sister to breast cancer. She left a husband and three children."

"I'm sorry for your loss," Pamela said.

"Thank you."

"Excuse me," the Eleven Madison Park waiter said. "Are you folks ready to place your order?"

"Give us a few minutes, please," Moses said. "I'll signal you when we're ready."

"Of course."

Moses drank the chilled water, savored the ice. "Well, Pamela Brighton, it's been a long time since I've been invited to lunch by a beautiful and, I might add, elegant lady. I don't think my charm or good looks put me here."

"Don't sell yourself short."

Pointing to himself, Moses chuckled. "An ol' bear like me? Thank you again." Changing his demeanor to serious, he asked, "Now, young lady, what can I do to help you?"

"I feel like a school girl telling you this."

"Try me."

"A week ago I met a man on a flight to pick up my daughter. I know his first name and your name. I want to talk to him again."

"Must be important to you. You hired a detective to find me."

"How did you know?"

"Pamela, it's my business to know things."

"Sounds mysterious."

"Not really. The man you met is Seth Collins."

"Seth Collins."

"What did you imagine his last name to be?"

"I didn't have any idea, but I like the name Collins. What can you tell me about him?"

"He and I met for the first time a week ago. We're both former Marines with multiple tours. He impressed me. In fact, he impressed me so much I had my people do a thorough background check on him. I called him this week and offered him a partnership with me here in the city."

"Is he going to take it?"

"Yes. Does that please you?"

"Yes." Pamela's enthusiastic answer surprised and embarrassed her. Studying her napkin, she said, "He was so sad when I saw him. . . and so gentle."

"When you met him, Seth had just lost a good friend."

"That explains a lot. What else can you tell me about him?"

"He's a cop or used to be. Right now, he has a full plate. He's in the middle of a drug war and, until this morning, he was a federal fugitive."

Pamela was stunned.

"You're surprised?"

She reviewed the placement of the linen napkin for the second time. She said, "Yes, I am. I don't know anything about drug wars. I just know I saw a part of him I want to see again. Is that silly?"

"No. It's honest. Finding Seth is important to you?"

"Yes."

"And you want a phone number?"

"Yes," Pamela said, biting her lip. She chided herself to keep her calm demeanor. Despite her control, if necessary, she would plead for Seth's number.

Moses revealed a glint of amusement, the beginnings of a smile. "I have a policy. I only divulge confidential information to my clients. Seth's phone number is confidential."

Pamela sagged in her chair.

Moses wasn't uncomfortable with her disappointment.

"If I gave Seth your phone number, he would never call you. He'd think you're way out of his league. I'm a pretty good judge of character. Seth should see you. It would be good for him."

Pamela's eyes brightened.

"Now, if I recall, earlier, you asked me to represent you in finding Seth Collins. Am I correct?"

Anxious, Pamela steepled her fingers, touched her lips. "Yes."

"That makes you a client. If you have a piece of paper and a pen, I have a phone number."

"Oh God, I can't begin to tell you how much I appreciate this."

"Hungry, Pamela?"

"Now I am starved."

***

It'd been a long time since Seth cooked himself dinner. No longer a federal fugitive, he wanted routine back into his life. The cooking effort was a mistake. He looked at the spaghetti and meatballs. The glued spaghetti stared back at him and an overdose of cayenne pepper destroyed the meatballs. Seth was an unhappy, hungry man.

Dammit.

The thought of another night of greasy fried food at a drive-thru was depressing. No choice. Greasy food or starve. Grabbing his keys and coat, he was one step from leaving the house when the phone rang. It'd be either Drummond, Porter, or Kat. That was good. They'd keep his mind busy until he satisfied his demanding stomach. Standing in the kitchen at the door to the garage, he answered the phone.

"Seth?" a soft voice asked.

No response.

Seth gaped at the caller's name in disbelief.

He stood in place, unable to move. He felt the sudden wetness of sweat on the bridge of his nose, the exaggeration in his breathing. Staring into the darkened living room with the over-stuffed blue couch, his eyes glazed over. Pamela. It can't be. . .it has to be some kind of trick, an illusion. Pamela would never call him. I didn't leave anything on the plane or pick up something of hers.

"Pamela?" he said.

"Hello, Seth."

"From the airplane?"

"Yes. . .from the airplane."

All thought of hunger was gone. He wiggled out of his coat, returned to the couch.

"Pamela," he said, with a tightness in his throat.

"I had everything rehearsed on what I was going to say to you, Seth. Now I can't remember any of it. Isn't that silly?"

Sitting on the edge of the couch, Seth saw himself in a near-by mirror. Unshaven, unkempt, seated on an overstuffed, stained couch talking to Pamela. What in the hell could he say to her?

"Seth, I can hear you breathing."

The sound of her voice was strange to him, gentle, almost an intimate tone. "I never thought I would hear from you." He'd struggled for a week trying to remember the sounds of her voice, the beauty of her face, the smell of her perfume. He wanted her memory to stay with him—forever.

"Did I call at a bad time?"

"No."

"How have you been?"

The question restored some sense of the present and his voice returned to his usual baritone. "Good. And you?"

"I'm doing well, Seth. Thank you for asking."

"And your daughter, Dusty. She's home now?"

"You remembered her name?" Seth heard the happiness in her voice.

"You're not easily forgotten nor is the name of your daughter. How did you ever find me?"

"Your friend Moses Remington. He said you were a good man. Are you sure I didn't catch you at a bad moment? I can call back when—"

"No, threw my dinner into the garbage. I was going out to eat."

"Kitchen a struggle for you?"

"Not my strongest suit."

Pamela laughed. A high-pitched, nervous laugh. "Has my call upset you?"

Silence. If he spoke the truth it could change everything.

"Seth?"

"No."

"Words are hard for you."

"They are now. I wasn't expecting this." Seth remained on the edge of the sofa. He kicked away a newspaper laying on the floor.

"May I risk it all and say what I have wanted to say to you all week?"

Another tough question. It required an honest answer. "Yes."

"Something happened on the plane. Something happened between you and me. Did you feel it, too?"

"Pamela. . .you're asking for the truth."

"I have to know, Seth. Did you feel it?"

"You're full of tough questions."

"Sorry. Am I alone in this?"

"Yes. . .I felt it."

"Oh God, I wanted to hear you say those words. Seth, I've never done this before. I had to know if you felt the same. Moses said you'd never call me."

Seth shook his head. "Why me, Pamela? You could pick anyone."

"Because you turn on something inside of me that won't quit running. I want to see you again."

"Stuff happening at the moment."

"Moses told me about it. Will you call me when you come to New York?"

"You won't quit with the questions."

"Will you?"

"Pamela, I was burned once. I don't want that again."

"You didn't get burned with me."

Seth felt it—the sense of entering into a room filled with serenity.

"Yes. . . I'll call you."

Chapter 24

"Police chief, no less." DEA Special Agent Quinton said. "What do I call you now with all those stars you'll be wearing? General?"

"Works for me."

Quinton hugged Drummond, patting him on the back.

Returning to his desk, Drummond asked, "Seth, did you see Kat this morning?"

"Saw her for a minute. The doctor is going to release her in a day or two. I asked him to keep her longer. Make my life simpler. She threw a box of tissues at me."

"Sounds like our girl is back to her old tricks. Gentlemen. Shall we start? Tell us what you have, Quinton?"

"Washington gave us reinforcements. Right now, there are a dozen DEA men in the field. Six more are coming later this morning. I appreciate the help your narcotics division is giving us. How many are on desk duty?"

"Four are confined to their desks. I wish it were more. I'm hopeful Boyd's dregs will be unemployed in the next sixty days."

"It's unfortunate. We could use the manpower. So far, we've rattled the cage of every dealer and junkie we can find. Tejano is in town. Haven't found the hole he's crawled into. There's so much heat in the city we think he's hiding out in a farmhouse.

Maybe a barn. We're going out ten miles trying to check everything. It's all we can cover, but if we're lucky, someone saw something."

"How about Angel?" Seth asked.

"No sign of her. An officer thought he saw a man called Garcia yesterday. We believe he's working for her. She has to be somewhere, and she's after Tejano. He's the key, find Tejano, we find Angel."

"When do you expect him to hit?" Drummond asked.

"Tonight. Sometime between midnight and four. All of our agents will be on duty."

"Do you have a clue what he is going to hit?"

"Don't know. Know your family needs protection. They're prime targets."

"I'll have three units outside the house," Drummond said, "and four officers inside. We think Kat's a target too. We'll have two officers outside the door and Sergeant Porter inside. Every officer will pull graveyard tonight. We've set up a grid so each neighborhood will have a drive-by every five minutes."

"Gentlemen," Quinton said, "I think we have all the bases covered. Let's hope we get lucky."

"You know, Seth," Drummond said. "I can't ask you to stay. I'm grateful for what you have done. We can handle it from here."

"If you don't mind, like to see it through. Kat's still a target. Not going to let that happen."

"Thanks."

"What's your plan, Seth?" Quinton asked.

"Think I'll snoop around town. Don't know about Tejano hiding in a barn. Might want to be closer to the target."

"Great," Quinton said. "I'd love for you to prove me wrong."

***

Sitting on an overturned box in a shaft of light coming from a window high on the warehouse wall, Tejano said, "Good job with Carlos."

"Got the job done," Fidel Acosta said, sitting on another box.

"Nice bonus when you go back to LA."

"Saul too?"

"Yeah, Saul too."

"The men with us, have you worked with them before?" Tejano asked.

"Yeah, we've done some jobs together."

Tejano knew the answer. He still had to ask the question before he could plan his counterattack.

"Cidro told you to kill me if I failed?"

"*Sí*," Fidel said.

"I'd kill you first."

"Maybe. . .we'll find out."

Tejano cast a bored look at Fidel. Fidel wasn't good enough to kill him. He spit to register his disgust. "Enough of this bullshit. We have work to do."

Fidel spit on the floor. Tit for tat. Two animals circling each other in a cage.

Tejano said, "Were the Fed license plates included with the guns you bought?"

"*Sí.*"

"Put them on three of our four cars. Send one car out at four with two men in suits. Check travel time and the number of cops in front of the hospital, police chief, and the mayor's homes. I have addresses.

"At ten tonight, a three-man team will do a drive-by shooting at Chase's twenty-four-hour Supermarket. That'll draw the chief out of his house. Have Kesara follow wearing a nurse's uniform and a baby car seat in the back. Police won't suspect her. No government plates on her car. Hide the first car and Kesara brings the three-man team back to the warehouse. Another team goes out and does a drive-by at the mayor's house. Same drill. Hide the car and Kesara brings them back. That completes her assignment.

"We'll have two men wearing U.S. Marshall shirts and vests. They should be able to get past any cop cars. Have them do a drive-by at the chief's house if there aren't any cops out front. While they're doing the drive-by, we'll send two men to the hospital to ask for Kat's room number. Scare the receptionist before leaving. Seth will come to the hospital. The two men will ambush him in the hospital parking lot."

"You've forgotten Angel."

"We'll kill her when she returns to Chicago. I want to see everyone at three. We'll go over the details and assignments."

"I have a couple of ideas to make it better," Fidel said.

"We'll talk at three," Tejano snapped.

***

They all started to appear the same. The old, neglected warehouses didn't offer any suggestion Tejano was in one of them. Still, Seth thought he was on the right track. Tejano was in town. He was convinced Quinton was wrong in thinking he was in a barn or farmhouse. Too far from his targets in the city and too conspicuous to hide men and cars. No, Tejano was in the city. The only places he could hide were in a house or an empty industrial building. A house wouldn't work. He'd have the same problem as a farmhouse. Tejano had to be in a warehouse. A

333

big open warehouse. Warehouses were everywhere in Hillsdale. What made one a better hiding place than another?

No other option. Drive around, hope he was lucky.

Turning the corner to another warehouse, he saw it again. The same van he noticed in the past hour. In the same area. A warehouse complex. Mario's Plumbing Service.

The driver's checking out warehouses.

Damn.

Angel. No other explanation.

***

"We have finished," Cesar said into the cell phone. "There are no more."

"I still have a few left," Angel said. "We will not fail. Link up with Garcia and Pedra. Load up the equipment and stand by for further instructions."

***

Using his Steiner M830r 8x30 binoculars from a block away and across an open field, Seth watched two men and a young woman load up equipment from a self-storage unit into the two vans. Included were Blackhawk S.T.R.I.K.E. Tactical Armor Vests, HK 416 A5 carbines with 11 inch barrels and HK MK 24 MOD O combat assault pistols. Included with the weapons were suppressors. Combat pants and shirts together with ceramic body armor and cummerbunds were also loaded. SRX 2200 combat radios were laid on top of the equipment.

Unreal.

Seth was stunned at the quality of the weapons. He'd used the same equipment in Afghanistan. Finished, the drivers drove to a remote corner of the storage yard and parked. Motors off, they waited—for Angel?

***

Despite her best effort to remain upbeat, Angel recognized failure to find Tejano could become a real option. It loomed larger as reality. Garcia, Cesar, and Pedra spent the morning reducing the number of warehouses down to seventeen. She lost two hours driving by fourteen of them. None of them sparked any signal she'd found Tejano's hiding place.

Three left.

Failure was unacceptable. Stubborn since birth, she refused to acknowledge defeat.

Stillwater Industrial Park was the closest. The remaining two were across town. Turning right off DuPont Avenue onto Industrial Way into the park, Angel didn't see an office curtain move when she passed the third of the five blocks.

Standing behind the curtain peering out, the man rushed his words into the phone, "Tejano, a car is coming."

Tejano crushed his cigarette on the floor. "What is it?"

"A woman is driving."

"Is there any writing on the car door?"

"The writing is small. I can read the larger letters. R. . .E. . .A. . .L."

"Real estate. Don't worry about it. It's just a real estate agent."

The man watched Angel stop in front of the storage yard. He did not see what caught her attention.

The glint of sun on steel piqued Angel's interest. A new lock on a worn chain-link security gate. Breaking into the warehouse, Tejano made the blunder of replacing the old lock with a new one. Angel was pleased. Tejano's error would cost him his life.

Headed back toward the frontage street. the curtain moved again. Mistake. She saw the movement. A fatal error. She parked in the fourth block from the entrance to the industrial park and forty yards across the street from the sentry. Turned on her acting skills. First, a telephone call followed with an inspection of the property. The sentry would relax. She was a real estate agent inspecting a listing. Leaning against the hood of the car studying her surroundings and the curtain, she placed her call.

"Cesar, I am at the Stillwater Industrial Park."

"*Sí.*"

Now, more acting. Changing shoes, she circled the Richmond Fabrication Warehouse located across the side street from Tejano's hiding place. She wasn't worried about being seen. The windows on the side street of the Sunland warehouse were high up on the walls under the roof. She carried a Beretta 92FS Inox semi-automatic pistol and a DTA MK9 MOD0 suppressor in her tote bag.

An occasional glance at her watch enhanced her performance as she leaned against the hood of the car. The perfect model of an impatient real estate agent, wearing dark sunglasses, bored, while she waited for her team.

***

With the plumbing van in the lead, the two trucks began the slow crawl out of the self-storage complex. The lead driver was again cautious. The small two-vehicle caravan wandered through side streets while Seth watched the drivers search back and forth for any suspicious vehicles. They didn't see Seth hidden in traffic a block away, nor did they realize Seth was a master at tracking people. He'd traveled for three months in small, unmarked cars following terrorists throughout the streets of Baghdad.

It surprised him. The vans turned into the Stillwater Industrial Park. He stopped there earlier. Saw nothing. Stopping on DuPont Avenue, short of the park entrance, he walked back to the north side of the park, next to a railroad spur line and began to reconnoiter the area.

The block-long warehouse complex had an open storage yard in front facing the street. An eight-foot chain-link security fence, topped with barbed wire, surrounded the yard. A steel roll-up door, big enough to accommodate an eighteen-wheeler truck is at the end of the building facing the open storage yard. A metal door also emptied into the yard. A fire escape door is at the other end of the warehouse next to the spur line. Connected to the distribution center in the front is a small one-story office building.

Close to the street and four feet inside the chain-link fence were two rows of four intermodal containers. The containers were parallel to the street and the steel roll-up door. There were two metal storage boxes in each row.

***

Angel was amused. She stole a glance at the curtain when Garcia and Cesar drove up. This time, she saw a face. It didn't disturb her. The sentry would report his latest observations and be instructed to report when they left. Despite her meticulous study of her surroundings, she failed to catch Seth peering at her in a thicket of weeds on the far side of the railroad berm.

"Join me," Angel said. Garcia, Cesar, and Pedra hurried to

her side.

"Pedra, you will drive my car to the first side street next to the entrance and turn left. Turn around facing the street where we stand. There is a sentry watching us from across the street."

Pedra started to turn toward the sentry.

"No! Don't look."

"Be sure to park alongside the warehouse where he cannot see you. You will report all movement of people and cars into the park. Do you understand my instructions?"

"*Sí, señorita.*"

"Are you armed. Suppressor screwed on?"

"*Sí, señorita.*"

"You may leave us." Angel watched Pedra drive away, stole another glance at the curtain. It moved again.

"Garcia and Cesar. You two will buckle on your tool belts, and follow me around the building. You must study the building and discuss what you see with each other. Your performance must entertain the guard."

Seth saw a young woman drive away, park on the side street. Time to introduce himself.

First, he had to make some immediate assumptions. It would govern what he did next. The driver was a young woman, new to the business of killing people. She had to be a sentry to protect Angel from unwanted intruders coming into the park. Her focus would be on what was in front of her. She would not expect someone to sneak up from behind.

Her inexperience would keep her eyes straight ahead.

She'd have a gun. He imagined her caressing it in her lap to ease her nervousness. If surprised, she would be terrified. Calming her would be the first order of business. Armed with his assumptions, he began to sneak up behind her.

Hidden from the rearview mirror and out of sight of Angel, Seth ran the first thirty yards from the railroad tracks to the back of the warehouse. Running fifty yards out in the open from the back of the structure to the car would not be easy. Detection would be unavoidable. He needed a diversion. A quick call solved the problem.

"Sergeant Porter. Can you help me out? Send an unmarked unit to the Stillwater Industrial Park. It's on DuPont Avenue. How long do I have to wait?"

"Should have someone there in a couple of minutes. Do you want backup?"

"No. Have the unit go in one block and stop. There'll be a gray Chevrolet parked on their right. Stay thirty seconds and leave."

"Done."

The wait was less than two minutes. Pedra sat straight up, her eyes fixated on the car, a phone pressed to her ear. Twenty seconds later, Seth reached the back of the car. A passenger in the unmarked police car rubbed his nose signaling he'd seen Seth run to the car. Satisfied, the driver turned the unmarked car around and left.

Pointing a Sig Sauer P226 at Pedra, Seth said through the closed passenger window, "Don't even think of picking up the gun, young lady. It's too nice a day to get yourself shot. Now unlock the door."

Eyes wide in shock, mouth frozen shut, Pedra leaned away when Seth sat in the passenger seat. She didn't offer any resistance when he removed the gun from her lap, placed it on the floorboard between his legs. A woman's voice yelled through the phone receiver demanding answers.

Seth removed the phone from Pedra's ear.

"Hello, Angel."

Chapter 25

Silence.

Seth waited.

More silence before Angel said, "Seth?"

"Yeah."

Angel digested the answer. "Only you could have snuck up on Pedra."

"I'm coming in."

"That is unacceptable. You are my enemy."

"We'll deal with that problem later. What's your girl's name?"

"Pedra."

"You need to talk to her. Right now, she can't breathe. Tell her to play nice. Then she can leave."

"Pedra."

"*Sí señ—*"

"—Do not be afraid. He will not harm you. Do as he tells you. Seth, there is a sentry at the warehouse, third block on the left behind a curtain."

"Thanks. Need some time to cross over and move up to him. I'll figure something out. Angel. Are you going to play nice?"

"Till the battle is over."

"Reasonable answer."

"Seth. . .never mind." She wanted to tell him to be careful.

Seth glanced at the sentry's hiding place. "Which window, Angel? There are two." Pedra had rejoined Angel.

"The one closest to me."

"I'm sure our boy locked himself in. Which one of you is the lock picker?"

"Cesar."

"Have him watch for my signal to move his butt over here."

"He will watch for a signal."

"Show time, Angel. Give me time to sneak up on the sentry."

Thirty seconds later after coming up on the sentry from the rear of the building, Seth waited. Noise. A boot hit the wall when the sentry moved closer to the window. Opened the curtain several more inches.

Seth checked Pedra's MK 24 MOD O pistol for a round in the chamber. She had screwed the suppressor tight onto the barrel. Satisfied, he stood up, shot the startled sentry in the face. Still staring into the room, Seth raised his left hand, circled his index finger.

"Grab his phone," Seth said when he passed Cesar in the street.

"Garcia," Angel barked. "Electrical van. Turn right. Hide it at the end of the block. Cesar, plumbing van. Pedra, car. Follow Garcia. No time, No time. Move! Move! Move!"

Time for war. He was in Afghanistan again. Only the dust and heat were missing.

Ready for battle, Angel and her crew again pulled on combat pants and shirts from the vans along with tactical body armor vests with ceramic plate inserts. Strapped around the vests, were cummerbunds with pockets for the carbine and pistol magazines.

Secured in thigh holsters were MK 24 pistols and each carried an HK 416 A5 carbine. Camouflage Boonie hats and Motorola SRX 2200 combat radios completed their uniform. Cesar also carried heavy-duty bolt cutters, while Garcia carried two cell phone IEDs on plywood bases in a canvas tote bag. Angel had divided a-quarter-pound C4 brick to make two bombs.

Seth stared at Angel.

"Why are you looking at me? Are you undressing me with your eyes?"

For the first time, Seth looked at Angel as a woman. "You're different than I imagined."

"What?" Angel said. "You imagined me repulsive or with fangs to drain the blood of my enemies."

"No, just surprised. You're beautiful. Taller than I expected."

"I am a beautiful woman," Angel said without embarrassment. "Men fear me. Do you fear me?"

Amused with the question, Seth said, "No."

Seth's answer unsettled Angel. Recovering, she said, "You are a strong man. I believe you. We must work together to kill our enemies. Then we will meet."

"Looking forward to it."

Seth was pleased Angel revealed surprise at his answer. Her sudden sense of uneasiness was the edge to stay alive when they faced off after the battle.

"Enough talk. Time to move. Angel, I need a rifle and radio."

"Pedra, give him yours."

Seth sprinted to the corner of the warehouse, studied the storage yard and warehouse. Stepping one foot forward confirmed someone had closed the large industrial shutter and steel doors. Sprinting around the corner of the yard, he stopped along the fence next to an intermodal container.

"Clear," Seth said into the radio microphone.

Angel and the others joined him. Cesar cut the fence into a swinging gate. Inside, he used tie wire to close the gate. Task completed, he joined the others who'd gathered in the lateral space between the two containers. They were now committed. Behind them was the closed fence. It was time.

Kill the enemy.

Except for the containers fifty yards away from the warehouse, the storage yard was empty. Fifty yards without any cover. Unacceptable. A sniper could kill all of them before they were halfway.

Angel signaled quiet. No movement or noise. Now the wait. Five minutes or five hours. Whatever it took.

Seth knew they couldn't begin their attack until the industrial door was up. The other option was to blow open a door with an IED. Good chance he'd lose Angel or some of her team. No. Better to sneak in through an open door.

"Pedra, you will stay close to me at all times," Angel said. "Watch my signals. You will have your pistol. Fire often, even if you do not see a target. The enemy will fear you and hide. Do you understand my orders?"

"*Sí, señorita.*"

"You and Garcia will take the first watch." Pointing to the inside edge of the container, four feet away from the other container in the same row, Angel said, "Pedra, you will lie there. "

Checking no one was in front of the warehouse, Angel barked, "Go, Pedra."

Pedra jumped four feet to the next container, dropped

into position. Angel followed, pulled out a small steel mirror, dropped beside Pedra. With the sun behind them, there wouldn't be any reflection on the mirror. Leaning it against the container, adjusting it, Pedra said she saw the large door.

Returning, Angel said, "Garcia, you will go to the end of the next container. Do not let them see you. Listen for the sound of the steel door opening. Signal if you hear or see movement."

"*Sí*," and he was gone.

"Impressive," Seth said. "You've done this before."

"Some," Angel said. "And you?"

"Some."

"You are a strange man, Seth. Why is it you are here? Tejano is not your fight."

"Yeah it is."

"You confuse me."

"Tejano wants to kill my friends, Kat and the police chief. Maybe their families. That makes it personal."

"It is good you are here," Angel said. She studied the strange man who called himself Seth. He sat across from her, relaxed, his eyes closed. Could he be her equal?

Pedra and Garcia left for their second watch while Seth, Angel, and Cesar rested on the hard asphalt, their backs against a metal intermodal container.

A scene of warriors at rest, without any suggestion of movement. The prelude to carnage, the death of men.

The first ring had them alert, muscles tense.

The sentry's phone rang.

Angel pointed. Cesar pulled it out of his pocket.

"*Sí*," he muttered. Listening for a moment, he said "*Sí*,"disconnected.

"They're changing sentries," Cesar said.

Angel's mind raced for a decision while former Marine Corps Staff Sergeant Seth Collins assumed command.

"You there at the end—"

"Garcia," Angel said.

"Garcia and Cesar, open the goddamn fence now."

"Pedra, keep watch till I tell you to move."

Angel was stunned watching Seth's reaction to the crisis. He was indeed her equal. She was astonished.

"Angel, once you're out of the fence, hold your position. Drop the new sentry when he turns the corner of the yard fence. Then you and the others go to the office, hide along the side closest to us. I checked. No windows on that side. Tejano will know something is wrong when the other sentry fails to show up. He'll realize someone has him surrounded. The only option he has to escape is through the office or the yard. I want you, Garcia and Cesar, to have full magazines if they try and break out through the office. No one makes it outside. Pedra and I will cover the yard. Questions, people?"

Angel stood motionless, transfixed by the presence of Seth. He was fighting to give her victory over her enemies. In a moment, she would have to kill him.

"Move out!'" Dropping his voice he said, "Angel."

Angel stared at him, unable to recover from her shock.

Seth gave her a fist bump. "Don't worry about Pedra. I'll keep her safe. You worry about the others."

It was her first fist bump.

For the first time in a long time, Angel was overwhelmed with the feeling of connection. "Thank you, Seth."

The fleeting moment evaporated.

Seconds later, Seth heard the suppressed sound of a carbine

spit out a bullet, and a body fall to the sidewalk. Angel and the others sprinted to the side of the office.

"We're at the office, Seth," Angel said.

"Wait 'til you hear the sound of voices in the office. Should be at least a couple. Pedra and I will cover the two doors in the yard. Stay safe, Angel."

Angel was unable to speak. No one urged her to stay safe.

"Pedra, follow me," Seth said. "We're going to cover the two doors. Anyone steps outside you shoot them. Understand?"

"*Sí, señor.*"

Seth and Pedra lay in a prone firing position on the sidewalk parallel to the fence and on the left flank of the office.

"Scared, Pedra?"

"*Sí,*" she said in a shaky voice.

"Me, too," Seth lied. "Listen. If one hostile comes out the door, he's mine. If two or more, you shoot the one on the right. Don't think. Just shoot. Remember, Pedra. They want to kill you."

"*Sí, señor.*" Pedra said. Lying next to the man who gave orders to Angel, the fear on her face vanished.

Sound. Distinct.

The pulling of a chain. The large overhead industrial door began to open. The steel door burst open with Kesara jumping out into the yard along with another man to her left. Armed with HK MP5 submachine guns pressed into their shoulders, they began firing at the intermodal containers, the bullets disintegrating off the walls.

More explosion of sound.

The roar of a car engine joined with the grinding of the chain. Seth saw the grill and headlights of a car. Tejano was one-step away from careening into the storage yard and crashing through the fence to freedom.

"Now, Pedra!"

They fired with one sound. The man dropped, didn't move. Kesara also collapsed. She tried to raise up, crawl. Her short life ended.

Seth fired a long burst into the car's radiator while someone inside released the chain, dropping the door to the pavement with a loud crash. The door narrowly missed hitting the car. Someone else stepped out to grab the steel door, slamming it shut.

Yelling.

Men argued inside the warehouse. Death was outside waiting for them. Then it began. The echoes of gunfire as Tejano and his men shot out all the windows high up on the walls.

Smart move.

The open windows would dissipate the blast pressure from a bomb tossed into the warehouse.

More arguing. Some yelling, even screaming. Then nothing. Not a sound. Seth knew why. They had a new plan to escape.

What in the hell was it?

Seth had his answer. Sustained gunfire erupted in all directions from the office. Their new route of escape. It had to be at least two men. They fired continuously through the windows and iron bars to stop anyone from returning fire. Bullets ricocheted off the bars into the blue sky. Satisfied the enemy was pinned down, Tejano and the others would join the men to escape on foot across the railroad tracks into the vacant fields and the trees beyond.

They'd shoot Angel if she jumped out from behind the wall to return fire.

Listening to the firing pattern coming from the office, Seth realized it was two men inside, not three. That was good. Now it was Seth's time.

Jumping up, yelling, "Follow me, Pedra," he sprinted toward the office while firing a full magazine into the office wall above Angel and the others. "Pedra, shoot your goddamn pistol."

The two men in the office expected their enemy to be in front of them, not coming from their left flank. Surprised, they stopped shooting. Ducked for cover.

The horrific explosions of battle and fighting to stay alive can create a telepathic communication between comrades. Un-explainable. One stopped so the other could start. When Seth ejected a magazine, Angel, Garcia and Cesar jumped out from behind the wall, emptying their magazines into the office.

One man alongside a counter dropped his rifle, fell to the floor. Another shooter fired.

"Aaaaaah." Cesar collapsed.

"Cesar's hit," Angel shouted.

The remaining man in the office retreated, pulling the pocket door shut into the warehouse. He cried out in death when Garcia emptied a magazine into the door.

With Garcia providing cover, Angel pulled Cesar away from the windows to the safety of the lateral wall of the office. She saw the two holes in his vest.

"*Hijo de puta*," Cesar said. The ceramic plate inside the vest stopped two 9 mm rounds, three inches apart.

"Breathe, Cesar, breathe," Angel said. Seth watched.

"*Yo sólo fui golpeado por un camión maldito*," Cesar said.

"Yeah, Cesar," Seth said. "I've been hit by a friggin' truck before, too. On your feet."

Cesar stood up, stumbling before he gained a sense of balance. He pressed his chest trying to suck in some air.

"Angel, have a medic check him out. Make sure the ribs are

okay."

"It will be done. Listen to my words. They will now try to come out the emergency door at the other end of the building. We must be ready for them. Cesar, can you still fight?"

Continuing to suck in air, Cesar said, "I can still fight."

"There are a couple of dirt mounds across from the office. You and Pedra cover the office. Watch for anyone trying to run away at the end of the building. Go! Garcia, give me the tote bag. You cover the other exit door on the side of the warehouse next to the vans. Watch for runners."

Again, without speaking, Garcia raced around the corner of the yard, disappearing behind the containers.

Angel reassumed command.

For the moment.

Or until Seth saw her make a mistake.

They retreated to their former position between the two rows of containers. A standoff. Tejano inside. Seth and Angel patiently waiting outside with two cell phone bombs. Men on the inside argued on how to stay alive and escape.

Listening to the sound of a door opening to signal escape, Seth said, "Suggestion?"

What had she missed? What oversight had she made?

"Speak," Angel said.

"Move Pedra to the end of the building. They can run straight out the exit door facing the tracks, and you'll never see them. I've walked the tracks."

"Thank you." The words were foreign to her.

Speaking into the microphone, she ordered Cesar to move Pedra to the end of the building to cover the exit while still covering him.

"Is there anything else I have missed?"

"No," Seth said. "You're doing just fine."

"You have seen much battle?"

"Yeah, some. Tell you one thing."

"What?"

"I'd have you on my flank anytime."

Again stunned, Angel wondered who was this man? Why did she feel a sense of achievement for receiving his compliment? Why had she said those foreign words, "Thank you," twice within seconds of each other.

"Angel, the only way we can chase them out is to be inside."

Recovered, Angel said, "Agreed. We can blow the steel door with one bomb and use the second to move into the building."

"Perfect plan. Give me the duct tape, cover me."

Two minutes later, Seth returned, the IED with the C4 taped to the steel door next to the lock. He listened to Angel alerting the others what to expect.

"Angel. Had some experience. May I?"

"Of course."

"Everyone inside is going to empty their weapon into the doorway when we blow it. I want you to the left of the door, close to the corner of the building. You'll be out of the line of fire. Have your phone ready with the last number to punch. Same for the second bomb. I'm going to skid the second one in on the floor. When it explodes, you go inside, cover the left flank. I'll cover the right. Tell me what you see. The windows should give us enough light."

"It is a good plan, Seth."

Someone inside fired two shots followed by three more shots. A man swore.

"I know the voice," Angel said. "It is Tejano. Someone is trying to escape. They're fighting each other inside."

"The back door into the office opened," Cesar said. "Some-one fired four shots."

Angel heard Tejano yelling.

"The door closed. I hear noise inside the office," Cesar yelled into the radio, his words rushed. "Men are in the office."

"Cesar," Angel said. "How many?"

"Maybe three."

"Someone is trying to break out. Signal Pedra to be alert."

"*Sí*"

"Angel, I'm on it," Seth said. "Garcia, watch your door. They're busting out."

"*Sí, señor.*"

"A head popped up," Cesar said.

"Wait till you have a clean shot. Pedra has your flank."

Someone fired a long burst of muffled shots from the office. Cesar hugged the ground behind the mound. "*Hijo de la puta*," he whispered. "They know I'm here."

Two pistol shots.

Pedra.

Two long bursts of automatic fire came from inside the of-fice.

"There are two, *señor* Seth. One is shooting at me, the other at Pedra."

"Don't let them out," Seth said.

"*Hijo de la puta*," Cesar said. "I'm trying."

"Is Pedra safe?" Angel asked.

"*Sí*. Wait, the door opened behind the two men. A man is in the doorway."

The man emptied the remainder of a full magazine into the backs of Fidel and Saul Acosta.

"He shot them," Cesar said, shocked.

"Cesar, it was Tejano," Angel said. "The men tried to escape from him."

"*Hijo de la puta.*"

"Garcia, move to the corner of the building," Seth said. "Cover the side and rear door. Cesar, join Pedra. Someone else may try to leave. Angel, you ready?"

"I am ready."

"Blow the goddamn door."

The C4 exploded in an orange ball of flame and smoke, blowing the door and frame deep into the building. Jumping up, Angel ran to the left side of the cavernous hole while Seth charged to the right.

"They're not shooting, Seth?"

"Trust me, Angel. They will."

Seconds later, someone fired a short burst through the jagged cavity, followed by two more shooters. Seth heard the bullets sing through the cavity, striking a warehouse in the adjacent complex. He charged up to the blown-in door, dropped to the asphalt. Reaching back, he slid the IED deep into the building.

"Now, Angel."

A second orange ball of flame illuminated the interior accompanied by the sound of a man screaming and a car blown off the floor onto its side.

Seth and Angel charged into the warehouse, dropped to the floor into a firing position on each side of the door. A man lay crumpled beside Angel, his lungs crushed from the pressure of the first bomb blast.

"Angel, I see four cars in the center. Can you see anything?"

"I have a big I-beam in my way."

Two men, on each side of the last car, stood up, firing a short burst into the front wall of the warehouse. The rounds were above Seth and Angel lying on the floor.

"Can you move, Angel?"

"There is a four-foot wall in front of me. Think it's a partition. Maybe ten yards away."

"Me too. On the count of three, let's move it to the wall. One. . . two. . . three."

They moved up to the wall while the two men moved from behind the fourth car to the third one.

"Hear it, Angel?"

"Yes. Two men. They are now behind the third car."

Tejano said from the back of the warehouse, "You're dead, Angel."

Angel said nothing.

Seth said, "Angel, on my mark, I'm going to give the two behind the car a target. Can you take them out?"

"I have to move around the wall to the next one. Think there's a bunch of walls in here."

"Must be bays to store equipment."

"Seth, I'm ready to move."

"Quiet, Angel, like a mouse."

"A little mouse."

Angel crawled to the next wall. Risky. She didn't have any other choice. She'd have to stand up to take a shot at the two men.

"I'm ready, Seth."

"Here we go. Mark!"

Seth stood up, fired a short burst, dropped before the two men returned fire.

Angel and Tejano stood up at the same time. Angel fired, killing the two men, ducked. Tejano missed hitting Angel by an inch when two bullets spit by her head.

"Angel, you okay?"

"Close, Seth. Too close."

"Angel, I think there's two, maybe three left."

"Agree."

"The last of the cars—"

Someone stood up in the left corner, fired a long burst, hitting cars and the front wall of the building.

"That has to be a kid," Seth whispered.

"That was stupid. Now we know his position."

"There isn't any talking back there," Seth said. "My guess is the kid is in the left corner and Tejano in the right."

"Agree."

"Are you still a little mouse, Angel?"

"Yes."

"Two more walls puts us fifteen meters from Tejano. You ready?"

"Wait. Garcia, Pedra. Step out from the corner. On my command, fire a full magazine across the back of the building, four feet off the ground."

"Damn, you're good, Angel."

"Now," Angel said. They began firing while she and Seth advanced to the last partition before the end wall.

"Kid, you in the corner? I am Angel. Throw your gun out and I'll let you live."

Tejano stood up, fired a long burst at Angel's voice.

Mistake.

Seth raised up, extended his arms, fired into Tejano's corner. Tejano cried out in pain.

"Seth." Angel said. "Cover me. Watch the kid. Tejano is mine. Kid, don't move and you'll live."

Tejano fired a short burst, killing the kid. Shot in the forearm and shoulder, Tejano ejected the empty magazine, struggled to slap in a new one.

Focused, Angel jumped up, darted to the corner. She leveled her carbine at Tejano. Tejano's rifle remained pointed at the kid's body.

Four inches. Could he raise the rifle up four inches? Shoot Angel first?

No.

Could he live knowing Angel had defeated him twice?

No.

"I have defeated you, Tejano," Angel said. "It is finished for you. Drop your rifle and I will let you live. You can dream of me for the rest of your miserable life in prison."

"Bitch," Tejano said, raising his rifle.

Angel shot him twice in the chest.

***

"Garcia, Cesar, Pedra, You have served me with honor. I shall reward you for your service. Now, you must step away. I must be alone with this warrior."

Angel stepped over to Seth. Guns hanging at their sides, they were within easy killing distance of each other.

She appeared pensive, almost sad. Soon she would be free to fly with the eagles. First, she must complete what she'd agreed to do. The thought of what she must do gave her pause, reflection on why it should end this way.

"It is now time we should meet. We must finish that which is between us."

Seth said nothing.

"You are a fearsome warrior."

Silence.

"I have given an oath that I would kill you."

Seth focused on any signal of movement in her right hand.

"I must honor the oath I have made."

Not a sound.

"Are you mute?" she barked. "You make no sound."

Seth refused to speak.

"Your eyes are studying my hand. Do you wish to kill me?"

"No," Seth said.

"At last, you speak. Words are difficult for you?"

"Not when something needs to be said."

"I love words. They are my companion."

"Your friends fought well."

"It is their destiny to serve me."

Seth tapped his right heel, studied Angel's eyes.

"I must kill you now. Are you prepared to die?"

More silence.

Angel's eyes didn't give any signal when she raised her pistol, fired. Seth heard the rush of air when the bullet passed next to his ear. He flinched. His gun didn't move. He knew what she would do.

"I have missed," Angel said. "I never miss. Why is that, Seth? Why are you still alive?"

"You twisted your hand away. Just enough. I saw it."

"Perhaps I did. I've never killed a warrior before."

Seth said nothing.

"You must kill me now," Angel said.

"No."

"Why? I am your enemy. You must kill your enemies."

Seth dropped his carbine. "I have no quarrel with you. I've killed my enemies. You weren't one of them."

"You're a strange man. I have not met a warrior such as

you." Angel became aware of her heart beating faster. She honored this man.

"Words have left you?" Seth asked.

Sighing, she studied his unreadable face. "It is done between us."

Seth exhaled, weary death had surrounded him again.

"I have honored my oath to kill you. I tried, but I missed." Angel dropped her pistol. "Where do you go from here?"

"New York. A friend wants me to work with him."

"Is there a woman in New York?"

No answer. Angel saw the struggle in Seth's eyes.

"Is she beautiful?"

"Yes."

"Am I beautiful?"

"Yes."

"Do you love her?"

"I just met her."

"Could you love her?"

Seth blinked. Exhaustion was taking hold. "Interesting question."

"Could you love me?"

"No."

The answer gave pause to Angel. To cover the sudden silence, she said, "I am not surprised. Love would be hard for me."

"Why?"

"I've never loved a man."

They heard the distant sound of sirens.

"We have to leave," Seth said.

"Seth?"

"What?"

"I honor you. You are a warrior who walks with the Aztec Jaguar Warriors, the *Cuāuhocēlōtl*. They are my brothers. It is sad. There are so few of us now. Will I see you again?"

"No way. Never going to happen," Seth said.

Angel offered a hint of a smile. Just enough for Seth to note its presence. She said with certainty in her voice.

"I will make it happen."

A PERSONAL NOTE:

Thank you for taking the time to read SETH. I hope you enjoyed reading the novel as much as I did writing the story. Book reviews are important to writers. They are like a report card the student brings home from school. They tell authors their successes or what needs to be improved.

I would appreciate if you would take a moment of your time to write a brief, honest review and send it to Goodreads and Amazon.

It will help me to write a better story. It will also help readers make their choice on the next book to read.

Have an awesome day.

JB Morris

ABOUT THE AUTHOR

JB Morris saw corruption in government, taught military tactics, and witnessed homicide violence. He pooled his experiences to write the crime novel SETH, the first of five books in a series about people whose lives changed when their paths crossed.

BOOK ONE: *SETH* (Published)
Seth Collins' combat experience protected his family.

BOOK TWO: *THE BEIJING MEMORANDUM* (2016)
Moses Remington caught up in China's invasion of Mexico.

BOOK THREE: *PAMELA* (2017)
Pamela Brighton did not walk away from an impossible love.

BOOK FOUR: *THE RESCUE OF LIDDIE MacARTHUR* (2017)
President Terrill Green lacked political courage.

BOOK FIVE: *ANGEL* (On the drawing board)
Angel struck fear with her unmatched assassin skills.

These stories and more come from the prolific pen of JB Morris. JB is active in the writing community with membership in Willamette Writers and The Writer's Chatroom. He also participates in a number of social media websites. JB blogs at http://www.jbmorrisbooks.com. Retired, he lives with his wife in the Willamette Valley in Oregon.

OTHER BOOKS BY JB MORRIS

BEIJING MEMORANDUM

Combat Outpost Cukela

Helmand Province, Afghanistan

Back ramrod straight, with an enigmatic expression, Marine Corps Gunnery Sergeant Moses Remington watched the four men drop to their knees in the desert dust. The intense July sun soaked their combat shirts with sticky sweat. Frozen in place, they waited for the signal to pick up the brown, human remains pouch and sprint forward. Two hundred feet overhead, a basket attached to a cable began its descent from a UH-60 Black Hawk helicopter. A UH-1Y "Venom" helicopter circled above the Black Hawk. The "Venom" helicopter's two 7.62 mm GAU-17/A Gatling guns ready for close air support. The four men shielded their faces in a vain effort to escape from the dust, and rock fragments stirred up from the Black Hawk's rotor downwash.

Moses swallowed hard, struggled to watch with opaque eyes. He wanted to cry, but Marines weren't permitted—especially gunnery sergeants. Had to be a regulation somewhere.

Behind the four men, his face grim, Captain Dana Palmer nodded in his direction. The captain understood. He saw Moses' pain. The pouch held the remains of Staff Sergeant Tucker Williams, Moses' closest friend.

Moses bit his lip in search of relief. Didn't work. The body bag and memory of the quiet sunrise turned lethal became overwhelming. Goddamn you, Williams. Look what in the hell you went and did.

He watched a stone he kicked bounce off the Hesco barrier. He and Williams played the game of who could kick a rock the closest to the wall. William's had a magic touch. Moses owed him his monthly salary until he reached the age of seventy-five. Jesus Christ, Williams. I told you to stay down. . . But no, not you. . .you had to move. A tear fell on Moses' tactical vest. Turned dark brown.

Moses lost it, and the pain of loss surprised him. He was mortal, not the robotic warrior he set for himself. Flesh and blood people die, including gunnery sergeants. You know, Moses, you're next. Can't live forever. Won't be long before they dump your sorry ass into a pouch.

He refused to think about buying a bullet or an IED. He couldn't protect his men if he worried about his own survival. A simple philosophy anchored him. One minute you're alive. The next minute you're dead. Can't change it. So deal with it.

RESCUE OF LIDDIE MacARTHUR

My expansive imagination could not construct a story when I read her nametag.

Madison.

Nor did her cold eyes stir any suggestion of what she was hiding from me. Her face empty, devoid of emotion, of life. A tight bun on the top of her head shielded the natural beauty of her auburn hair. Her oval face, bronze skin, and chestnut eyes remained hidden behind a mask of plainness. Her lack of make-up stirred up the idea her plainness must be a disguise. She wore dark-framed glasses that appeared out of place, out of character. Her loose-fitted, silk blouse did not highlight her statuesque figure.

Even her name was one I would have never have guessed. Madison. Where in the hell did she get the name, Madison? Who gave her the name? Why? Not even a hint of a smile on her face. A robot ready to take our order.

My secretary Paige and I were sitting in the Desert Oasis Steakhouse for dinner when our waitstaff Madison first rounded the corner. The rich tones of mahogany walls, candlelight, and thick alabaster linen tablecloths surrounded her. Added to the ambiance. An original oil painting of the Spanish Steps in Rome crowned our table hidden in a corner. I imagined Madison's toned, smooth, silky legs as she climbed the steps.

"Hello, Madison," I said. "How are you tonight?"

"I'm fine, sir," Her voice crisp, curt. "Are you ready to place your order?"

"It all looks good," I said, pleased with what I had reviewed on the menu. "What do you recommend?"

"Our master chef prepares all of our entrees," she said in a monotonous, mechanical voice.

"Okay, we'll order the New York steaks, medium rare, tossed green, with bleu cheese on the side."

"Thank you, sir."

"Excuse me," I said as she picked up the menus, prepared to

leave. "May I ask you a question? How long have you lived in Palm Springs?"

Madison's face froze. She bit her lower lip. Said nothing.

"We want to find a drug store. Thought you might be able to help us."

She gave me a hard, penetrating stare, left without speaking.

"What the hell happened?"

"You didn't see it?"

"See what?"

"You scared her," Paige said.

"What are you talking about?"

"She was terrified when you asked how long she'd lived in Palm Springs. She's hiding something. Thinks you're a threat to her."

A short, plus-sized server name Edith returned later with our meal. Remained with us through dessert.

I gave my credit card to Edith. "What happened to Madison?"

"I'm sorry, sir. Madison left."

I have to stop. Go back to where my story began.

PAMELA

It was a day like none other. He saw it in the mirror shaving and tasted it in the eggs at breakfast.

Fear.

Not the catastrophic fear of death. A veteran of six combat tours with the Marines in Iraq and Afghanistan, Seth Collins, discarded those fears years ago. Fear in combat equaled hesitancy. Hesitancy equaled death. Seth's focus became singular.

Kill or be killed. An outlook that awarded him a Navy Cross in Helmand Province, Afghanistan.

That was then. Unlike before, Seth's new fear robbed him of sleep, focus. It was fear of the unknown—rejection. And it had a name.

Pamela Brighton.

She terrified him. Her elegance, grace, and beauty were foreign to him. But most of all, she puzzled him. Why did you pick me, Pamela? Look at me. I'm a bum. How can you relate to that? You can't. There's no way this will work. You have a daughter. What do I know about children? She'd write me off the first time she sees me.

Overwhelmed with self-consciousness, he studied his face in the mirror, muttered to himself. He couldn't escape his anxiety. He retreated to the window, gazed down at the Canal Bar across the street. The bar anchored a three-story brick apartment building highlighted with a fire escape cascading down the front and a faded American flag wrapped around a flagpole. An old man sat on a bench in front of the bar, asleep.

I wonder where you live, Pamela?. You sure don't live here in Brooklyn. Seth pulled out the folded piece of paper with her address, 110 Breckenshire House, W 59th Street. Creases had begun to tear the faded note No matter. He'd memorized the address. The message helped to remind him of her poetic voice, soft and gentle. He carefully folded it to avoid further wrinkling. Slid it back into a shirt pocket.

"This is nuts," he said to the chair.

I mean, we met on the plane. Yes, it was nice. No, Pamela, it was better than nice. But it's over. The plane landed. We'd never see each other again. Just walk away. It happens all the time. Seth rubbed his clean-shaven face, glanced at a cumulus cloud that mirrored a cauliflower. And I'd spend the rest of my life thinking about you.

Seth became weary of self-analysis. It hadn't solved any-thing. He promised to meet her at eleven. Time to leave. With a hand on the doorknob, he paused.

Where in the hell is this taking me?

CONNECT WITH JB MORRIS

My email address is jbmorris37@gmail.com

My website is www.jbmorrisbooks.com

Like me on Facebook
www.facebook.com/JBMorrisBooksAuthorPage

Connect with me on Twitter
www.twitter.com/JBMorrisAuthor

Friend me on Goodreads
www.goodreads.com/goodreadscomjbmorrisauthor

Follow me on Pinterest
www.pinterest.com/jbmorris37